William M. Punshon

Lectures and Sermons

William M. Punshon

Lectures and Sermons

ISBN/EAN: 9783337264352

Printed in Europe, USA, Canada, Australia, Japan

Cover: Foto ©Andreas Hilbeck / pixelio.de

More available books at **www.hansebooks.com**

AND

SERMONS

BY THE

REV. W. MORLEY PUNSHON. LL.D.

&c., &c.

NEW YORK

R. WORTHINGTON, 750 BROADWAY.

1877.

CONTENTS.

DANIEL IN BABYLON.

DANIEL IN BABYLON.

THERE were giants in the earth in those days, for those old Hebrew prophets were a marvellous race of men. It is difficult for us to regard them as parts of the ordinary creation of God. Only in such an age, when Revelation was a simple thing, and men felt, as they saw the symbol or the vision, that the Divine was "not far away from any one of them:" only beneath such a sky, whose sun, as it blasted the desert into desolation, or greened the olive slope into beauty, was a perpetual monition both of threatening and of promise : only among such a people, of deep religious instincts, and impressible in a high degree, could they have lived, and flourished, and become the powers they were. They were not soldiers, but when they rebuked kings, theirs was a courage which the most stalwart crusader might have envied. They were not priests, but never priest spake solemn words with greater seemliness of utterance, nor with diviner power. As we trace their long and lofty line, and their notable ones crowd upon our memories, we seem to shrink from any discussion of their characters, as if they were creatures from the spirit-land. Some such feeling steals over us, as might have prompted the affrighted Gadarenes, when they prayed for the departure of the Saviour, or as might have burdened the wondering soul of Peter, when in his first vision of Christ's miraculous power, he said, "Depart from me, for I am a sinful man, O Lord." They seem to be *in* the nature of humanity rather than *of* it, to be surrounded by conditions, and to dwell in an existence of their own, with which the rest of the world can have but a scanty sympathy, or rather a mingled feeling, which is half admiration and half awe. They are not men so much as distinct individual influences, passive beneath their swelling inspiration, standing before the Lord, like the lightnings, which are his messengers, or as the "stormy wind, fulfilling His word."

It is evident that the peculiarities of their office, and their comparative isolation from the experiences of common humanity, prevent us, in the general, from acknowledging their fitness as examples by which to regulate our own life and conduct. There is a shrewd impiety in human nature, which has formed its own estimate of what its patterns ought to be, and which demands that certain initial conditions shall be rigidly fulfilled. There must be identity of nature, and there must be similarity of circumstance. The man must have like passions, and those passions must have been powerfully tried. Failure in these conditions would at once neutralize the force of the example, even as a blemish in physical beauty would, to a Greek of the olden time, have ostracised Apollo from the fellowship of the Gods.

There is none among the brotherhood of the Prophets, who so thoroughly comes home to us as that Hebrew youth, of the royal line of Judah, from whose history we are purposing to be instructed now. He was inspired, but he had a life apart from his inspiration, and we recognize in it the common elements of which lives are made. Principle and persecution—sorrow and success—the harp-song of thankfulness and the breeze-like voice of grief—all the constituents which are shapely in the formation of character ; we meet with them in his experience, just as we have felt them in our own. He comes to us, therefore, no stranger, but robed in our own humanness. He is no meteor vision—sweeping out of darkness to play for a brief space the masque of human living, and then flitting into darkness as unbroken—he comes eating and drinking, doing common things, thrilled with common feelings—though those feelings prompt him to heroic action, and those common things are done in a majestic way. My object is to teach lessons from the life and character of Daniel. My chief purpose, I am not ashamed to avow, is to do my listeners good, and though the platform is broader than the pulpit, and may be indulged with wider latitude of range and phrase, I should be recreant to my great, loved life-work, if I were not to strive mainly to make my words tell upon that future when eternity shall flash upon the doings of time.

It is affirmed of the religion of Jesus, that it is adapted for all changes of human condition, and for all varieties of human character. Clearly, a religion which aims to be universal must possess this assimilating power, or, in the complexities of the world, it would be disqualified for the post which it aspires to fill. The high claims which its advocates assert for Christianity, have been passed through the crucible of the ages, and have been verified by the experience of each generation. It is not hemmed in by parallels of latitude. It is not hindered by any "wall of partition." It can work its marvels in every clime. It can translate its comforts into every language. Like its founder, its delight is in the "*habitable* parts of the earth," and wherever man is, in rich metropolis or in rude savannah, whether intellect has exalted, or savagery degraded him, there, in the neighbourhood and in the heart of *man*, is the chosen sphere of Christianity, where she works her changes, diffuses her blessings, raises up her witnesses, and proves to every one who embraces her his angel of discipline and of life. It may be that you are thinking, some of you, that your circumstances are exceptional, that Religion is a thing only for stream-side villages and quiet hours—not for the realm of business, nor "the tragic hearts of towns." That is a grave error, my brother. Heaven is as near the great city as the breezy down. You can preserve as bright an integrity, you can hold as close a fellowship with the true and the Divine in the heart of London, the modern Babylon, as did Daniel in Babylon, the ancient London.

This brings me to my first thought—*the earnest piety which was the foundation-fact of Daniel's consistent life.* He was a religious man. His religion influenced his character, kindled his heroism, and had largely to do with his success. His religion, moreover, was not a surface sentiment, traditionally inherited, and therefore loosely held. Opinions have often been entailed with estates, handed down as reverenced heir-looms from one generation to another. Men have rallied round a crimson banner, or shouted lustily for the buff and blue, for no better reason than that the same colours had sashed and rosetted their fathers perhaps for a century of years. In the history of human opinion it would be curious to enquire how much of it has been the pride of partisanship, or the inheritance of affection, how little of it the force of conviction, and the result of honest thought and study. But Daniel's was an inwrought piety, whose seat was in the heart, and it was of that brave sort which no disaster was able to disturb.

And it was no easy matter to maintain it. Look at him as he is first introduced to our notice. He was lonely, he was tempted, he was in peril. Loneliness, temptation, danger,—these are words which perhaps from painful personal experience, some of us can understand. Add to these the further condition of bondage, a word, thank God, whose full meaning a free people does *not* understand, and you have some conception of the position of Daniel, when we first become acquainted with him in the palace of the King of Babylon.

Moreover, the circumstances of Babylon, at the time when he was carried there, would necessarily expose his piety to greater hazards. It is always difficult for a slave to profess a faith other than the faith of his master. The victory which Nebuchadnezzar had gained would barb the tongue of the Chaldean scoffer with sharper sarcasms against the Hebrew creed. Babylon was wholly and earnestly given to idolatry. There Belus was magnificently worshipped. There the soothsayer wrought his spells, and the astrologer affected to read in the heavens, as in a sparkling Bible. There the followers of Zoroaster lingered, and clung tenaciously to their pure and ancient error, for of all idolatries fire-worship is at once the most primitive and the most plausible. There the commonest things of life were linked with idol associations, and consecrated by idol ceremonies ; so that the conscience of the Hebrew was in momentary danger of attack, and active resistance became the duty of every day.

But Daniel's piety did not fail, because it was thorough in its consistency and in its grandeur. It has been a favourite scoff in all ages ever, since the words "Doth Job serve God for nought?" fell from the lips of the old original liar, that Christians are Christians only when no motive tempts them to the contrary, and when their policy is on the side of their religion. Hence, some Chaldean sceptic, or some captive of a Sadducean spirit, might have flung the gibe at the young enthusiast Hebrew, "Ah! there will come a change upon him soon. He has breathed a Hebrew atmosphere, and been bound by Hebrew habits. His soul is but the chrysalis just emerging from the cocoon of dormant thought and dull devotion. Wait until he is fledged. Wait until he has preened his wings amid the sunshine and the flowers of Babylon. The Jordan is but a sluggish stream, the Euphrates rolls grandly in its rushing silver. Translate him from the slopes of Olivet to the plains of Shinar. Let him taste the luxury of Chaldean living, and join in the pomp of Babylonish worship, you will soon hear of his abandonment of his former friends, and he will plunge, as eagerly as any, into the gaieties of the capital." But that scoffer, like most others of his kindred, would have been grievously mistaken. Did Daniel's piety fail him? Was he entangled in the snare of pleasure, or frightened by the captor's frown? Knelt he not as fervently in the palace at Shushan as in the temple at Jerusalem? Amid the devotees of Merodach or Bel, his Abdiel-heart went out, as its manner was, after the one Lord of earth and heaven. Oh, what are circumstances, I wonder, that they should hinder a true man when his heart is set within him to do a right thing? Let a man be firmly principled in his religion, he may travel from the tropics to the poles, it will never catch cold on the journey. Set him down in the desert, and just as the palm tree thrusts its roots beneath the envious sand in search of sustenance, he will manage somehow to find living water there. Banish him to the dreariest Patmos you can find, he will get a grand Apocalypse among its barren crags. Thrust him into an inner prison, and make his feet fast in the stocks; the doxology will reverberate through the dungeon, making such melody within its walls of stone that the gaoler shall relapse into a man, and the prisoners, hearing it, shall dream of freedom and of home.

Young men, you who have any piety at all, what sort is it? Is it a hot-house plant, which must be framed and glassed, lest March, that bold young fellow, should shake the life out of it in his rough play among the flowers?—or is it a hardy shrub, which rejoices when the wild winds course along the heather or howl above the crest of Lebanon? We need, believe me, the bravery of godliness to bear true witness for our Master now. There is opposed to us a manhood of insolence and error. The breath of the plague is carried on the wings of the wind. Ours must be a robust piety—which does not get sick soon in the tainted air. The forces of evil are marshalled in unwonted activity—and there are liers in wait to surprise and to betray. Ours must be a watchful piety which is not frightened from its steadfastness by the "noise of the captains and the shouting." Through the heavy night, and beyond the embattled hosts, there glitters the victor's recompense. It must be ours to press towards it on our patient way, saying to all who differ from us, "Hinder me not, I mean to wear that crown."

One main cause of Daniel's consistency, which I would fain commend for your imitation, was this. He made the stand at once, and resisted on the earliest occasion of encroachment upon conscience and of requirement to sin. He purposed in his heart that he "would not defile himself with the king's meat, nor with the portion of wine which he drank." Now, as a true Hebrew, bound by the rescripts of the Mosaic law, certain meats were forbidden to him which other nations ate without scruple. Moreover, the chances are that the bread and the wine had been idolatrously consecrated, for those old Pagans were not ashamed, *as we are*, to pervade the common things of life with their religion. To Daniel, therefore, these things were forbidden, forbidden by their ceremonial uncleanness, forbidden equally by their idolatrous association, and it was his duty to refuse them.

I see that curl of the lip on the face of that unbeliever, and as it might hurt him, possibly, if his indignation had not vent, I will try to help it into words. "A small thing, a very insignificant occasion for a very supercilious and obstinate display! What worse would he have been if he had not been so offensively singular? He was not obliged to know that there had been any connection with idolatry about it. Why obtrude his old-world sanctimoniousness about such a trifle as this?" A trifle! Yes! but are not these trifles sometimes among the mightiest forces in the universe? A falling apple, a drifting log of wood, the singing and puffing of a tea-kettle! Trifles all— but set the royal mind to work upon them, and what comes of the trifles then? From the falling apple, the law of gravitation. From the drifting log of wood, the discovery of America. From the smoke and song of the tea-kettle, the hundred-fold appliances of steam. There are no trifles in the moral universe of God. Speak me a word to-day;—it shall go ringing on through the ages. Sin in your heedless youth;—I will shew you the characters, long years afterwards, carven on the walls of "the temple of the body." Hence the good policy as well as piety of Daniel. He made the stand at once, and God honoured it; and, the foremost champion of the enemy slain, it was easy to rout the rest. Do I address some one now over whom the critical moment impends? You are beset with difficulties so formidable that you shudder as you think of them. Does wealth allure, or beauty fascinate, or endearment woo, or authority command you to sin? Does the carnal reason gloss over the guiltiness, and the deprecating fancy whisper "Is it not a little one?" and the roused and vigorous passion strive with the reluctant will? Now is the moment, then, on your part for the most valorous resistance, on my part for the most affectionate and solemn warning. It is against this beginning of evil, this first breach upon the sacredness of conscience, that you must take your stand. It is the first careless drifting into the current of the rapids which speeds the frail bark into the whirlpool's wave. Yield to the temptation which now invites you, and it may be that you are lost for ever. Go to that scene of dissipation, enter that hell of gambling, follow that "strange woman" to her house, make that fraudulent entry, engage in that doubtful speculation, make light of that Sabbath and its blessings—what have you done? You have weakened your moral nature, you have sharpened the dagger for the assassin who waits to stab you, and you are accessory, in your measure, to the murder of your own soul. Brothers, with all a brother's tenderness, I warn you against a peril which is at once so threatening and so near. 'Now, while time and chance are given, while, in the thickly-peopled air there are spirits which wait your halting, and other spirits, which wait to give their ministry to the heirs of salvation—now, let the conflict be decided. Break from the bonds which are already closing around you.   Frantic as a bondsman to escape the living hell of slavery, be it yours to hasten your escape from the pursuing evil of sin. There, close at your heels, is the vengeful and resolute enemy. Haste! Flee for your life! Look not behind you, lest you be overtaken and destroyed. On—though the feet bleed, and the veins swell, and the heart-strings quiver. On—spite of wearied limbs, and shuddering memories, and the sobs and pants of labouring breath. Once get within the gates of the city of refuge and you are safe, for neither God's love nor man's will ever, though all the world demand it, give up to his pursuers a poor fugitive slave.

Having mentioned the piety of Daniel, the Corinthian pillar of his character, we may glance at some of the acanthus leaves which twine so gracefully round it.

It will not be amiss if we learn to be as contented, under all change of circumstance, as Daniel's piety made him. He is supposed to have been about twenty years old when he was carried away to Babylon. He was then in the flower of his youth; at an age when the susceptibilities are the keenest, when the visions of the former time have not faded from the fancy, when the future stretches brightly before the view. His connexion with the royal family of Judah might, not unnaturally, have opened to him the prospect of a life of state and pleasure, haunted by no pangs of ungratified desire. It was a hard fate for him to be at once banished from his fatherland and robbed of his freedom. Every sensibility must have been rudely shocked, every temporal hope must have been cruelly blighted, by the transition from the courtly to the menial, and from Jerusalem to Babylon. How will Daniel act under these altered circumstances, which had come upon him from causes which he could neither control nor remedy? There were three courses open to him, other than the one he took. He might have resigned himself to the dominion of sorrow, have suffered grief for his bereavement to have paralyzed every energy of his nature, and have moaned idly and uselessly, as, beneath the trailing willows, he "wept when" he "remembered Zion." He might have harboured some sullen purpose of revenge, and have glared out upon his captors with an eye whose meaning, being interpreted, was murder. Or he might have abandoned himself to listless dreaming, indolent in present duty, and taking no part at all for the fulfilment of his own dreams. But Daniel was too true and brave a man, and had too reverent a recognition of the Providence of God to do either the one or the other. He knew that his duty was to make the best of the circumstances round him, to create the content, and to exhibit it, though the conditions which had formerly constrained it were at hand no longer. Hence, though he was by no means indifferent to his altered fortunes; though there would often rise upon his softened fancy the hills and temples of his native land, he was resigned and useful and happy in Babylon. It may be that some among yourselves may profitably learn this lesson. Wearied with hard work, done for the enrichment of other people, you are disposed to fret against your destiny, and to rebel against the fortune which has doomed you to be the toiler and the drudge. Ambition is, in some sort, natural to us all, and could we borrow for a night a spirit more potent than the lame demon of Le Sage, and could he unroof for us hearts as well as houses, there would perhaps be discovered a vast amount of lurking discontent, poisoning the springs both of usefulness and of happiness for many. Under the influence of this embittered feeling some rail eloquently at class distinctions in society, and sigh for an ideal equality with an ardour which the first hour of a real equality would speedily freeze, while some drivel into inglorious dreamers, and are always on the look-out, like the immortal Micawber, for something to "turn up," which will float them into the possession of a Nabob's fortune, or into the notoriety of some easily-acquired renown.

I am not sure whether our dispensation of popular lecturing is altogether guiltless in this matter. Young men, especially, have been so often exhorted to aspire, to have souls above business, to cultivate self-reliance, to aim at a prouder destiny, and all that sort of thing; and we have heard so much of the men who have risen from the ranks to be glorified in the world's memory—Burns at the plough-tail, and Claude Lorraine in the pastry-cook's shop, and Chantrey the milk boy, and Sir Isaac Newton with his cabbages in the Grantham market, and John Bunyan mending the kettles, and Martin Luther singing in the streets for bread—that it is hardly surprising if some who have listened to these counsels have been now and then excited into an anti-commercial frenzy; not, it is hoped, so fiercely as that silly lad who attempted, happily in vain, to destroy himself, and left a note for his employer, assigning as the reason of the rash act, as the newspapers always call it, that "he was made by God to be a man, but doomed by man to be a grocer." Well, if we lecturers have fostered the evil, it should be ours to atone by the warning exhibition of its peril. I can conceive of nothing more perilous to all practical success, more destructive of everything masculine in the character, than the indulgence in this delirious and unprofitable reverie. The mind once surrendered to its spell has lost all power of self-control, and is passive, like the opium-eater, under the influence of the horrible narcotic. Real life is discarded as unlikely, and the dream is arranged with all the accuracy, and very much of the adventure of a three-volumed novel. A high-born maiden becomes suddenly enamoured of the slim youth who serves her with the silks she rustles in, or, some rich unheard of uncle dies, just at the critical time, or he turns out to be somebody's son, and by consequence heir to a fortune or a large-acred landed proprietor, or he is hurtling an imaginary senate with very imaginary eloquence; or, fired with the hope of hymeneal bliss, he is whirled off with a bride and a fortune (always a fortune) in a chariot and four; and so he revels in these impossible heavens, until, as in the dream of Alnaschar, crash goes the crockery, or down falls the bale of muslin upon his most bunioned toe, or an equivocal river of gamboge is too sure prediction of the annihilation of the basket of eggs. But how unreal and foolish all this is! how hurtful to all healthiness of moral sentiment, and to all industry of patient toil. How nearly akin to the spirit of the gambler, who has lost all his fortune at hazard and then risks his last quarter just because it is so small. "But," says some indignant youth, "what do you mean? Are all the counsels to which we have listened in the former time to go for nothing? Are we not to aspire? Are we to grovel always? Are we never to rise above the sphere of society in which we moved to-day?" Oh yes! some of you may, and if the elements of greatness are in you *they will come out*, aye, though an Alp were piled upon them, or though the sepulchre hewn out of the rock hid them in its heart of stone. But it is no use hiding the truth; ninety out of every hundred of you will remain as you are. "Grocers" to-day, you will be grocers or something like it to the end of the chapter. Well, and what of that ? Better the meanest honest occupation than to be a dastard, or a deceiver, or a drone. Better the weary-footed wanderer, who knows not where the morrow's breakfast will be had, than to be the sordid or unworthy rascal, whirled through the city in a carriage, built, cushioned, horsed, harnessed, all with other people's money. God has placed you in a position in which you can be honest and excel. Do your duty in the present, and God will take care of the future. Depend upon it, the way to rise in life, is neither to repine, and so add to the troubles of misfortune the sorer troubles of passion and envy, nor to waste in dreams the plodding energy which would go far to the accomplishment of the dreamer's wealthiest desire. If the Passions rule you, there will be a Reign of Terror. If Imagination be suffered to hold the reins, you will make small progress, if indeed there be no catastrophe, for though Phæton was a very brilliant driver, yet he burnt the world.

Don't aim, then, at any impossible heroisms. Strive rather to be quiet heroes in your own sphere. Don't live in the cloudland of some transcendental heaven ; do your best to bring the glory of a real heaven down, and ray it out upon your fellows in this work-day world. Don't go out, ascetic and cowardly, from the fellowships of men. Try to be angels in their houses, that so a light may linger from you as you leave them, and your voice may echo in their hearing, " like to the benediction that follows after prayer." The illumination which celebrates a victory is but the vulgar light shining through various devices into which men have twisted very base metal ; and so the commonest things can be ennobled by the transparency with which they are done. Seek then to make trade bright with a spotless integrity, and business lustrous with the beauty of holiness. Whether fortune smile on you or not, you shall "stand in your lot," and it shall be a happy one. The contentment of the soul will make the countenance sunny ; and if you compare your heritage with that of others who are thought higher in the social scale, dowered more richly with the favours of that old goddess who was said to be both fickle and blind, the comparison will not be a hopeless one if you can sing in the Poet's stirring words—

> "Cleon hath a thousand acres,
>   Ne'er a one have I ;
> Cleon dwelleth in a mansion,—
>   In a lodging, I.
> Cleon hath a dozen fortunes,
>   Hardly one have I ;—
> Yet the poorer of the twain
>   Is Cleon and not I.
>
> "Cleon, true, possesseth acres,
>   But the landscape I ;—
> Half the charms to me it yieldeth
>   Money cannot buy.
> Cleon harbours sloth and dulness,
>   Freshening vigour, I ;—
> He in velvet—I in broadcloth—
>   Richer man am I.
>
> "Cleon is a slave to grandeur,
>   Free as thought am I ;—
> Cleon fees a score of doctors ;—
>   Need of none have I.
> Wealth-surrounded—care-environed,
>   Cleon fears to die ;—
> Death may come, he'll find me ready,
>   Happier man am I.

> " Cleon sees no charms in nature,
>   In a daisy, I ;—
> Cleon hears no anthems ringing
>   In the earth and sky ;—
> Nature sings to me for ever,
>   Earnest listener I,
> State for state with all attendants,
>   Who would change?   Not I."

The religion of Daniel influenced him further to be *courteous* to those by whom he was surrounded. In the early years of his residence in Babylon, he won " the favour and tender love of the prince of the eunuchs." His resistance to what he deemed unworthy subserviency was not rudely nor harshly manifested. " He requested of the prince of the eunuchs that he might not defile himself." He bore himself respectfully, yet without an atom of servility ; never compromising his fidelity to God, but neither insolent in his contempt of idolatry, nor forward to withhold honour and custom where honour and custom were due. It will not, perhaps, be amiss to commend him in this matter to the age in which we live ; and amid many incentives to independence, original thought, intolerance of shams and scorners, and the like, to whisper a word in favour of good manners. There is so much of outspokenness now-a-days, and it has been so much and so eloquently enforced that there is some danger lest in our re-action from servility, we should exhibit the " falsehood of extremes." Some men fancy themselves extremely clever when they are only extremely coarse, and obtrude before all comers a boorishness which they mistake for bravery.   I covet for you all, the more if you be Christians, the grand old name of gentleman—manhood and gentleness—inborn and influencing energy, but with affability and courtesy to temper it. You have heard of the Nasmyth hammer. It can chip an egg-shell without breaking it, or can shiver with a stroke the ponderous bar of iron. We are awed by the wonderful force, but we are especially attracted by the machinery which holds it in control. So a rough strength of character will repel even while it attracts us, but a frank and winning courtesy comes stealing into our hearts like a sunbeam, and flings an otto of July over the chillest November air.

This courtesy which I recommend you to exhibit is not only auxiliary to your religion, but a part of it. "The wisdom which is from above," I leave you to guess where the other wisdom comes from, is "gentle, and easy to be entreated." "Christ," Emerson says, "was a prince in courtesy, as well as in beneficence and wisdom," and a Christian is not more bound to maintain his own rights than to be tolerant of the feelings and opinions of others. Even Fashion, at the bottom, (though, as in a muddy road, the bottom may be a long way down) is based upon religion, and is a sort of Rabbinical perversion of Christianity. There is not a usage of cultivated society to-day which had not its origin in some real or fancied benevolence. Love is the essence of religion, and courtesy is but love in society— the "good Samaritan" genial in the drawing-room, as on the occasion he was self-sacrificing on the highway and in the field. The golden rule of all the politeness which it is worth A MAN's while to seek after, is in the old music-master's counsel to his pupil when she asked him the secret of performing with expression and effect—"Cultivate your heart, Miss, cultivate your heart." There is no reason surely why you should be otherwise than courteous. Good men are not necessarily abrupt and disagreeable.   There is no inevitable connection between Christianity and cynicism. Truth is not a salad, is it? that you must always dress it with vinegar.   It will be foul shame if some of your quondam friends should be able, with any truth, to say, "He was a fine, frank, generous, open-hearted fellow *before he became a Christian*," as if that had contracted the sympathies, which only can rightly expand them, as if that had frosted the heart, under whose warmth alone spring up "all that is of good report and lovely."   Have a care to wipe away this reproach, even if it has but begun to cleave to you, or, so far as you are concerned, your religion will be "wounded in the house of her friends." You should be so firm in your principles that you can afford to be kind. Let yours be the heroism which can sing even from a shattered heart,

> "Ten thousand deaths in every nerve.
> I'd rather suffer than deserve."

Preserve this unfailing kindliness whatever betide; though you are deafened by the strife of tongues, though, loudest in the scoff or the slander, you hear the changed tones of your own familiar one; though your heart be wrung until its very fibres start,—yet beseem yourself as becomes God's child, the child of one who bears with "the unthankful and the evil." You will find your account in it, and in earnest prayers, and charity which never faileth, and compassions delicately shewn, and opportunities eagerly embraced for piling up "coals of fire," you may secure the nobility of revenge.

And not for your own comfort only, but in your work of Christian witness-bearing, there must be gentleness in the rebuke and in the testimony, if either of them are to prevail.   A bluff countryman once strayed into Westminster Hall, and sat, with edifying patience for two mortal hours, while two lawyers wrangled over the merits of a case which was as much Greek *to him* as Curran's famous quotation from Juvenal was to the jury of Dublin shopkeepers. Some bystander, amused at his bewilderment, and amazed at his attention, asked him "which he thought had the best of it?" His reply was ready—"The little one, to be sure, *because he put the other man in a passion.*" There was shrewdness, if not logic, in the answer, and it shews how all argument is likely to shape itself to the bucolic mind. Believe me, neither Christianity, nor sound political dogma, nor any other good thing was ever yet permanently advantaged, either by the sword of the bigot, or by the tongue of the scold. The one only elevates the slaughtered into martyrdom, even though they were in life "lewd fellows of the baser sort ;"—the other rouses resistance, and enlists manliness upon the side of error. Brothers, in all seriousness I protest against grafting upon our holy religion a spirit that is truculent and cruel. Speak the truth, by all means ! Speak it so that no man can mistake the utterance. Be bold and fearless in your rebuke of error, and in your keener rebuke of wrong-doing, all Christ's witnesses are bound to be thus "valiant for the truth ;" but be human, and loving, and gentle, and brotherly, the while. If you must deliver the Redeemer's testimony, deliver it with the Redeemer's tears. Look, straight-eyed and kindly, upon the vilest, as a man ought to look upon a man, both royal, although the one is wearing, and the other has pawned, his crown.

The religion of Daniel constrained *his fidelity to duty and his diligent fulfilment of every trust confided to him.* It is a grievous error, but partly from the mistakes of religionists, and partly from the malignity of infidels, it is one which has very largely obtained, that the interests of the life that now is are in direct antagonism to the interests of the life that is to come. You may hear it reiterated from many a Sanhedrim of worldly self-sufficiency, and from many a Rabbi's supercilious lips. They will tell you that high moral excellence and deep religious feeling are inconsistent with shrewd business habits, and with the effective discharge of the commoner duties of life; and that, if a man would serve his God aright, he must forthwith abandon all hope of temporal advantage, and transfer his thought exclusively to the inheritance which awaits him in the sky. There is in this view, as in all prevalent errors, a sub-stratum of important truth. A Christian will not hesitate to tell you that he lives in the recognition of Eternity, and there is that in his glad hope of the future which will smite down his avarice, and turn away his footsteps from the altar of Mammon, but he has not forgotten, that as the heir of promise, he inherits this world too. The present is his by a truer charter than that by which the worldling holds it, and his eye may revel in its beauty, and his ear may listen to its music, and he may gather up its competence with a thankful heart, while yet his faith pierces through the cloud, and sees in the wealthier heaven his treasure and abiding home.

How fine an illustration of diligent and successful industry we have in the character of Daniel! He rose rapidly in the king's favour, and by his administrative ability secured the confidence of four successive monarchs who sat upon the throne of Babylon. Darius the Median, who succeeded to the empire after Belshazzar had been slain, discerned early the excellent spirit that was in him, promoted him to be chief of the presidents, to whom the hundred and twenty princes were amenable, and thought to set him over the whole realm. The duties thus devolved upon Daniel must have been of the most onerous and responsible kind. The empire extended southward to the Persian Gulf and northward to Mesopotamia. Naturally fertile, it had been cultivated to the uttermost. Babylon, the capital, to which Herodotus assigns dimensions of almost fabulous magnitude, had, on the lowest computation, an area twice as large as that of modern London, and enclosed within its walls a population of a million and a quarter souls. How complicated must have been the problems of government which Daniel was called upon to solve! He had to deal, in a foreign language, with foreign customs, and under different dynasties of kings. Many of those with whom he had to work were the "wise men of Babylon," not inconsiderably versed in starry lore and bearing a high reputation among their fellows. He must have therefore political sagacity and scientific research. His must be the ruling mind to disentangle a sophistry, and the seer's foresight to perceive the end from the beginning. Then the administration of justice formed no small part of his duty. Before him, as he sat in the gate, appellant and defendant came. It was his to hear the cause, to weigh the probabilities of evidence, to adjudicate, to execute the decision. Then, further, he must make provision for the contingencies which in those turbulent times were constantly occurring. He must be Argus-eyed against intestine faction, and against aggressions from beyond: quick to catch and quiet the murmurs of discontent at home; equally quick to scent the battle from afar. On him also devolved, in the last event, the financial administration of the realm. He had to get from each reluctant satrap the tribute assessed upon his province, to check the accounts of the presidents, and to see, as the tale was told into the treasury, that the king suffered no damage. Now, when you think of all the responsibility thus thrust upon one busy man, how he was at once Finance Minister, Lord Chief Justice, Home and Foreign Secretary, War Minister, and Premier to boot, you will readily conceive that Daniel had about enough on his hands, and that he would require, rightly to discharge his duty, both tact and energy, and a rigid and conscientious frugality of time.

In the differing play of mind before me, this consideration may have suggested different thoughts just now. I will imagine one or two of them, and turn them to profit as we proceed.

There may be perhaps what I will venture to call the narrowly pious thought ; the thought of a mind, evil from the extreme of good; the apprehension of a sensitive spirit, which like the mollusc of the rock, thrusts out its long antennæ at the barest possibility of danger. " Enough on his hands ! yes ! and far too much, more than any man ought to have who has two worlds to think about and provide for. It would be impossible, in this round of ceaseless secularity, to preserve that recognition of Eternity, and that preparation for its destinies which it is so needful for man to realize." The apprehension does you honour, my brother. I won't chide you for it ; there are sadly too few who are thus jealous for the Lord in the midst of us : but you need not fear. See him ! He comes out of the presence-chamber, where he has been having audience of the king. Whither will he go ? Ah ! he goes to the closet, and the lattice is reverently opened, and the knees are bent towards the unforgotten temple at Jerusalem, and there trembles through the air the cadence of some Hebrew psalm, followed shortly by some fervent strain of prayer. Oh! there is no fear, while the track to that chamber is a beaten one, while the memories of home and temple are so fragrant; while through the thrown-back lattice the morning sun shines in upon that silver-haired statesman on his knees. He who can thus pray will neither be faithless to man nor recreant to God. In that humiliation, and thrice-repeated litany of prayer, he finds his safety and his strength, and he exhibits for your encouragement and mine that it is possible to combine, in grandest harmony of character, fidelity to duty and to God; and amid the ceaselessness of labour, whether of the hand or of the brain, to keep a loyal heart within, whose every pulse beats eagerly for heaven.

Then out speaks a frank and manly worldling, knowing little and caring less about religion, but delighted with Daniel because he is so clever; almost worshipping the diplomacy which is astute, and sagacious, and above all successful. " Time for thought of eternity. No, and why should he? His deeds are his best prayers. Surely if ever a man might make his work his worship, it is he. He is a brave, true man, doing a man's work in a right manly way. What needs he to pray, except perhaps that his own valued life may not come to a close too soon." Ah! so you think that the thought of Eternity must paralyze the effort of Time. You think that your nature, when a strong man wears it, may claim its own place among the Gods. You, to whom prayer is an impertinence, and the acknowledgment of sin hypocrisy, alas for you that you are not in the secret! Why, this prayer is the explanation of everything which you admire in the man. Is he brave? What makes him so? Because the fear of God has filled his heart so full that there is no room for the fear of man to get in. Does he walk warily on a giddy height, which would make weaker brains dizzy? It is because he knows that the sky is higher than the mountain, and cherishes in all his ways the humbled feeling of dependence and faith. Is he rigid and conscientious in the discharge of daily duty? It is because he has learnt, and recollects, that "every one of us must give account of himself to God." Go then, and learn his piety, and humble thyself in thy chamber as he does. It will teach thee higher views of life than thou hast ever realized yet. Immortality shall burst upon thee, as America burst upon Columbus, a new world, flashing with a new heaven, and thou shalt be shewn that not in stalwart arm nor cunning brain shall be thy strength, but in quietness, and confidence, and in "the joy of the Lord."

It may be, though I would fain believe it otherwise, that a third discordant voice is speaking, the voice of one who hides beneath a seemly exterior, a scoffing soul. "He a statesman! what! that man of psalm and prayer, who cants along about right, and conscience, and duty,—you will find out differently by-and-bye. I am greatly mistaken if he does not turn out incompetent or wicked; they will have a hard life who bear office under him. I hate these saints. Look narrowly into his accounts, perhaps you will make some discoveries; there'll be a fine exposure some day of his blundering, and rapacity, and wrong." It would please you, I dare say to find yourself among the prophets, but happily the answer is at hand. Your ancestors shall come forward (you are not the first of the line) and with their own reluctant lips they shall refute your sarcasm. Mark them how they gather, presidents and princes, and counsellors, and captains—"vile conspirators all of them, devising mischief against the beloved of the Lord." Now we shall know the worst, you may be sure. If Daniel's administration has been faulty or fraudulent, all the world will be privy to it now. Malice is on his track, and it has a keen scent for blemishes. Envy is at work, and if *it* cannot see, it will suborn witnesses to swear *they* see, spots upon the sun. All his administration is brought into unfriendly review. Home and Foreign politics, Finance, Justice, all are straitly canvassed. Well, what is the result? Come scoffer, and hear thy fathers speak. "We shall not be able to find any occasion against this Daniel, except we find it against him concerning the law of his God." What? Did we hear aright? No occasion of charge against the chief minister of a great empire, when men are seeking for it with all their hearts! Was ever such a thing heard in this world? No failure of foresight! No lack of sagacity, which they might torture into premeditated wrong! no personal enrichment! no solitary nepotism in the distribution of patronage! This is very marvellous, and it is very grand. Speak it out again, for it is the noblest testimony which malice ever bore to virtue. "We shall not be able to find *any* occasion against this Daniel!" There he stands, spotless on the confession of his enemies. It matters not what becomes of him now, the character—*which is the man*—has been adjudged free from stain. Cast him to the lions, if you like, his faith will stop their mouths. Fling him into the sevenfold heated furnace, you can't taint his garments with the smell of fire. Heir of two worlds, he has made good his title of inheritance for both:—Daniel, faithful among men! Daniel, the beloved of the Lord.

Brothers, if the exhibition of this character has produced the effect upon you which I fondly hope, you will have learnt some lessons, which will make all your after-life the brighter. You will learn that though there may be, here and there, a favourite of fortune who goes up in a balloon to some high position without the trouble of the climbing, the only way for ordinary men is just to foot it, up the "steep and starry road." You will learn that Labour is the true alchemist which beats out in patient transmutation the baser metals into gold. You will learn that atheistic labour and prayerful idleness are alike disreputable, and you will brand with equal reprobation the hypocrite who is too devout to work, and the worldling who is too busy to pray. You will learn how hollow is the plea of the procrastinator that he has no time for religion, when the Prime Minister of a hundred and twenty provinces can retire for prayer three times a day. Above all you will learn that a reputation, built up by the wise masonry of years, does not fall at the blast of a scorner's trumpet, that God thrones the right at last, in kinglier royalty, because its coronation is delayed, and that neither earth nor hell can permanently harm you, if you be "followers of that which is good."

It needs only that I should remind you that *when the interests of the two worlds came into collision*, and there are periods in every man's life when they will, *Daniel dared the danger*, *rather than prove faithless to his God.* The vile council which met to compass his ruin laid their scheme cunningly. They knew him to be faithful, faithful in all respects, and it may be that like that other famous council of which Milton sings, they were about to separate in despair without accomplishing their purpose, when some Belial-spirit suggested that his fidelity to man should be pitted against his fidelity to God. The scheme succeeded. The King's consent was hastily gained to the promulgation of a decree, that for thirty days no petition should be offered to God or man, save to the King's own majesty, and the men, who knew Daniel's habit of prayer, exulted as they deemed his ruin sure.

And what has he done, this man, whom they thus conspire to destroy? Alas! for the baseness of human nature, his only faults are merit and success. It is the same world still. The times are changed from those of Smithfield and the Lollard's Tower; men fear not now the stake and the headsman, but the spirit which did the martyrs to the death is the spirit of the carnal heart to-day.

How will Daniel meet this new peril? It is inevitable—Darius cannot relent, for "the law of the Medes and Persians altereth not." Then shall Daniel yield? shall there be evasion, compromise, delay? His manner was to retire, that he might commune with God undisturbed; to kneel, in the prostration of a spirit at once contrite and dependent; to open his window towards Jerusalem, that the prayer which Solomon, as if prescient of their exile, invoked at the dedication of the temple, might be realized and answered. Shall he omit an observance, or suspend, even for an hour, the constancy of his devotion to his God? I think you could answer these questions from what you already know of the man. *He did exactly as he had been accustomed to do.* He did not then, for the first time throw open his window. If he had done that, he would have been a Pharisee. He did not close his window, because, for the first time, there was danger in opening it. If he had done that, he would have been a coward. He was neither the one nor the other, but simply, a brave, good man, who loved life well, but who loved God better; and who when a thing was put before him, when Timidity whispered, "Is it safe?" and Expediency hinted, "Is it politic?" and Vanity suggested, "Will it be popular?" took counsel of his own true heart, and simply enquired, " Is it right?" You can see him as on the fated day he retires for his accus-tomed worship, and with a quickened pulse, for he knows that his foes are in ambush, he enters his room, and opens his west-ern window. Now he reads in the law of the Lord—then the psalm rises, a little tremulous in its earlier notes, but waxing louder and clearer as the inspiration comes with the strain; then the prayer is heard—adoration, confession, supplication, thanksgiving, just as it had arisen from that chamber through the seasons of some seventy years. And now the room is filled with the envious ones, their eyes gleaming with triumph, and they accuse him fiercely of a violation of the King's decree. He does not falter, though he might have faltered as he thought of the cruel death, from which the King laboured vainly until sun-down to deliver him; though he might have faltered as he thought of the hungry lions, kept without food on purpose that they might the more fiercely rush upon their prey; but he does not falter; and rather than betray his conscience goes calmly down to death, with the decision of the martyr, with the deci-sion of the martyr's Lord.

Surely this is true heroism. It is not physical daring, such as beneath some proud impulse will rush upon an enemy's steel; it is not reckless valour, sporting with a life which ill-fortune has blighted, or which despair has made intolerable; it is not the passiveness of the stoic, through whose indifferent heart no tides of feeling flow; it is the calm courage which re-flects upon its alternatives, and deliberately chooses to do right; it is the determination of Christian principle, whose foot resteth on the rock, and whose eye pierceth into Heaven.

And now surely the enemies are satisfied. They have com

passed the ruin of the Minister, they have wounded the heart of the King ; they have removed the watchfulness which prevented their extortion, and the power which restrained them from wrong ; now they will enjoy their triumph ! Yes ! *but only for a night.* The wicked do but boast themselves a moment, and the shrewd observers, who meditate upon their swift destruction, remember the place where it is written, " They digged a pit for the righteous, and into the midst of it they are fallen themselves." Oh vain are all the efforts of slander, *permanently* to injure the fair fame of a good man ! There is a cascade in a lovely Swiss valley, which the fierce winds catch and scatter so soon as it pours over the summit of the rock, and for a season the continuity of the fall is broken, and you see nothing but a feathery wreath of apparently helpless spray ; but if you look further down the consistency is recovered, and the Staubbach pours its rejoicing waters as if no breeze had blown at all ; nay, the blast which interrupts it only fans it into more marvellous loveliness, and makes it a shrine of beauty where all pilgrim footsteps travel. And so the blasts of calumny, howl they ever so fiercely over the good man's head, contribute to his juster appreciation and to his wider fame. Preserve only a good conscience toward God, and a loving purpose toward your fellow-men, and you need not wince nor tremble, though the pack of the spaniel-hearted hounds snarl at your heels—

> Never you fear, but go ahead
>   In self-relying strength ;
> What matters it that Malice said,
>   " We've found it out at length."
> Found out ! Found what ? An honest man
>   Is open as the light,

> So search as keenly as you can,
>   You'll only find—all right.
>
> Aye ! blot him black with slander's ink,
>   He stands as white as snow,
> You serve him better than you think,
>   And kinder than you know.
> Yes ! be the scandal what you will,
>   Or whisper what you please ;
> You do but fan his glory still
>   By whistling up a breeze.

I trust there are many of you who are emulous of Daniel's heroism. The brutality of the olden persecutions has passed away. Saul does not now make havoc of the Church, nor Caligula nor Adrian purify it by lustrations of blood, but the spirit of the oppressor lives, and there is room enough in the most uneventful life for exemplary religious decision. The exigencies of the present times, regard for your own character and honour, the absolute requirement of God, all summon you to this nobleness of religious decision. Resist all temptations to become recreant to the truth. Remember that the Christian ought to be like Achilles, who could be wounded only in the heel, a part of the body which good soldiers *do not generally show*. Don't let the question ever be asked about you, " Is such an one a Christian ? " The very necessity to ask suggests a negative answer. Some painters in the rude times of art are said to have put under their works, " This is a horse ! " Of course ! it was necessary, for no one could possibly recognize it without being told. But it is a poor sign when either a work of art or a work of grace needs to be labelled. Who thought of asking where Moses had been when he came down from the mount? They looked at him, and they saw the glory. Let your consistency be thus steadfast and pure. If you know that the "writing is signed" which will throw you upon the world's cold pity or cruel scorn because you will keep your conscience inviolate, take heart from the example of Daniel. Don't shut your lattice-window. Men may ridicule you, but they will respect you notwithstanding; and if they do not, you can afford to do without their good opinion, while God looks down upon you with complacency, and the light of His countenance shines, broad and bright, upon your soul.

I have never despaired of the future of the world in which I live. I leave that to infidelity, with its sad scorn of the immortal and its vaunt of brotherhood with the brutes that perish. Humanity has been at once ransomed and glorified by Christ, and though there are still dark omens round us, though "this dear earth which Jesus trod is wet with tears and blood," yet there is a power abroad to whose call there is something in every man responsive, and the glad gospel of peace and blessing shall yet hush the voices of earth's many wailings, and speak of resurrection amid the silence of its many tombs.

And the work is being done. When I think of the agencies which are ceaslessly at work to make this bad world better, I am thankful that I live. From the eminence of the proud To-day, as from an Alp of clear and searching vision, I have looked backward on the past and forward on the illimitable future. I look, and that former time seemeth as a huge primeval forest, rioting in a very luxury of vegetation; with trees of giant bole, beneath which serpents brood, and whose branches arch overhead so thickly that they keep out the sun. But as I look there is a stir in that forest, for "the feller has come up against the trees." All that is prescriptive and all that is venerable combine to protest against the intrusion. Custom shudders at the novelty ; Fraud shudders at the sunlight ; Sloth shudders at the trouble ; "grey-bearded Use" leans upon his staff and wonders where all this will end ; Romance is indignant that any should dare to meddle with the old ; Affection clinging to some cherished association, with broken voice and with imploring hands, says, "Woodman, spare that tree." But as I look the woodman hath no pity, and at every stroke he destroys the useless, or dislodges the pestilent, or slaughters the cruel. The vision vanisheth, but again—

> "I look, aside the mist has rolled,
>   The waster seems the builder too ;
> Upspringing from the ruined old
>   I see the new !
>
> "Twas but the ruin of the bad,
>   The wasting of the wrong and ill ;
> Whate'er of good the old time had,
>   Is living still."

The woodman is there still, but he has thrown his axe aside, and now drives the ploughshare through the stubborn soil, or delves in the earth as lustily as though he knew that the colours of Eden were slumbering in the clods, and close upon him come the planter and the sower, and soon upon the *cleared ground*, there is the laugh of harvest, as reapers with their sickles bright

> "Troop, singing, down the mountain-side."

That vision of the present vanisheth, and, yet further away, there dawns on me the sight of the To-morrow. The woodman and his co-workers are dead—all dead !—but the work lives on. The seeds of the former time have ripened into a goodly growth, and there, on the spot where once the swamp was sluggish, and where once the serpent writhed, lo! a Paradise, wherein is man the loving and the happy, into which angels wander as of yore, and where the "voice of the Lord is heard speaking in the cool of the day."

Brother, this vision is no fable. It is for an appointed time, and it will not tarry. It is nearer for every outworn lie, and for every trampled fraud, for each scattered truth-seed, and each kindly speech and deed. Each of us may aid it in its coming. Children who fling seeds about in sport—Youth in its prime—Age in its maturity—Manhood in his energy of enterprise—Womanhood in her ministry of mercy—all may speed it onward. In a reverent mingling of Faith and Labour, it is ours to watch and to work for it. Do not mourn the past, my brother, it has given place to better times. Do not dread the coming of the future. It shall dawn in brighter and in safer glory. Come, and upon the altars of the faith be anointed as the Daniels of to-day, at once the prophet and the worker— the brow bright with the shining prophecy, the hands full of earnest and of holy deeds.

> "Thine the needed Truth to speak,
> Right the wronged, and raise the weak ;
> Thine to make earth's desert glad,
> In its Eden greenness clad.
> Thine to work as well as pray,
> Clearing thorny wrongs away,
> Plucking up the weeds of sin,
> Letting Heaven's warm sunshine in.

Watching on the hills of Faith,
Listening what the Spirit saith,
Catching gleams of temple-spires,
Hearing notes from angel-choirs.
Like the seer of Patmos, gazing
On the glory downward blazing,
Till, upon earth's grateful sod,
Rests the city of our God."

MACAULAY.

MACAULAY.

I AM in difficulties. There are three pictures vivid to my mental eye, which will haply illustrate these difficulties better than any long array of words. The first is that of a gleaner, by the dim light of the moon, searching painfully among the unwealthy stubble, in a harvest-field from which the corn has been reaped, and from which the reapers have withdrawn. I am that gleaner. About **the** great man who is my subject there has been as much said as would suffice for a long course of lectures, and as much written as would almost furnish a library. Where is the tongue which has not been loosened to utter his eulogy? Where is the pen which has not been swift in his praise? I have, therefore, to deal with matters which are already treasured as national property. If I am to furnish for you any but thin and blasted ears, I must of necessity enrich myself from the full sheaves of others. The second picture is that of an unfortunate individual, who has to write an art-criticism upon a celebrated picture, but who finds himself, with a small physique and with a horror of crowds, jammed hopelessly into the front rank of the spectators at the Academy, with the sun dazzling his eyes, and so near to the picture that he sees little upon the canvas but a vague and shapeless outline of colour. I am that unhappy critic, dazzled as I look upon my subject—and both you and I are too near for perfect vision. Macaulay, as every one knows, was through life identified with a political party. Even his literary efforts were prompted by political impulses, and tinged necessarily with political hues. It would seem, therefore, that to be accurately judged he must be looked at through the haze of years, when the strife of passion has subsided, and prepossession and prejudice have alike faded in the lapse of time. The third picture is that of a son, keenly affectionate, but of high integrity, clinging with almost reverent fondness to the memory of a father, but who has become conscious of one detraction from that father's excellence, which he may not conscientiously conceal. I am that mourning son. There are few of you who hold that marvellous Englishman more dear, or who are more jealous for the renown which, on his human side, he merits, and which has made his name a word of pride wherever Anglo-Saxons wander. If this world were all, I could admire and worship with the best of you, and no warning accompaniment should mingle with the music of praise; but I should be recreant to the duty which I owe to those who listen to me, and traitorous to my higher stewardship as a minister of Christ, if I forbore to warn you that, without godliness in the heart and in the life, the most brilliant career has failed of its allotted purpose, and there comes a paleness upon the lustre of the very proudest fame. It is enough. Your discernment perceives my difficulties, and your sympathy will accord me its indulgence while we speak together of the man who was the marvel of other lands, and who occupies no obscure place upon the bright bead-roll of his own—the rhetorician, the essayist, the poet, the statesman, the historian—Thomas Babington, first and last Baron Macaulay.

From a middle-class family, in a midland county in England, was born the man whom England delights to honour. The place of his birth was Rothley Temple, in Leicestershire, at the house of his uncle, Mr. Thomas Babington, after whom he was named; and the time the month of October, when the century was not many moons old. His grandfather was a minister of the Kirk of Scotland, who dwelt quietly in his manse at Cardross on the Clyde. His father, after the manner of Scotchmen, travelled in early life toward the south, that he might find wider scope for his enterprise and industry than the country of Macallum More could yield. His mother was the daughter of a bookseller in Bristol, who was a member of the Society of Friends. Some of his critics, on the "*post hoc propter hoc*" principle, have discovered in these two facts the reasons of his after severity against Scotchmen and Quakers. When, in these times, we ask after a man's parentage, it is not that we may know by how many removes he is allied to the Plantagenets, nor how many quarterings he is entitled to grave upon his shield. Estates and names are not the only inheritances of children. They inherit the qualities by which estates are acquired or scattered, and by which men carve out names for themselves, the prouder because they are self-won. Influences which are thrown around them in the years of early life are vital, almost creative in their power, upon the future of their being. You look upon a child in the rounded dimples of its happiness, with large wonder in its eyes, and brow across which sun and shadow chase each other ceaselessly. It is all unconscious of its solemn stewardship, and of the fine or fatal destiny which it may achieve; but you take the thoughts of responsibility and of influence into account, and you feel that of all known and terrible forces, short of Omnipotence, the mightiest may slumber in that cradle, or look wistfully from out those childish eyes. You look at it again when the possible of the child has developed into the actual of the man. The life purpose has been chosen, and there is the steady striving for its accomplishment. The babe who once slumbered so helplessly has become the village Hampden, or the cruel Claverhouse; the dark blasphemer, or the ready helper of the friendless; the poet, in his brief felony of the music of Paradise, or the missionary in his labour to restore its lost blessings to mankind. You might almost have predicted the result, because you knew the influences, subtle but mighty, which helped to confirm him in the right, or which helped to warp him to the wrong. And who shall say in the character of each of us, how much we are indebted to hereditary endowments, to early association, to the philosophy of parental rule, and to that retinue of circumstances which guarded us as we emerged from the dreamland of childhood into the actual experiences of life?

In the character and habits of Macaulay the results of these influences may be very largely discovered. Those of you who are familiar with the wicked wit of Sydney Smith will remember his reference to " the patent Christianity of Clapham;" and in Sir James Stephen's inimitable essay, the worthies of the Clapham sect are portrayed with such fidelity and power that we feel their presence, and they are familiar to us as the faces of to-day. Let us look in upon them on a summer's eve some fifty years ago. We are in the house of Henry Thornton, the wealthy banker, and for many years the independent representative of the faithful constituency of Southwark. The guests assemble in such numbers that it might almost be a gathering of the clan. They have disported on the spacious lawn, beneath the shadow of venerable elms, until the evening warns them inside, and they are in the oval saloon, projected and decorated, in his brief leisure, by William Pitt, and filled, to every available inch, with a well-selected library. Take notice of the company, for men of mark are here. There is *Henry Thornton* himself, lord of the innocent and happy revels, with open brow and searching eye; with a mind subtle to perceive and bright to harmonize the varied aspects of a question; with a tranquil soul, and a calm, judicial, persevering wisdom, which, if it never rose into heroism, was always ready to counsel and sustain the impulses of the heroism of others. That slight, agile, restless little man, with a crowd about him, whose rich voice rolls like music upon charmed listeners, as if he were a harper who played upon all hearts at his pleasure, can that be the apostle of the brotherhood? By what process of compression did the great soul of *Wilberforce* get into a frame so slender? It is the old tale of the genius and the fisherman revived. He is fairly abandoned to-night to the current of his own joyous fancies; now contributing to the stream of earnest talk which murmurs through the room, and now rippling into a merry laugh, light-hearted as a sportive child. There may be seen the burly form, and heard the sonorous voice of *William Smith*, the active member for Norwich, separated from the rest in theological beliefs, but linked with them in all human charities; who at threescore years and ten could say that he had no remembrance of an illness, and that though the head of a numerous family, not a funeral had ever started from his door. Yonder, with an absent air, as if awakened from some dear dream of prophecy, sits *Granville Sharp*, that man of chivalrous goodness; stern to indignation against every form of wrong-doing, gentle to tenderness towards the individual wrong-doer. The author of many publications, the patron of many societies, the exposer of many abuses, there was underlying the earnest purpose of his life a festive humour which made the world happy to him, and which gladdened the circle of his home. His leisure was divided, when he was not called to the councils of Clapham, between his barge, his pencil, and his harp, the latter of which he averred was after the precise pattern of David's; and strollers through the Temple Gardens in the early morning might often hear his voice, though broken by age, singing to it, as in a strange land, and "by the river" of the modern "Babylon," one of the songs of Zion. In his later years the study of prophecy absorbed him, and we smile at the kindly aberrations which devised portable wool-packs to save the lives at once of exposed soldiers in the Peninsula, and of starving artizans at home; which thought that in King Alfred's law of frankpledge there was a remedy for all the sorrows of Sierra Leone, and which mourned over the degeneracy of statesmen, because Charles Fox, whom he saw at the Foreign Office, had never so much as heard of Daniel's " Little Horn." Approaching with a half-impatient look, as if he longed to be breathing the fresh air in some glen of Needwood Chase, comes *Thomas Gisborne*, the sworn friend of Nature, to whom she whispered all her secrets of bird and stream and tree, and who loved her with a pure love, less only than that which he felt for the souls in his homely parish to whom he ministered the Word of Life. There, in a group, eagerly conversing together, are the lamented *Bowdler*, and the elder *Stephen*,—*Charles Grant*, then the reputed autocrat of that Leadenhall Street whose glory has so recently departed, and *John, Lord Teignmouth*, whose quiet, gentlemanly face one could better imagine in the chair of the Bible Society, than ruling in viceregal pomp over the vast empire of India. Summoned up from Cambridge to the gathering there is *Isaac Milner*, "of lofty stature, vast girth, and superincumbent wig," charged perhaps with some message of affection from good old John Venn, who then lay quietly waiting until his change should come; and *Charles Simeon*, redeemed from all affectations, as he is kindled by the reading of a letter which has just reached him from the far East, and which bears the signature of Henry Martyn. Are we mistaken, or did we discover in the crowd, lighted up with a fine benignity, the countenance of the accomplished *Mackintosh?* And surely there flitted by us, with characteristic haste, that active, working, marvellously expressive face which could answer to no other name than that of *Henry Brougham.* There is just one more figure in the corner upon whom we must for a moment linger, and as we pass towards him that we may get a nearer vision, look at that group of three ingenuous youths, drinking in the rich flow of soul with feelings of mingled shyness and pride. Can you tell their fortunes? The interpreting years would show them to you—the one dying beloved and honoured as the Professor of Modern History at Cambridge, the second living, as the active and eloquent Bishop of Oxford,* and the the third the future historian of his country, and one of her most renowned and most lamented sons.

With beetling brows, and figure robust but ungainly, slow of

---

* Now of Winchester.

speech, and with a face which told no tale, described as the man "whose understanding was proof against sophistry, and his nerves against fear," and who, though his demeanour was "inanimate, if not austere, excited among his chosen circle a faith approaching to superstition, and a love rising to enthusiasm."—What was the secret of *Zachary Macaulay's* power? Just this, the consecration of every energy to the one purpose upon which his life was offered as a living sacrifice—the sweeping from the face of the earth of the wrong and shame of slavery. An eye-witness of its abominations in Jamaica, a long resident at Sierra Leone, with the slave-trade flourishing around him, he became impressed with the conviction that God had called him to do battle with this giant sin, and from that moment he lived apart, lifted above ordinary cares and aims by the grandeur of this solemn inspiration. For this cause he laboured without weariness, and wrote with force and vigour. For this cause he suffered slander patiently, made light of fame and fortune, wasted health, and died poor. His friends marked this self-devotion, and respected it. They bowed in homage to the majesty of goodness. They regarded him almost as a being of superior order, while so deep was his humility, and so close his fellowship with God, that it became easy to imagine that he dwelt habitually in the presence of the shining ones, and that the glory of the mount upon which his footsteps often lingered, shone about him as he sojourned among men.

Such were the men who, as leaders of the "Clapham sect," as it was called, drew down the wonder of the worldly, and provoked the scoffing of the proud.

Oh rare and sacred fellowship! Where is the limner who will preserve for us these features upon canvas? Already

upon our walls we can live with the renowned and the worthy.
We see the great Duke in the midst of his companions-in-arms;
we are at home with Dr. Johnson and his friends; we are present when John Wesley dies; we can nod familiarly to a group
of free-traders; we can recognise noble sheep-breeders and
stalwart yeomen at an agricultural show; why should our moral
heroes be forgotten?   Who will paint the Clapham sect for us?
Their own age derided them; let us, their posterity, enthrone
them with double honour.   They sowed the seeds of which the
harvest waveth now.   It was theirs to commence, amid unfriendly watchers, those wide schemes of philanthropy which
have made the name of England blessed.   Catching the mantle of those holy men who in the early part of the last century were the apostles of the second Reformation, they had
perhaps a keener sense of the difficulties of evangelism, and a
more practical knowledge of the manners and customs of the
world.   Fearlessly as their fathers had testified in attestation of
some vital doctrine, they bore their heroic witness against insolent oppression and wrong; and to them we owe the creation
of that enlightened public opinion which has made the nation a
commonwealth, and the world a neighbourhood, which is so
prolific in its merciful inventions in the times in which we live;
and which, while it screens the peasant's thatch, protects
the beggar's conscience, and uplifts the poor man's home, is so
world-wide in its magnificence of charity, that it has an ear for
the plaint of the exile, a response to the cry of the Sudra, and
a tear for the sorrows of the slave.

With such healthy and stirring influences surrounding him,
Macaulay passed his childhood; and though in after years he
became the student rather than the worker,—"brought over,"

as Mr. Maurice significantly says, "from the party of the saints to the party of the Whigs,"—the results of the association stamped themselves upon his character, and we can trace them in his sturdy independence and consistent love of liberty, in his rare appreciation of the beauty of moral goodness, and in the quiet energy of perseverance which urged him to the mastery of every subject he handled, and which stored his mind so richly that he grew into a living encyclopædia of knowledge. The world has recently been enriched with information upon the subject of Macaulay's childhood, from the letters addressed to his father by the venerable Hannah More. This remarkable woman—sprightly at seventy as at twenty-five—was a living link between the celebrities of two ages, and wielded, from her retirement at Barley Wood, an influence of which it is scarcely possible for us to estimate the extent and value. Rich in recollections of Garrick, Burke, Walpole, and Johnson, she entered heartily into the schemes and interests of the world of later times, and many were the eminent names who sought her counsel, or who prized her correspondence and friendship. Her interest in the Macaulay family was increased by the fact that the Selina Mills, whom Zachary Macaulay afterwards married, had been under her charge as a pupil, when she and her sister kept a school in Bristol. From her letters we learn the impression of extraordinary endowment which the young Macaulay gave. When he had attained the mature age of eight, she rejoices "that his classicality has not extinguished his piety," and adds—"his hymns were really extraordinary for such a baby." What better illustration can there be of the old adage that poets are born, not made! "He lisped in numbers, and the numbers came." In his twelfth year, when the momentous question of a public school was debated in the parental councils, Hannah More gives her judgment in favour of his being sent to Westminster by day—thus, as she thought, securing the discipline and avoiding the danger. And in the same letter she says, "Yours, like Edwin, is no vulgar boy, and will require attention in proportion to his great superiority of intellect and quickness of passion. He ought to have competitors. He is like the prince who refused to play with anything but kings. I never saw any one bad propensity in him; nothing except natural frailty and ambition, inseparable, perhaps, from such talents and so lively an imagination. He appears sincere, veracious, tender-hearted, and affectionate." It would seem that private tuition was thought to have the advantage over public schools, for the Rev. Matthew M. Preston, then of Shelford, Cambridgeshire, and subsequently of Aspden House, Herts, was entrusted with the educational guardianship of young Macaulay. During his residence here, he is described as a studious, thoughtful boy, rather largely built than otherwise, with a head which seemed too big for his body, stooping shoulders, and pallid face; not renowned either at boating or cricket, nor any of the other articles in the creed of muscular Christianity, but incessantly reading or writing or repeating ballad-poetry by the yard or by the hour. Hannah More says that during a visit to Barley Wood, he recited all Bishop Heber's prize poem of " Palestine," and that they had "poetry for breakfast, dinner, and supper." She laboured hard to impress him with Sir Henry Saville's notion that poets are the best writers of all, *next* to those who have written prose, and seems to have been terribly afraid lest he should turn out a poet after all. It was about this period that he wrote an epitaph on Henry Martyn, which has been published as his earliest effort, and which other judges than partial ones will pronounce excellent, to have been written by a boy of twelve :—

> " Here Martyn lies ! in manhood's early bloom,
> The Christian hero found a Pagan tomb !
> Religion, sorrowing o'er her favourite son,
> Points to the glorious trophies which he won.
> Immortal trophies ! not with slaughter red,
> Not stained with tears by helpless orphans shed ;
> But trophies of the Cross ! In that dear Name,
> Through every scene of danger, toil, and shame,
> Onward he journeyed to that happy shore,
> Where danger, toil, and shame are known no more."

In the fifteenth year of his age, we find the young student, with characteristic energy, coming out as a church reformer, assailing the time-honoured prerogative of parish clerks, and making " heroic exertions " to promote, in the village where he worshipped, the responses of the congregation at large. The same period was signalised by the appearance of his first critical essay, and of his earliest published work—the criticism, however, ventured only in a letter to Barley Wood, and the work being neither an epic nor a treatise, but an index to the thirteenth volume of the *Christian Observer*. It seems that his father shared the jealousy of his poetical tendencies which Hannah More so frequently expressed ; and to curb his Pegasus, imposed on him the cultivation of prose composition, in one of its most useful, if not of its most captivating styles. The letter in which Macaulay talks the critiques, and alludes to the forthcoming publication, shall tell its own tale, and you may forget or remember, as you please, that the writer was not yet fifteen. After alluding to the illness of Mr. Henry Thornton, and to Hannah More's recovery from the effects of an accident by fire, he says:

"Every eminent writer of poetry, good or bad, has been publishing within the last month, or is to publish shortly. Lord Byron's pen is at work over a poem as yet nameless. Lucien Buonaparte has given the world his 'Charlemagne.' Scott has published his 'Lord of the Isles,' in six cantos—a beautiful and elegant poem ; and Southey his 'Roderick, the last of the Goths.' Wordsworth has printed 'The Excursion' (a ponderous quarto of five hundred pages), being a portion of the intended poem entitled 'The Recluse.' What the length of this intended poem is to be, as the Grand Vizier said of the Turkish poet—'n'est connu qu'à Dieu et à M. Wordsworth '—this forerunner, however, is to say no more, almost as long as it is dull ; not but that there are many striking and beautiful passages interspersed ; but who would wade through a poem

> "Where perhaps one beauty shines
> In the dry desert of a thousand lines."

To add to the list, my dear Madam, you will soon see a work of mine in print. Do not be frightened ; it is only the Index to the thirteenth volume of the *Christian Observer*, which I have had the honour of composing. Index-making, though the lowest, is not the most useless round in the ladder of literature ; and I pride myself upon being able to say that there are many readers of the *Christian Observer* who could do without Walter Scott's works, but not without those of

> "My dear Madam, your affectionate friend,
>
> "THOMAS B. MACAULAY."

From Mr. Preston's roof Macaulay proceeded in due course to Trinity College, Cambridge, the alma mater of so many distinguished sons, proud in the past of the fame of those whose "*mens divinior*" first developed itself within her classic precincts—her Bacon, Newton, Milton, Barrow—as she will be proud in the future of her later child, who spake of their greatness to the world. Such is reported to have been his distaste for mathematics that he did not compete for honours, but he twice carried off the Chancellor's medal for prize-poems on the subjects respectively of "Pompeii," and "Evening;" gained the Craven scholarship; and in 1822 obtained his Bachelor's degree. It should not be forgotten, and the mention of it may hearten into hope again some timid youth who has been discouraged by partial failure, that a third poem, on the inspiring subject of "Waterloo," failed to obtain the prize. In 1825 his Master's degree was taken, and in the year following he was called to the bar.

It was during his residence at the University that he started as an adventurer into that world of letters, which is so stony-hearted to the friendless and the feeble, but which, once propitiated or mastered, speeds the vigorous or the fortunate to the temple of fame. He was happy in the enterprising individual who first enlisted his ready pen. There were times when the publisher was as a grim ogre, who held the writer in his thrall; and there would be material for many an unwritten chapter of the "Calamities of Authors," if one could but recount the affronts put upon needy genius by vulgar but wealthy pride. They are to be congratulated who find a publisher with a heart to sympathise and a soul to kindle, as well as with brows to knit and head to reckon. It was well for

Macaulay, though his genius would have burst through all trammels, that he was a genial leader under whose banners he won his spurs of literary fame. There are few names which the literature of modern times should hold in dearer remembrance than the name of Charles Knight, at once the Mecænas of youthful authorship, and a worthy fellow-labourer with the band whom he gathered around him. He yet lives in the midst of us, though in the winter of his years. Long may it be ere Jerrold's apt epitaph be needed, and the last "Good Knight" be breathed above the turf that wraps his clay !

A goodly band of choice spirits those were, who, under various names, enriched the pages of "Knight's Quarterly Magazine." It is not too much to say, however, that though John Moultrie, Nelson Coleridge, and Winthrop Praed were among the valued contributors, the great charm of the magazine, during its brief but brilliant existence, was in the articles signed "Tristram Merton," which was the literary *alias* of Thomas Macaulay. In these earlier productions of his pen there are the foreshadowings of his future eminence, the same flashes of genius, the same antithetical power, the same prodigious learning, the same marvellous wealth of illustration, which so much entrance and surprise us in his later years. His versatility is amazing. Nothing comes amiss to him : Italian poets and Athenian orators—the revels of Alcibiades, and the gallantries of Cæsar, the philosophy of history, and the abstruser questions of political science,—all are discussed with boldness and fervour by this youth of twenty-four summers ; while those who read his fragments of a parish law-suit, and a projected epic, will pronounce him " of an infinite humour ;" and those who read his "Songs of the Huguenots," and of the "Civil

War," will recognise the first martial outbursts of the poet-soul which flung its fiery words upon the world in the "Lays of Ancient Rome." His old love of the ballad, which had been a passion in his schoolboy life, was not entirely overborne by his application to graver studies. Calliope had not yet been supplanted by Clio, and he sung the Battle of Naseby, for example, with a force of rushing words which takes our hearts by storm, in spite of olden prejudice or political creed, and which, in what some critics would call a wanton perversion of power, carries away the most peace-loving amongst us in a momentary insanity for war :

> "Oh ! wherefore come ye forth, in triumph from the North,
>   With your hands and your feet and your raiment all red ?
> And wherefore doth your rout send forth a joyous shout ?
>   And whence be the grapes of the wine-press which ye tread ?

> "Oh ! evil was the root, and bitter was the fruit,
>   And crimson was the juice of the vintage that we trod ;
> For we trampled on the throng of the haughty and the strong,
>   Who sate in the high places and slew the saints of God.

> "It was about the noon of a glorious day of June,
>   That we saw their banners dance and their cuirasses shine ;
> And the Man of Blood was there, with his long essenced hair,
>   And Astley, and Sir Marmaduke, and Rupert of the Rhine.

> " Like a servant of the Lord, with his Bible and his sword,
>   The General rode along us to form us for the fight,
> When a murmuring sound broke out, and swelled into a shout,
>   Among the godless horsemen upon the tyrant's right.

> " And hark ! like the roar of the billows on the shore,
>   The cry of battle rises along their charging line—
> For God ! for the Cause ! for the Church ! for the Laws!
>   For Charles, King of England, and Rupert of the Rhine!

" The furious German comes, with his clarions and his drums,
　　His bravoes of Alsatia and pages of Whitehall;
　They are bursting on our flanks.　Grasp your pikes:—close your
　　ranks :
　　For Rupert never comes but to conquer or to fall.

　　*　　*　　*　　*　　*　　*　　*　　*

" Stout Skippon hath a wound :—the centre hath given ground :—
　　Hark ! hark !—What means the trampling of horsemen on our rear?
　Whose banner do I see, boys? 'Tis he, thank God, 'tis he, boys,
　　Bear up another minute.　Brave Oliver is here !

" Their heads all stooping low, their points all in a row,
　　Like a whirlwind on the trees, like a deluge on the dykes,
　Our cuirassiers have burst on the ranks of the Accurst,
　　And at a shock have scattered the forests of his pikes.

" Fast, fast the gallants ride, in some safe nook to hide
　　Their coward heads, predestined to rot on Temple-Bar.
　And he—he turns, he flies,—shame on those cruel eyes
　　That bore to look on torture, and dared not look on war.

　　*　　*　　*　　*　　*　　*　　*

" Fools ! your doublets shone with gold, and your hearts were gay and
　　bold,
　　When you kissed your lily hands to your lemans to-day,
　And to-morrow shall the fox, from her chambers in the rocks,
　　Lead forth her tawny cubs to howl above the prey.

" And she of the seven hills shall mourn her children's ills,
　　And tremble when she thinks on the edge of England's sword;
　And the kings of earth in fear shall shudder when they hear
　　What the hand of God hath wrought for the Houses and the Word.'

It has been said that a speech delivered by Macaulay, on
the great question which absorbed his father's life, attracted
the notice of Jeffrey, then seeking for young blood wherewith

to enrich the pages of the "Edinburgh Review," and that this was the cause of his introduction into the guild of literature, of which he became the *decus et tutamen.* The world is now familiar with that series of inimitable essays, which were poured out in rapid and apparently inexhaustible succession, for the space of twenty years. To criticise them, either in mass or in detail, is no part of the lecturer's province; and even to enumerate them would entail a pilgrimage to many and distant shrines. As we surrender ourselves to his masterly guidance, we are fascinated beneath a life-like biography, or enchained by some sweet spell of travel we pronounce upon canons of criticism, and solve problems of government with a calm dogmatism which is troubled by no misgivings; we range unquestioned through the Court at Potsdam, mix in Italian intrigues, and settle Spanish successions; and, under the robe of the sagacious Burleigh, peer out upon the presence chamber of Elizabeth herself. Now, with Clive and Hastings, we tread the sultry Ind—our path glittering with "barbaric pearl and gold" —now on bloody Chalgrove we shudder to see Hampden fall, and anon we gaze upon the glorious dreamer, as he listens musingly to the dull plash of the water from his cell on Bedford Bridge. We stand aside, and are awed while Byron raves, and charmed while Milton sings. Addison condescendingly writes for us, and Chatham declaims in our presence; Madame d'Arblay trips lightly along the corridor, and Boswell comes ushering in his burly idol, and smirking like the showman of a giant. We watch the process curiously as an unfortunate poet is impaled amid the scattered Sibyllines of the reviews which puffed him; and we hold our breath while the Nemesis descends to crucify the miscreant Barère. In all moods of mind, in all varieties of experience, there is something for us of instruction or of warning. If we pause, it is from astonishment; if we are wearied, it is from excess of splendour; we are in a gorgeous saloon, from whose walls flash out upon us a long array of pictures, many of them Pre-Raphaelite in colour; and we are so dazzled by the brilliant hues, and by the effective grouping, that it is long ere we can ask ourselves whether they are true to nature, or to those deeper convictions which our spirits have struggled to attain. Criticism, for a season, becomes the vassal of delight; and we know not whether most to admire the prodigality of knowledge or the precision of utterance—the sagacity which foresees, or the fancy which embellishes—the tolerant temper, or the moral courage.

In these essays Macaulay has written his mental autobiography. He has done for us in reference to himself what, with all his brilliancy, he has often failed to do for us in his portraitures of others. He has shown us the man. He has anatomised his own nature. As in a glass we may here see him as he is. He is not the thinker—reverent, hesitating, troubled, but the rare expositor of the thoughts of elder time. He is not the discerner of spirits, born to the knowledge of others in the birth-pangs of his own regeneration, but the omnivorous reader, familiar with every corner of the book-world, and divining from the entrails of a folio, as the ancient augurs from the entrails of a bird. He is not the prophet, but has a shrewdness of insight which often stimulates the prophet's inspiration. He is not the philosopher, laying broad and deep the foundations of a new system, but the illustrator, stringing upon old systems a multitude of gathered facts; not dry nor tiresome, but transmuted into logic or poetry by the fire that burned within him. He is not the mere partisan, save only "in that unconscious disingenuousness from which the most upright man when strongly attached to an opinion is seldom wholly free," but the discriminating censor, who can deride the love-locks and fopperies of the Cavalier, and yet admire his chivalrous loyalty; who can rejoice in the stern virtues of the Puritan, and yet laugh at his small scruples and his nasal twang. He is not, alas! the Christian apostle, the witness alike amid the gloom of Gethsemane and on the Mount of Vision; not for him are either those agonies or that mountain-baptism; "he would have feared to enter into the cloud." He is rather the Hebrew scribe, astonished at the marvellous works, eager and fluent in recording them, and yet retaining his earthward leanings, and cherishing his country's dream of the advent of a temporal Messiah.

The first essay, that on Milton, at once established Macaulay's fame. In later years, he spoke of it as overloaded with gaudy and ungraceful ornament, and "as containing scarcely a paragraph such as his matured judgment approved." There are many yet, however, with whom its high moral tone, courage, and healthy freshness of feeling will atone for its occasional dogmatism, and for the efflorescence of its style. Who has not glowed to read that description of the Puritan worthies, "whose palaces were houses not made with hands; their diadems crowns of glory which should never fade away. On the rich and the eloquent, on nobles and priests, they looked down with contempt, for they esteemed themselves rich in a more precious treasure, and eloquent in a more sublime language; nobles by the right of an earlier creation, and priests by the imposition of a mightier hand?"

Scarcely less eloquent, though much less known, is the

description of the influence of the literature of Athens, which I quote as a fair example of the essayist's early style :

"It is a subject on which I love to forget the accuracy of a judge in the veneration of a worshipper, and the gratitude of a child. If we consider merely the subtlety of disquisition, the force of imagination, the perfect energy and eloquence of expression, which characterise the great works of Athenian genius, we must pronounce them intrinsically most valuable; but what shall we say when we reflect that from hence have sprung, directly or indirectly, all the noblest creations of the human intellect—that from hence were the vast accomplishments and the brilliant fancy of Cicero; the withering fire of Juvenal; the plastic imagination of Dante; the humour of Cervantes ; the comprehension of Bacon ; the wit of Butler; the supreme and universal excellence of Shakspeare? All the triumphs of truth and genius over prejudice and power, in every country and in every age, have been the triumphs of Athens. Wherever a few great minds have made a stand against violence and fraud, in the cause of liberty and reason, there has been her spirit in the midst of them—inspiring, encouraging, consoling; by the lonely lamp of Erasmus; by the restless bed of Pascal ; in the tribune of Mirabeau ; in the cell of Galileo; on the scaffold of Sidney. But who shall estimate her influence on private happiness? Who shall say how many thousands have been made wiser, happier, and better, by those pursuits in which she has taught mankind to engage?—to how many the studies which took their rise from her have been wealth in poverty, liberty in bondage, health in sickness, society in solitude ? Her power is indeed manifested at the bar, in the senate, in the field of battle, in the schools of philosophy. But these are not her glory. Wherever literature consoles sorrow, or assuages pain, wherever it brings gladness to eyes which fail with wakefulness and tears, and ache for the dark house and the long sleep, there is exhibited in its noblest form the immortal influence of Athens. The dervise, in the Arabian tale, did not hesitate to abandon to his comrade the camels with their load of jewels and gold, while he retained the casket of that mysterious juice which enabled him to behold at one glance all the hidden riches of the universe. Surely it is no exaggeration to say that no external advantage is to be compared with that purification of the intellectual eye which gives us to contemplate the infinite wealth of the mental world, all the hoarded treasures of its primeval dynasties, all the shapeless ore of its yet unexplored mines. This is the gift of Athens to man. Her freedom and her power have for more than twenty centuries been annihilated; her people have degenerated into timid slaves; her language into a barbarous jargon; her temples have been given up to the successive depredations of Romans, Turks, and Scotchmen; but her intellectual empire is imperishable. And when those who have rivalled her greatness shall have shared her fate; when civilization and knowledge shall have fixed their abode in distant continents; when the sceptre shall have passed away from England; when, perhaps, travellers from distant regions shall in vain labour to decipher on some mouldering pedestal the name of our proudest chief—shall hear savage hymns chanted to some misshapen idol over the ruined dome of our proudest temple, and shall see a single naked fisherman wash his nets in the river of the ten thousand masts—her influence and her glory will still survive, fresh in eternal youth, 'exempt from mutability and decay, immortal as the intellectual principle from which they derived their origin, and over which they exercise their control."

You will not fail to perceive in the last sentence of this quotation the first sketch of the celebrated New Zealander, who has certainly earned the privilege of a free seat on London Bridge, by the frequency with which he has "pointed a moral and adorned a tale." In his finished form, and busy at his melancholy work, he appears in an article on "Ranke's History of the Popes," to illustrate Macaulay's principle of the perpetuity of the Roman Catholic Church :—"She saw the commencement of all the governments, and of all the ecclesiastical establishments that now exist in the world ; and we feel no assurance that she is not destined to see the end of them all. She was great and respected before the Saxon had set foot in Britain, before the Frank had passed the Rhine, when Grecian eloquence still flourished at Antioch, when idols were still worshipped in the temple of Mecca. And she may still exist in undiminished vigour when some traveller from New Zealand shall, in the midst of a vast solitude, take his stand on a broken arch of London Bridge to sketch the ruins of St. Paul's." As one reads this oracular announcement, one is ready to enquire, 'Is it really so ? Is the tide to roll back so far ? Are all the struggles of the ages fruitless ? Has the light streamed into the darkness only that the darkness may not comprehend it ? The blood of our fathers, shed in the battle for dear life, that life of the spirit which is costlier far than this poor life of the body—has it flowed in vain ?' Ah ! he sees but events on the level, and the mists of the past dim the eyes that would penetrate the future. Let us get up higher, higher than the plain, higher than the plateau, higher than the table-land, even on to the summit where Faith rests upon the promises and awaits patiently their fulfilment; and in the light of that clear azure, which is unclouded by the fog or by the shadow, we shall learn other lessons than these. We shall see one purpose in the history of the nations, in the preparation of agencies, in the removal of hindrances, in the subordination, both of good and evil fortune, to the unfolding of one grand design. We shall see a profound religious movement awakened, growing, gathering strength, and preparing in secret for the ministry which its manhood is to wield. We shall see that Protestantism has hold of the world's intellectual wealth, spreads herself among new peoples as a missionary power, breathes even in Romish countries as a healing and salutary breath, and is heaving unconsciously in every trampled land which yearns and groans for freedom. We shall see science extending her discoveries, and Popery is at variance with science; Education diffusing her benefit, and Popery shrinks from knowledge; Liberty putting forth her hand that serfs may touch it, and leap at the touch into freemen, and Popery cannot harbour the free; Scripture universally circulated, and Popery loves not the Bible; and then, remembering that we have a sure word of prophecy, we know that its doom is spoken, and that in God's good time, Popery shall perish—thrown from the tired world which has writhed beneath its yoke so long,—perish, from its seven hills, and from its spiritual wickedness, utterly and for ever, before the Lord, "slain by the breath of His mouth, and consumed by the brightness of His coming."

To the wealth of Macaulay in illustration we have already

made reference, and also to the fact that his images are drawn but rarely from external nature. In books he found the enchanted cave which required but his " open sesame " to disclose to him the needed treasure; and in his discursive reading the highest book was not forgotten. The reader of his various works will not fail to be struck with his frequent scriptural allusions; and if he is in search of a peroration, and hits upon an image which rings more musically on the ear, or which lingers longer in the memory than another, it will be strange if he has not drawn it from that wonderful Bible which dispenses to all men, and is none the poorer for all the bounties of its magnificent giving. I select but two brief passages; the one from the essay on Lord Bacon, and the other from that on Southey's Colloquies of Society : " Cowley, who was among the most ardent, and not among the least discerning followers ot the new philosophy, has, in one of his finest poems, compared Bacon to Moses standing on Mount Pisgah. It is to Bacon, we think, as he appears in the first book of the Novum Organum, that the comparison applies with peculiar felicity. There we see the great lawgiver looking round from his lonely elevation on an infinite expanse, behind him a wilderness of dreary sands and bitter waters, in which successive generations have sojourned, always moving, yet never advancing, reaping no harvest, and building no abiding city; before him a goodly land, a land of promise, a land flowing with milk and honey ; while the multitude below saw only the flat sterile desert in which they had so long wandered, bounded on every side by a near horizon, or diversified only by some deceitful mirage, he was gazing from a far higher stand on a far lovelier country, following with his eye the long course of fertilising rivers, through ample pastures, and under the bridges of great capitals, measuring the distances of marts and havens, and portioning out all those wealthy regions from Dan to Beersheba." The other extract represents the evils of the alliance between Christianity and Power, and commends itself to our literary taste, even if we suppose that there are two sides to the shield: "The ark of God was never taken till it was surrounded by the arms of earthly defenders. In captivity its sanctity was sufficient to vindicate it from insult, and to lay the hostile fiend prostrate on the threshold of his own temple. The real security of Christianity is to be found in its benevolent morality, in its exquisite adaptation to the human heart, in the facility with which its scheme accommodates itself to the capacity of every human intellect, in the consolation which it bears to every house of mourning, in the light with which it brightens the great mystery of the grave. To such a system it can bring no addition of dignity or strength, that is part and parcel of the common law. It is not now for the first time left to rely on the force of its own evidences, and the attractions of its own beauty. Its sublime theology confounded the Grecian schools in the fair conflict of reason with reason. The bravest and wisest of the Cæsars found their arms and their policy unavailing, when opposed to the weapons that were not carnal, and the kingdom that was not of this world. The victory which Porphyry and Diocletian failed to gain, is not, to all appearance, reserved for any of those who have in this age, directed their attacks against the last restraint of the powerful, and the last hope of the wretched. The whole history of Christianity shows that she is in far greater danger of being corrupted by the alliance of power, than of being crushed by its opposition. Those who thrust temporal sovereignty upon her, treat her as their prototypes treated her Author. They bow the knee, and spit upon her; they cry ‘ Hail !’ and smite her on the cheek; they put a sceptre in her hand, but it is a fragile reed; they crown her, but it is with thorns; they cover with purple the wounds which their own hands have inflicted on her; and inscribe magnificent titles over the cross on which they have fixed her to perish in ignominy and pain.”

Every reader of the essays must be impressed with the marvellous versatility of knowledge which they disclose. What has he not read? is the question which we feel disposed to ask. Quotations from obscure writers, or from obscure works of great writers ; multitudinous allusions to ancient classics, or to modern authors whom his mention has gone far to make classic—references to some less studied book of Scripture— names which have driven us to the atlas to make sure of our geo- graphy—or to the Biographical Gallery to remind us that they lived ;—they crowd upon us so thickly that we are wildered in the profusion, and there is danger to our physical symmetry from the enlargement of our bump of wonder. It is said that, in allusion to this accumulation of knowledge, his associates rather profanely nicknamed him “ Macaulay the Omniscient ;” and indeed, the fact of his amazing knowledge is beyond dispute. Then, how did he get it? Did it come to him by the direct fiat of heaven, as Adam's, in Paradise ? Did he open his eyes and find himself the heir of the ages, as those who are born to fair acres and broad lands? Did he spring at once, like Minerva, from the brain of Jupiter, full-armed, a ripe and furnished scholar ? Or was he just favoured, as others, with a clear mind and a resolute will—with a high appreciation of knowledge, and a keen covetousness to make it his own? He had a wonderful memory, that is true; so that each fragment of his amassed lore seemed to be producible at will. He had a regal faculty, that also is true; by which all that he had gathered goldened into a beauty of its own; but it was the persevering industry of labour which brought stores to the retentive memory, and material to the creative mind. Work, hard work, the sweat of the brain through many an exhausting hour, and through many a weary vigil, was the secret after all, of his success. Many who slumber in nameless graves, or wander through the tortures of a wasted life, have had memories as capacious, and faculties as fine as he, but they lacked the steadiness of purpose, and patient thoughtful labour, which multiplied the "ten talents" into "ten other talents beside them." It is the old lesson, voiceful from every life that has a moral in it—from Bernard Palissy, selling his clothes, and tearing up his floor to add fuel to the furnace, and wearying his wife and amusing his neighbours with dreams of his white enamel, through the unremunerative years; from Warren Hastings, lying at seven years old upon the rivulet's bank, and vowing inwardly that he would regain his patrimonial property, and dwell in his ancestral halls, and that there should be again a Hastings of Daylesford; from William Carey, panting after the moral conquest of India, whether he sat at the lap-stone of his early craft, or wielded the ferule in the village school, or lectured the village elders when the Sabbath dawned. It is the old lesson,—a worthy purpose, patient energy for its accomplishment, a resoluteness that is undaunted by difficulties, and, in ordinary circumstances, success. Do you say that you are not gifted, and that therefore Macaulay is no model to you?—

that yours is a lowly sphere or a prosaic occupation, and that
even if you were ambitious to rise, or determined to become
heroic, your unfortunate surroundings would refuse to give you
the occasion? It is quite possible that you may not have the
affluent fancy, nor the lordly and formative brain. All men
are not thus endowed, and the world will never be reduced
to a level uniformity of mind. The powers and deeds of some
men will be always miracles to other men, even to the end of
time. It is quite possible, too, that the conditions of your life
may be unfavourable, that your daily course may not glow with
poetical incident, nor ripple into opportunities of ostentatious
greatness. But, granted all these disadvantages, it is the part
of true manhood to make its own occasions. The highest
greatness is not that which waits for favourable circumstances,
but that which compels hard fortune to do it service, which
slays the Nemæan lion, and goes on to further conquests.
robed in its tawny hide. The real heroes are the men who
constrain the tribute which men would fain deny them,—

> " Men who walk up to Fame as to a friend,
>   Or their own house, which from the wrongful heir
>   They have wrested : from the world's hard hand and gripe,
>   Men who—like Death, all bone, but all unarmed—
>   Have ta'en the giant world by the throat, and thrown him,
>   And made him swear to maintain their name and fame
>   At peril of his life."

There are few of you, perhaps, who could achieve distinction ; there are none of you who need be satisfied without
an achievement that is infinitely higher. You may make your
lives beautiful and blessed. The poorest of you can afford

to be kind; the least gifted amongst you can practise that loving wisdom which knows the straightest road to human hearts. You may not be able to thrill senates with your eloquence, but you may see eyes sparkle and faces grow gladder when you appear; you may not astonish the listeners by your acquirements of varied scholarship, but you may dwell in some spirits, as a presence associated with all that is beautiful and holy; you may neither be a magnate nor a millionaire, but you may have truer honours than of earth, and riches which wax not old. You may not rise to patrician estate, and come under that mysterious process by which the churl's blood is transformed into the nobleman's, but you may ennoble yourselves in a higher aristocracy than that of belted earl. Use the opportunities you have; make the best of your circumstances, however unpromising. Give your hearts to God, and your lives to earnest work and loving purpose, and you can never live in vain. Men will feel your influence like the scent of a bank of violets, fragrant with the hidden sweetness of the spring. Men will miss you when you cease from their communions, as if a calm, familiar star shot suddenly and brightly from their vision; and if there wave not at your funeral the trappings of the world's gaudy woe, " eyes full of heartbreak" will gaze wistfully adown the path where you have vanished, and in the long after-time, hearts which you have helped to make happy will recall your memory with gratitude and tears.

The union of great acquirements and great rhetorical power so manifest in Macaulay's mind, could not fail to render him a desirable acquisition to any political party; and as he had imbibed, and in some sort inherited, Whig principles, an opportunity was soon found for his admission into Parliament, where he appeared in time to join in the discussions on the first Reform Bill. He was returned, in February, 1830, by the influence of the Marquis of Lansdowne, for the nomination borough of Calne. He sat for Calne until the passing of the Reform Bill, when he was elected one of their first representatives by the newly created constituency of Leeds. In 1834 he was appointed a Member of Council in India, and devoted himself to the construction of a new penal code for that part of her Majesty's dominions. This was his sole legislative offspring, and, from the best estimate which we can form from imperfect knowledge, it would seem to have been exquisite on paper, but useless in working—a brilliant, but impracticable thing. During his residence in India he continued on the staff of the "Edinburgh," and contributed some of his superb criticisms from beneath an Eastern sky. Here, also, it is probable that he gathered the material and sketched the plan of those masterly articles which, perhaps, more than most others, aroused English sympathies for India—the articles on Warren Hastings and Lord Clive. In May, 1839, he reappeared in Parliament, on the elevation to the peerage of Mr. Speaker Abercromby, as the representative of Edinburgh. He was re-elected at the general election of 1841, and twice on occasion of his accession to office. In 1847, at the general election, he failed to obtain his seat, partly, as it is said, from the brusque manner in which he treated his constituents, and partly from his consistent support of the enlarged Maynooth grant, to which many of those who had previously supported him were conscientiously opposed. The papers were loud in condemnation of the Edinburgh electors, who were represented as having disgraced themselves for ever by their rejection of a man of so much excellent renown. Well, if a representative is to be chosen for his brilliant parts, or for his fluent speech, perhaps they did; but if men vote for conscience sake, and they feel strongly on what they consider a vital question, and if a representative is to be what his name imports—the faithful reflex of the sentiments of the majority who send him—one can see nothing in the outcry but unreasoning clamour I cannot see dishonour either in his sturdy maintenance of unpopular opinions, or in his constituents' rejection of him because his sentiments were opposed to their own ; but I can see much that is honourable to both parties in their reconciliation after temporary estrangement,—on their part, that they should honour him by returning him in 1852, unsolicited, at the head of the poll,—on his part, that he should, with a manly generosity, bury all causes of dissension, and consent to return to public life, as the representative of a constituency which had bidden him for a season to retire. There is, indeed, no part of Macaulay's character in which he shows to more advantage than in his position as a member of parliament. We may not always be able to agree with him in sentiment, we may fancy that we discover the fallacies which lurk beneath the shrewdness of his logic, we may suffer now and then from the apt sarcasm which he was not slow to wield ; but we must accord to him the tribute that his political life was a life of unswerving consistency and of stainless honour. In his lofty scorn of duplicity he became, perhaps, sometimes contemptuous, just as in his calm dogmatism he never seemed to imagine that there were plausible arguments which might be adduced on both sides of a question; but in his freedom from disguise, and abhorrence of corruption, in his refusal to parley when compromise would have been easy, and in his refusal to be silent when silence would have wounded his conscience but saved his seat, in the noble indignation with which he denounced oppression, and in his independence of all influences which were crafty and contemptible, he may fairly be held up as a model English statesman. Before the Reform Bill, the members for the city usually subscribed fifty guineas to the Edinburgh races, and shortly after the election of 1841, Mr. Macaulay was applied to on this behalf. His reply was a fine specimen of manly decision. " In the first place," he says, " I am not clear that the object is a good one. In the next place, I am clear that by giving money for such an object in obedience to such a summons, I should completely change the whole character of my connection with Edinburgh. It has been usual enough for rich families to keep a hold on corrupt boroughs by defraying the expense of public amusements. Sometimes it is a ball, sometimes a regatta. The Derby family used to support the Preston races. The members for Beverley, I believe, find a bull for their constituents to bait. But these were not the conditions on which I undertook to represent Edinburgh. In return for your generous confidence I offer faithful parliamentary service, and I offer nothing else. The call that is now made is one so objectionable, that I must plainly say I would rather take the Chiltern Hundreds than comply with it." All honour to the moral courage which indited that reply. Brothers, let the manly example fire you. Carry such heroism into your realms of morals and of commerce, and into all the social interlacings of your life; let no possible loss of influence or patronage or gold tempt you to the doing of that which your judgment and conscience disapprove.   Better a thousand times to be slandered than to sin; nobler to spend your days in all the bitterness of unheeded struggle, than become a hollow parasite to gain a hollow friend. Worthier far to remain poor for ever, the brave and self-respecting heir of the crust and of the spring, than, in another sense than Shakspeare's, to " coin your heart," and for the " vile drachmas," which are the hire of wrong, " to drop your " generous " blood."

Macaulay's speeches, published by himself in self-defence against the dishonest publication of them by other people, bear the stamp and character of the essay rather than of the oration, and reveal all the mental qualities of the man—his strong sense and vast learning, his shrewdness in the selection of his materials, and his mastery over that sort of reasoning which silences if it does not convince.   They betray also, very largely, the idiosyncrasy which is, perhaps, his most observable faculty, the disposition to regard all subjects in the light of the past, and to treat them historically, rather than from the experience of actual life.   Thus in his speeches on the East India Company's charter, on the motion of want of confidence in the Melbourne ministry, on the state of Ireland, on the Factories Bill, on the question of the exclusion of the Master of the Rolls from parliament, he ransacks for precedents and illustrations in the histories of almost every age and clime, while he gives but vague and hesitating solutions on the agitating problems of the day.   Hence, though his last recorded speech is said to have been unrivalled in the annals of parliamentary oratory for the number of votes which it won, the impression of his speeches in the general was not so immediate as it will, perhaps, be lasting.   Men were conscious of a despotism while he spoke, and none wished to be delivered from the sorcery; but when he ceased the spell was broken, and they awoke as from a pleasant dream. They were exciting discussions in which he had to engage, and he did not wholly escape from the acrimony of party strife. There are passages in his speeches of that exacerbated bitterness which has too often made it seem as if our politicians acted upon the instructions which are said to have been once endorsed upon the brief of an advocate—" No case, but abuse the plaintiff's attorney."

There is one extract from the speeches which I quote with singular pleasure. It will answer the double purpose of affording a fair specimen of his clear and earnest style, and of revealing what, to a resident in India, and one of the most shrewd and sagacious observers, appeared sound policy in reference to the method in which that country should be governed. It is from his speech on Mr. Vernon Smith's motion of censure on Lord Ellenborough anent the celebrated gates of Somnauth. " Our duty, as rulers, was to preserve strict neutrality on all questions merely religious; and I am not aware that we have ever swerved from strict neutrality for the purpose of making proselytes to our own faith. But we have, I am sorry to say, sometimes deviated from the right path in an opposite direction. Some Englishmen, who have held high office in India, seem to have thought that the only religion which was not entitled to toleration and respect was Christianity. They regarded every Christian missionary with extreme jealousy and disdain; and they suffered the most atrocious crimes, if enjoined by the Hindoo superstition, to be perpetrated in open day. It is lamentable to think how long after our power was firmly established in Bengal, we, grossly neglecting the first and plainest duty of the civil magistrate, suffered the practices of infanticide and suttee to continue unchecked. We decorated the temples of the false gods. We provided the dancing girls. We gilded and painted the images to which our ignorant subjects bowed down. We repaired and embellished the car under the wheels of which crazy devotees flung themselves at every festival to be crushed to death. We sent guards of honour to escort pilgrims to the places of worship. We actually made oblations at the shrines of idols. All this was considered, and is still considered, by some prejudiced Anglo-Indians of the old school, as profound policy. I believe that there never was so shallow, so senseless a policy. We gained nothing from it. We lowered ourselves in the eyes of those whom we meant to flatter. We led them to believe that we attached no importance to the difference between Christianity and heathenism. Yet how vast that difference is! I altogether abstain from alluding to topics which belong to divines; I speak merely as a politician, anxious for the morality and the temporal well-being of society; and so speaking, I say that to countenance the Brahminical idolatry, and to discountenance that religion which has done so much to promote justice, and mercy, and freedom, and arts, and sciences, and good government, and domestic happiness, which has struck off the chains of the slave, which has mitigated the horrors of war, which has raised women from servants and playthings into companions and friends, is to commit high treason against humanity and civilization." I should like to commend this manly and Christian utterance to our rulers now. The old traditional policy is yet a favourite sentiment with many, though it has borne its bitter fruits of bloodshed. While we thankfully acknowledge an improved state of feeling, and the removal of many restrictions which in former times hindered the evangelization of India, we must never forget that at this day, not by a company of traders, but the government of our beloved Queen, there is in all government schools on that vast continent, a brand upon the Holy Bible. It may lie upon the shelf of the library, but for all purposes of instruction it is a sealed book. The Koran of the Mussulman is there, the Shastras of the pagan are there, the Zend Avesta of the Parsee is there; and their lessons, sanguinary or sensual or silly, are taught by royal authority, and the teachers endowed by grants from the royal treasury; but the Book which England acknowledges as the fountain of highest inspiration, and the source of loftiest morals; from whose pure precepts all sublime ethics are derived; which gives sanction to government, and majesty to law; on which senators swear their allegiance, and royalty takes its coronation oath,—that Book is not only ignored but proscribed, subjected to an Index Expurgatorius as rigid as ever issued from Rome; branded with this foul dishonour before scoffing Mussulmen and wondering pagans at the bidding of state-craft, or spurious charity, or fear. It is time that this should end. Our holy religion ought not to be thus " wounded in the house of her" enemies, by the hands of her professed "friends." An empire which extends " from Cape Comorin to the eternal snow of the Himalayas," " far to the east of the Burrampooter and far to the west of the Hydaspes," should not demean itself before those whom it has conquered by a proclamation of national irreligion. We ask for Christianity in India neither coercive measures nor the boastful activity of government proselytism. Those who impute this to the Christians of England are either ignorant of our motives, or they slander us for their own ends. The rags of a political piety but disfigure the Cross around which they are ostentatiously displayed, and to bribe a heathen into conformity were as bad as to persecute him for his adhesion to the faith of his fathers. All we ask of the government is a fair field; if Alexander would but stand out of the way, the fair sunshine would stream at once into the darkness of the Cynic's dwelling; if they will give freedom to the Bible, it will assert its own supremacy by its own power, and Britain will escape from the curse which now cleaves to her like a Nessus' robe—that in a land committed to her trust, and looking up to her for redress and blessing, she has allowed the Word upon which rest the dearest hopes of her sons for eternity, to be forbidden from the Brahman's solicitude, and trampled beneath the Mollah's scorn.

In the year 1842 Mr. Macaulay appeared in a new character, by the publication of the " Lays of Ancient Rome." This was his first venture in acknowledged authorship. It is often not safe to descend from the bench to the bar. The man who has long sat in the critic's chair must have condemned so many criminals that he will find little mercy when he is put upon his own trial, and has become a suppliant for the favour which he has been accustomed to grant or refuse. The public were taken by surprise, but surprise quickly yielded to delight. Minos and Rhadamanthus abdicated their thrones to listen; every pen flowed in praise of that wonderful book, which united rare critical sagacity with the poetic faculty and insight; and now, after the lapse of years, the world retains its enthusiasm, and refuses to reverse the verdict of its first approval. By one critic, indeed, whose opinions are entitled to all respect, the ballads are said to be as much below the level of Macaulay, as the

" Cato" of Addison was below all else which proceeded from his pen. But there is surely more in them than " rattling and spirited songs." These are expressions which hardly describe those minutely accurate details; that gorgeousness of classic colouring, those exquisite felicities of word; and, above all, that grand roll of martial inspiration which abounds throughout their stirring lines. Another critic strangely says that " none of the characters have the flesh and blood, the action and passion of human nature." The test of this, I suppose, should be the effect which they produce upon those who hear or read them. It has not been an unfrequent charge against Macaulay that he had no heart, and that he was wanting in that human sympathy which is so large an element of strength. He who has no heart of his own cannot reach mine and make it feel. There are instincts in the soul of a man which tell him unerringly when a brother soul is speaking. Let me see a man in earnest, and his earnestness will kindle mine. I apply this test in the case of Macaulay. I am told of the greatest anatomist of the age suspending all speculations about the mastodon, and all analyses of the lesser mammalia, beneath the spell of the sorcerer who drew the rout at Sedgemoor and the siege of Derry. I see Robert Hall lying on his back at sixty years of age, to learn the Italian language, that he might verify Macaulay's description of Dante, and enjoy the " Inferno" and the " Paradiso" in the original. I remember my own emotions when first introduced to the Essays; the strange, wild heart-throbs with which I revelled in the description of the Puritans; and the first article on Bunyan. There is something in all this more than can be explained by artistic grouping or by the charms of style. The man has convictions and sympathies of his own, and the very strength of those convictions and sympathies forces an answer from the "like passions" to which he appeals. It is just so with the poetry. It were easy to criticise it, and perhaps to find in it some shortcomings from the rules of refined melody, and a ruggedness which the linked sweetness of the Lakers might not tolerate; but try it in actual experiment, sound it in the ears of a Crimean regiment, and see how it will inspirit them to the field; rehearse it with earnestness and passion to a company of ardent schoolboys, at the age when the young imagination has just been thrilled with its first conscious sense of beauty and of power; and you shall have the Bard's best guerdon in their kindling cheeks and gleaming eyes. "The Prophecy of Capys" is perhaps the most sustained, "Virginia" the most eloquent, and "The Battle of the Lake Regillus" the one which contains the finest passages; but I confess to a fondness for "Horatius," my first and early love, which all the wisdom which ought to have come with maturity has not been able to change. Perhaps you will bear with a few stanzas of it, just to try the effect upon yourselves:

> "But the Consul's brow was sad,
>   And the Consul's speech was low,
> And darkly looked he at the wall,
>   And darkly at the foe.
> 'Their van will be upon us
>   Before the bridge goes down;
> And if they once but win the bridge,
>   What hope to save the town?'
>
> "Then out spake brave Horatius,
>   The Captain of the Gate:
> 'To every man upon this earth
>   Death cometh soon or late.

And how can man die better
  Than facing fearful odds,
For the ashes of his fathers,
  And the temples of his gods?'

*   *   *   *   *   *

"'Hew down the bridge, Sir Consul,
  With all the speed ye may;
I, with two more to help me,
  Will hold the foe in play.
In yon strait path a thousand
  May well be stopped by three,
Now who will stand on either hand,
  And keep the bridge with me?'

"Then out spake Spurius Lartius;
  A Ramnian proud was he:
'Lo, I will stand at thy right hand,
  And keep the bridge with thee.'
And out spake strong Herminius;
  Of Titian blood was he:
'I will abide on thy left side,
  And keep the bridge with thee.'

"'Horatius,' quoth the Consul,
  'As thou sayest, so let it be.'
And straight against that great array
  Forth went the dauntless Three.
For Romans in Rome's quarrel
  Spared neither land nor gold,
Nor son nor wife, nor limb nor life,
  In the brave days of old.

"Then none was for a party;
  Then all were for the state;
Then the great man helped the poor,
  And the poor man loved the great:

Then lands were fairly portioned ;
  Then spoils were fairly sold :
The Romans were like brothers
  In the brave days of old.

*　　*　　*　　*

" But all Etruria's noblest
  Felt their hearts sink to see
On the earth the bloody corpses,
  In the path the dauntless Three !
And, from the ghastly entrance
  Where those bold Romans stood,
All shrank, like boys who unaware,
Ranging the woods to start a hare,
Come to the mouth of the dark lair
Where, growling low, a fierce old bear
  Lies amidst bones and blood.

" Was none who would be foremost
  To lead such dire attack :
But those behind cried 'Forward !'
  And those before cried ' Back !'
And backward now and forward
  Wavers the deep array ;
And on the tossing sea of steel
To and fro the standards reel ;
And the victorious trumpet peal
  Dies fitfully away.

" But meanwhile axe and lever
  Have manfully been plied ;
And now the bridge hangs tottering
  Above the boiling tide.
' Come back, come back, Horatius !'
  Loud cried the Fathers all.
' Back, Lartius! back, Herminius !
  Back, ere the ruin fall !'

'Back darted Spurius Lartius ;
   Herminius darted back ;
And, as they passed, beneath their feet
   They felt the timbers crack.
But when they turned their faces
   And on the farther shore
Saw brave Horatius stand alone,
   They would have crossed once more.

"But with a crash like thunder
   Fell every loosened beam,
And, like a dam, the mighty wreck
   Lay right athwart the stream ;
And a long shout of triumph
   Rose from the walls of Rome,
As to the highest turret-tops
   Was splashed the yellow foam.

    *   *   *   *

"Alone stood brave Horatius,
   But constant still in mind ;
Thrice thirty thousand foes before,
   And the broad flood behind.
'Down with him !' cried false Sextus,
   With a smile on his pale face.
'Now yield thee,' cried Lars Porsena,
   'Now yield thee to our grace.'

"Round turned he, as not deigning
   Those craven ranks to see ;
Nought spake he to Lars Porsena,
   To Sextus nought spake he !
But he saw on Palatinus
   The white porch of his home ;
And he spake to the noble river
   That rolls by the towers of Rome.

F

" ' Oh, Tiber ! father Tiber !
  To whom the Romans pray,
A Roman's life, a Roman's arms,
  Take thou in charge this day ! '
So he spake, and speaking sheathed
  The good sword by his side,
And with his harness on his back,
  Plunged headlong in the tide.

" No sound of joy or sorrow
  Was heard from either bank ;
But friends and foes in dumb surprise,
  With parted lips and straining eyes,
Stood gazing where he sank ;
  And when above the surges
  They saw his crest appear,
All Rome sent forth a rapturous cry,
And even the ranks of Tuscany
  Could scarce forbear to cheer.

  *   *   *   *   *   *

" Never, I ween, did swimmer,
  In such an evil case,
Struggle through such a raging flood
  Safe to the landing place :
But his limbs were borne up bravely
  By the brave heart within,
And our good father Tiber
  Bare bravely up his chin.

" ' Curse on him ! ' quoth false Sextus ;
  ' Will not the villain drown ?
But for this stay, ere close of day
  We should have sacked the town.'
' Heaven help him ! ' quoth Lars Porsena.
  'And bring him safe to shore ;
For such a gallant feat of arms
  Was never seen before.'

"And now he feels the bottom;
    Now on dry earth he stands;
Now round him throng the Fathers
    To press his gory hands;
And now, with shouts and clapping,
    And noise of weeping loud,
He enters through the River-gate,
    Borne by the joyous crowd.

"They gave him of the corn land,
    That was of public right,
As much as two strong oxen
    Could plough from morn till night;
And they made a molten image,
    And set it up on high,
And there it stands unto this day
    To witness if I lie.

*   *   *   *   *   *

"And in the nights of winter,
    When the cold north winds blow,
And the long howling of the wolves
    Is heard amidst the snow;
When round the lonely cottage
    Roars loud the tempest's din,
And the good logs of Algidus
    Roar louder yet within—

"When the oldest cask is opened,
    And the largest lamp is lit;
When the chestnuts glow in the embers,
    And the kid turns on the spit;
When young and old in circle
    Around the firebrands close;
When the girls are weaving baskets,
    And the lads are shaping bows—

> "When the goodman mends his armour,
>   And trims his helmet's plume ;
> When the goodwife's shuttle merrily
>   Goes flashing through the loom ;
> With weeping and with laughter
>   Still is the story told,
> How well Horatius kept the bridge
>   In the brave days of old."

It is undoubtedly as the historian that Macaulay will be longest remembered. His work, fragment though it is, possesses a sort of dramatic unity, will survive at once flattery and criticism, and will be shrined among the classics of our literature in calmer times than ours. It is amusing to read the various opinions of reviewers, each convinced after the manner of such literary craftsmen that he is nothing if not critical, and gloating over some atom of inaccuracy as if he had found hidden treasure. I deemed it my duty in the preparation for this lecture to go through a course of review reading, if haply I might find confirmation of the sentiments I had entertained, or some reason to change them ; and while I was delighted with and proud of the vast and varied talent of the articles, the result as to opinion was only to unsettle my own, and to induce a mental dyspepsia from which I was long to recover. I was told that it is *the* History of England—*a* history of England—an attempt at history—a mistaken notion of history—an historiette—an historical picture gallery— an historical novel. I was informed that it is thoroughly impartial, and I was informed that it is thoroughly factious : one critic tells me that his first object is to tell the story truly ; another, that his first object is picturesque effect. Some christen him Thucydides, and others Walter Scott. One eulogist exalts my confidence by assuring me that "he does not lie, even for the Whigs;" and just as I have made up my mind to trust him thoroughly, I am thrown into terrible bewilderment by the averment of another learned Theban, that "his work is as full of political prejudice as any of his partizan speeches, and is written with bad taste, bad feeling, and bad faith." The impression left upon my mind by all this conflict of testimony is a profound conviction of Macaulay's power. All the faults which his censors charge upon him reappear in their own writings, as among the supple courtiers of Macedon was reproduced the wry neck of Alexander. They charge him with carelessness, but it is in flippant words. If they call him vituperative, they become atrabilious. If he is said to exaggerate, not a few of them out-Herod him; and his general impartiality may be inferred from the fact, that while his critics are indignant at the caricatures which they allege that he has drawn of their own particular idols, they acknowledge the marvellous fidelity of his likenesses of all the world beside. Moreover, for the very modes of their censorship they are indebted to him. They bend Ulysses' bow. They wield the Douglas brand. His style is antithetical, and therefore they condemn him in antitheses. His sentences are peculiar, and they denounce him in his own tricks of phrase. There can be no greater compliment to any man. The critics catch the contagion of the malady which provokes their surgery. The eagle is aimed at by the archers, but "he nursed the pinion which impelled the steel." To say that there are faults in the history is but to say that it is a human production, and they lie on the surface and are patent to the most ordinary observer. That he was a "good hater" there can be no question; and Dr. Johnson, the while he would have called him a vile Whig, and a sacreligious heretic, would have hugged him for the heartiness with which he lays on his dark shades of colour. That he exaggerated rather for effect than for partizanship, may be alleged with great show of reason, and they have ground to stand upon who say that it was his greatest literary sin. There are some movements which he knew not how to estimate, and many complexities of character which he was never born to understand. Still, if this be not history, there is no history in the world. Before his entrance history, for the masses of English readers, was as the marble statue ; he came, and by his genius struck the statue into life.

We thank him that he has made history readable ; that it is not in his page the bare recital of facts, names and deeds inventoried as in an auctioneer's catalogue, but a glowing portraiture of the growth of a great nation, and of the men who helped or hindered it. We thank him that he has disposed for ever of that shallow criticism, that the brilliant is always the superficial and unworthy, and that in the inestimable value of his work he has confirmed what the sonorous periods of John Milton, and the long-resounding eloquence of Jeremy Taylor, and the fiery passion-tones of Edmund Burke had abundantly declared before him, that the diamond flashes with a rarer lustre than the spangle. We thank him for the happy combination which he has given us of instruction and literary enjoyment, of massive truth decorated with all the graces of style. We thank him for the vividness of delineation by which we can see statesmen like Somers amd Nottingham in their cabinets, marshals like Sarsfield and Luxembourg in the field, and men like

Buckingham and Marlborough, who dallied in the council-room and plotted at the revel.

We thank him for the one epical character which he has left us—William, the hero of his story, whom he has taxed himself to the utmost to pourtray—the stadtholder adored in Holland—the impassive monarch who ' lived apart' in the kingdom which he freed and ruled—the audacious spirit of whom no one could discover the thing that could teach him to fear—the brave soldier who dashed about among musketry and sword-blades as if he bore a charmed life—the reserved man upon whom " danger acted like wine, to open his heart and loosen his tongue"— the veteran who swam through the mud at the Boyne, and retrieved the fortunes which the death of Schomberg had caused to waver—" the asthmatic skeleton who covered the slow retreat of England " at Landen—the acute diplomatist who held his trust with even-handed wisdom—the faithful friend who, when he loved once, loved for a lifetime—who kept his heart barred against the multitude, but gave pass-keys to the chosen ones so that they might go in and out at pleasure—the stern and stoical sufferer who wrote, and hunted, and legislated, and devised, while ague shook the hand which held the pen or the bridle, and fever was burning away the life which animated the restless brain—the rigid predestinarian, who though he grieved over noble works unfinished, and plans which could never become deeds, submitted himself calmly as a child when the inevitable hour drew nigh. We feel that, if there had been nothing else, the working out of that one character, its investiture with " newer proportions and with richer colouring," the grand exhibition which it gives us of the superiority of mind over matter and circumstance, and native repulsiveness and alien habits, is in itself a boon for which the world should speak him well.

Above all, we thank Macaulay for the English-heartedness which throbs transparently through his writings, and which was so marked a characteristic of his life. It may be well said of him as he said of Pitt, " he loved his country as a Roman the city of the Seven Hills, as an Athenian the city of the Violet Crown." Herein is his essential difference from the hero whom he celebrated, and whom in many things he so closely resembles. William never loved England. She was but an appanage of Holland to him. One bluff Dutch burgomaster would outweigh with him a hundred English squires, and he was never so happy as when he could escape from the foggy Thames to the foggier Meuse, or be greeted with a Rhenish welcome by a people to whom an enthusiasm was as an illness which came once in a lifetime, and was over. But with Macaulay the love of country was a passion. How he kindles at each stirring or plaintive memory in the annals he was so glad to record! Elizabeth at Tilbury; the scattering of the fierce and proud Armada; the deliverance of the Seven Bishops; the thrilling agony and bursting gladness which succeeded each other so rapidly at the siege of Derry; the last sleep of Argyle; Lord Russell's parting from his heroic wife; the wrongs of Alice Lisle; the prayer upon whose breath fled the spirit of Algernon Sydney; they touch his very soul, and he recounts them with a fervour which becomes contagious until his readers are thrilled with the same joy or pain.

It is not unfashionable among our popular writers to denounce the England of to-day, and to predict for us in the future auguries of only sinister omen. There is a school of prophets to whom everything in the present is out of joint; who can see nothing around them but selfishness, and nothing beyond them but the undiscoverable bourn, to whom there is "cold shade" in an aristocracy, and in the middle classes but a miserable mammon-worship: and beneath a trampled people in whom the sordid and the brutal instincts strive from day to day. Of these extremes of sentiment, meeting on the common ground of gloomy prophesyings about England, her history, as Macaulay has told it, is the best possible rebuke. He has shown us the steps by which, in his own eloquent words, "the England of the Curfew and the Forest laws, the England of Crusaders, monks, schoolmen, astrologers, serfs, outlaws, became the England which we know and love, the classic ground of liberty and philosophy, the school of all knowledge, the mart of all trade." He has shown us how, through the slow struggles of years, the component forces of society become equalized in their present rare and happy adjustment; how each age has added to the conquests of its predecessors, by the truer solution of political problems; by the readier recognition of human rights; by the discovery of richer resources in nature, and of more magnificent capabilities in man. He has shown us how in health, in intelligence, in physical comfort, in industrial appliances, in social and moral culture, the tide of progress has rolled on without a refluent wave. He has shown us how the despairs and hopes, the passions and lassitudes of the former generations have helped our national growth; how our country has been rallied by her very defeats, and enriched by her very wastefulness, and elevated by her disasters to ascendancy; how the storms which have howled along her coast have only ribbed her rocks the more firmly; and the red rain of her slaughtered sires has but watered the earth for the harvest of their gallant sons. Oh, if the young men of our time would glow with a healthy pride of race ; if they would kindle with the inspirations of patriotism ; if they would find annals wealthier in enduring lesson, and bright with the radiance of a holier virtue than ever Rome embraced or Sparta knew, let them read their own land's history, as traced by the pen of its most fervent recorder ; and while grateful for the instruction of the past, let its unwavering progress teach them to be hopeful for the future. What hinders that the growth of England's past should be but the type of the yet rarer splendours of its coming time ? There are many who wait for her halting, " wizards that peep and that mutter" in bootless necromancy for her ruin ; but let her be true to herself and to her stewardship, and her position may be assured from peril. On the " coign of vantage " to which she has been lifted, let her take her stand ; let her exhibit to the wondering nations the glad nuptials between liberty and order ; let her sons, at once profound in their loyalty and manly in their independence, be fired with ambition greater than of glory, and with covetousness nobler than of gain ; let her exult that her standard, however remote and rocky the islet over which it waves, is ever the flag of the freeman ; let her widen with the ages into still increasing reverence for truth and peace and God, and " she may stand in her lot until the end of the days," and in the long after-time, when the now young world shall have grown old, and shall be preparing, by reason of its age, for the action of the last fires, she may still live and flourish, chartered among the nations as the home of those principles of right and freedom which shall herald the coming of the Son of man.

The one great defect in Macaulay's life and writings, viewed from a Christian standpoint, is his negativism, to use no stronger word, on the subject of evangelical religion. Not that he ever impeaches its sacredness; no enemy of religion can claim his championship: he was at once too refined and too reverent for infidelity, but he nowhere upholds Divine presence or presidency; nowhere traces the unity of a purpose higher than the schemes of men; nowhere speaks of the precepts of Christianity as if they were Divinely-sanctioned; nowhere gives to its cloud of witnesses the adhesion of his honoured name. As we read his essays or his history, when he lauds the philosophy of Bacon, or tells of the deliverances of William, we are tempted to wonder at his serene indifference to those great questions which sooner or later must present themselves to the mind of every man. Did it never occur to him that men were deeper than they seemed, and restless about that future into which he is so strangely averse to pry? Did the solemn problems of the soul, the whence of its origin, the what of its purpose, the whither of its destiny, never perplex and trouble him? Had he no fixed opinion about religion as a reality, that inner and vital essence which should be "the core of all the creeds?" or did he content himself with "the artistic balance of conflicting forces," and regard Protestantism and Popery alike as mere schemings of the hour, influences equally valuable in their day and equally mortal when their work was done? Did it never strike him that there was a Providence at work when his hero was saved from assassination, when the fierce winds scattered the Armada, when the fetters were broken which Rome had forged and fastened, when from the struggles of years rose up the slow and stately growth of English freedom? Did he never breathe a wish for a God to speak the chaos of events into order, or was he content to leave the mystery as he found it, deeming "such knowledge too wonderful for man?" Why did he always brand vice as an injury or an error? Did he never feel it to be a sin? Looking at the present, why always through the glass of the past, and never by the light of the future? Did he never pant after a spiritual insight, nor throb with a religious faith? Alas, that on the matters on which these questions touch, his writings make no sign! Of course, no one expected the historian to become a preacher, nor the essayist a theologian; but that there should be so studious an avoidance of those great, deep, awful matters which have to do with the eternal, and that in a history in which religion, in some phase or other, was the inspiration of the events which he records, is a fact which no Christian heart can think of without surprise and sorrow.

It has become fashionable to praise a neutral literature which prides itself upon its freedom from bias, and upon the broad line of separation which it draws carefully between things secular and things sacred; and there are many who call this liberality, but there is an old Book whose authority, thank God, is not yet deposed from the heart of Christian England, which would brand it with a very different name. That Book tells us that the fig-tree was blasted, not because it was baneful, but because it was barren; and that the bitter curse was denounced against Meroz, not because she rallied with the forces of the foe, but because in her criminal indifference she came not up to the help of the Lord. Amid the stirring and manifold activities of the age in which we live, to be neutral in the strife is to rank with the enemies of the Saviour. There is no greater foe to the spread of His cause in the world than the placid indifferentism which is too honourable to betray, while it is too careless or too cowardly to join Him. The rarer the endowments, the deeper the obligation to consecrate them to the glory of their Giver. That brilliant genius, that indefatigable industry, that influencing might of speech, that wondrous and searching faculty of analysis, what might they not have accomplished if they had been pledged to the recognition of a higher purpose than literature, and fearless in their advocacy of the faith of Christ! Into the secret history of the inner man, of course we may not enter; and we gladly hope, from small but significant indications which a searcher may discover in his writings, as well as from intimations, apparently authentic, which were published shortly after his death, that if there had rested any cloud on his experience, the Sun of righteousness dispersed it, and that he anchored his personal hope on that "dear Name" which his earliest rhymes had sung; but the regret may not be suppressed that his transcendant powers were given to any object lower than the highest. And when I see two life courses before me, both ending in Westminster Abbey, for the tardy gratitude of the nation adjudged to Zachary Macaulay's remains, the honour which it denied to his living reputation; when I see the father, poor, slandered, living a life of struggle, yet secretly but mightily working for the oppressed and the friendless, and giving all his energies in a bright summer of consecration unto God; and when I see the son, rich, gifted, living a life of success, excellent and envied in everything he undertook, breathing the odours of a perpetual incense-cloud, and passing from the memory of an applauding country to the tomb, but aiming through his public lifetime only at objects which were "of the earth, earthy," I feel that if there be truth in the Bible, and sanction in the obligations of religion, and immortality in the destinies of man, "he aimed too low who aimed beneath the skies;" that the truer fame is with the pains-taking and humble Christian worker, and that I had rather have the amaranth which encircles the father than the laurel which crowns the forehead of the more gifted and brilliant son.

In 1856 he resigned his seat for Edinburgh, in consequence of failing health; and in 1857 literature was honoured with a peerage in the person of one of the noblest of her sons, and the peerage was honoured by the accession of Lord Macaulay's illustrious name. Thenceforward in his retirement at Kensington he devoted himself to his History, "the business and the pleasure of his life." The world rejoiced to hope that successive volumes might yet stimulate its delight and wonder, and wished for the great writer a long and mellow eventide, which the night should linger to disturb. But suddenly, with the parting year, a mightier summons came, and the majestic brain was tired, and the fluttering heart grew still. Already, as the months of that fatal year waned on, had the last harvestman multiplied his sheaves from the ranks of genius and of skill. There had been mourning in Prussia for Humboldt, and across the wide Atlantic there had wailed a dirge for Prescott and Washington Irving; Brunel and Stephenson had gone down in quick succession to the grave; men had missed the strange confessions of De Quincey, and the graceful fancies with which Leigh Hunt had long delighted them; Hallam and Stephen had passed the ivory gates; but, as in the sad year which closed upon our national sorrow, it seemed as if the spoiler had reserved the greatest victim to the last, that he might give to the vassal world the very proudest token of his power.

If Macaulay had an ambition dearer than the rest, it was that he might lie in " that temple of silence and reconciliation where the enmities of twenty generations lie buried ; " and the walls of Westminster Abbey do enclose him "in their tender and solemn gloom."   Not in ostentatious state, nor with the pomp of sorrow, but with hearty and mourning affection, did rank and talent, and office and authority, assemble to lay him in the grave.   The pall was over the city on that drear January morning, and the cold, raw wind wailed mournfully, as if sighing forth the requiem of the great spirit that was gone ; and amid saddened friends—some who had shared the sports of his childhood, some who had fought with him the battles of political life—amid warm admirers and generous foes, while the aisles rang with the cadences of solemn music, and here and there were sobs and pants of sorrow, they bore him to that quiet resting-place, where he "waits the adoption, to wit, the redemption of the body."   Not far from the place of his sepulture are the tablets of Gay, and Rowe, and Thomson, and Garrick, and Goldsmith ; on his right sleeps Isaac Barrow, the ornament of his own Trinity College ; on his left, no clamour breaks the slumber of Samuel Johnson ; from a pedestal at the head of the grave, serene and thoughtful, Addison looks down ; the coffin, which was said to have been exposed at the time of the funeral, probably held all that was mortal of Richard Brinsley Sheridan ; Campbell gazes pensively across the transept, as if he felt that the "pleasures of hope" were gone ; while from opposite sides, Shakspeare, the remembrancer of mortality, reminds us from his open scroll that the "great globe itself, and all that it inhabit, shall dissolve, and, like the baseless fabric of a vision, leave not a rack behind ;" and Handel, comforting us in our night of weeping by the glad hope of immortality, seems to listen while they chant forth his own magnificent hymn, "His body is buried in peace, but his name liveth for evermore." There are strange thoughts and lasting lessons to be gathered in this old Abbey, and by the side of this latest grave. From royal sarcophagus, and carven shrine ; from the rustling of those fading banners, which tell of the knights of the former time ; yonder where the Chathams and Mansfields repose; here where the orators and poets lie, comes there not a voice to us of our frailty, borne into our hearts by the brotherhood of dust upon which our footsteps tread? How solemn the warning ! Oh for grace to learn it !

> "Earth's highest glory ends in—' Here he lies !'
> And 'dust to dust ' concludes her noblest song."

And shall they rise, all these? Will there be a trumpet blast so shrill that none of them may refuse to hear it, and the soul, re-entering its shrine of eminent or common clay, pass upward to the judgment? "Many and mighty, but all hushed," shall they submit with us to the arbitrations of the last assize? And in that world is it true that gold is not the currency, and that rank is not hereditary, and that there is only one name that is honoured? Then, if this is the end of all men, let the living lay it to heart. Solemn and thoughtful, let us search for an assured refuge; childlike and earnest, let us confide in the one accepted Name; let us realise the tender and infinite nearness of God our Father, through Jesus our Surety and our Friend ; and in hope of a joyful resurrection for ourselves, and for the marvellous Englishman we mourn, let us sing his dirge in the words of the truest poet of our time :—

" All is over and done :
    Render thanks to the Giver !
    England, for thy son.
    Let the bell be tolled.
    Render thanks to the Giver,
    And render him to the mould.
    Let the bell be tolled
    And the sound of the sorrowing anthem rolled,
     And a deeper knell in the heart be knolled.
    To such a name for ages long
    To such a name
    Preserve a broad approach of fame,
    And ever-ringing avenues of song.

  * * * * * *

    Hush ! the dead march wails in the people's ears,
    The dark crowd moves, and there are sobs and tears ;
    The black earth yawns—the mortal disappears ;
    Ashes to ashes—dust to dust ;
    He is gone who seemed so great.
    Gone, but nothing can bereave him
    Of the force he made his own
    Being here, and we believe him
    Something far advanced in state,
    And that he wears a truer crown
    Than any wreath that man can weave him.
     But speak no more of his renown,
    Lay your earthly fancies down,
    And in the solemn temple leave him :
    God accept him, Christ receive him."

JOHN BUNYAN.

JOHN BUNYAN.

IT were impossible to gaze upon the Pyramids, those vast sepulchres which rise, colossal, from the Libyan desert, without solemn feeling. They exist, but where are their builders? Where is the fulfilment of their large ambition? Enter them. In their silent heart there is a sarcophagus with a handful of dust in it, and this is all that remains to us of a proud race of kings !

Histories are, in some sort, the pyramids of nations. They entomb in olden chronicle, or in dim tradition, peoples which once filled the world with their fame, men who stamped the form and pressure of their character upon the lives of thousands. The historic page has no more to say of them than that they lived and died. "Their acts and all that they did" are compressed into scantiest record. They are handed down to us, shrivelled and solitary, only in the letters which spelt out their names. It is a serious thought, sobering enough to our aspirations after that kind of immortality, that multitudes of the men of old have their histories in their epitaphs, and that multitudes more, as worthy, slumber in nameless graves.

But although the earlier times are wrapt in a cloud of fable; though tradition, itself a myth, gropes into mythic darkness;

though Æneas and Agamemnon are creations rather than men —made human by the poet's "vision and faculty divine;" though forgetfulness has overtaken actual heroes, once "content in arms to cope, each with his fronting foe;" it is interesting to observe how rapid was the transition from fable to evidence, from the uncertain twilight to the historic day. It was necessary that it should be so. "The fulness of time" demanded it. There was an ever-acting Divinity caring, through all change, for the sure working of His own purpose. The legendary must be superseded by the real; tradition must give place to history, before the advent of the Blessed One. The cross must be reared on the loftiest platform, in the midst of the ages, and in the most inquisitive condition of the human mind. Hence the atonement has been worked out with grandest publicity. There hangs over the cross the largest cloud of witnesses. Swarthy Cyrenian and proud son of Rome, lettered Greek and jealous Jew, join hands around the sacrifice of Christ —its body-guard as an historical fact—fencing it about with most solemn authentications, and handing it to after ages, a truth, as well as a life, for all time. In like manner we find that certain periods of the world—epochs in its social progress— times of its emerging from chivalric barbarism—times of reconstruction or of revolution—times of great energy or of nascent life, seem, as by divine arrangement, to stand forth in sharpest outline; long distinguishable after the records of other times have faded. Such, besides the first age of Christianity, was the period of the Crusades, of the Reformation, of the Puritans, and such, to the thinkers of the future, will be the many-coloured and inexplicable age in which we live. The men of those times are the men on whom history seizes, who are the studies of the aftertime; men who, though they must yield to the law by which even the greatest are thrown into somewhat shadowy perspective, were yet POWERS in their day: men who, weighed against the world in the balance, caused " a downward tremble" in the beam. Such times were the years of the seventeenth century in England. Such a man was JOHN BUNYAN.

Rare times they were, the times of that stirring and romantic era. How much was crowded into the sixty years of Bunyan's eventful life! There were embraced in it the turbulent reign of the first Charles—the Star-chamber, and the High Commission, names of hate and shuddering—Laud with his Papistry, and Strafford with his scheme of Thorough—the long intestine war —Edgehill, and Naseby, and Marston, memories of sorrowful renown—a discrowned monarch, a royal trial, and a royal execution. He saw all that was venerable and all that was novel changing places, like the scene-shifting of a drama; bluff cavaliers in seclusion and in exile; douce burghers acting history, and moulded into men. Then followed the Protectorate of the many-sided and wondrous Cromwell; brief years of grandeur and of progress, during which an Englishman became a power and a name. Then came the Restoration, with its reaction of excesses—the absolutism of courtiers and courtezans—the madness which seized upon the nation when vampyres like Oates and Dangerfield were gorged with perjury and drunk with blood; the Act of Uniformity, framed in true succession to take effect on St. Bartholomew's day, by which, " at one fell swoop," were ejected two thousand ministers of Christ's holy gospel; the Conventicle Act, two years later, which hounded the ejected ones from the copse and from the glen; the great plague, fitting sequel to enactments so foul, when the silenced clergy, gathering in pestilence immunity from law, made the Red Cross the sad badge of their second ordination, and taught the anxious, and cheered the timid, at the altars from which hirelings had fled. Then followed the death of the dissolute king—the accession of James, at once a dissembler and a bigot—the renewal of the struggle between prerogative and freedom—the wild conspiracy of Monmouth—the military cruelties of Kirke and Claverhouse, the butchers of the army, and the judicial cruelties of Jeffreys, the butcher of the bench—the martyrdoms of Elizabeth Gaunt, and the gentle Alice Lisle—the glorious acquittal of the seven bishops—the final eclipse of the house of Stuart, that perfidious, and therefore fated race—and England's last revolution, binding old alienations in marvellous unity at the foot of a parental throne. What a rush of history compressed into a less period than threescore years and ten ! These were indeed times for the development of character—times for the birth of men.

And the men were there—the wit, the poet, the divine, the hero—as if genius had brought out her jewels, and furnished them nobly for a nation's need. Then Pym and Hampden bearded tyranny, and Russell and Sydney dreamed of freedom. Then Blake secured the empire of ocean, and the chivalric Falkland fought and fell. In those stirring times Charnock, and Owen, and Howe, and Henry, and Baxter, wrote, and preached, and prayed. "Cudworth and Henry More were still living at Cambridge ; South was at Oxford, Prideaux in the close at Norwich, and Whitby in the close of Salisbury. Sherlock preached at the Temple, Tillotson at Lincoln's Inn, Burnet at the Rolls, Stillingfleet at St. Paul's Cathedral, Beveridge at St. Peter's, Cornhill. Men," to continue the historian's eloquent description, " who could set forth the majesty and beauty of

Christianity with such justness of thought and such energy of language that the indolent Charles roused himself to listen, and the fastidious Buckingham forgot to sneer." But twelve years before the birth of Bunyan, all that was mortal of Shakespeare had descended to the tomb. Waller still flourished, an easy and graceful versifier; Cowley yet presented his "perverse metaphysics" to the world; Butler, like the parsons in his own Hudibras,

> " Proved his doctrine orthodox
> By apostolic blows and knocks."

Dryden wrote powerful satires and sorry plays "with long-resounding march and energy divine;" George Herbert clad his thoughts in quaint and quiet beauty; and mid the groves of Chalfont, as if blinded on purpose that the inner eye might be flooded with the "light which never was on sea or shore," our greater Milton sang.

In such an era, and with such men for his contemporaries, John Bunyan ran his course, " a burning and a shining light," kindled in a dark place, for the praise and glory of God.

With the main facts of Bunyan's history you are most of you, I presume, familiar; though it may be doubted whether there be not many—his hearty admirers withal,—whose knowledge of him comprehends but the three salient particulars, that he was a Bedfordshire tinker, that he was confined in Bedford jail, and that he wrote the "Pilgrim's Progress." It will not be necessary, however, to-night, to do more than sketch, succinctly, the course of his life, endeavouring—Herculean project—to collate, in a brief page, Ivimey, and Philip, and Southey, and Offor, and Cheever, and Montgomery, and Macaulay; a sevenfold biographical band, who have reasoned about the modern, as a seven-fold band of cities contended for the birth of the ancient Homer.

He was born at Elstow, a village near Bedford, in the year 1628. Like many others of the Lord's heroes, he was of obscure parentage, "of a low and inconsiderable generation," and, not improbably, of gipsy blood. His youth was spent in excess of riot. There are expressions in his works descriptive of his manner of life, which cannot be interpreted, as Macaulay would have it, in a theological sense, nor resolved into morbid self-upbraidings. He was an adept and a teacher in evil. In his 17th year we find him in the army—"an army where wickedness abounded." It is not known accurately on which side he served, but the description best answers certainly to Rupert's roystering dragoons. At 20 he married, receiving two books as his wife's only portion—"The Practice of Piety," and "The Plain Man's Pathway to Heaven." By the reading of these books, and by his wife's converse and example, the Holy Spirit first wrought upon his soul. He attempted to curb his sinful propensities, and to work in himself an external reformation. He formed a habit of church-going, and an attachment almost idolatrous to the externalisms of religion. The priest was to him as the Brahman to the Pariah; "he could have lain down at his feet to be trampled on, his name, garb, and work did so intoxicate and bewitch him." While thus under the thraldom which superstition imposes, he indulged all the licence which supersition claims. He continued a blasphemer and a Sabbath-breaker, running to the same excess of riot as before. Then followed in agonizing vicissitude a series of convictions and relapses. He was arrested, now by the pungency of a powerful sermon, now by the reproof of an abandoned woman, and anon by visions in the night, distinct and terrible. One by one, under the lashes of the law, "that stern Moses, which knows not how to spare," he relinquished his besetting sins—from which he struggled successfully to free himself while he was yet uninfluenced by the evangelical motive, and with his heart alienated from the life of God. New and brighter light flashed upon his spirit from the conversation of some godly women at Bedford, who spake of the things of God and of kindred hopes and yearnings "with much pleasantness of scripture," as they sat together in the sun. He was instructed more perfectly by "holy Mr. Gifford," the Evangelist of his dream, and, in "the comment on the Galatians" of brave old Martin Luther, he found the photograph of his own sinning and troubled soul. For two years there were but glimpses of the fitful sunshine dimly seen through a spirit-storm, perpetual and sad. Temptations of fearful power assailed and possessed his soul. Then was the time of that fell combat with Apollyon, of the fiery darts and hideous yells, of the lost sword and the rejoicing enemy. Then also he passed, distracted and trembling, through the Valley of the Shadow of Death, and a horror of great darkness fell upon him. At length, by the blest vision of Christ "made of God unto him wisdom, and righteousness, and sanctification, and redemption," the glad deliverance came—the clouds rolled away from his heart and from his destiny, and he walked in the undimmed and glorious heaven. From this time his spiritual course was, for the most part, one of comfort and peace. He became a member of the Baptist Church under Mr. Gifford's pastorate, and when that faithful witness ceased his earthly testimony, he engaged in earnest exhortations to sinners, "as a man in chains speaking to men in chains," and was urged forward, by the concurrent call of the Spirit and the bride, to the actual ministry of the gospel. His ministry was heartfelt, and therefore powerful, and was greatly blessed of God. In 1660 he was indicted "as a common upholder of unlawful meetings and conventicles," and by the strong hand of tyranny was thrown into prison; and though his wife pleaded so powerfully in his favour as to move the pity of Sir Matthew Hale, beneath whose ermine throbbed a God-fearing heart like that which beat beneath the tinker's doublet, he was kept there for twelve long years. His own words are, "So being again delivered up to the jailor's hand, I was had home to prison." *Home* to prison. Think of that, young men! See the bravery of a Christian heart! There is no affectation of indifference to suffering—no boastful exhibition of excited heroism; but there is the calm of the man "that has the herb heart's-ease in his bosom."

Home to prison! And wherefore not? Home is not the marble hall, nor the luxurious furniture, nor the cloth of gold. If home be the kingdom where a man reigns, in his own monarchy over subject hearts—if home be the spot where "fireside pleasures gambol," where are heard the sunny laugh of the confiding child, or the fond "what ails thee?" of the watching wife—then every essential of home was to be found, "except these bonds," in that cell on Bedford Bridge. There, in the day-time, is the heroine wife, at once bracing and soothing his spirit with her womanly tenderness, and, sitting at his feet, the child—a clasping tendril—blind and therefore best beloved. There, on the table, is the "Book of Martyrs," with its records of the men who were the ancestors of his faith and love; those old and heaven patented nobility whose badge of knighthood was the hallowed cross, and whose chariot of triumph was the ascending flame. There, nearer to his hand, is the Bible, revealing their secret source of strength; cheering his own spirit in exceeding heaviness, and making strong, through faith, for the obedience which is even unto death. Within him the good conscience bears bravely up, and he is weaponed by this as by a shield of triple mail. By his side, all unseen by casual guest or surly warder, there stands the Heavenly Comforter; and from overhead, as if anointing him already with the unction of the recompense, there rushes the stream of glory.

And now it is nightfall. They have had their evening worship, and, as in another dungeon, " the prisoners heard them." The blind child receives the fatherly benediction. The last good night is said to the dear ones, and Bunyan is alone. His pen is in his hand and his Bible on the table. A solitary lamp dimly relieves the darkness. But there is fire in his eye, and there is passion in his souL " He writes as if joy did make him write. " He has felt all the fulness of his story. The pen moves too slowly for the rush of feeling as he graves his own heart upon the page. There is beating over him a storm of inspiration. Great thoughts are striking on his brain, and flushing all his cheek. Cloudy and shapeless in their earliest rise within his mind, they darken into the gigantic, or brighten into the beautiful, until at length he flings them into bold and burning words. Rare visions rise before him. He is in a dungeon no longer. He is in the palace Beautiful, with its sights of renown and songs of melody, with its virgins of comeliness and of discretion, and with its windows opening for the first kiss of the sun. His soul swells beyond the measure of its cell. It is not a rude lamp that glimmers on his table. It is no longer the dark Ouse that rolls its sluggish waters at his feet. His spirit has no sense of bondage. No iron has entered into his soul. Chainless and swift, he has soared to the Delectable Mountains —the light of Heaven is around him—the river is the one, clear as crystal, which floweth from the throne of God and of the Lamb—breezes of Paradise blow freshly across it, fanning his temples and stirring his hair—from the summit of the Hill Clear he catches rarer splendours—the new Jerusalem sleeps in its eternal noon—the shining ones are there, each one a crowned harper unto God—this is the land that is afar off, and THAT is the king in His beauty; until the dreamer falls upon his knees and sobs away his agony of gladness in an ecstasy of prayer and praise. Now, think of these things—endearing intercourse with wife and children, the ever fresh and ever comforting Bible, the tranquil conscience, the regal imaginings of the mind, the faith which realized them all, and the light of God's approving face shining, broad and bright, upon the soul, and you will understand the undying memory which made Bunyan quaintly write "I was had home to prison."

In 1672, Richard Carver, a member of the Society of Friends, who had been mate of the vessel in which King Charles escaped to France after his defeat at Worcester, and who had carried the king on his back through the surf and landed him on French soil, claimed, as his reward, the release of his co-religionists who crowded the jails throughout the land. After some hesitation, Charles was shamed into compliance. A cumbrous deed was prepared, and under the provisions of that deed, which was so framed as to include sufferers of other persuasions, Bunyan obtained deliverance, having lain in the prison complete twelve years.

From the time of his release his life flowed evenly on. Escaped alike from Doubting Castle and from the net of the flatterer, he dwelt in the Beulah land of ripening piety and hope. The last act of the strong and gentle spirit brought down on him the peace-maker's blessing. Fever seized him in London on his return from an errand of mercy, and after ten days' illness, long enough for the utterance of a whole treasury of dying sayings, he calmly fell asleep.

> "Mortals cried, 'a man is dead :'
> Angels sang 'a child's born ;'"

and in honour of that nativity "all the bells of the celestial city rang again for joy." From his elevation in heaven his whole life seems to preach to us his own Pentecostal evangel, "There is room enough here for body and soul, but not for body, and soul, and sin."

There are various phases in which Bunyan is presented to us which are suggestive of interesting remark, or which may tend to exhibit the wholeness of his character before us, and upon which, therefore, we may not unprofitably dwell.

As a WRITER he will claim our attention for a while. This is not the time to enter into any analysis of his various works, nor of the scope and texture of his mind. That were a task rather for the critic than the lecturer; and although many mental anatomists have been already at work upon it, there is room for the skilful handling of the scalpel still. His fame has rested so extensively upon his marvellous allegories, that there is some danger lest his more elaborate works should be depreciated; but as a theologian he is able and striking, and as a contributor to theological literature he is a worthy associate of the brightest Puritan divines. His terse, epigrammatic aphorisms, his array of "picked and packed words," the clearness with which he enunciates, and the power with which he applies the truth, his intense earnestness, the warm soul that is seen beating through the transparent page, his vivacious humour, flashing out from the main body of his argument like lightning from a summer sky, his deep spirituality, chastening an imagination princely almost beyond compare—all these combine to claim for him a high place among that band of masculine thinkers who were the glory of the Commonwealth, and whose words, weighty in their original utterance, are sounds which echo still. The amount of actual good accomplished by his writings it would be difficult to estimate. No man since the days of the Apostles has done more to draw the attention of the world to matters of supremest value, nor painted the beauty of holiness in more alluring colours, nor spoken to the universal heart in tenderer sympathy or with more thrilling tone. In how many readers of the " Grace Abounding " has there been the answer of the heart to the history. What multitudes are there to whom "the Jerusalem Sinner Saved " has been as ",yonder shining light" which has led through the wicket gate, and by the house of the Divine Interpreter, to the blest spot "where was a cross, with a sepulchre hard by ;" and at the sight of that cross the burden has fallen off, and the roll has been secured, and, sealed and shining, they have gone on to victory and heaven. How many have revelled in silent rapture in his descriptions of the " Holy City" until there have floated around them some gleams of the "jasper light," and they felt an earnest longing to be off from earth—that land of craft, and crime, and sorrow—

> " And wished for wings to flee away,
> And mix with that eternal day."

Oh, to thousands of the pilgrims that have left the city of Destruction—some valiant and hopeful, others much afraid and fearing—has Bunyan come in his writings, to soothe the pang or to prompt the prayer, to scare the doubt or to solve the problem — a Great-heart guide, brave against manifold ill favoured ones—a faithful Evangelist, pointing the soul to the Saviour.

Of the " Pilgrim's Progress " it were superfluous to speak in praise. It seizes us in childhood with the strong hand of its power, our manhood surrenders to the spell of its sorcery, and its grasp upon us relaxes not when " mingles the brown of life with sober gray," nay, is often strongest amid the weariness ot waning years. Its scenes are familiar to us as the faces of home. Its characters live to our perceptions no less than to our understanding. We have seen them, conversed with them, realized their diversities of character and experience for ourselves. There never was a poem which so thoroughly took possession of our hearts, and hurried them along upon the stream of the story. We have an identity of interest with the hero in all his doubts and dangers. We start with him on pilgrimage; we speed with him in eager haste to the Gate; we gaze with him on the sights of wonder; we climb with him the difficult hill; the blood rushes to our cheek, warm and proud, as we gird ourselves for the combat with Apollyon ; it curdles at the heart again amid the Valley of the Shadow of Death ; we look with him upon the scoffing multitude from the cage of the town of Vanity; we now lie, listless and sad, and now flee, fleet and happy, from the cell in Doubting Castle; we walk with him amid the pleasantness of Beulah ; we ford the river in his company; we hear the joy-bells ringing in the city of habitations;

H

we see and greet the hosts of welcoming angels ; and it is to us as the gasp of agony with which the drowning come back to life, when some rude call of earthly concernment arouses us from our reverie, and we wake, and, behold, it is a dream.

There must be marvellous power in a book that can work such enchantment, wrought withal with the most perfect self-unconsciousness on the part of the enchanter himself. "The joy that made him write" was, in no sense, the prospect of literary fame. With the true modesty of genius he hesitated long as to the propriety of publication, and his fellow-prisoners in the jail were empanelled as a literary jury, upon whose verdict depended the fate of the story which has thrilled the pulses of the world. In fact his book fulfilled a necessity of his nature. He wrote because he must write: the strong thoughts within him laboured for expression. The "Pilgrim's Progress" was written without thought of the world. It is just a wealthy mind rioting in its own riches for its own pleasure ; an earnest soul painting in the colours of a vivid imagination its olden anguish, and revelling at the prospect of its future joy. And while the dreamer thus wrote primarily for himself—a "prison amusement" at once beguiling and hallowing the hours of a weary bondage —he found to his delight, and perhaps to his surprise, that his vision became a household book to thousands ;—worldlings enraptured with its pictures, with no inkling of the drift of its story ; Christians pressing it to their hearts as a "song in the night" of their trouble, or finding in its thrilling pages "a door of hope" through which they glimpsed the coming of the day.

It has been often remarked that, like the Bible, its great model, the "Pilgrim's Progress" is, to a religious mind, its own best interpreter. It is said of a late eminent clergyman and commentator, who published an edition of it with numerous expository notes, that having freely distributed copies amongst his parishioners, he sometime afterwards inquired of one ot them if he had read the " Pilgrim's Progress." " Oh, yes, sir !" "And do you think you understand it ?" " Yes, sir, I understand *it*, and I hope before long I shall understand the notes as well."

One of the most amusing and yet conclusive proofs of the popularity of this wonderful allegory is to be found in the liberties which have been taken with it in the versions into which it has been rendered, and in the imitations to which it has given rise. Mr Offor, in his carefully-edited edition of Bunyan's works, has enumerated between thirty and forty treatises, mostly allegorical, whose authors have evidently gathered their inspiration from the tinker of Elstow. The original work has been subjected to a thousand experiments. It has been done into an oratorio for the satisfaction of play-goers ; done into verse at the caprice of rhymesters ; done into elegant English for the delectation of drawing-rooms ; done into catechisms for the use of schools. It has been quoted in novels ; quoted in sermons innumerable ; quoted in Parliamentary orations ; quoted in plays. It has been put upon the Procrustes' bed of many who have differed from its sentiments, and has been mutilated or stretched as it exceeded or fell short of their standard. Thus there has been a Supralapsarian supplement, in which the Interpreter is called the Enlightener, and the House Beautiful is Castle Strength. There has been a Popish edition, with Giant Pope left out. There has been a Socinian parody, describing the triumphant voyage, through hell to heaven, of a Captain Single-eye and his Unitarian crew ; and last, not least noteworthy, there has been a Tractarian travesty, in which the editor

digs a cleansing well at the wicket-gate, omits Mr. Worldly
Wiseman, ignores the town of Legality, makes no mention of
Mount Sinai, changes the situation of the cross, gives to poor
Christian a double burden, transforms Giant Pope into Giant
Mahometan, Mr. Superstition into Mr. Self-indulgence, and
alters, with careful coquetry towards Rome, every expression
which might be distasteful to the Holy Mother. Most of those
who have published garbled or accommodated editions have
done their work silently, and with some sense of shame; but
the editor of the last mentioned mutilation dwells with ineffable
complacency upon his deed, and evidently imagines that he has
done something for which the world should speak him well.
He defends his insertions and omissions, which are many, and
which affect important points of doctrine, in a somewhat curious
style. "A reasonable defence," he says, "is found in the following consideration:— The author whose works are altered
wished, it is to be assumed, to teach the truth. In the editor's
judgment, the alterations have tended to the more complete
setting forth that truth, that is, to the better accomplishment of
the author's design. If the editor's views of the truth, then, are
correct, he is justified in what he does; if they are false, he is
to be blamed for originally holding them, but cannot be called
dishonest for making his author speak what he believes that,
with more knowledge, the author would have said." Exquisite
logic! How would it avail in the mouth of some crafty forger,
at the bar of the Old Bailey! "I am charged with altering a
cheque, drawn for my benefit, by making £200 into £1,200.
I admit it, but a reasonable defence may be found in the following consideration. The gentleman whose cheque I altered
wished, it is to be assumed, to benefit me and my family. In

my judgment, the alteration has tended to the better accomplishment of the gentleman's design. If my views in this matter are correct, I am justified in what I have done; if they are incorrect, I may be blamed for originally holding them, but cannot be called dishonest for doing what, with more knowledge of my circumstances and his own, the gentleman himself would have done." Out upon it! Is there one shade of sentiment, from the credulousness which gulps the tradition and kisses the relic, to the negativism of "the everlasting No," which might not lay the flattering unction to its soul, that "with more knowledge" Bunyan would have been ranged under its banner. Rejoicing as I do in substantial oneness of sentiment with the glorious dreamer, I might yet persuade myself into the belief that, with more knowledge, he would have become an Evangelical Arminian, and would hardly have classed the election doubters among the army of Diabolus: but shall I, on this account, foist my notions into the text of his writings? or were it not rather an act from which an honest mind would shrink with lordly scorn? I cannot forbear the utterance of an indignant protest against a practice which appears to me subversive of every canon of literary morality, and which in this case has passed off, under the sanction of Bunyan's name, opinions from which he would have recoiled in indignation, which war against the whole tenor of his teaching, and which might almost disturb him in his grave; and especially is my soul vexed within me that there should have been flung by any sacrilegious hand, over those sturdy Protestant shoulders, one solitary rag of Rome.

Though the "Pilgrim's Progress" became immediately popular, the only book save the Bible on the shelf of many a rustic dwelling, and though it passed in those early times through twelve editions in the space of thirty years, the "inconsiderable generation" of its author long prevented its circulation among the politer classes of the land. There was no affectation, but a well-grounded apprehension in Cowper's well-known line :

"Lest so despised a name should move a sneer."

At length, long the darling of the populace, it became the study of the learned. Critics went down into its treasure-chambers and were astonished at their wealth and beauty. The initiated ratified the foregone conclusion of the vulgar; the tinker's dream became a national classic; and the pontificate of literature installed it with a blessing and a prayer.

No uninspired work has extorted eulogies from a larger host of the men of mark and likelihood. That it redeemed into momentary kindliness a ferocious critic like Swift; that it surprised, from the lips of Johnson, the confession that he had read it through and wished it longer; that Byron's banter spared it, and that Scott's chivalry was fired by it ; that Southey's analysis, and Franklin's contemplation, and Mackintosh's elegant research, and Macaulay's artistic criticism, should have resulted in a symphony to its praise; that the spacious intellect and poet-heart of Coleridge revelled with equal gladness in its pages ; that the scholarly Arnold, chafed by the attritions of the age, and vexed by the doubt-clouds which darkened upon his gallant soul, lost his trouble in its company, and looked through it to the Bible, which he deemed it faithfully to mirror;—all these are testimonies that it established its empire over minds themselves imperial, and constrained their acknowledgment of its kingly power.

It would, we suspect, be of no account with Bunyan now

that critics conspire to praise him; that artists, those bending worshippers of beauty, have drawn sumptuous illustrations from his works; or that his statue, the tinker's effigy, standing in no unworthy companionship with statesmen, and heroes, and men of high degree, should decorate the British House of Commons. But if the faithful in glory have earthly sympathies and recognitions still; if, from the region where they "summer high in bliss upon the hills of God," they still look down lovingly upon the world which has missed and mourned them; if their inviolate joy may be enhanced from aught below—it might surely thrill the heart of the dreamer with a deeper ecstacy, that his Pilgrim yet walks the earth, a faithful witness for Jesus; that it has guided thousands of the perplexed, and cheered thousands of the fearing; and that it has testified to multitudes, of many a clime and colour, "in their own tongues, the wonderful works of God." No book but God's own has been so honoured to lift up the cross among the far off nations of mankind. The Italian has read it under the shadow of the Vatican, and the modern Greek amid the ruins of Athens; it has blessed the Armenian trafficker, and it has calmed the fierce Malay; it has been carried up the far rivers of Burmah; and it has drawn tears from dark eyes in the cinnamon gardens of Ceylon. The Bechuanas in their wild woods have rejoiced in its simple story; it has been as the Elim of palms and fountains to the Arab wayfarer; it has nerved the Malagasy for a Faithful's martyrdom, or for trial of cruel mockings, and tortures more intolerable than death. The Hindoo has yielded to its spell by Gunga's sacred stream; and, crowning triumph! Hebrews have read it on the slopes of Olivet, or on the banks of Kedron, and the tender hearted daughters of Salem, descendants of those who wept for the sufferings of Jesus, have "wept" over it "for themselves and for their children."

Dr. Johnson, in his life of Waller, advances the strange opinion that spiritual subjects are not fit subjects for poetry; and he dogmatizes, in his usual elephantine style of writing, upon the alleged reason. He says: "The essence of poetry is invention; such invention as, by producing something unexpected, surprises and delights. The topics of devotion are few, and being few are universally known; but few as they are they can be made no more; they can receive no grace from novelty of sentiment, and very little from novelty of expression." Such an unworthy definition of poetry might answer for an age of lampooners, when merry quips and conceits passed muster as sparks from the Heaven-kindled fire. We prefer that of Festus, brief and full:

> "Poets are all who love, who feel great truths
> And tell them."

And the greatest truths are those which link us to the invisible, and show us how to realize its wonders. If, then, there be within each of us a gladiator soul, ever battling for dear life in an arena of repression and scorn—a soul possessed with thought, and passion, and energy invincible, and immortal hope and yearnings after the far off and the everlasting, which all the tyranny of the flesh cannot subdue; if there be another world which sheds a holy and romantic light upon every object and upon every struggle of this,—if by the Word and Spirit divine there can be opened the soul's inner eye, that sublime faith which is "the substance of things hoped for, and the evidence of things not seen"—to the visions of which our nature becomes a treasury of hidden riches, and which instates us in the heirship of "the powers of the world to come;"—then there can be poetry in this world only because light from heaven falls on it, because it is a subtle hieroglyph full of solemn and mystic meanings, because it cradles a magnificent destiny, and is the type and test of everlasting life. It must be so. All conceptions of nature, or of beauty, or of man, from which the spiritual element is excluded, can be, at best, but the first sweep of the finger over the harpstrings, eliciting, it may be, an uncertain sound, but failing to evoke the soul of harmony which sleeps in the heart of the chords. Macaulay shall answer Johnson : " In the latter half of the seventeenth century there were only two minds which possessed the imaginative faculty in a very eminent degree. One of those minds produced the 'Paradise Lost;' the other the 'Pilgrim's Progress.'" Religious epics these ! the one painting the lapse and the doom of our race in all shapes of beauty or of grandeur ; the other borrowing nothing from voluptuous externalisms, dealing only with the inner man in his struggles and yearnings after God. We want to see, in this age of ours, more and more of the genius that is created by piety ; of a literature informed with the spirit of the Gospel of Christ. Critics have predicted the decay of poetry with the spread of civilization ; and literary men speak with diffident hope of its "ultimate recovery from the staggering blows which science has inflicted ;" and, in truth, if its inspiration be all of earth, there may be some ground for fear. As mere secular knowledge has no antiseptic power, so mere earthly beauty has no perennial charms. But draw its subjects from higher sources, let it meddle divinely with eternal things, and it can never die.

> " O say not that poesy waxeth old,
>   That all her legends were long since told !
>   It is not so ! It is not so !
>   For while there's a blossom by summer drest,
>   A sigh for the sad, or a smile for the blest,
>   Or a changeful thought in the human breast,
>   There'll be a new string for her lyre, I trow.
>   Do you say she is poor, in this land of the free ?
>   Do you call her votaries poor as she ?
>   It may be so ! It may be so !
>   Yet hath she a message more high and clear,
>   From the burning lips of the heaven-taught seer;
>   From the harp of Zion that charms the ear,
>   From the choir where the seraph minstrels glow."

Not, of course, that the monotone should be the measure of every life-song: rather should it flow after Scriptural precept and precedent, now in "psalms," grand, solemn, stately, the sonorous burst of the full soul in praise, now in "hymns," earnest, hopeful, winning—the lyrics of the heart in its hours of hope or pensiveness,—and now in "songs" light and hearty— the roundelay, the ballad, the carol of a spirit full of sunshine, warbling its melodies out of its own exuberance of joy. Nor, of course, that literary men should write only on Christian themes. We would have them illustrate the goodliness of nature, the inductions of science, the achievements of art. They should speak to us in the language of the sweet affec- tions, give soul and sentiment to the harmony of music, and strike the chords of the resounding lyre. They should take, in comprehensive and sympathetic survey, all nature and all man. But they must submit to the baptism of Christianity, and be leavened with her love divine, ere they can be chroniclers of the august espousals, or guests at the happy bridal of the beautiful and true.

Young men, lend your energies to this hallowed consummation. You are not poets, perhaps, and according to the old " *Poeta non fit* " adage, you are not fit to be. If you have the " divine afflatus," by all means give it forth ; but if you have not, do not strain after it to the neglect of nearer and more practicable things. One would not wish to see a race of Byronlings,— things of moustache and turn-down collar,— moody Manfreds of six feet three, with large loads of fine frenzy and infinitesimal grains of common sense. And it is woful enough to meet the weird youth of a later day, with his jargon of " subjective " and " objective," who looms dimly upon us through the blended smoke of mist and meerschaum, and who goes floundering after transcendental nonsense until he is nearly run over in Cheapside. It is given to very few of us to live ethereal lives, or to be on familiar terms with thunder. But if you are not the writers, you are the readers of the age. You have an appreciation of the beautiful, an awakened intelligence which pants hard after the true. Terminate, I beseech you, in your own experience, the sad divorce which has too often existed between intellect and piety. Take your stand, unswerving, heroic, by the altar of truth ; and from that altar let neither sophistry nor ridicule expel you. Let your faith rest with a child's trust, with a martyr's gripe upon the truth as it is in Jesus. Then go, humbly but dauntlessly, to work, and you can make the literature of the time. Impress your individuality upon others, and in so far as you create a healthier moral sentiment and a purer taste, the literature of the future is in your hands. The literature of any age is but the mirror of its prevalent tendencies. A healthy appetite will recoil from garbage and carrion. Pestilent periodicals and a venal press reveal the depraved moral feeling which they pamper. Work for the uplifting of that moral feeling, and by the blessing of God upon the efforts of the fair brotherhood who toil for Him, the dew of Hermon shall descend upon the hill Parnassus, and there shall be turned into the fabled Helicon a stream of living waters. Religion shall be throned in her own queenly beauty, and literature shall be the comeliest handmaid in her virgin train.

There is no feature more noticeable in Bunyan's character than *the devout earnestness with which he studied the Divine Word*, and *the reverence which he cherished for it* throughout the whole of his life.

In the time of his agony, when, "a restless wanderer after rest," he battled with fierce temptation, and was beset with Antinomian error, he gratefully records, "the Bible was precious to me in those days;" and after his deliverance it was his congenial life-work to exalt its honour and to proclaim its truths. Is he recommending growth in grace to his hearers?— The Word is to be the aliment of their life. " Every grace is nourished by the Word, and without it there is no thrift in the soul." Has he announced some fearless exposition of truth ?— Hark how he disarms opposition and challenges scrutiny! "Give me a hearing : take me to the Bible, and let me find in thy heart no favour if thou find me to swerve from the stand-ard." Is he uplifting the Word above the many inventions of his fellows?—Mark the racy homeliness of his assertion: " A little from God is better than a great deal from men. What is from men is often tumbled over and over ; things that we receive at God's hand come to us as things from the minting-house.   Old truths are always new to us if they come with the smell of Heaven upon them." Is his righteous soul vexed with the indifference of the faithful, or with the impertinences of the profane?   How manfully he proclaims his conviction of a pressing want of the times ! "There wanteth even in the hearts of God's people a greater reverence for the Word of God than to this day appeareth among us; and this let me say, that want of reverence for the Word is the ground of all the disorders that are in the heart, life, conversation, or Christian communion."

If ever Bunyan saw with a seer's insight, and spoke with a prophet's inspiration, he has in this last quoted sentence foreseen our danger, and uttered a solemn warning for the times in which we live.   There never was an age in which reverence for the Word needed more impressive inculcation.   There never was an age when there were leagued against it fiercer elements of antagonism.   Not that infidelity proper abounds—the danger from this source is over.   Some rare specimens of this almost extinct genus do occasionally flounder into sight, like the ichthyosaurus of some remote period, blurting out their blasphemies from congenial slime ; but men pity their foolishness or are shocked with their profanity.   That infidelity is the most to be dreaded which moves like the virus of a plague, counterfeiting, by its hectic glow, the flush of health and beauty, unsuspected till it has struck the chill to the heart, and the man is left pulseless of a living faith, and robbed of the rapture of life —a conscious paralytic who " brokenly lives on." This kind of scepticism,—a scepticism which apes reverence and affects candour—which, by its importunity, has almost wearied out some of the sturdy guardians of the truth—which seems to have talked itself into a prescriptive right, like other mendicants, to exhibit its sores among the highways of men,—has, it is not to be denied, done its worst to infect society, and to wither the energy of religion in multitudes of souls. It may be that some amongst yourselves have not altogether escaped the contagion. Could I place the young men of this country in the confessional to-night, or could their various feelings be detected, as was the concealed demon at the touch of Ithuriel's spear, I might find not a few who would tell that stranger doubts had come to them which they had not forborne to harbour—that distrust had crept over them—that unbelief was shaping out a systematic residence in their souls—that they had looked upon infidelity, if not as a haven of refuge amid the conflicts of warring faiths, at least as a theatre which gave scope for the ideal riot of fancy, or the actual riot of sense, in indulgences and excesses far fitter for earth than heaven?

And there are, unhappily, many around us, at the antipodes of sentiment from each other, and yet all after their manner hostile to the Divine Word, who fan the kindled unbelief, and whose bold and apparently candid objections are invested to the unsettled mind with a peculiar charm.

The Jew, with prejudice as inveterate as ever, rejects the counsel of God against himself, and crushes the Law and the Prophets beneath a load of rabbinical traditions, the Mishna and Gemara of his Talmuds. The papist still gives to the decretals of popes and the edicts of councils co-ordinate authority with the Scriptures, and locks up those Scriptures from the masses, as a man should imprison the free air while men perish from asphyxia around him. The rationalist spirits away the inspiration of the Bible, or descants upon it as a fascinating myth, to be reviewed like any other poem, by ordinary criticism, or postpones it to the proud reason of Eichhorn and Paulus, or Strauss and Hegel, or Belsham and Priestley. The mystic professes to have a supplemental and superior revelation drafted down into his own heart. Printing furnishes unprecedented facilities for the transmission of thought, and man's perdition may be cheapened at the stall of every pedlar. And finally, some ministers of religion, yielding to the clamour of the times, have lowered the high tone of Scriptural teaching, and have studiously avoided the terminology of the Bible. What wonder, with influences like these, that upon many over whom had gathered a penumbra of doubt before, there should deepen a dark and sad eclipse of faith?

Brothers, nothing will avail to preserve you amid the strife of tongues but to cherish, as a habit ingrained into the soul—as an affection enfibred with your deepest heart—continual reverence for the Divine Word. We do not claim your feudal submission to its sovereignty. It recks not a passive and unintelligent adhesion. Inquire by all means into the evidences which authenticate its divinity. Bring keenest intellects to bear upon it. Try it as gold in the fire. Satisfy yourselves, by as searching a process as you can, that the Eternal has really spoken it, and that there looms from it the shadow of a large immortality ; but do this *once for all.* Don't be "*ever* learning, and never able to come to the knowledge of the truth." Life is too short to be frittered away in endless considerings and scanty deeds. There can be no more pitiable state than that of the eternal doubter, who has bid the sad " vale, vale, in æternum vale," to all the satisfactions of faith, and who is tossed about with every wind of doctrine—a waif upon the wreckage of a world. Settle your principles early, and then place them "on the shelf," secure from subsequent assault or displacement. Then in after years, when some rude infidel argument assails you, and, busied amid life's activities, you are unable, from the absorption of your energies otherwhere, to recall the train of reasoning by which you arrived at your conclusion, you will say, "I tried this matter before—I threw these doctrines into the crucible, and they came out pure—the assay was satisfactory—the principles are on the shelf;" and when the Sanballats and Tobiahs gather malignantly below, you will cry with good Nehemiah, girt with the sword, and wielding the trowel the while, "I am doing a great work—I cannot come down—why should the work stop while I come down to you?" Oh it will be to you a source of perennial comfort, that in youth, after keen investigation of the Bible—the investigation, not of frivolity or prejudice, but of candour, and gravity, and truth-loving, and prayer—you bowed before it as God's imperishable utterance, and swore your fealty to the monarch-word. Depend upon it the Bible demands no inquisition, and requires no disguises. It does not shrink before the light of science, nor crouch abashed before the audit of a scholarly tribunal. Rather does it seem to say, as it stands before us in its kingliness, all pride humbled and all profanity silenced in its majestic presence—Error fleeing at its approach—Superstition cowering beneath the lightning of its eye, "I will arise, and go forth, for the hour of my dominion is at hand."

As a PREACHER OF THE TRUTH Bunyan had a high reputation in his day. Sympathy, earnestness, and power, were the great characteristics of his successful ministry. He preached what he felt, and his preaching therefore corresponded to the various stages of his personal experience. At first, himself in chains, he thundered out the terrors of the law, like another Baptist, against rich and poor together; then, happy in believing, he proclaimed salvation and the blessedness of life by Christ, "as if an angel stood at his back to encourage him;" and then, with advancing knowledge, he disclosed the truth in its rounded harmony—"the whole counsel of God." Instances of conversion were frequent under his ministry—many churches were founded by his labours. Dr. Owen assured King Charles that for the tinker's ability to prate he would gladly barter his own stores of learning; and in his annual visit to London, twelve hundred people would gather, at seven in the morning of a winter's working day, to hear him. Nor can we wonder that his ministry should have had "favour both with God and man," when we listen to his own statements of the feelings with which he regarded it. "In my preaching I have really been in pain, and have, as it were, travailed to bring forth children to God. If I were fruitless, it mattered not who commended me; but if I were fruitful, I cared not who did condemn." "I have counted as if I had goodly buildings and lordships in those places where my children were born; my heart hath been so wrapped up in the glory of this excellent work that I counted myself more blessed and honoured of God by this, than if He had made me the emperor of the Christian world, or the lord of all the glory of the earth without it." This is what we want now. We will not despair of the speedy conversion of the world if you give us an army of ministers who have, burned into their hearts, this passionate love for souls.

There are those, indeed, who tell us that the mission of the pulpit is fulfilled. They acknowledge that in the former ages—

in the times of immaturity, when men spelt out the truth in syllables, it did a noble work. But the world has outgrown it, they tell us. It is an anachronism now. Men need neither its light nor its warning. The all-powerful press shall direct them —from the chair of criticism they shall learn wisdom—the educational institute shall aid them in heavenward progress— they shall move upward and onward under the guidance of the common mind. But the divine institution of the ministry is not to be thus superseded. It has to do with eternity, and the matters of eternity are paramount. It has to deal with the most lasting emotions of our nature—with those deep instincts of eternal truths which underlie all systems, from which the man can never utterly divorce himself, and which God himself has graven on the soul. This opposition to the pulpit, however the inefficiency of existing agencies may have contributed to it, however the memories of olden priestcraft may have given it strength, cannot be explained but as originating in the yet unconquered enmity of the carnal mind to God. The teaching of the political theorizer, of the infidel demagogue, of the bene- volent idealist—why are they so popular? The teaching of the religious instructor—why is it so repulsive to the world? The main secret will be found in the fact that the one exalts, the other reproves, our nature—the one ignores, the other insists upon, the doctrine of the fall. If you silence the ministry, you silence the only living agency which, of set purpose, appeals to the moral sense of man, and brings out the world's conscience in its answer to moral obligation and to the truths of the Bible. The minister divides empire over the other faculties. He may speak to the intellect, but the philosopher will rival him ; he may charm the imagination, but the poet is his master ; he may rouse the passions, the mob orator will do it better : but in his power over conscience he has a government which no man shares, and, as a czar of many lands, he wields the sceptre over the master faculty of man. It is absolutely necessary, in this age of manifold activities and of spiritual pride, that there should be this ever-speaking witness of man's feebleness and God's strength. That witness dares not be silent amid the strife of tongues; and however the clamour may tell—and it does tell and ought to tell, upon the time-serving and the indolent, upon the vapid and the insincere—it is an unanswerable argument for the mission of the ministry itself, even as the blast which scatters the acorns roots the oak more firmly in the soil.— Standing as I do to-night, in connection with an association * which I dearly love, and which has been so highly honoured as an instrument of good, I must yet claim for the pulpit the foremost place among the agencies for the renovation of the world. Neither the platform nor the press can supersede it. So long as they work in harmony with its high purpose, and aim at the elevation of the entire man, it will hail their helpings with glad heart and free, but God hath set it on the monarchy, and it may not abdicate its throne.

One great want of the times is a commanding ministry—a ministry of a piety at once sober and earnest, and of mightiest moral power. Give us these men, "full of faith and of the Holy Ghost," who will proclaim old truths with new energy, not cumbering them with massive drapery, nor hiding them beneath piles of rubbish. Give us these men ! men of sound speech, who will preach the truth as it is in Jesus, not with faltering tongue and averted eye, as if the mind blushed at its own credulity—

* The Young Men's Christian Association of London, England.

not distilling it into an essence so subtle and so speedily decomposed that a chemical analysis alone can detect the faint odour which tells it has been there—but who will preach it apostlewise, that is, "first of all," at once a principle shrined in the heart and a motive mighty in the life—the source of all morals, and the inspiration of all charity—the sanctifier of every relationship, and the sweetener of every toil. Give us these men! men of dauntless courage, from whom God-fear has banished man-fear—who will stand unblenched before the pride of birth, and the pride of rank, and the pride of office, and the pride of intellect, and the pride of money, and will rebuke their hypocrisies, and demolish their false confidences, and sweep away their refuges of lies. Give us these men! men of sympathy, who dare despise none, however vile and crafty, because the "one blood" appeals for relationship in its sluggish or fevered flow—by whom the sleeper will not be harshly roused, and who will mourn over the wanderer, "My brother—ah! my brother!" Give us these men! men of zeal untiring—whose hearts of constancy quail not although dull men sneer, and proud men scorn, and timid men blush, and cautious men deprecate, and wicked men revile; who

> "Think
> What others only dreamed about, and do
> What others did but think, and glory in
> What others dared but do."

Give us these men! in whom Paul would find congenial reasoners; whom the fervent Peter would greet with a welcome sparkle in the eye; to whom the gentle John would be attracted as to twin souls which beat like his own—all lovingly. Give us these men! and you need speak no more of the faded greatness of the pulpit; the true God-witnesses shall be reinstated in their ancient moral sovereignty, and " by manifestation of the truth shall commend themselves to every man's conscience in the sight of God."

One main reason of Bunyan's repute among the people was *his thorough humanness.* He was no bearded hermit, sarcastic in his seclusion upon a world which he had forsaken, or which he never knew. He was no dark ascetic, snarling at his fellows from some cynical tub, inveighing against pleasures which were beyond his reach, and which he had toiled in vain to enjoy. He was a brave, manly, genial, brotherly soul, full of sympathy with the errors and frailties of men, mingling in the common grief and in the common cheerfulness of life. See him as he romps with the children in their noisy mirth, himself as great a child as they. Listen to him as he spins out of his fertile brain riddles to be guessed by the pilgrims, such as " keep Old Honest from nodding." Mark the smile that plays over his countenance as he writes how Ready-to-halt and Much-afraid footed it right merrily, in dance of joy, for the destruction of Giant Despair. Observe the ineffable tenderness with which he describes Feeblemind and Fearing. See in his real life the wealth of affection which he lavishes upon his sightless child. Oh ! it is charming—this union of the tender and the faithful in a master-mind—this outflow of all graceful charities from a spirit which bares its breast to danger, and which knows not to blench or quail ! Beautiful are these gushes of sensibility from a manly soul,—as if from some noble mountain, with granite heart and crest of cedar, there should issue a crystal rill, brightening the landscape with its dimpled beauty, or flashing archly beneath the setting sun.

Strength and gentleness are thus combined, in grandest harmony, only under the humanizing rule of Christianity. We might expect, under the old stoical morality, to find endurance and bravery—the perfection of an austere manhood—Roman virtue and Spartan pride. Under the precepts of a philosophy which never compromised with human weakness, we do not wonder at a Leonidas at the pass of Thermopylæ, or at a Miltiades on the plains of Marathon, at a high-souled Epaminondas or a meditative Numa, at an Aristides consenting to his own ostracism, or a Brutus pronouncing the death-doom of his son. They are the natural efflorescence of such culture and such soil. And, in truth, there is a hardy endeavour, an heroic self-abandonment, a capacity for deed and suffering, in some of these brave old Heathen, that would make many a modern Christian dwindle into the shadow of a man. But it was reserved for Christianity, by the inspiration of her faith and love, to exhibit human nature in its "highest embodied possibility," to show the bravery of heroes chastened by the meekness of children—an endurance more resolute than stoicism ever knew, combined with an all-embracing tenderness that would "clasp the universe to keep it warm." In Christianity, and in Christianity alone, can be discovered character in harmonious wholeness, at once the "*righteous* man," high in the practice of all social virtues, stern in his inflexible adhesion to the utter right, and the "*good* man," who has won for himself a revenue of affection—at whose name men's eyes sparkle and their spirits glow as in a sunbeam glinted in—and for whom some, in their strength of tenderness, would even dare to die.

It would seem, indeed, to be God's usual method to prepare men for extensive usefulness by the personal discipline of trial.

Hence, when we see Bunyan encompassed by terrible temptations, and immured in bondage; Luther in the fortress on the Wartburg, pining in sore sickness, and battling, in fancy, with embodied evil; Wesley wandering to Georgia and back, led through doubt and darkness to the long deferred moment which ended his "legal years," and then welcomed on his evangelistic journeys with ovations of misrepresentations and mud;—we remember that this protracted suffering is but the curriculum of heavenly discipline by which they are shriven of self and pride, and which superadds to the fortitude which bears all, and to the courage which dares all, the meekness and gentleness of Christ. You will remember a notable instance of the teaching of the Master on this matter in the history of the disciples. On one occasion, misers of that wealth divine which could have enriched every man of the five thousand, and have been none the poorer for the sumptuous dole, they exhibited a sad lack of needful sympathy, and impatiently murmured, "Send the multitudes away." Mark the sequel. "Straightway He constrained His disciples to get into a ship, and go before Him to the other side, while He sent away the people." *They* must be sent away like the multitudes, that they might know what such banishment meant, and feel, by bitter experience, the pangs of an absent Lord. Stormfully howled the wind on Tiberias' lake that night; deep would be the disquietude as the vexed waves tossed the vessel, and the eyes of the watchers, straining wistfully through the darkness, saw no star of hope nor glimpse of Saviour. But there came blessing to the world out of that storm. They would be better apostles for that night's anxious vigil; more thoroughly human in their sympathy; better able to proclaim to the benighted nations the overcoming might of love.

If you look from the Master's teaching to the Master's example, who fails to remember that for this purpose He became " touched with the feeling of our infirmity," and was tempted, that He might succour the tempted—that hunger and thirst, and weariness, and pain came upon Him—that He felt the pangs of desertion when those whom He trusted forsook Him, and the pangs of bereavement when those whom He loved had died—that He sorrowed with human tears over a freshly opened grave, and feared, with human apprehension, under the shadow of impending trial?

Brothers, he must be no fiery recluse who shall preach the people into a new crusade. The great work of the world's uplifting now-a-days is not to be wrought by the stern prophet of wrath, moving amongst men with the austerity as well as with the inspiration of the wilderness, but by the mild and earnest seer who comes, like the Son of Man, " eating and drinking," of genial soul, and blithe companionship, and divinest pity ; who counsels without haughtiness, and reproves without scorn ; and who bears about with him the reverent consciousness that he deals with the majesty of man. Neither the individual nor the aggregate can be lectured out of vice nor scolded into virtue. There is a relic of humanness, after all, lingering in every heart, like a dear gage of affection, stealthily treasured amid divorce and estrangement, and the far wards where it is locked up from men can be opened only by the living sympathy of love. Society is like the prodigal, whom corrective processes failed to reform, and whom gaol discipline only tended to harden, and whom enforced exile only rendered more audacious in his crime, but down whose bronzed cheek a tear stole in a far off land at some stray thought of home, and whose heart of adamant was broken by the sudden memory of dead mother's prayer. Let us recognize this truth in all our endeavours for the benefit of men. It is quite possible to combine inflexibility of adhesion to the right with forbearing tenderness towards the wrong-doer. Speak the truth, by all means,—let it fall upon the hearts of men with all the imparted energy by which the Spirit gives it power ; but speak the truth in love, and, perchance, it may subdue them by its winsome beauty, and prompt their acknowledgment that it is altogether lovely.

Such a one in his teachings will be equally remote from lax indifferentism and from cynical theology. He will not dare a hair's breadth deviation from the Bible ; but he will not graft upon it his own moroseness, nor mutilate it into his own deformity. Such an one will not complain that he has no neighbours. He will find neighbours, aye, even in the heart of London. He will be a kind husband and tender father ; but his hearthstone will not bound his sympathy. He will be a patriot ; he will be a philanthropist. His love, central in his home and in his country, will roll its far ripples upon all men. He will see in the poorest man a brother, and in the worst man a nature of divine endowment, now sunk in darkness, which he is to labour to illumine and to save. Such an one will not call earth a howling wilderness. He will not slander this dear old world because some six thousand years ago an injury befel it which disfigured it sadly, and has embittered its subsequent history. Against that which did the wrong he will cherish intensest hatred—he will purge it from himself—he will root it out of others, if he can. He will love the world as a theatre for the display o. noble energies, or rich benevolence, of manly strength, of godlike pity ; and he will work in it with an honest heart and loving purpose, until the finger beckons him into the wealthier heaven.

Young men, the age of chivalry is not over. The new crusade has already begun. The weapons are not shaped by mortal skill, nor is the battle with garments rolled in blood. Strong-souled, earnest men—knights, of the true Order of Jesus, are leagued in solemn covenant, and are already in the field. " Theirs are the red colours, and for a scutcheon they have the Holy Lamb and Golden Shield." " Good-will to man " is their inspiring banner-text. " Faith working by love " is broidered on their housings. Not to prance in the tilt-yard, amidst the sheen of bright lances and bright eyes, don they their armour. They have too serious work on hand to flaunt them in a mimic pageant, or to furnish a holiday review. They have caught the spirit of their Master. As, with eyes dimmed by their own sym-pathy, He looked upon the fated Jerusalem, they have learnt to look upon a fallen but ransomed race. They war for its rescue from the inexorable bondage of wrong. Ignorance, im-providence, intemperance, indifference, infidelity ; these are the giants which they set lance in rest to slay. I would fain, like another Peter the Hermit, summon you into the ranks of these loving and valiant heroes. The band will admit you all. In this, the holier chivalry, the churl's blood is no bar to honour. The highest distinctions are as open to the peasant's offspring as to the scion of the Plantagenets and Howards. Go, then, where glory waits you. The field is the world. Go where the abjects wander, and gather them into the fold of the sanctuary. Go to the lazarettos where the moral lepers herd, and tell them of the healing balm. Go to the haunts of crime, and float a gospel message upon the feculent air. Go wherever there are ignorant to be instructed, timid to be cheered, and helpless to be succoured, and stricken to be blessed, and erring to be reclaimed. Go wherever faith can see, or hope can breathe, or love can work, or courage can venture. Go and win the spurs of your spiritual knighthood there.

> " Oh ! who would not a champion be,
> In this, the lordlier chivalry ?
> Uprouse ye now, brave brother band,
> With honest heart and working hand.
> We are but few, toil-tried, but true,
> And hearts beat high to dare and do ;
> Oh ! there be those that ache to see
> The day-dawn of our victory !
> Eyes full of heart-break with us plead,
> And watchers weep, and martyrs bleed ;
> Work, brothers, work ! Work, hand and brain,
> We'll win the Golden Age again,
> And love's millennial morn shall rise
> In happy hearts and blessed eyes ;
> We will, we will, brave champions be,
> In this, the lordlier chivalry."

It remains only that we present Bunyan before you as a CONFESSOR FOR THE TRUTH. One would anticipate that a character like his would be sustained during the hour of trial, and that, like Luther, whom in many points he greatly resembled, he would witness a good confession before the enemies of the Cross of Christ. A warrant was issued for his apprehension in the dreary month of November. The intention of the magistrate was whispered about beforehand, and Bunyan's friends, alarmed for his safety, urged him to forego his announced purpose to preach. Nature pleaded hard for compliance, and urged the claims of a beloved wife and four children, one of them blind. Prudence suggested that, escaping now, he might steal other opportunities for the preaching of the truth. He took counsel of God in prayer, and then came to his decision. " If I should now run, and make an escape, it will be of a very ill savour in the country ; what will my weak and newly converted brethren think of it ? If God, of His mercy, should choose me to go upon the forlorn hope, if I should fly, the world may take occasion at my cowardliness to blaspheme the Gospel." At Samsell, in Bedfordshire, the people assembled ; there were about forty persons present. Some of the timid sort advised, even then, that the meeting should be dismissed. Bravely he replied, " No, by no means ! I will not stir, neither will I have the meeting dismissed. Come, be of good cheer, let us not be daunted ; our cause is good ! we need not be ashamed of it ; to preach God's word is so good a work that we shall be well rewarded if we suffer for that." Accordingly he was cast into prison. After seven weeks imprisonment the session was held at Bedford, and Bunyan was arraigned at the bar. This was his sentence : " You must be had back again to prison, and there lie for three months following ; then, if you do not submit to go to church to hear divine service, you must be banished the realm ; and after that, if you should be found in the realm, without the special license of the King, you must stretch by the neck for it, I tell you plainly." So spake the rude and arbitrary Judge Kelynge, who, like Scroggs and Jeffreys, enjoys the distinction. rare among English judges, of being in infamy immortal, Bunyan answered, inspired with Lutheran and Pauline courage,

" I am at a point with you ; if I were out of prison to-day, I would preach the Gospel again to-morrow, by the help of God." His spirit blenched not with the lapse of time, though he lay twelve years in that foul dungeon, the discovery of whose abominations, a century afterwards, first started John Howard in his " circumnavigation of charity." Towards the close of his imprisonment we hear the dauntless beatings of the hero-heart : " I have determined—the Almighty God being my help and my shield—yet to suffer, if frail life might continue so long, even until the moss shall grow over my eye-brows, rather than violate my faith and my principles." Oh, rare John Bunyan ! thy " frail life " has become immortal ; the world will not let thee die. Thou art shrined in the loving memory of thousands, while thy judges and persecutors are forgotten, or remembered only with ridicule and shame. " The righteous shall be in everlasting remembrance, but the memory of the wicked shall rot."

Our lot is cast in gentler times than these. No indictments are preferred against us now for " devilish and pernicious abstinence from church-going." Felons are not now let loose in honour of a monarch's coronation, while men of God are hailed to closer durance. Phœnix-like, out of the ashes of the martyr-fires, arose religious freedom. The flames of outward persecution have well nigh forgotten to burn. And yet the offence of the cross has not ceased. The profession of the Gospel does not always bring peace, but a sword. Trouble is yet the heritage " of all that will live godly in Christ Jesus," and there is strong need in all of us for the exhibition of the main element in a confessor's character—nobleness of religious decision. We must have convictions of duty wrought so strongly into our souls, that neither opposition nor difficulty, nor even disaster, shall make us falter in the course which we have intelligently chosen. For lack of these sincere and abiding convictions many have erred from the faith, and have manifested an instability of character that is truly deplorable. Many young men have run well for a season—have formed large plans of usefulness, and have been full of promise in all that was of good report and lovely ; but a fatal indecision has blighted the promise and rendered the plans abortive ; and their course has reminded us of Emerson's ludicrous account of the American roads, starting fair and stately, between avenues of branching pines, but narrowing gradually as they proceed, and at last ending in a squirrel track, and running up a tree. It may be questioned, indeed, whether any of us, in this matter, approximate to the standard. Let us ask ourselves, if we had lived in the days of the Master, should " we have left all and followed Him ? " As we look at Him in the garb of a peasant, and a Nazarene, of ignoble origin and vagrant life, opposed by all recognized authorities, alone against the world, shocking every ancient prejudice, and pronouncing the doom of a ritual, gorgeous in its ceremonial, and enfibred, by the ties of ages, round the hearts of men, what should we have thought of such a questionable man ? Should we have dared to have come to him, even by night, while living, much less to have gone boldly and begged His body when dead ? Should we have foregone, for His sake, the chief seats of synagogues, and the uppermost rooms at feasts, and for the pleasure of His Divine discourse, have cast ourselves on His fidelity, even for daily bread ? Let us look into the glass of our own consciousness, that we may be humbled and reproved. And, in the present, with the light of

His teaching and of His example, how are we living? Would it please us that the hidden man of the heart should be unveiled to our neighbour's scrutiny? Do we the right always, because it is the right—without thought of profit—and at the sure risk of ill? Do we rejoice to be brought into contact with *a man*, that we may put our own manhood to the proof? Can we resolve to work ever for the good of this bad world, not bating from weariness, nor deterred by ingratitude, nor palsied with fear? Dare we speak honestly and act bravely, though loss and shame should follow speech and deed? Is there in us no division of activity against itself; are our thought and action mutually representative of each other? In one word, are we sincere? Do we serve one Master? with no reserve of our endowments? with every fragment of our influence? at every moment of our time? Oh! let us search our hearts on this matter. There is a great deal more of this sincere and decisive godliness wanted in the world, and you are to furnish it. I assume, of course, that you are decided for God; that the great change has taken place in you, and that you are walking in the fear of the Lord, and in the comforts of the Holy Ghost. If it be not so with you, seek first, for yourselves, the kingdom of God. It will be a terrible thing if the " Perdidi diem " of the regretful Roman should deepen into a " Perdidi vitam " for you; or if there be one torturing thought of unforgiven sin, which, like Poe's raven

> " Never flitting, still is sitting, still is sitting
> On the pallid bust of Pallas just above your chamber door ;
> And its eyes have all the seeming of a demon's that is dreaming,
> And the lamplight o'er it streaming, throws its shadow on the floor ;
> And your soul from out that shadow that lies floating on the floor
>   Shall be lifted—Nevermore."

But I rejoice to know that many of you are already the Lord's, living in the conscious enjoyment of religion, and anxious to make the world the better for your presence. To you we make our appeal. Of you, Christian young men, it is asked that you cast out of yourselves the false, and the selfish, and the defiling, and that you be sincere workers for the glory of God and for the benefit of men. We ask it in the name of Truth, that you may man her bulwarks and tell her to the generation following. We ask it in the name of Christianity, that you may join her in her brave battle with world, and flesh, and devil. We ask it in the name of Society, that she may not be convulsed by the crimes of the lawless, nor by the frenzy of the despairing. We ask it in the name of our common country, bewildered as she is by the burdens which oppress her, and distracted as she is by the contentions of her children. We ask it in the name of Humanity, struggling to deliver herself from a thousand wrongs. We ask it in the name of multitudes, sharing your own manhood, who are passing down to darkness, wailing as they go— " No man hath cared for my soul." We ask it in the name of the Redeemer, who has shed for you His own most precious blood, and who waits, expecting to see of the travail of His soul.

Wearily have the years passed, I know: wearily to the pale watcher on the hill who has been so long gazing for the daybreak: wearily to the anxious multitudes who have been waiting for His tidings below. Often has the cry gone up through the darkness, " Watcher, what of the night?" and often has the disappointing answer come, " It is night still; here the stars are clear above me, but they shine afar, and yonder the clouds lower heavily, and the sad night winds blow." But the time shall come, and perhaps sooner than we look for it, when the countenance of that pale watcher shall gather into intenser expectancy, and when the challenge shall be given, with the hopefulness of a nearer vision, "Watcher, what of the night?" and the answer will come, "The darkness is not so dense as it was; there are faint streaks on the horizon's verge; mist is in the valleys, but there is a radiance on the distant hill. It comes nearer—that promise of the day. The clouds roll rapidly away, and they are fringed with amber and gold. It is, it is the blest sunlight that I feel around me—MORNING!"

IT IS MORNING!

And, in the light of that morning, thousands of earnest eyes flash with renewed brightness, for they have longed for the coming of the day. And, in the light of that morning, things that nestle in dust and darkness cower and flee away. Morning for the toilworn artisan! for oppression and avarice, and gaunt famine, and poverty are gone, and there is social night no more. Morning for the meek-eyed student! for doubt has fled, and sophistry is silenced, and the clouds of error are lifted from the fair face of Truth for aye, and there is intellectual night no more. Morning for the lover of man! for wrongs are redressed, and contradictions harmonised, and problems solved, and men summer in perpetual brotherhood, and there is moral night no more. Morning for the lover of God! for the last infidel voice is hushed, and the last cruelty of superstition perpetrated, and the last sinner lays his weapons down, and Christ the crucified becomes Christ the crowned. Morning! Hark how the earth rejoices in it, and its many minstrels challenge the harpers of the sky—"Sing with us, ye heavens! The morning cometh, the

J

darkness is past, the shadows flee away, the true light shineth now." Morning! Hark how the sympathetic heavens reply, "Thy sun shall no more go down, neither shall thy moon withdraw herself, for the Lord shall be thine everlasting light, and the days of thy mourning shall be ended!"

IT IS MORNING!

"The planet now doth, like a garment, wear the beauty of the morning." And the light climbeth onward, and upward, for there is a sacred noon beyond. That noon is HEAVEN!

"AND THERE SHALL BE NO NIGHT THERE."

WESLEY AND HIS TIMES.

WESLEY AND HIS TIMES.

THE history of Christianity has not been a continuous progress. It has had its times of decay and of revival. Now it has appeared as though all hearts would welcome it—and as though, like an undisputed king, it had only to proclaim itself to be received and crowned. Again it has languished from the affections of a people, and has seemed to live only by effort and struggle. In the time of the Apostles its march was a triumph. Ere the last of them fell asleep beneath the purple sky of Ephesus, it had reached and subdued the most considerable cities of the world, and everything seemed fair and promising for the speedy conversion of men. But then came a season of indifference. Through the dreary ages succeeding, the light shone more dimly, until, like the torches at a funeral, it shone only on the mourners for the dead. The Church became formal and haughty, ambition seized upon the truth, and established upon its possession a vast ecclesiastical power, and thus the Popery of Hildebrand overlaid the Christianity of Paul. Then again came a season of revival. The world was weary for the light. Morality and faith were languishing together—men's minds brooded over the state of things, some with a strange disquiet, some with a stranger hope—the hour was ripe for

change, either by amendment or by ruin. From German clois-
ters, amid Alpine heights, from the plains of France, there rose
the simultaneous cry of multitudes of spiritual bondsmen. God
heard and answered, and the Reformation came. Yet again,
as if with the regularity of a law, there came a period of decay.
The zeal of the churches became fitful, their faith loosely held,
the morals of the people dissolute, until there grew a need of
a second Reformation, which should put life into the truth
which had been established by the struggles of the first. All
accounts agree to represent the sad religious state of England
when George the Second succeeded to the throne. The righteousness which exalteth a people was hidden in secret places,
and, to the mourning eyes of the few faithful, it seemed as if a
cloud hung darkly over the land, and as if the vials of Divine
wrath were almost full. The literature of the age, which may
be regarded as the index to its prevalent tendencies, was for the
most part corrupt or irreligious. There were exceptions, of
course, for this was the period at which the British classics
started into being, but the design of Steele and Addison, and,
still later, of Johnson, was to counteract the follies and vices
whose desolations they deplored ; and it may be easily conceived
that the moral aspects of society were of no doubtful badness
when Pope's Pantheism and Bolingbroke's Infidelity were
fashionable ; when, according to Dryden, the loose wit of Con-
greve was the only prop of a declining stage ; when the popular
novelists were Smollett and Fielding, and Mrs. Aphia Behn;
and when even divinity could so far forget its sacred calling as
to pen the ribaldries of Swift and Sterne. If you look into the
churches the decline is equally lamentable, and you find, even
among the reputedly orthodox, the looseness of thought which

too frequently introduces to looseness of life. There had been hard thinkers and great preachers, men of massive thought and burning word, both in the established and non-conforming churches, but the words of the preachers fell powerless, and it was as though the theology of the writers was embalmed. The works of Collins and Tindall were more in vogue than those of Baxter and Howe. Men sat at the feet of Chesterfield rather than of Tillotson. Whiston lapsed into Arianism at Cambridge, and Clarke dispensed it at the church of St. James. Among Dissenters, if the truth was held it was as a sentiment rather than as a power, and while a large number of the clergy sought relief from subscription to articles which they had long disavowed, others drank or dreamed away their lives; shepherds were profligate or idle, while the hungry sheep looked up and were not fed.

It would be easy to multiply testimonies that these are not random shafts from a bow that is drawn at a venture. Butler, Burnet, Secker, Leighton, and many others in the Establishment, Watts, Guyse, Doddridge, and many more among the Non-conformists, have left their sorrowful witness on record, and there is everything to assure us that, in Isaac Taylor's forcible words, "the Anglican Church was a system under which men had lapsed into heathenism," and that "languishing non-conformity was in course to be found nowhere but in books."

There are strange omens in the midst of us to-day—the sneer and the scoff mingle with the welcomes which are given to godliness—the truth is still cast into "the place for gold where they fine it;" the ravens wander forth from the ark and return not; but there is morality in place of shameless vice, and we breathe a bracing atmosphere instead of tainted air ; and in view of the times of rebuke and trouble to which we have referred, there is much to make us thankful for present privilege, and that with all our faults our condition has not fallen so low.

The Rectory of Epworth—a small town among the flatlands of Lincolnshire, where ague is a frequent visitant, and melancholy pollard-willows rise, on dreary winter's days, through levels often lying under water—was held, in the first years of the last century, by a brave and much enduring man, who, with a noble wife, like minded, struggled with a small income to rear and educate a large family. This man was SAMUEL WESLEY. His own sturdy independence was rooted in him by the like virtue in his ancestors. Bartholomew Wesley, his grandfather, was one of the ejected ones at the Restoration. John Wesley, son of Bartholomew, attained still higher rank in the spiritual peerage than his father, for he endured repeated imprisonment, and at length sank into the grave a brave confessor for the truth he loved so well. Samuel Wesley inherited the strong soul of his father, with a more robust habit of body. Designed originally for a Non-conformist minister, he saw reason to review and change his opinions, and with characteristic decision he trudged off to Oxford, and entered himself as a poor scholar at Exeter College. He was known through his University life as a devout, laborious man, whose leisure was occupied in maintaining himself by his pen, save when he snatched an hour for a visit to a poor man's cottage, or to the felons' prison. After his marriage he accepted a cure in London, and was "passing rich on thirty pounds a year." A brave fearlessness distinguished him through life, and sustained him under the trials to which, sometimes by his imprudence, sometimes by his fidelity, he was exposed. For years he had but fifty pounds, and one child additional, per annum. His dedication of a work to Queen Mary procured for him the Rectory of Epworth, where he struggled on a nominal salary of two hundred pounds to sustain the nineteen hostages which he had given to society, ten of whom grew up to adult years. He eked out his living by his verses, and his thoughts ran in rhyme so swiftly that his publisher declares that two hundred couplets were born, on the average, per day. His searching ministry and his unpopular politics gave great offence to the rabble of his parish, who vented their spleen, sometimes by drumming beneath his windows to the damage of the symmetry of his sermons, and sometimes by acts of more serious annoyance and cruelty. They broke his doors, they wounded his cattle, they stole his tithe corn, they cut off the legs of his house-dog, and, on two several occasions, they set fire to his house. His friends advised him to remove, but he said that would be cowardly, and by his fierce crusade against evil he earned his right to the escalop-shell which was graven upon his family arms. Arrested at the doors of the church for a small debt which he could not at the moment discharge, he remained three months in Lincoln prison; but there, like the Vicar of Wakefield, he began to preach to the prisoners, and wrote to the Archbishop of York that " he expected to do far more good *in his new parish* than in the old one." He had a stubborn will and a firmness which bordered upon obstinacy, and withal a relish for joking, and a rich vein of native humour. He lived long enough to rejoice in the labours of his noble sons, to see, with an insight which approaching death had sharpened, the dawn of a brighter moral day for England; to testify to his own inward witness of acceptance with God; to exult, though in the chastening of strong pain, that he could

" thank, love, and bless God for all," and then the brave heart broke, and the strong and gentle spirit mounted to Heaven upon the breath of the communion prayer.

Yet even more largely than to his father, was John Wesley indebted to "the elect lady" who shared her husband's fortunes, and gave him heart by the sight of an endurance that was even more heroic than his own. In all galleries of noble and illustrious women SUSANNA WESLEY deserves a foremost place. Dr. Annesly, her father, was a noted Puritan leader, and his daughter inherited his spirit and his bravery. At thirteen years of age she examined for herself the points of difference between Dissenters and Churchmen, and though familiar with her father's wrongs, and " rich," as Isaac Taylor says, "in a dowry of non-conforming virtues," she became a zealous Churchwoman. After her marriage with Samuel Wesley she was most exemplary in her discharge of every social and parental duty, and exhibited the completeness of her character in all sweet sanctities of home. She bestowed great pains and skill upon the education of her children, watching over them with a vigilance which never slumbered, and teaching them with a patience which was never tired. She was asked, "Why do you tell that boy the same thing twenty times over?" "Because nineteen times telling were not enough," was her common-sense reply. During her husband's absence she established services for her poor neighbours in the kitchen of the rectory, which so scandalized the affrighted curate that he sent post haste to apprize the rector that a conventicle had been set up in his house. In answer to her husband's remonstrances she calmly stated her reasons for the step she had taken, and the results which had followed, and then said, " If you wish me to desist, do not advise, but command me," thus recognizing her conjugal duty, and preserving, at the same time, her own good conscience towards God. Her healthful piety enabled her to warn her son sagainst the mysticism towards which they often wavered. Her sagaciousness saw the good which lurked in the employment of lay agency, and she urged the early recognition of Thomas Maxfield and others, foremost of a bright succession of true workers for the kingdom of God. Her cheerful soul smiled on amidst various fortune, through years of struggle, almost of hunger—when sharper sorrows came,—when the rings from her fingers went to comfort her husband in his prison,—when she bowed heavily over nine fair children claimed early by the covetous grave,—when she waded with scorched hands and face through the fires of her own dwelling,—when she mourned over the sorrows of her living children with a fiercer pang than had smitten her at the burial of her dead. Of rare classic beauty, dignified and graceful, as became her noble blood, one of those firm but gentle natures which, like sunbeams, shine without an effort, and leave us genial like themselves ; with a far-seeing sagacity and with excellent common-sense—a pattern of all womanly virtues—a lightener of all manly cares, ruling her household with a quiet power, yet alive to the accomplishments of society, and ready to pass her verdict upon books and men—faithful in the common things of life, withal an heiress of the heavenly, and holding daily converse with the place where she had hid her treasure, she moved on in her course, a queen uncrowned and saintly—

> "Not perfect, nay, but full of tender wants,
> No angel, but a dearer being, all dipt
> In angel instincts ; breathing Paradise ;

> Interpreter between the gods and men ;
> Who looked all native to her place, and yet
> On tip-toe seemed to touch upon a sphere
> Too great to tread."

Wise in counsel, with a discernment which was almost prophetic, attracting to herself the reverent love of her children, she lived for years in the house which John Wesley had provided for her, a very marvel of green and kindly age, until at length, in an almost absolute negation of death, she finished her course whispering, " Children, as soon as I am released, sing a psalm of praise to God." Then, leaving a fragrant name and an affluent inheritance of prayer, she looked calmly upward, and all was still until the hymn arose in the death-chamber, and Heaven was the richer for another of those "honourable women" who with gladness and rejoicing "are to be brought into the palace of the King."

Of such parents was John Wesley born. The world is familiar with his marvellous deliverance from the burning house in the sixth year of his age. When thirteen years old he was sent to the Charter House to proceed with the education which had been commenced beneath the home discipline of his mother. That discipline had wonderfully prepared him for life at a public school, so that, though the fagging system was in full operation, and he had to bear his share of oppression and robbery, he was neither crushed into the spirit of a slave, nor goaded to be the despot when his own upper-form days came. The little Methodist preserved his health by a morning scamper, in which he thrice made the circuit of the garden, nor would he suffer any gloom either of spirits or of weather to frighten him from his trinity of rounds. There was even thus early a combination of buoyancy and manliness about him which attracted the notice of his masters, and made the shrewder among them predict that his life would not be an unnoticed calm. The half-confessed presentiment of ordination to distinguished service seems to have been upon him almost unconsciously, and as a student of Christ Church, and subsequently as a fellow of Lincoln College, he subordinated everything to the preparation for that future which as yet he knew not, save in the high hopes which bounded in his breast, and in the patient watching for the light, as a sleepless one watcheth for the morning.

Thomas A'Kempis, William Law, and Jeremy Taylor, were the three writers who, at this period of his history, took the greatest hold upon his mind. It is needless to dwell in detail upon the methods in which his convictions of sin prompted him to seek rest of soul. He toiled painfully through an ascetic discipline which almost consumed him. He was rigid in the observance of each rite and rubric, mapping out every moment of his time, and accounting for every farthing of his property as if with a morbid hope that he might lacerate himself into holiness, or purchase acceptance by a devotion which ceased not from its prayers. At one time he contemplated flight from the fellowship of men, and sought a school in some wild Yorkshire dale as most congenial to the temper of his soul. He went to Georgia on a bootless journey, where his rigorous interpretation of the glad tidings brought "not peace but a sword" throughout the whole colony. He returned to England to discover that he, who had been labouring for the conversion of the Indians, was not himself converted, for in those ends of the earth Moravian cheerfulness had rebuked his severity, and Moravian simplicity had chided his ritualism, and Moravian resignation had contrasted with his unbelief. And we see, in all these incidents of his life, parts of the great discipline by which he was prepared for service, by which he was taught sympathy and patience and courage—those apostolic graces which his apostle's life required.

How marvellous are the ways in which God works to fulfil his plans ! The sower sows his seed, rejoices over the filled furrows, mourns over that which the birds of the air snatch and scatter ; but those winged wanderers are often, like the ravens of Elijah, charged to bear food to some famishing prophet, or to sow the germs of harvests where plough was never driven. Slight as the thistledown may be the breath of prayer, but God marks it as it rises to Heaven. Quietly, as the acorn to the earth, the pleading word may fall, but its influence shall be fruitful and mighty, even as the "oak which looseneth golden leaves in a kind largess to the soil it grew on." Man, in the ardour of enterprise, sounds a trumpet to the living, but when God gives his clarion-call, He gives it in the valley full of bones, and among the corpses breathes the generous life which springs armed and eager to the battle. The feeblest agency and the lowliest worker, the heart which has strange struggles between the hero's purpose and the coward's fear, with God's help may drive the aliens before them, and shout in the raptures of victory. Aye, and when the dank grass waves over the sepulchres of wearied or slaughtered ones who have died disheartened for the cause they loved, their spirits may walk the earth in a prophetic resurrection. Like the Bruce's heart, they may be silent leaders of armies, and thousands of exulting followers, catching inspiration from their memory, may be proud to follow where their ashes lead the way.

More than 300 years had rolled away since the sky of Constance reflected the fires by which the initial martyrs of the Reformation were consumed. The sapient council which offered Jerome and Huss in sacrifice, and wreaked its puny vengeance upon Wickliffe's bones, wist not that they were both rooting and spreading the doctrines they were wishful to destroy. Scarcely had the council been dissolved when the Bohemian peasantry arose to avenge their teachers, and to battle for their own religious freedom. For twenty years, under the brave Count Ziska, did they maintain the strife with varying fortune, but with a spirit which never quailed ; and though persecution afterwards arose, and the Hussites filled the prisons, the truth was preserved and handed down from the father to the children as a heritage more precious than of lands or gold.

In the early part of the 18th century one of these Bohemian confessors, Christian David by name, led a few followers into Lusatia, where dwellings were built for them upon the domain of the young Count Zingendorf. Hence arose the establishment of the Moravian brotherhood, who, starting from Herrnhut, as they named their settlement, spread their earnest missions into many a land, won grand gospel triumphs among the most forlorn and hopeless, and became, in the providence of God, powers for good to lead into the perception of a better life some who were to accomplish yet mightier works than theirs. About a week after his arrival from Georgia, John Wesley, still striving to establish his own righteousness, went to a select meeting which these indefatigable Moravians had established in London. Here he met with PETER BÖHLER, a name never to be forgotten in connection with Wesley's history, because God chose him to be the Ananias to his later Paul. Böhler convinced him of his unbelief, pressed home upon him the necessity and happiness of a living faith in Christ, urged him to immediate reliance, and thus cleared away the mists which had obscured to him the shining of the sun. At length, on the 24th May, 1738, the hour of deliverance came. In a meeting in Aldersgate Street, while a layman was reading Luther's preface to the Epistle to the Romans, John Wesley says "I felt my heart strangely warmed; I felt I did trust in Christ alone for salvation, and an assurance was given me that he had taken away my sins, even mine, and saved me from the law of sin and death." Thus it is that truth can never die, that the good which men do lives after them, reproducing itself like multiplying grain. Through the intervening centuries John Huss becomes an instrument in the conversion of John Wesley, and the Apostle of the Second Reformation is quickened from the death of sin through the living words of the dead Apostle of the First.

Here then we have the starting point of Wesley's labours—the key to the solution of all his mysteries of toil and triumph. Consciously reconciled to God, and having peace by faith in Jesus, he burned to declare the glad tidings which had made himself so happy. All estimates of his character will be unworthy if they do not start from his conversion. All histories of him will be unsatisfactory if this great fact fails to be apprehended. The real reason which barbed many a contemporaneous slander, and guided the pens of such critics as Lavington and Nightingale, which led Sydney Smith to scoff profanely at the thing he knew not, which threw a warp over the fine mind of Southey, so that he understood but dimly the character he would fain have drawn, is perhaps to be found, not in personal malignity, not in wilful disingenuousness, but in the simple postulate of Scripture: "The natural man knoweth not the things of the spirit of God, neither can he know them, because they are spiritually discerned."

While John Wesley was thus receiving his fitness for his great mission, his coadjutors were led, by the same Providence, to the same end. A bright rosy lad, with the blue apron of a common drawer in an inn, struggling with a confusion of great thoughts about himself and about his destiny, which he could neither exclude nor comprehend—a pale servitor of Pembroke College, choosing the meanest drudgery, wearing the coarsest serge, eating the homeliest food, and but little of that; standing in the biting frost until he had no feeling either in feet or fingers; wandering in Christ Church meadows at the gloomy nightfall;—trying hard to fast through the whole forty days of Lent;—the chosen butt for the ridicule and insult both of town and gown—these are the glimpses we get of the childhood and youth of GEORGE WHITEFIELD, who afterwards became an evangelist such as the world has never known since Peter the Fisherman witnessed a Pentecost under the first Gospel sermon. Rescued from his self-righteousness in an illness, and opening his heart to receive the love of the Saviour, he went forth to his loved work of preaching, beginning in the church where he had been baptized and had humbly knelt to receive his first communion. His directness offended the sinful, and his earnestness startled the timid, so that church after church was closed against him, until at length, thinking little of irregularity, and less of the revival he was beginning to inaugurate, he went forth into the open air, and proclaimed to listening thousands the unsearchable riches of Christ. The effects which followed were extraordinary. As he stood forth, his frank, manly

K

countenance seemed to bespeak a hearing, and when once his voice was heard, so exquisitely was it toned, and so skilfully wielded, that high and low were subject to its spell. Add to this a wealth of eloquent action which made every sentence dramatic, an earnestness which the heat of holy passion kindled, and above all a subject which had stirred his strongest convictions, and which bore him as with a torrent's force upon its stream; and you will not wonder that with all these advantages, and withal the " demonstration of the Spirit," his should be a mighty and transforming word. His power of description must have been marvellous. Men saw the scenes he painted. They heard the ripple of the Galilean waters. They felt the awful shadows of the Tabor cloud. They shivered as the fierce wind swept among the olives, or the pale moon gleamed upon the paler brow of the sufferer in Gethsemane. They crouched as if they heard the tramp of nearing demons when he prophesied of doom. Not only were Garrick and Pulteney, themselves orators, eager listeners to his burning words, but David Hume hearkened till he forgot to sneer; the philosophic Franklin acknowledged the sorcery, and emptied his pockets like a common man; the artificial Chesterfield yielded for once to an impulse of real feeling, and sprang forward to arrest the fall of the blind beggar whom the speaker pictured on the cliff's extremest verge. Among the rude and turbulent his triumphs were greater still. " I came to break your head, and you have broken my heart," said a ruffian, as the brick-bat dropped out of his nerveless hand. " He preaches like a lion," was the testimony of one whom he had terrified by some strong appeal. In single-handed defiance he went into Bartholomew Fair, and while he spoke the booths were deserted, the acrobats tumbled in vain, and the baffled showmen found their occupation gone. The deaf old woman who had cursed him as he passed along the street was found presently clambering up the pulpit stairs that she might not lose a syllable of his sermon. "The prisoners heard him," and they wept and trembled. The flowing tears made little rills of cleanliness down the swarth faces of Kingswood colliers, ruder than the foresters who dwelt in the old Chase before them. Children hung upon his lips with loving, earnest eyes ; and perhaps the most touching illustration of his influence was in the case of a little boy, who sickened after he had heard him preach, and whose sole cry in the pauses of his pain was, "Let me go to Mr. Whitefield's God." All description must fail to make us realize his wonderful power, unless we could transfer the countenance, and fix the flashing eye and sweeping hand upon the page. And this power was not, as has been said, "the power of the cambric handkerchief or of the simulated tears." He could not help being an orator, but he aimed to be an evangelist, and so great was his success that he is said in one week to have received 1,000 letters from those who had been blessed by his ministry. He had no great grasp of mind, nor was he born to organize or to command. "I hate to head a party. If I were to raise societies, I should only be weaving a Penelope's web." These were his words. When he went to Scotland he was received by the Associate Presbytery, who were about to elect a Moderator and proceed to business. "What about?" he asked. They told him it was to set him right on some matters of church government. He answered that they might save themselves the trouble, that his time was wanted for highways and hedges, and that, if the Pope himself would only lend his pulpit, he would gladly preach the righteousness of Christ therein. His work was preaching, and he knew it. The pulpit was his throne, and never monarch filled a regal seat with kinglier presence. Worn down with labour, the physicians prescribed a perpetual blister. He says he tried perpetual preaching and found that it answered as well. When winter prevented his journeys he mourned like a smitten child—when spring opened his way he bounded to his beloved labour, glad as a gazelle upon the hills. His seal had for its device a winged heart, soaring above the globe, with the motto "*Astra petamus*," and this was emblematic of the business to which he had consecrated his life. "I hope to die in the pulpit, or at least soon after I come out of it. It is your cowardly Christians, who have borne no witness while they live, whom God honours at the last. I shall die in silence; my testimony has been given in my life." Such was his language as, after thirty-four years of labour, he gathered himself up for what proved a final discourse. For two hours, though he had recently suffered from the cruel asthma which destroyed him, he spoke with a pathos and power which he had never surpassed, to a people who lingered like the hosts on Carmel, and as if they knew that for another Elijah there awaited a chariot of fire. The pavement and entrance hall of the house in which he lodged were thronged with people, who craved a parting word. Exhausted with his labours he requested another minister to speak to them, and with the candle in his hand was ascending the stairs to rest. Suddenly he turned, and, as if with a sense of opportunity rapidly vanishing, and of moments more precious than gold, addressed them from the stairway, and paused not in his labour of love until the candle burned down into the socket as he held it in his hands. The next morning he was not. In the night the messenger came, and, like his

Master, he ascended from the summit of the mountain of prayer. Such was George Whitefield, strangely reviled in his day, but whom time has amply avenged:

> "We need not now beneath well-sounding Greek,
> Conceal the name the poet dared not speak."

His praise is in all the churches and he belongs to them all. You can no more chain him to a sect than you can tame the libertine breezes or control the wilful spring. The works that follow the good man will keep his memory green, and cause his fame to grow, until world-wide as his benevolence and his ministry shall be the estimation in which he is held, and ages yet unborn, as they read the marvel of his 'life, shall bless God for this Prince of Preachers, this noblest, grandest embodiment of the Revelation angel, who "flies through the midst of heaven having the everlasting Gospel to preach to every nation, and people and tongue."

"Let me make the ballads of a people, and I care not who makes their laws," was a great man's saying. If there be force in this statement, and it is a just recognition of the marvellous power of song, CHARLES WESLEY deserves a more extended notice than our time will allow us to render. Like his brother, he was below the middle stature, but of stouter build. He was shortsighted, warm-tempered (for did he not belong to the "genus irritabile" of the poets?) and had an abrupt and rapid manner. It is said that his visits at college used to be dreaded by his exacter brother, for he would stumble against the table, disarrange the papers, offend against the small proprieties which neat men covet, and perhaps ask a dozen questions, and bounce out of the room before he had heard the answer to any one of the number. A child of feeling, with a soul formed for friendship, and blessed with the endearments of a happy home, he entered more deeply than most men into the common grief and cheerfulness of life. With less evenly balanced faculties than his brother, and with a more limited range of vision, he had a heart which yearned as tenderly over sinners, and an eloquent tongue which spoke with warmth and freedom of the things concerning the King. As a linguist he greatly excelled. He was well acquainted with five languages, had a critical knowledge of the Scriptures, and was so enamoured of Virgil that he had the Æneid almost by heart. This latter accomplishment sometimes stood him in good stead. Dr. Johnson is said to have once silenced an abusive fishwife by calling her an isosceles and a parallelogram. Charles Wesley defended himself in Latin against a drunken sea-captain with whom he sailed from Charleston; and when John Wesley's unhappy wife had secured the brothers in a room and opened upon them, like a very Xantippe, the whole battery of her feminine wrath, Charles Wesley pelted her with Virgil until he obtained for them respite from clamour and permission to escape. His joy in the great work of Reformation was ardent and sincere, though checked often by alarm about irregularity, and by a misgiving of the consequences whereunto these things might grow. He neither soared above the times nor looked keenly beyond them, but, with a uniform inconsistency of which he was hardly conscious, his mind clung to opinions which his heart prompted him daily to violate. Hence, though in theory a rigid Churchman, so much so that he requested he might not be buried in any but consecrated ground, in practice he was the most daring innovator of his time. He preached in church hours without scruple; was the first, it is believed, to administer the

Lord's Supper in a Methodist place of worship ; defended lay preaching when bishops impugned it ; and, in fine, he manifested through a long course of years, that while his mind reposed in all the seemliness of ecclesiastical order, the glorious irregularities which he witnessed and shared commanded the deeper passion of his soul, and all the activities of his honoured life. He publicly censured some of his brother's proceedings, but he would allow no one else to blame him. He declined to write an epitaph for Hervey's tomb, because he conceived that the " letters" which were posthumously published did a great wrong to John Wesley's name, and when Lady Huntingdon attempted to alienate them, he endorsed her letter with the words, " unanswered by John Wesley's brother." Though the brothers were sometimes opposed in their views of polity, their love for each other was inviolate, and their influence to some extent mutually beneficial. If John went often too fast for Charles, Charles not unfrequently moved considerably too slow for John. Charles was prudential when John was sanguine, timid when John was daring, the drag upon the wheel not always put on when the coach was going down hill—the brake, perhaps of safety, upon the flying train. The difference between the brothers was once quaintly illustrated. " Brother John," said Charles, " if the Lord were to give me wings I'd fly." " Ah ! Brother Charles," was John's reply, " if the Lord told me to fly I'd do it, and leave Him to find the wings." In his later years he resided principally in London and Bristol, preaching as often as he was able, and pouring out his soul in song. He lingered until close upon eighty years of age, though oft "in feebleness extreme," and then, with a hymn to Christ upon his lips, he sweetly fell asleep. In the terse obituary which his brother inserted in the " Minutes," he says, "his least praise was his talent for poetry," but it will be by his incomparable hymns that he will be longest remembered. Few have left a wealthier legacy than these noble lyrics, which he has bequeathed to the church and to the world. Entering into the hearts' deep secrets; striking every chord of subtlest and holiest feeling; giving forth, not echoes from old harp songs, but melodies of the present, poured from a soul which enacts all the melodies that it sings; now plaintive as the breath of evening, now with a grand roll, like that of the thunder of God; expressing every variation in the changing music of life, and moreover piercing the invisible and standing like a seraph in the full vision of the throne—seldom has the sacred lyre been swept by a more skilful hand. It is renown enough to satisfy the most covetous seeker after fame that he has furnished to tens of thousands their happiest utterances of religious hope and joy. His words abide in the memory of multitudes, second only to the words of inspiration in their charm and power. They have chased away trouble from the sorrowful, as David from the melancholy Saul. They have inspired the Christian warrior as the " Marseillaise " the passions of France, or the " Ranz des Vaches," the patriotism of the brave Swiss peasantry, and, greatest triumph,—in cases without number they have been the Hallelujahs of the dying, who have lingered upon the notes of the song until they caught the notes of the trumpet which was " sounding for them upon the other side."

I cannot do more than mention other names which deserve to be remembered in connection with the great revival : Selina, COUNTESS OF HUNTINGDON, who, in spite of the contempt of courtiers, threw the influence of her rank into the movement, and, by her piety and benevolence, conciliated the esteem of the many who derided her enthusiasm. HOWELL HARRIS, the fervent and successful herald of the Gospel in Wales. JAMES HERVEY, the pious and the scholarly, whose fancy revelled in the beauty of the truth, and whose zeal wasted his frail body till you could almost see the spirit through the veil; whose gay style has allured towards godliness many who have been after. wards charmed by its native loveliness, just as the child, whose first love of flowers is awakened by the tulip-bed, becomes enamoured in manhood of the rarer beauty of the algæ and the ferns. JOHN BERRIDGE, the wise and witty Vicar of Everton, of whom it was said that he thought in proverbs, whose quaintness attracted the sinners who were slain from his quiver, and who feathered his arrows so pleasantly that men were scarcely conscious of their flight until the barb was in their heart, and they cried with the sore smart of pain. WILLIAM ROMAINE, who early in life committed the unpardonable offence of overcrowding St. George's, Hanover Square, and disturbing the calm devotions of its worshippers by the intrusion of a mob of vulgar people who had souls; and who for fifty years bore sturdy witness which threats could not silence—preaching, when they put out the lights of the church, by a solitary candle which he held in his hand. WILLIAM GRIMSHAW, the gallant West Riding evangelist,—hardy as the heather which grew upon the moors around him, humble and lowly as the mosses which peep from out their shadow—a brave trooper in his Master's service who used to chase men out of the taverns while they were singing the hymns before the sermon, and who made such head against the heathenism of his little parish that his name was a terror to evil-doers long years after his death. JOHN NEWTON, the tamed lion, transformed from a marvel of profanity to a miracle of grace, with the old sailor's fondness for yarns and the old sailor's shrewdness in telling them, the kindly adviser of half the godly people in the city— the sweet correspondent who wrote and warbled by turns his hymns, setting to music the "cardiphonia" which his letters traced. JOHN NELSON, whom the clergy of his neighbourhood contrived to get pressed for a soldier, and who sang hymns in the dungeon with a chorus of friends outside,—a mason who shaped many stones for the temple, "polished after the similitude of a palace." THOMAS OLIVERS, one of the "consecrated cobblers" against whom Sidney Smith would have sneered, but a poet of no mean order, and who in the tilt of controversy bore himself so bravely that his adversary lost his temper, and for once a baronet forgot to be a gentleman. THOMAS COKE, Wesley's tried friend and counsellor, who belted the globe in his missionary travel, and at last sank down in death with the great sea for a sepulchre, as if so mighty a heart could not rest in a narrower grave. CHARLES SIMEON, moulding the University to an evangelical type, and standing in his commanding pulpit, like a pharos on a hill, a light for the storm-tossed who were anxiously making for the land. And last, not least, JOHN FLETCHER, in many respects the goodliest in the band, so that "no tree in the garden of God was like unto him in his beauty." Of fine talents, accurate scholarship, and almost seraphic piety, his face shining as if, like Moses, he had lingered on the mount until he had stolen the glory; keen in irony and powerful in rebuke, but with a temper which no abuse could ruffle, and a zeal which no labour could satisfy; preaching with the death-dews on his forehead,—exclaiming, as he passed feebly from the pulpit to the altar, "I am going to throw myself under the shadow of the Mercy-seat"—then carried fainting to his bed, from which he rose only to ascend to his reward. Oh, they are a bright brotherhood—never country boasted truer hearts and purer lives. Though the godless deride them, and the annals of common fame pass them by, their record is on high, and in the majority of the world, that grand coming time when it shall "put away childish things," and enter upon its moral manhood, these will be the names which will be treasured as its choicest inspirations, and which will stir the pulses of its holiest pride.

With such helpers did John Wesley enter upon that course of marvellous labour which continued for half a century almost without pause, certainly without holiday. With no aim but to warn the careless and save the lost, never dreaming of personal enrichment, either of wealth or fame, with no ambition but a passion for saving souls, with no enthusiasm but a strong faith in God, and, perhaps, a too ready trust in man, these evangelists of the later time emulated the first heralds of the Gospel in toil, in peril, in success. The record of Wesley's labours is something wonderful, whether you consider their kind, their number, or the circumstances under which they were done. Rapid, punctual, earnest, he is the "man of one business" throughout. One day of his work would furnish some of us with ample employment for three. One of his weeks would tell heavily upon the relaxed nerves and feeble throats of his degenerate sons. At the rate of 15 sermons a week and 5,000 miles a year, done on horseback, when railways were not, and when roads, uneducated by Macadam, were often feeble compromises between swamp and sludge, he manfully journeyed,— at all hours, in all weathers, riding himself into a fever, and then preaching himself out of it,—now entertained hospitably, now treated like an angel, and, by consequence, offered no food,—now hooted in the streets, now honoured by the authorities, but never faltering in his purpose, whether the learned would bribe him to silence, or the persecutor snarled at his heels. Outwardly calm, while his heart burned within him ; with an even temper held in almost perfect control, with a fine flow of animal spirits which, he says, he never remembers to have been for a quarter of an hour below zero; never unemployed, but never in a hurry; moving everyone around him to activity, but keeping, calm and lordly, the possession of his own soul, and, above all, smitten with a high sense of duty whose spell bore him onward through every discouragement, he had all human conditions of success ; and when the Divine influence breathed upon his ministry, it is not wonderful that the startled people heard and wept and lived. His preaching was not the announcement of novelties ; the doctrines he taught lay in the formularies of the Church, and had been enforced by other lips before him ; he was no iconoclast of ancient institutions, nor did he gain a hearing by exposure of the errors of others. Man a sinner, all men sin-ners, exposed to wrath, but embraced in a covenant of mercy ; another world close at hand, with its unalterable and solemn issues—so near that men could almost see the gleams of glory or the forks of flame; the truth pressed home upon the conscience, · "You are lost ;" and when that was apprehended, that other golden sentence, "God is love," presented for the soul's com_ fort, like a sheltering splendour to relieve and scatter the cloud, These were the burden of the message which he spake, and he spake it with a prophet's singleness, authority and power.

It is not needed that we should dwell either in analysis or in apology upon the physical phenomena which at times waited upon the word. These phenomena, which have staggered the philosophers and furnished scoffers with choice material for derision, were no essential parts of the revival,—were produced under calm and logical preaching, and, when the subjects of discourse were rather comforting than terrible, seized upon both sexes and often upon those who had been bitterest in their complaint against the scandal, and astonished the preachers full as much as their critics, leaving them in doubt whether they were the works of confusion, or whether they were done by the finger of God. The proof of success, however, was not in bodily convulsions, but in reclaimed lives. Out of the inevitable disorder Christianity could recognize its own, and the result was a revived life in the churches, a large recovery from among the vilest to Christ, and a moral reformation more complete and lasting than had ever before been dreamed of.

The spots in which Wesley preached were, in many cases, highly romantic, and added as secondary causes to the effect of his ministry. In quiet rural glens which nestle here and there in the neighbourhood of large towns; on green hillsides, with fair branches of the woodland above, and a lively stream laughing on its course below; in the Gwennap Amphitheatre; on the fragment of rock at St. Ives, with the great sea in sight, and the clear swell of the preacher's voice finding a grand accompaniment in the low murmur of the waves; on his father's tombstone, overhung by the funeral cypress, and with " the grassy barrows " of the dead around him ; under the spreading sycamore, screened from the heat of the summer, or sheltered by the roofless walls of a ruined cathedral while frost was in the air and the hills still white with snow; in places like these, as well as in every available building, from the university church and the large Foundry chapel to the court-house in Alnwick and the St. Ives round-house, built of brazen slags, which he supposes "will last as long as the world," he rejoiced to preach the Gospel. By the blessing of God upon His word, the drunkards became sober, the dishonest upright, the licentious chaste; "sharp arrows of the mighty" fastened in the hearts of turbulent and scornful sinners; and, when the results were not so marked and decisive, there was a leavening power, as if there broke upon society the air-waves of a fresher atmosphere: and the health, and the beauty, and the manliness remain as our heritage to-day.

It could hardly be expected that a work like this could be suffered without hindrance and insult. The prince of this world had reigned too long in quiet to be dispossessed without a struggle. Hence the work of the Wesleys and their compatriots was subjected to the oddest misunderstandings, assailed with foulest slanders, and hunted by a persecution as malignant in its spirit as those of the early church, though the power of the oppressor was not always equal to his rage. Many among that species of the clergy, now happily almost extinct, to whom a full church was an impertinence, and a consistent life a perpetual rebuke, were the bitterest enemies of the revival. They instigated, in some cases even headed the mob. They coaxed or threatened the magistrates. They abused the teachers, repelled them and their converts from communion, and punished them as vagrants for whom the most effectual remedy was the duck-pond or the pillory. The cold dislike of the gentry chimed with the coarse passions of the baser sort, until Methodism became a thing for or against which nearly every man took up his parable, and the nation was divided into those whose delight it was to listen to the earnest preachers and those whose delight it was to hunt them down. The most absurd ideas had currency about the men and about their communications. In Oxford they were the " Bible moths " and the " Godly club." Some said they were Atheists and allies of the Pretender. In Cornwall they were called, with some propriety, considering their sufferings and their valour, the Maccabees. In Ireland, from the text of one of their preachers, who preached about the child in swaddling-bands on a Christmas-day morning, they were christened Swaddlers. One sapient critic thought he had hit upon the thing exactly when he said they were " Presbyterian Papists." " The Methodists !" asked an acute Irish Colonel of Dragoons, " isn't that the new sect which has risen up whose religion it is to wear long beards and whiskers ? " (Some of you may, perhaps, imagine that the honest colonel was for once, like Saul, " among the prophets," and that his chief mistake was in speaking of the new sect about a century before its time.) Wesley was said to be a Jesuit, a correspondent of the Pope, in league with France, in the pay of Spain, and so thorough and deep-rooted was the enmity against them that, in his own forcible words, they were " forbidden from Newgate lest they should make men wicked, and from Bedlam lest they should drive men mad." Nor were ruder assaults wanting. They were arrested, imprisoned, drafted into the ranks of the army. Churchwardens and constables panted for the chase after the Methodists like a leash of eager hounds. The mob were too glad to gratify their love of disorder and their hate against religion together, and outrages were perpetrated, now by the impulse of passion—now by bands organized for purposes of cruelty, by which many were seriously injured, and others driven into a martyr's grave.

John Wesley was often in personal danger ; often had he to confront enraged mobs and suffer personal violence at their hands. But his faith in God sustained him, and, with a courage which might shame many of the world's chartered heroes, he blenched not from his duty and from his work. Meeting with hard fare and little food during a tour in Cornwall, he congratulates himself that "blackberries are plentiful," and after three weeks lying upon the floor, in the same county, with the brave John Nelson beside him, one having an overcoat and the other "Burkitt's Notes" for a pillow, he cries out in the middle of the night, " Be of good cheer, the skin is only off one side yet." Alone with the rabble at Walsall, with torn clothes and bleeding mouth, he subdued a noted prize-fighter by his calmness and by his words, with his strange escort passed harmless through the crowd, and records in his journal that at the door of his lodgings they " parted with much love." Threatened with being thrown into the river, he says that he was as collected as if seated in his study, and that his only thought was that the papers in his pocket would he spoiled. Told that the mob were coming to pull down the house at Epworth in which he was preaching, he assured the congregation that if the report was true they had better make good use of it while it was still standing. Like Paul, he knew when to stand upon his privilege—" a Roman and uncondemned." A pompous chief magistrate, big with the small dignities of his office, sent to discharge him from preaching within the limits of his borough. " Tell his worship," was Wesley's cool rejoinder, " that as long as King George gives me leave to preach I shall not ask the

Mayor of Shaftesbury." When his moral character was slandered by fierce opponents, from whom better things might have been hoped, and to whom I grant in this lecture the mercy of my silence, his faith rose into sublimity. "Brother, when I gave to God my life, my time, my all, I did not leave my reputation out." When asked how he would spend the intervening time if he knew that he should die on the morrow, he answered with the same cheerful calmness, "Just as I intend to spend them now. I should preach at Gloucester to-night, and at five o'clock in the morning, ride on to Tewksbury, preach in the afternoon, and meet the societies in the evening. I should then repair to Friend Martin's house, who expects to entertain me, converse and pray with the family as usual, retire to my room, commend myself to my Heavenly Father, lie down to rest, and wake up in glory." Surely neither legends of chivalry nor annals of authentic heroism can surpass the grandeur of this simple trust in God. You talk of heroes, large, world renowned, kingly men, men of colossal fame, who have filled the great spaces of the world with their names ; men who have leaped into renown from the corpses of the trampled, or cleaved their stern way to it through the battle's dust and blood. What are their claims to his ? Look at his brave life from the time of its devotion to the Gospel. See him as he loosens his grasp upon the things he loved the most, mortifies his desire after honour, spurns the lust of wealth as only nobler natures can, foregoes the endearments of social and the delights of cultivated life. Mark him as, little in stature but great in soul, he stands calmly amid the mob who burn to kill him, and they are subdued at his glance, as the manly eye can awe the lion into fear. See him as, in conscious integrity, still as the patient stars, he

L

bids slander do her worst to defame him, smiles at nearing
danger, holds all hardship light, and regards death but as a
vassal—a vassal without a terror and without a sting ;—and
then tell me whether in that life-long devotion, fearless out-
speaking of the truth, and fervent trust in God, there is not
greatness as lofty as was ever recompensed by glittering orders
or embalmed in minstrel's song.

My time fails me to proceed further with the history on which
I have already lingered too long. On the separation from
Whitefield ; on the dignity with which he offered the costliest
sacrifice to God—the sacrifice of slain affections ; on his ill-
judged and unfortunate marriage, three days after which he
makes the significant entry in his journal, " Met the single men
of the society and exhorted them to continue single ;" on his
accurate and varied scholarship,—an accomplished logician, and
one of the first Greek scholars of his time,—on his subsequent
labours prosecuted without intermission through a long course
of years ; on the organization of his societies, and his care for
their purity and extension ;—on all these matters I must forbear
to dwell. Neither can I do more than mention the gradual
growth of honour which sat upon his forehead like a crown—
how prejudice changed into respect, and " troops of friends "
gave reverence in his kindly age ; how John Howard blessed
his loving words, and under their inspiration went forth to his
prison journeys with greater heart than ever ; how Bishop Lowth
sat at his feet and hoped he might be found there in another
world ; how Samuel Johnson delighted in his conversation, and
was only vexed because he would take his leave just when the
great Moralist had stretched his legs for the luxury of an
intellectual evening ; how Alexander Knox kindled in rapture

as he recalled the fine old man, "with a child's heart and a seraph's faith," realizing his notion of angelic goodness, and impressing him with the pang at parting that he "ne'er should look upon his like again;" and finally how, in perfect peace, and leaving a reformed nation and a flourishing church as his monument, the good John Wesley died: these are tempting subjects for enlargement, but the inexorable hand moves on.

A brief estimate of some of the more noticeable features of John Wesley's character must not, however, be omitted. During his life he endured more abuse than any man of his time, and since his death so many Daniels have "come to judgment" upon him, that he has been credited with almost every fault and virtue that can be named. Many failings have been gratuitously ascribed to him, and some from which I am by no means concerned to defend him. It is said he was *ambitious*. He was, but not with the vulgar lust of power or fame, or gold. His ambition was a large and lofty thing, a yearning magnanimity, like that of Moses—a ceaseless self-sacrifice, like that of Paul. It is said that he was *enthusiastic*. He was, but his enthusiasm was neither a wild rant nor a delusive expectation of the end without the means; it sprang from a passion to do good, and was sustained by faith in God,—the results justified him. It is said that he was *arbitrary*. In the true sense of the word, he was— for never man was born who exerted more influence upon other men; but he valued and used his power, not for its own sake, but as a trust. His was the legitimate influence of mind and character; and was neither got by despot force nor wielded for despot ends. From the charge of credulity he cannot be deemed wholly free, but those who consider that the age in which he lived was an age of scepticism, and that it was necessary for the doing of his great work that he should realize the nearness of the other world, will hardly wonder that he shared, though in no excess by comparison with others of his time, the prevalent infirmity of noble minds. That in fifty years he sometimes erred in judgment; that he chose not a helpmeet worthy of him; that his ideas of the education of children were severe and impracticable, as proved by the successive failures of his plans at Kingswood school; that his continual submission to what he believed to be the will of God involved him in inconsistencies which he was not careful to reconcile, and which gloriously vindicate the disinterestedness of his life; these things may be admitted, with no other result, on the part of those who love him, than that they can look without being dazzled upon a brightness which would otherwise be insufferable. But after you have made all the subtractions which candour and even honest prejudice demand, the manhood of his excellence remains, and it is a manhood of loftiest type and truest soul—human, and therefore leavened with human frailty, but living as near to Heaven as merely human may :

> " Who never sold the truth to serve the hour,
> Nor paltered with Eternal God for power ;
> Who let the turbid streams of rumour flow,
> Through either babbling world of high and low ;
> Whose life was work—whose language rife
> With rugged maxims hewn from life ;
> Whose eighty winters freeze with one rebuke,
> All great self-seekers trampling on the right :
> Greatest, yet with least pretence,
> Foremost-hearted of his time.
> Rich in saving common sense,
> And, as the greatest only are,
> In his simplicity sublime."

This *simplicity* was indeed the great feature of his character, to which everything else must be referred as to a central motive power. From the time of his entrance upon his public work he was a man of one purpose. That purpose absorbed him, and against that purpose he would not harbour a thought that was disloyal. If ever man was perfectly devoted to the service of God it was he. He was a "living sacrifice." The usual and strong instincts which prevail among men, love of ease, fame, wealth, were almost trampled out of his soul. Even the fondest affections were crucified, though he had as warm a heart as ever beat in the breast of man ; and, at the bidding of the high purpose which possessed him he could surrender the dearest friend, and expend the costliest tribute, endure the keenest pang, and be unmoved under the foulest slander, with a courage which to us, who dwell in lower regions, seems well nigh stoical, and which we must breathe the upper air to understand. The secret of this self-control, as of the marvellous power of his ministry, was in the morning hour, which for many years he was accustomed to spend in the closet. If in Luther's prayers was the mystery of the Reformation, in Wesley's prayers may be found one explanation of the great revival. He could afford to be calm in human tumult, who had memories of the lone mountain-top and of the manifested glory. To him it was a necessity to be in earnest, who had just come from the ford of Jabbok, where the strange wrestler had striven with him until the breaking of the day. He could surely calculate upon a blessing to whom the Lord had pledged it in the secret place of his pavilion. And it is so still—prayer can preserve any peace unbroken and any arm in strength. If the pulpit be powerless, the churches feeble, the truth wounded in the house of her friends, the source of the languor is here. Let the closet fires be bright and the flame is sure to spread, and, like that which brave Hugh Latimer saw in the vision of his martyrdom, it shall never be put out. Give us the men of prayer, and from every hill of Zion there shall be baptisms of power from on high.

Wesley's *indefatigable industry* has already been noticed, and when we consider the object for which he redeemed the time, his frugal and conscientious use of it cannot be sufficiently admired. Incessantly travelling, constantly preaching, he conducted an extensive correspondence, dealt with cases of conscience, settled family disputes, wrote or abridged 200 volumes, kept himself abreast of the literature of the times, maintained his classical studies, and managed the whole concerns of a society which numbered at his death more than 70,000 souls. With all this, as he once said, " he had no time to be in a hurry," was always ready for a visit of sympathy, for a sight of a fair landscape or a fine building, for a cheerful evening or part of one with a friend ; and now and then for recreation, as when he listened to the oratorios of " Judith " and " Ruth," and " The Messiah." Do you ask how he managed to have this wealth of leisure at command ? I answer, by his practice of early rising, by his methodical habits, and by the patient avarice with which he hoarded each moment as it flew. Thus he tells us that he read " History, Philosophy, and Poetry, for the most part, on horseback." We do not wonder, by the way, that his poor steed so often stumbled. Detained in Wales because the tide was over the sands, so that he could not cross them, he tells us : " I sat down in a little cottage and translated Aldrich's Logic." His mind could not fail to be stored so richly when he thus diligently fed it. If a man will pile up the moments of life he will be sure to have a pyramid at last. It is hard work washing in the cradle the sand of the gully-stream, but it hath dust of gold.

Wesley's *benevolence* was, perhaps, never surpassed. Beyond what was absolutely necessary to sustain and clothe him, he gave all he had in charity. There were no bounds to his generosity save his means. "Two silver spoons in London and two silver spoons in Bristol," thus he made his return of plate to the astonished Commissioners of Excise, "and I shall not buy any more while so many around me want bread." He was accustomed to declare that his own hands should be his executors, and said, in print, that if he died worth ten pounds, independent of his books, he would give the world leave to call him a thief and a robber. Although this was an incautious announcement, made in the excess of his zeal, yet, as his friends expected, he almost literally kept his word, for when the silver cord of his great life was loosed, his chaise and horses and his clothes were about all that he left behind him, except, as has been quaintly said, "a good library of books, a well-worn clergyman's gown, a much abused reputation, and—the Methodist Church."

His *charity*, in the wider sense, was as remarkable as his beneficence. With a temper naturally quick, as is perhaps inevitable in all lively natures, he was enabled so far to conquer himself that he bore personal injury not only without anger, but without apparent emotion, and it was as easy for him as to breathe. Gathering the materials of his judgment from his own transparent goodness, he suspected no evil in others, and it was difficult to make him think that any had intended to deceive him. Although this trustful spirit exposed him to the schemes of the designing, it sets forth in beautiful relief the guilelessness of his own blameless life. His moderation in controversy was remarkable, and was maintained under provocation which might well have kindled any storm which "ran in the shifting currents of the blood." On the testimony of one of his unfriendly critics, "he kept his temper and his ground," and it is refreshing to find him receiving the sacrament from the hands of Bishop Lavington, and sitting down to a cosy breakfast with his old antagonist, Father O'Leary. His catholicity, indeed, was extraordinary. He had as a keen a scent for goodness as slanderers have for evil. Even among the nightshade and the nettles it was hard if he could not discover some fragrant violet or balm of healing. Hence he speaks of the "strong faith" mingled with the "gross superstition" of the Church of Rome; commends and publishes the life of Thomas Firmin, a Unitarian, "whose real piety—notwithstanding his erroneous notions on the Trinity—he says he dares not deny," and "makes no doubt that Marcus Antoninus, the heathen Emperor of Rome, shall be of the many who shall come from the east and from the west and shall sit down in the kingdom of God."

While Wesley thus preached and lived a high state of religious purity, his *freedom from asceticism* was a marked and fine characteristic. There was about him, especially as he grew in years, a courtesy and grace which made him the charm of social circles, and which especially attracted the young. He often selected them as the companions of his walks, and was wont to give them his blessing and some small trifle of money. Alexander Knox speaks of his "sportive sallies of innocent mirth, which delighted the young and thoughtless," and when his wit had play, his conversation would sparkle as when the moon glances upon the silver sea. He often used his native humour to record his observations on men and things, to silence a trouble-some opponent, or teach a lesson to some refractory helper. Thus he records: "Spent an agreeable hour with Dr. S., the greatest genius in little things that ever fell under my notice. I really believe, were he seriously to set about it, he could invent the best *mouse-trap* that ever was in the world." Again, with a sly hit at the glorious uncertainties of the law, he says: "To oblige a friendly gentlewoman I was a witness to her will, wherein she bequeathed part of her estate to charitable uses, and part, during his natural life, to her dog Toby. I suppose, though she should die within the year, her legacy to Toby may stand good, but that to the poor is void by the statute of mortmain." He was troubled by a visit from some pretended prophets, who told him he was to be *born'd* again, and that they were to wait till it was done. He politely shewed them into what he calls a "tolerably cold room," and kept them twelve hours without food or fire, after which, he says, "they quietly went away." One came to him professedly with a warning from the Lord, that he was living in luxury, and heaping up treasure upon earth. He told her the Lord knew better, and that if He had sent her He would have given her a more proper message. A very weak little man, one of Wesley's helpers, Michael Fenwick by name, came to him with an imploring countenance and begged a favour, which was that as Wesley was revising his journals for the press, and as these journals would live, Michael might have a place in them, and so stand some chance of immortality. Wesley promised compliance, and the entry appeared: "About one preached at Clayworth; I think none was unmoved but Michael Fenwick, who fell fast asleep under an adjoining hay-rick." These are but random instances of a wit which ever played across the clear sky of Wesley's life, like summer lightning, having no fork to wound, and only seen in the still evening, when the labours of the day were done.

It marks a great man that he is before his age, and that he initiates plans upon which after ages can improve. It would be difficult to name a man more endowed with this prophetic and forecasting goodness than John Wesley. There is scarcely an enterprise of the church or an active form of charity, scarcely an acknowledged good at work amongst us, which he did not attempt, and often with a success which later times can only strive to parallel. You talk of a cheap press and its blessings. John Wesley was the first man to write for the million, and that not for gain but for the people's benefit. His were the first popular Grammars, Dictionaries, Histories, Compendiums, and they were issued not in learned leisure, but in the intervals of the busiest life of the age. You rejoice in the Tract Society's labours. Though the "Jubilee Memorial" makes no mention of his name, he was a diligent writer and systematic distributor half a century before the Tract Society was born. Do you hail the Strangers' Friend Society, with its open hand for the friendless and the alien? It was of Wesleyan origin. Do you believe in Ragged Schools? Wesley's Orphan Houses were the germinant idea. Do you subscribe to Loan Libraries? He established them a hundred years ago. Are you proud of your country as you see the sick huddling together before the Dispensary gates, and think that charity has furnished them with the skill and the medicines which they are too poor to buy? The first Dispensary that I read of was set up by John Wesley at the Foundry. And not only in matters of active charity did he thus anticipate

the future, but in the silent revolutions of opinion. Take his
" Primitive Physic," with which wits make merry, and which is
certainly funny enough to win even Niobe from her tears ; but it
compares very favourably with a treatise published but a little
earlier by the celebrated Robert Boyle ; and the Pharmacopœia of
the day, which was in constant use among the faculty, contains
offensive and frivolous prescriptions which Wesley disdains to
mention.   He was a Temperance advocate when Total Abstinence Societies were not.   He was a Law Reformer, speaking of
that " foul monster—a Chancery Bill," and declares that he
will " no more encourage that villainous tautology of lawyers,
which is a scandal to the nation at large."   He believed in
the marvels of electricity while the sceptic world yet sneered at
Franklin's name.   With a far-sighted view of the magnificent
capabilities of India, he spoke of it as " enslaved to a
company of merchants " while Leadenhall Street was still in its
glory.   And, finally, when the nation was only half alive to the
evils of slavery—when Lady Huntingdon trafficked in human
nature, when George Whitefield held slaves—John Wesley
roused himself in behalf of the poor trampled bondsmen ;
denounced slavery in general as " the sum of all villanies,"
and American slavery in particular as " the vilest that ever saw
the sun."

Looking at these things, who shall say how much of our
present philanthropy and privileges are the results of the
merciful shadow which John Wesley projected upon the coming
age ? If you decorate the conqueror with stars, who at the
head of his gallant armies achieves a victory, look upon the
man whose genius drew the plan of the battle, and let his breast
glitter too. If you reward the reaper who gathers amid the

inspiration of plenty and the voice of singing, put by—of your justice I claim it—for the sower, who alone, under the grey wintry sky, went forth for the scattering of the seed.

And now, to sum up the whole, look upon this character, at first "like the young moon with a ragged edge, still in its imperfection beautiful," but waxing lovelier and larger, until, full-orbed and calm, it shines in its completeness before men. Think of the elements which you suppose necessary to moral greatness. Fervent piety, strong faith in God, a self-sacrificing purpose in life, manly daring, womanly tenderness, an industry which never tires, a benevolence which never says " it is enough," an almost perfect control over passion, an almost perfect abnegation of selfishness, a catholic heart and a world-wide sympathy, a gentleman's courtesy and a scholar's learning ;—if these things, combining in an individual, make up an artistic wholeness of character which the world should reverence, then look at that little old man with the band and cassock, walking at a brisk pace down the street, neat in his dress and busy in his manner, "with aquiline nose and quick bright eye, silver hair, and clear smooth forehead, and colour fresh as a boy's." Go, mark him well, for that wholeness of character is his, and his name is John Wesley, and, in the apt words of one who has deeply studied him, " a greater, and by the grace of God, a better man, the world has not known since the days of St. Paul."

And now for one parting word.   It is for us these great men labour.   All the past is ours.   Its splendour flashes that we may not walk in darkness.   Its manhood appeals to our own. The records of its greatness and goodness abide that we may be inspired by the example, and "quit ourselves like men " in the common struggles of every day.   Brothers, to your duty !   Let your lives show that the heritage has descended into no unworthy hand. Be not the poor pensioners upon the bounty of the past. Be not the gay spendthrifts of its riches. Be it yours to husband its resources that you may increase its returns, so that the legacy you bequeath, enriched by your own personal tribute, may be wealthier than the portion which you received. "Give me place for my lever," said a great one of old, "and I will move the world." We do not lack in our moral machinery either the fulcrum or the power. Of small account and limited sphere of action, considered as individuals, most of us may be, but from each of us there is shed an influence which, by the law of accelerated force, will gather intensity as it spreads, and will tell upon the future as with avalanche power. There is something grandly terrible in this aspect of it in an assembly like this. Flung upon life, unable to rid yourselves of life; compelled, whether you will or no, to wield the responsibilities of life, like charged clouds which must discharge their contents either in the havoc of storms or in the kind weeping of the summer rain, you must go on, influential every moment, a blast or a blessing for ever. Oh ! choose the good—choose it from this moment if you have never chosen it before—renew, if you have already chosen it, your high and grand consecration. I would fain bind it upon you by a spell from which you cannot disenchant yourselves, and under whose power you shall pass to your eternity. It is done—surely it is done. You *will* be the Lord's servants ; and, for His sake, the servants of men.

This is an age of transition, and, in many respects, of surprise Amidst its endless activities for good and evil, it is difficult to trace the progress which, in spite of all discouragements, is constantly going on. But that progress is not the less **real** because we cannot see it, for that our poor human eyes are dimmed by the films of sense or blinded by the tears of sorrow. There is a lesson for us in the recently published experiences of those intrepid voyagers who, for scientific purposes, have ventured into the regions of upper air. They tell us that " they experienced as they ascended a feeling of profound repose ; " by and by they record " that it was very dark beneath, but light above, with a clear sky," and " amid the solemn stillness the only sounds they heard were the striking of a clock and the sounding of a bell." Oh ! rare and beautiful teaching for us— tossed about with many fears, depressed by the clouds which hang over us, and longing for the coming of the day ! The rest and hope of the spirit must come with the faith which leaves this earth behind it. Though to us—the toilers—it is night still, to Him—the Master who watcheth our labour, and to then. —our fellows whose labour is done—" there is light with a clear sky." Though to us, down below, there is but the deafening roar, the shriek of discord, the wail of pain, blent in one jargon of strange sounds which have no chime ; to them, above in the high calm silence, there are heard only the striking of the hour which tells of the sure speed of time, and the voice of the joy-bells already ringing for the world's great bridal. And it is always so in respect of the matters which bewilder us and make our hearts sad. Down below, strange struggles between hope and fear, problems of existence which baffle our poor wit to solve, mourning over new-made graves of wise or kind ones snatched from the midst of us ere yet, to mortal thought, their life's great work is done. Up above, a throne that is never vacant, a King who sits assured of an accomplished purpose, and waiting an expected end,—grand solutions of life which make all

Heaven wonder, and stir the spirits of the just made perfect
with new throbs of joy—rest from earth's weariness, and rapture
in the stead of its sorrow—the joining of hands and hearts long
unclasped from each other's welcomes, in the eternal re-union
of the sky.

> Down beiow, a sad, mysterious music,
>   Wailing from the woods and on the shore ;
> Burdened with a grand, majestic secret,
>   Which keeps sweeping from us ever more
>
> Up above, a music that entwineth,
>   In eternal threads of golden sound,
> The great poem of this strange existence,
>   All whose wondrous meaning hath been fouud.
>
> Down below, the grave within the churchyard,
>   And the anguish on the young lace pale,
> And the watcher, ever as it dusketh,
>   Rocking to and fro with long, sad wail.
>
> Up above, a crowned and happy spirit,
>   Like an infant in the eternal years,
> Who shall grow in light and love for ever,
>   Ordered in his place among his peers.
>
> O, the sobbing of the winds of autumn !
>   O, the sunset streak of stormy gold !
> O, the poor heart, thinking in the churchyard !
>   Night is coming and the grave is cold.
>
> O, the rest forever, and the rapture !
>   O, the hand that wipes the tears away !
> O, the golden homes beyond the sunset !
>   O, the God—that watches o'er the clay !

FLORENCE

AND SOME NOTABLE FLORENTINES.

M

FLORENCE

AND SOME NOTABLE FLORENTINES.

A GREAT CITY is a great poem, a poem whose story unfolds through the ages, and whose characters are striving and suffering human hearts. Unheard often amid the rattle of its busy streets there are plaintive undertones of rarest music. Beneath its outer life there is an inner one, in which Tragedy and Passion, Pity and Enterprise, Wrong and Sorrow, are the daily actors. If, moreover, the city has a history, if it has passed through those sharp transitions which wring the hearts of nations as they wring the hearts of men ; if it kindle with the memories of a glorious past, or, amid present sorrow, glows with the prophecy of a more glorious future, the melody becomes more audible and strong—the voice has louder tones to soothe or to inspire ; and a ramble through the streets of such a city, or a visit to its shrines, becomes at once a profit and a pleasure.

With this intent let me lead you for a while to what, until lately, was the capital of the new Kingdom of Italy—beautiful for situation, affluent in annals of the former time ; far renowned in song ; and let us

> " Muse in hope upon the shore
>   Of golden Arno, as it shoots away
>   Through Florence' heart beneath her bridges four."

There are some pictures, world-wide in their reputation, the first sight of which disappoints the eye, and it is only by the study of their various parts that you grow into a perception of their wondrous beauty. Of such is Florence. Its river is the "golden Arno" only by a strong poetical license, and its narrow streets, unfinished churches, and massive, prison-like houses, look sombre to a stranger after the artistic symmetry of Milan, and the superb palaces of Genoa. Each day's sojourn, however, lessens the impression of disappointment, until it is not difficult to emulate the Tuscan enthusiasm for " Firenze la bella." The loveliness of Florence does not consist so much in separate gems as in the exquisite harmony of the whole. If you wish to see it to perfection, fix upon such a day as Florence owes the sun, and climbing the hill of Bellosguardo, or past the stages of the Via Crucis to the Church of San Miniato, look forth upon the scene before you. You trace the course of the Arno from the distant mountains on the right, through the heart of the city, winding along the fruitful valley toward Pisa. The city is beneath you, "like a pearl set in emerald." From the midst of it rises Brunelleschi's dome, high above all the minor spires which flash back the noontide rays. Hard by is the beautiful campanile lifted by Giotto, "like an unperplexed fine question heavenward." The hill behind the city is Fiesolé, of which Milton sings :

> " The moon, whose orb
> Through optic glass the Tuscan artist views
> At evening from the top of Fiesolé."

This is where Milton and Galileo met—neither of them then blind, but both heirs of such darkness as only purges the vision of the inner eye ; patricians of the nobility of Genius, whose meeting was grander than of monarchs on some field of the

Cloth of Gold. On the extreme right, dimly discernible, is the sanctuary of Vallombrosa, hidden in its wealth of beach and pine some twenty miles away. Far to the left is Pistoja, with the pillar of Catiline, and the majestic Appenines close up the view. All colours are in the landscape, and all sounds are in the air. The hills look almost heathery. The sombre olive and funereal cypress blend with the graceful acacia and the clasping vine. The hum of insect and the carol of bird chime with the blithe voices of men, while dome, tower, mountains, the yellow river, the quaint bridges, spires, palaces, gardens, and the cloudless heavens overhanging, make up a panorama on which to gaze in trance of rapture, until the spirit wearies from the exceeding beauty of the vision.

Florence is said to have sprung out of the ruins of the ancient Fiesolé. It is supposed to have been originally the place where the markets of Fiesolé were held, the commercial spirit of the age being not slow to perceive that there were fewer facilities for barter on the mountain summit than on the fertile plain. In pursuance of the wise policy of the time, a policy upon which after ages have been unable to improve, it was speedily colo-nized from Rome. The dwellings of the traders gathered other dwellings round them. It was politic to dwell in company, both for accommodation and for defence. By cultivation, also, the earth is cleared from many noxious vapours, the air is purified by the kindling of household fires, and so places formerly unhealthy become fitted for the habitation of men. In the sixth century the new city was destroyed by Totila, King of the Ostrogoths. It remained in ruins for two hundred and fifty years, when it was rebuilt by Charlemagne. From this time it grew in numbers and influence ; not rapidly, because of the oppression of its many rulers.   Its history for a long series of years is but a record of the alternate triumphs and misfortunes of Guelph and Ghibelline, Bianchi and Neri, Cerchi and Donati, —foolish partisans, who fretted for supremacy during their little hour, and heeded not that the city languished beneath the sickness of their perpetual distemper while the great world was moving on.   As we read these stormy Florentine annals, and remember that those of other nations can furnish parallels, it is humiliating to think how long great nations linger in the swaddling-bands and primers of their childhood.   The logic of the fist is a very juvenile branch of study, and is resorted to only until boys and nations become wise enough for the logic of the brain.

The history of Florence does not need to be followed until, about the middle of the fourteenth century, Cosmo de Medici appeared upon the stage.   He was born on the day of St. Cosmo, in the year 1389.   His early years were full of trouble, and the discipline prepared him for the government. He learned in captivity and exile the prudence which gained him a fortune, and which enabled him to wield an influence over a distracted state, admired both by friends and enemies for his consummate skill.   He was as generous as he was wealthy, and as moderate as he was powerful.   At the head of the state he remembered that he was one of the people ; a mighty ruler, he had sagacity to see that the strength of his power lay in the discretion with which he used it ; and amid a people so given to change as to be proverbs of inconstancy, he held his position until a generation had faded by his side.   He encouraged the learned to make Florence their home, for he had that prescient wisdom which foretold by how much the glory of letters transcends and will survive the glory of war. Some of his sayings are notable, as indicating a sprightly mind, with some portion of the gift of prophecy. The rebels who had been banished gave him to understand that they "were not dreaming." He said he believed it, for he had "robbed them of their sleep." Rinaldo, his great rival, to warn him that he must not consider himself secure, sent him the enigmatical message that "the hen has laid." His only reply was that "she did ill to lay so far from her nest." After his own return from banishment he was told by some citizens that he was injuring the city by driving out of it nobles and monks. His answer was : "It is better to injure a city than to ruin it ; two yards of rose-coloured cloth will make a gentleman, and it requires something more to direct a government than to play with a string of beads." In his later years he suffered much from bodily infirmity, and from apprehension lest the glory would depart from the Florence which he loved so well. As his illness increased he shut his eyes, as he quaintly said "to get them in the way of it ;" and so died in the zenith of his power, leaving a name honoured by princes and people, and justifying the proud title of the "Father of his Country," which the city inscribed upon his grave. He was no vulgar or sordid miser or authority, but stands out amid Florentine history a "bright particular star," to trace whose orbit it is worth while to sweep the heavens. He showed how, amidst perpetual tumult, there can be empire in one commanding mind, and was the founder of that wondrous family of the Medici, who were the good or evil angels of their city through so many stormful years.

The state of Florence, during the long years in which the Medici governed her, was in the main peaceful and prosperous. There were many conspiracies, of course, and the rulers were not equally competent, but Florence became a power in Italy under their ambitious rule. Their memorials are seen everywhere; in the palaces where they dwelt; in the magnificent galleries which they founded and enriched; in the Mausoleum which contains their dust, and sets forth their virtues as with a marble tongue. Arrogant, indeed, is the conception of this splendid sepulchre. The walls are covered with the richest Florentine mosaic, the roof of the dome is embellished with frescoes, and the shrines profusely ornamented with precious stones. Here are the urns and cenotaphs of six successive Grand Dukes, whose ashes are in the crypt below. Nowhere in the world can be seen such pomp of marble piled upon the grave. These Grand Dukes were inferior, both in address and excellence, to the citizen princes of the earlier time, of whom alone we think when we speak of the greatness of the Medici. Cosmo il Vecchio, of whom I have already spoken, and his grandson, Lorenzo the Magnificent, assume proportions of grandeur which dwarf their lesser kindred.

Of the character of Lorenzo de Medici it is not easy to speak, so conflicting is the evidence upon which any opinion must rest. His detractors are loud in their censure, his admirers indiscriminate in their praise. An air of romance attaches to him and his doings, through whose brilliant cloud one can hardly see him as he is. Judged by the light of his age, he must have been one of the Anakim, alike in the faults which were charged upon him and in the qualities which add lustre to his name. Born to a noble destiny, he leaped forth to meet it, as a war-horse scenteth the battle. Called to power while yet unripe to wield it, he gathered wisdom from the ready brain, and hope out of the boy's heart, and by his prudent enthusiasm became the man for the hour. Cautious as the most practised diplomatist, he had the reckless valour of the most daring soldier. Crafty in his policy, he was yet steady in his friendships, and generous, even to prodigality, with his wealth. Flung upon a rude, iron age, and forced to be a man of war, he was a munificent patron of letters, revelled in each golden legend or occult discovery, and peopled his city with the learned until it became the Etruscan Athens, no unworthy rival of the " city of the violet crown." Intent upon the aggrandizement of his family, and dreaded for his overshadowing authority, he made Florence a city of palaces, her neighbourhood a garden of delight, so that he seemed to rise only with the rise of the commonwealth, and was at once trusted by the citizens and the friend and counsellor of princes of ancient blood. With consummate address he rescued himself from the jaws of a conspiracy which had assassinated his brother, and won over, by his eloquence, the whole city to his side. With like address he concluded peace with the King of Naples, cajoled the Pope, courted the clergy, strengthened himself by alliances among the nobles, obtained diplomatic relations with other states, and had a son in the Roman Conclave, a Cardinal of Holy Church, not yet fourteen years old. His public policy was equally sagacious. Now he endowed a monastery, now he built and garrisoned a fortress. Now he startled the city by ostentatious conviviality, now he caused it to wonder by ostentatious devotion. He mingled freely with the people, but he kept train-bands in his pay and at his bidding. To-day he opens a University, to-morrow he will preside at a magnificent banquet. He held outwardly to the Church, but was an ardent patron of the philosophy which threatened to uproot it, and commemorated

All Saints' Day by a festival in honour of Plato, when that "Attic Moses" furnished at once liturgy and gospel, and received intellectual homage which was little short of idolatry. In counsel he was acute, and in execution prompt and resolute. He delighted equally in the play of wit and the play of children, and, indeed, seems to have had that union of the stronger and lighter qualities which are necessary to the full-orbed character of a man. His incessant anxieties told too early upon his constitution, and, like a sword so keen that it cuts through its scabbard, the fire of his soul consumed the tabernacle in which it was ordained to burn. In his 44th year, when the prepossessions of youth are commonly over and the infirmities of age are yet afar, when the speed of the spirit is not that of the breathless, when the eye can look calmly forward, nor be dazzled by a broad sweep of vision—he was called to sicken and to die. Leaving Florence for his country-seat at Careggi, he wasted through some months of suffering, "now comparing himself to Lot in Sodom, and again to Orpheus leaving his Eurydice in hell," borne down somewhat by the ingratitude of the people, burdened somewhat by the memory of sin, and giving vent to his feelings sometimes in plaintive song—as in the following stanzas, in which he breathes out his soul's wistful desire.

> "Go, devout soul, enjoy that sacred fire
> Which plenteous mercies in the heart inspire;
> Whither the shepherd bids thee haste away,
> Hie thee submissive, and his voice obey.
>
> "Or, if awhile thou weepest, and with sighs
> Art scattering seed upon a barren soil,
> Cherish thy holy madness, it shall rise
> In fruit eternal to repay thy toil.

> " The people have devised vain things, but thou
> Sit still ; to Jesus hearken ; let them say
> What lists them ; harmless is the tumult now—
> At home, in Bethany, thy refuge, stay."

As his illness increased, his physicians administered pearls in solution, and mixtures of amalgamated jewels, as if to conciliate that grim warder who is, after all, inaccessible to bribes. He received the viaticum with all humility on the 8th April, 1492, confessed to Savonarola, whom he especially desired to attend him, and shortly afterwards passed away. Many affirmed that there were portentous omens about the time of his dying, and that the highest pinnacle of the cathedral was struck with lightning, as if in token of disasters that were to follow. Shrewd observers regarded him as the only man who could moderate the distractions of Italy. He was said to be like the isthmus which connects the Peloponnesus with the rest of Greece, and prevents the waves of the Ægean and Ionian seas from battling in perpetual storm. Being midway in position, and having both a reputation for prudence and an arm of power, he was as the breakwater between the pride of the King of Naples and the ambition of the Duke of Milan, upon which the rival billows broke, indignant but harmless as the spray. When he died all Italy grieved, as though smitten by a common trouble ; while Florence wept over him with a genuine sorrow, and, despite the faults of his person and of his family, glories in his memory still.

There is not a picture nor a statue in Florence, of any reputation, about which the reading public of the world is not sufficiently informed. It would be impertinent, therefore, and an endless task withal, to lead you through the rich galleries of the Uffizi and Pitti palaces. The latter, which is now the palace of the King, owes its erection to Luca Pitti, a wealthy Florentine, and a great opponent of the Medici family. The Palazzo Strozzi was formerly the largest and richest in Florence. "I will build a palace," said Pitti, "large enough to hold the Strozzi in its courtyard." Before its completion, however, he had fallen from his high estate, and it was finished by other hands. Inferior in extent to the galleries of the Vatican and the Louvre, those in Florence are probably the richest in the world. "Here," to quote from one who has entranced thousands by his eloquent words, "in their beautiful and calm retreats, the ancient sculptors are immortal; those illustrious men of history beside whom its crowned heads and harnessed warriors shew so poor and small, and are so soon forgotten. Here the imperishable past of noble minds survives, placid and equal, when strongholds of assault and defence are overthrown, when the tyranny of the many, or the few, or both, is but a tale; when pride and power are so much cloistered dust."

There is one picture in the Pitti gallery which ought surely to be in English hands. It is an authentic portrait, painted by Sir Peter Lely, of Oliver Cromwell. It is said that the sturdy old Roundhead, heedless for the moment of that Puritan humour which objected to the imposition of hands, shook the artist roughly by the shoulder, and threatened him with severe displeasure if he dared to make the portrait one whit handsomer than the man. And there it is—the stern, rough face, with a world of energy latent in the mouth, and gleaming from the deep-set eyes; with every blotch and wart upon the countenance which Nature, or hard usage, or scrofula, or excess, had placed there; a face which requires the jack-boots and the buff jerkin ; which seems as if it would be more at home at Naseby than in St. James' ; and yet a face with such a *power* in it, that through seam and scar you can almost see the lordly soul it shrined. It was a present from the Protector to the Grand Duke of Tuscany, and as such things are not now, it is a pity that it should not lend its inspiration to the land which the King uncrowned did so much to uplift and to save.

On the way from the Arno to the Pitti palace, as the observant eye glances right and left with that eager restlessness which possesses one in a strange city, if the heart underneath the eye be susceptible, it will perhaps begin to beat quickly, as mine did, smitten by a sweet surprise. The cause of this emotion was a small square slab, inserted just above the door of a decent-looking house in a narrow street, bearing an Italian inscription, which, being translated, reads thus: "Here wrote and died *Elizabeth Barrett Browning*, who, to the heart of a woman joined the science of a scholar and the spirit of a poet, and who made with her golden verse a nuptial ring between Italy and England. Grateful Florence places this memorial." I could not help wondering how long it would be before similar tributes appealed to us from our walls at home. In the nineteenth century we are but beginning to learn that the pen is mightier than the sword, and that those who strike the harp of life, and sing to us its many toned music, leave worthier memories than those who spill its heart out on the stained sward of some field of blood. All honour to Florence for her appreciation and her gratitude, and all honour, too, to the great, true woman who wept over Cowper's grave, from whose wrung spirit wailed forth the " Cry of the Children," and who burned into the national soul the lessons of Aurora Leigh.

Among the charities of Florence there are two which are noticeable ; one because it verges on the ridiculous—one because it approaches the sublime. Close under the shadow of the church of San Lorenzo there is a unique asylum, endowed in perpetuity under the will of some spinster of the former time. It is an asylum for cats. Here foundling cats are taken, and distressed ones sheltered. Supernumerary cats are saved from the Arno ; all proper cat courtship is promoted within reasonable limits ; and aspiring cats, anxious to go out into the world, are provided with suitable situations, in which, as the advertisements say, "salary is not so much an object as a comfortable home." Oh, poor human nature ! If, sometimes, from our weaknesses our strongest principles of action are born, as the oak from the trampled acorn, how often are our best instincts warped to folly, and our virtues, by their own devious energy, become objects of derision.

Turn we from this eccentricity of benevolence to look at one of the noblest charities of Europe. Driving through the Piazza of the Duomo, I was met by what seemed to be a funeral procession. The coffin was borne on the shoulders of men, and they who bore and they who followed were dressed in long monastic robes of black, with crape hoods, masks concealing the face, into which holes were cut for the eyes and mouth. This was the " Compagna della Misericordia," which has existed in Florence for upwards of six hundred years. It is said to have had a moral origin, for it was established from a fund created by fines for profane swearing, imposed upon themselves by the porters in the cloth manufactories of the city. Gradually it assumed vaster proportions, until it grew into a corporation of honour, and the most distinguished citizens were proud to enrol themselves in its band. The city is divided into districts, and the members, of whom there are some hundreds, are told off for daily duty with all the discipline of military rule. Their office is to carry the sick to hospital, the wounded to some place of refuge, and the dead to burial. One of the bells in the Campanile is called the "Misericordia." It is tolled when their services are needed, and at the summons of that bell, whether it be heard at sunrise or on Sabbath ; whether it strike upon the silence of midnight, or boom solemnly through the hall of banquet, each member of the brotherhood is bound, forsaking all other engagement, to obey its bidding. It is not an ecclesiastical fraternity, notwithstanding its hideous dress. The Florentines raise the hat, and the military present arms, when the "Misericordia" passes, and the Grand Duke himself, in the days when there was such a personage, has been known to leave his guests at the banquet, and take his turn, perhaps with the humblest, as a helper in this work of mercy. What an illustration at once of the sweetness and of the immortality of charity ! Through all change of dynasty, amid the rise and fall of nobles, while the sky has been dark with troubles and the streets have been dishonoured with blood, while the tempest has uprooted governments which seemed so stable, and the fortunes of the city have been alternately on the crest and in the trough of the waves, this institution has survived—like a pharos in a stormy sea, flinging its white light across the waters, though the waves howled about it in fury, and the "broad shoulders of the hurricane" pressed heavily against its solid form. Oh, it is beautiful to think that wherever Christianity has gone, even in partial or corrupt manifestation, this human charity, a stranger from some other world, has found for itself a mission and a home.

Who shall despair of a world, however fallen, when "one touch
of sorrow can make all men kin." We may not substitute
charity for godliness, but there is room for the Divine love in
the heart which has been touched by the human ; and there is
more than poetry in that exquisite Arabic parable which Leigh
Hunt has crystallized into verse :

> " Abou Ben Adhem, may his tribe increase !
>   Awoke one night from a deep dream of peace,
>   And saw, within the moonlight in his room—
>   Making it rich, and like a lily in full bloom—
>   An angel writing in a book of gold.
>   Exceeding peace had made Ben Adhem bold,
>   And to the presence in the room he said,
>   " What writest thou ? " The vision raised its head,
>   And, with a look made all of sweet accord,
>   Answered : " The names of those who love the Lord."
>   " And is mine one ? " said Abou. " Nay, not so,"
>   Replied the angel. Abou spake more low,
>   But cheerly still, and said, " I pray thee, then,
>   Write me as one who loves his fellow-men."
>   The angel wrote and vanished. The next night
>   It came again, with a great wakening light,
>   And showed the names whom love of God had blest,
>   And lo ! Ben Adhem's name led all the rest."

One of the sacred spots which no stranger in Florence should
omit to visit is the Church of Santa Croce, where are grouped
the cenotaphs of the illustrious dead. In this " temple of silence
and reconciliation," the Westminster Abbey of Florence, lie
or are commemorated some of the greatest names in the history
of the fair city. Alfieri, the sweet poet, Lanzi, the historian of
the arts, Raphael Morghen, the engraver, Aretino, the illus-

trious scholar, live in company on the walls of this hallowed shrine. Here also is the monument of Galileo, sturdy Protestant of the pre-Protestant ages, whose "yet it moves," uttered in the moment of enforced recantation, startled the conclave who had condemned him, like thunder out of a clear sky. Boccaccio has his tablet here, whose "Decameron" is among the classics of Italy. Here also, by the efforts of an English nobleman, is perpetuated the memory of Niccolo Machiavelli, who has had charged upon him, as the tempter, political crimes without number,—Niccolo Machiavelli, "out of whose surname," says Macaulay, "we have coined an epithet for a knave, and out of his Christian name a synonyme for the devil." Here also, mourned by the three sister arts—Architecture, Sculpture, and Painting—is the tomb of Michael Angelo, the site said to have been chosen by himself, that when the doors of the church were open it might be in sight of the cupola of the cathedral. Here also the remorseful gratitude of Florence, swelling like the tide about a stranded wreck, too late, has given to the memory of Dante a monument, something less than a grave. There is an inspiration and a solemnity as you tread the marble pavement beneath, while, all unheeding of the feet which tramp above them, these great hearts lie still. But Italy has gazed into these graves somewhat too long. Her prophets have ceased out of the land ; it is some four hundred years since the last bright-browed one vanished. Is it *therefore* that she has ceased to pray ? Is she so enamoured of her sires' memory that she has no heart to imitate their example ? She, whose citizens so often clave their way to freedom, will she ever be content again to be " no nation, but the poet's pensioner, with alms from every land of song and dream ?" These men of cunning brain and stalwart arm, foster-

N

gods of her glorious former times, can their successors ever be serfs, or men degenerate and lazy?

> " Oil-eaters, with large, live, mobile mouths
> Agape for maccaroni."

Oh ! it were to desecrate the sepulchre only to wail upon its marble. We dishonour the dead when we entomb our manhood with theirs. They loom, large and solemn, upon the sky, not to dwarf our stature, but to show us to what bigness we may grow. Confessors witness that the holy seed may follow. It is for the birth of heroes that the martyrs bled, and that the conquering human angel standeth in the sun. Thermopylæ were a rash impertinence if Sparta be not free. He who swears by Marathon must fight for Athens, if the leaguers threaten or the Medes surround. The dead but oped the door through which the living were to pass to valorous deed, to enterprise, to victory. If we ourselves would not shame an ancestry that is honoured, we shall haste forward with their memory to speed us on, that so, when we have borne our age yet nearer to the paradise it panteth for, our children may strew violets on our sepulchres, and evoke from us, as we from our fathers, the inspiration of the immortal dead.

Modern Florence is not backward in her recognition of the memory of DANTE, and this is a name so illustrious that we may not pass it hastily by. In the narrow Via Ricciarda, a marble slab over a modern Gothic door tells you, " In this house was Alighieri born, the Divine poet." In the cathedral is his portrait, placed there by decree of the Republic in 1465. In the Palazzo del Podesta, which has an ancient chapel of its own, there is a fresco by Giotto, which with Vandal barbarism was covered with whitewash, nearly two inches thick, and with equally Vandal indifference was so suffered to remain for years, until English and American liberality subscribed to reveal it. On the south side of the Piazza del Duomo, a slab let into the pavement is inscribed, "Sasso di Dante," where he was wont

> "to bring his quiet chair out, turned
> To Brunelleschi's church, and pour, alone,
> The lava of his spirit when it burned,
> While some enamoured passer used to wai
> A moment in the golden day's decline,
> With ' Good night, dearest Dante.' "

And in the centre of the Piazza of Santa Croce, on the 12th of May, 1865, six hundred years after his birth, and on the spot where, just before he came into the world, the Florentine republic was proclaimed, his statue was uncovered amid flaunting of banners, and salvoes of cannon, and *vivas* of an enthusiastic people, by the king of a free Italian kingdom, holding his court in the Florence which the passionate exile loved so long and so well. At the time the poet-politician was born, Florence had become a considerable city. There were 100,000 inhabitants within its walls. Few cities exerted so imperial a command, and but for the intestine strifes which distracted it, it might have climbed to well nigh unapproachable renown. There was much in the aspect of affairs, in a past of tradition and legend, in a present of tumult and hope, to fire a youthful imagination with patriotism and valour. With the romantic love, all free from passion, which filled him for the Beatrice of his dream and song, he had no room for meaner attachments, and the young Guelph partisan rode in the fore front of the battle, and was a trusted counsellor when victory had purchased peace. So great was his reputation for wisdom, even in early life, that he was nominated to many foreign embassies, and indeed it was during his absence on one of these that the wheel of fortune turned his adversaries uppermost, and he was summoned to appear before the podesta within forty days, and pay a fine of 8,000 livres. The charge against him was that he had resisted the pacific mission of the French prince, to which was added an unworthy innuendo that he had misused the public money. We can fancy the high souled scorn with which he would treat an accusation like this. Failing to appear at the summons he was declared a rebel, and banished from the city for ever. Then began those long and regretful wanderings which ended only with his life, and which caused him to lament over the bitterness of the bread which is eaten at the table of a foreigner, and the weariness of the feet which travel up a patron's stairs. The celebrated Can Francesca received him at his court and paid him honour: but the iron had entered into his soul. It was the fashion to have buffoons and jesters in the prince's pay, and the more license and audacity they exhibited, the greater was the courtier's relish for their company. The Duke said to Dante, "I wonder that these buffoons, who are so grossly ignorant, should please us and be so much beloved, while you, who are reputed to be so learned, fail to win our love." The reply was bitter and bold : " Your grace would not wonder if you consider that friendship is always based upon similarity of disposition." After some years an offer of recall was made, but on degrading conditions which Dante indignantly refused, and after the failure of a negotiation on behalf of Ravenna with the Council of Venice, his mortification induced an illness of which he died, in the fifty-seventh year of his age. There were many considerations which hindered the early popularity of his works. Men could hardly read poetry while its most tragic scenes were being enacted around them. The poet had mingled too sternly in the strifes of the day to be favourably judged by all. Bigots hated his writings because, though an orthodox son of the Church, he was not insensible to her errors. He denounced the sale of pardons and indulgences, and was an unmistakeable foe to the temporal power of the Pope. It sounds like an utterance of the after ages when he represents the Church as one which,

> " Mixing two governments that ill assort,
> Hath lost her footing, fallen into the mire,
> And there herself and burden much defiled."

Moreover, it commonly requires a century to create a classic. But Dante, in spite of all hindrances, gradually climbed to the throne. Professorships were established in the Universities of Italy to expound the " Divina Commedia." The people, who rarely err on questions of standard reputation, when the matter submitted to them is one which they understand and teel, delivered their verdict of approval. The vernacular of modern Italian was henceforth as Dante had written it ; and Italy rose, sad with the remorse of ages, and crowned him as the bard of truth and of religion—the teacher, perhaps the prophet, of his country's freedom. Political error ! Misuse of funds out of the Treasury ! He scorned to answer these charges, but what dust of their defilement settles upon Dante now ? The ages have been empannelled as the jurors, and time has pronounced him free from sordid stain. Since his death the neglect and exile of his life have been mourned and atoned. If a man do the right, and can learn the secret of grandly waiting, he shall have a world to witness his acquittal or his triumph by and by.   Not only did powers, civil and ecclesiastical, gather to do honour to the man whom both had formerly decried, but the memory of Dante had an ampler atonement still.   On the day when the first charter (afterwards shamelessly withdrawn) was given by the Grand Duke Leopold, the people, bright with such new hope as can kindle only in the eyes of freemen, gathered by thousands to welcome the charter of their liberty.   But where was their trysting-place?   Not on the broad Cacine, dedicate to fashion and pleasure.   Not in front of the palace, laden with recollec-tions of many an illegitimate Cæsar.   Not by the Loggia, where stand superb the masterpieces of stone.   None of these were sacred enough for the solemnity of such an occasion.

> " Not there ! The people chose still holier ground ;
> The people, who are simple, blind and rough,
> Know their own angels, after looking round."

They met by Dante's stone.   The earliest charter of the modern liberties of Tuscany dated from the seat of Tuscany's most illustrious exile as if, on that spot, hallowed alike by the memo-ries of his rapture and of his banishment, it was meet that they should shake hands with Freedom.

Turn we to another shrine.   In the Via Ghibellina is the Palazzo Buonarotte, the house, the veritable home, of MICHAEL ANGELO.   It has been preserved inviolate, and much of the furniture is as it was in the artist's time.   Here, in a snug little closet, are the table at which he used to write, his inkstand, his sandals, the sword which he took on his journeys, the crutch-handled walking-stick which he daily used, notched with strong iron ferules, to prevent his falling on the slippery pavement;

many of his original drawings ; the model for his " David ;" his sketch for his greatest work, "The Last Judgment ;" his autograph correspondence with Vittoria Colonna ; an early sculpture, chiselled before he was sixteen ; the bronze bust of him, by John of Bologna, his favourite pupil, which is considered the most faithful likeness, and which shows the broken nose which Torrigiani's jealousy gave him ;—all are here, and you can enter into almost palpable communion with the proud, grand old man, whom one of his biographers describes as "unique in painting, unparalleled in sculpture, a perfect architect, an admirable poet, and a divine lover." He was born at the castle of Caprese, in Tuscany, of a good family, and his father was greatly chagrined at his son's attachment to art, for no amount of argument could teach him the difference between a sculptor and a stone-mason. The astrologers had cast the nativity of the young Buonarotti, and had predicted for him great distinction, because at the hour of his birth the conjunction of Mercury and Venus took place, and they were received into the house of Jupiter with benign aspect. After this starry prophecy his father could not brook the idea of his following a pursuit which he deemed fitted only for the lowly born. Genius, however, is not always to be restrained, even by parental authority, so the youth won his father's reluctant consent that he should be placed in the studio of Ghirlandajo, that sculpture and painting might contend for the mastery. Here he devoted himself to art with an assiduity which soon led him to distance all competitors, and was even bold enough to correct his master's errors. A tall dignified stranger one day entered, and scrutinizing the works of the students, paused before the easel of Michael Angelo. "By your leave," said he to the master, " I select this youth for the garden of St. Mark. Will it accord with his views?" "Ay," was the significant reply, "think ye the eagle does not ken his eyrie?" When the stranger left, Buonarotti asked of those near him who the noble was. "Do you not know?" they asked, in astonishment, "it was the Duke, Lorenzo di Medici." "I was not aware," the proud youth replied, "but henceforward we shall know each other." The death of Lorenzo, after three years of friendship, affected the artist so much that he retired to Caprese, brooding over his loss until he became misanthropical, but was softened at length by the tender preachings of nature, and by the wise patience of the healer, time. Pietro di Medici, Lorenzo's unworthy son and successor, was one of those feeble princelings whose rank is so much larger than themselves that their small souls crouch behind it. Though his taste was corrupt and his manners overbearing, he had just wit enough to know that a great artist would be an acquisition to his court. Hence he invited Michael to return, and lodged him in the same apartments which he had occupied in the time of the Magnificent. His estimate of his guest, however, may be gathered from his recorded boast: "I have two extraordinary persons in my house; the one a Spanish running footman, who is so rapid on foot, and so long breathed, that I cannot get before him when riding at full speed; and the other is—Michael Angelo." It was in this character of patron, and perhaps to humble the genius which was getting somewhat too manly for the palace serfdom, that on a winter's day, in the Via Larga, he bade him carve a statue in the snow, and as he watched the mighty worker at his toil, laughed his paltry laughter from the palace window. For three days the statue was the admiration of Florence, so grand and sharp were the proportions; on the fourth, the returning sun left nothing of it but a memory. It is not easy to divine the motives which bowed the artist-soul to consent to the humiliation. Perhaps the memory of the dead father threw a present halo round the meaner son. Perhaps he was conscious of power, and would impress upon the Florentines that genius is not dependent upon the fittest materials to create its forms of beauty. Perhaps he flung an eagle gaze into the future, and "read a wrong into a prophecy." You can fancy the world of scorn which would gleam through the honest eye, just lifted from its perishing labour to shoot a glance into the balcony where the Prince watched the people's enthusiasm.

> "I think thy soul said then, I do not need
>   A princedom and its quarries, after all,
>   For if I write, paint, carve a word indeed,
>   On book or board or dust, on floor or wall,
>   The same is kept of God, who taketh heed
>   That not a letter of the meaning fall,
>   Or ere it touch and teach the world's deep heart ;
>   Outlasting therefore all your lordships, sir !
>   So keep your stone, beseech you, for your part
>   To cover up your grave-place, and refer
>   The proper titles. I live by my Art !
>   The thought I threw into this snow shall stir
>   This gazing people when their gaze is done ;
>   And the tradition of your act and mine,
>   When all the snow is melted in the sun,
>   Shall gather up, for unborn men, a sign
>   Of what is the true princedom ; ay, and none
>   Shall laugh that day, except the drunk with wine."

There was a school of virtuosi in Florence who were never weary of decrying contemporary merit. To their sagacious criticism it was needful that a work should have the rust of years upon it before they would allow it to have any excellence at all. Michael Angelo taught these gentlemen a practical lesson. He made a statue of a Sleeping Cupid, which he stained to represent it as antique, and, having cut off an arm, he procured its burial in a vineyard, and its discovery in due course ; and, when all the works of modern artists were pronounced to be trash in the comparison, he quietly produced the arm, and covered the critics with confusion. Returning to Florence after a brief sojourn in Rome, he had to contend with Leonardo da Vinci for the sculptor's palm. The contest was on this wise. There was a huge block of marble, which had been embossed by Simon da Fiesolé for the statue of a giant, but he had failed in his attempt, and the marble had lain neglected for years. Leonardo was asked to finish it, but he declared it to be impossible without additional material, because it had been irreparably injured. Michael Angelo took hold of the marble, thus marred in the hands of the designer, and at his bidding it grew into a colossal statue of David, with a face of perpetual youth, and the firm, lithe limbs of the athletic shepherd boy. Not only did he require no additional marble, but it is said that he left some of his predecessor's work untouched, so that it was a common Florentine saying, that Michael Angelo had raised the dead. Soderini, the chief magistrate, who deemed himself bound, in his official capacity, to patronize art, and who, perhaps, imagined that criticism is at once the most enlightened and the most condescending form of patronage, said, as he looked at the statue, " The nose is too large." The artist mounted the scaffold with a chisel in one hand and a little marble dust in the other, and pretended to work upon the face, letting the dust fall as if he were. Shortly he turned about

" How is it now?" " Excellent," was the reply, " you have given it life." The critic was not undeceived, and Michael Angelo, with proverbial self-confidence, said that Soderini's was as good as most criticism.

On the accession of Julius II. to the Papal Chair, Michael was invited to Rome, and received a commission, unlimited as to expense, to decorate a mausoleum, so gorgeous that it should hand down patron and artist to posterity. The design was approved, and the Pope ordered San Gallo, the architect, to devise the best means for placing the work in St. Peter's. San Gallo, struck with the grandeur of the design, represented to His Holiness that such a monument required a chapel that was worthy of it, at the same time suggesting that St. Peter's was an old church, and that any alteration would mar the unity of the building. The Pope listened and pondered, until the purpose arose in his mind to rebuild St. Peter's itself; and this was the origin of that wonderful edifice, which grew slow and stately for a hundred and fifty years. What great events from tiniest causes spring ! What remote and subtle analogies run through life, like a silent spring through its bed of rock and sand ! It would startle you to be told that Michael Angelo began the Reformation ; but mark the unbroken chain of causes, and explain them as you may. The great sculptor designs a monument. The monument demands a worthy shrine. The existing buildings are all too poor, so that a new one must be built on purpose. Money is required to finish the building and to replenish the exhausted treasury. Indulgences are sold to raise the money. Tetzel the friar, licensed hawker in this sorry trade, travels into Saxony to sell them. Martin Luther is startled, protests, searches, is converted, becomes a witness, girds himself for the battle, shakes the world. And so Michael Angelo began the Reformation.

Upon the later years of this great man we may not longer dwell. His paintings in the Sistine Chapel establish his fame as a painter. His conspicuous share in the building of St. Peter's assures his architectural reputation. His works, as Master of the Ordnance in Florence, are monuments of his engineering skill. His sonnets shew a refined and tender soul, and no small mastery of the art of poetry. Sculptor, painter, architect, mechanician, poet; unparalleled in some, in others holding his own against the loftiest ; excellent in all ; living to enjoy the wealth which his labour had earned ; unable to rid himself of the flattery for which he cared so little ; the sternness and jealousy of his earlier years mellowing with the deeper study and the firmer faith ; not unloved, although Venus somehow dropped out of his horoscope, but receiving the homage of beautiful and gifted women. What crown could you put upon a destiny like his, except that " which fadeth not away ? " Add to his other names the name of Christian, which there is reason to believe you may lawfully do, and you have one of the highest styles of men, second only to those whose lives have been a grand self-sacrifice, or who, after years of unrewarded labour, have got the glory of the martyr's grave. Michael Angelo lived through a pilgrimage of ninety years, and then, in his will, committed his soul to God, his body to the earth, and his possessions to his nearest relatives, adding that he died in the faith of Jesus Christ, and in the firm hope of a better life. His own words will fittingly close this endeavour to recall and exhibit him :

> Sculpture and painting ! rival arts !
>   Ye can no longer soothe my breast
> 'Tis love Divine alone imparts
>   The promise of a future rest.
> On that my steadfast soul relies,—
>   My trust the Cross, my hope the skies

In the church of San Marco is the pulpit from which SAVONAROLA spoke in thunder ; in the adjoining convent is the cell in which he wrote, and in the Piazza Gran Duca, the fountain of Neptune stands upon the spot where his soul went out in fire. Any notice of Florence would be imperfect which should omit the reference to this courageous martyr for the truth. Just a generation after the ashes of John Huss had been given to the waters of the Rhine, he was born at Ferrara. He was early steeped in the works of Aristotle and Plato, Dante and Petrarch ; the masters of Grecian philosophy, the masters of Italian song. In early life also he entered a Dominican convent. Like many other men of ardent imagination and austere morals, he was disappointed in a monastic life. He expected to find absorbing devotion, Christian fellowship, the real deadness to the world which the cowl and the cloister simulated. He found only passions intensified by their professed renunciation, languor in the chapel, and worldliness in the cell. After a seven years' novitiate he entered upon priest's orders, and as the brotherhood of the monastery felt that the reputation of Friar Jerome reflected honour upon his order, they encouraged his desire to preach, and he accordingly essayed in the church of San Lorenzo at Florence. The congregation was numerous, and high in expectation ; but he delivered his sentiments with ungainly action, in a shrill, uncultivated voice, hesitatingly, and in meagre style, so that in a few days the thousands had dwindled down to twenty-five, and he vowed for the present to abjure the pulpit, saying " I could not have moved so much as a chicken; I had neither voice, lungs, nor style." He felt, however, that the Divine gift was in him, and like Demosthenes, he spared no pains to acquire the power of commanding speech. Hence in four years more we find him again in Florence, named by Lorenzo the Magnificent Prior of San Marco, no longer an ineffective preacher, but a master of the tribune, and of the hearts of men. The lecture-room soon became too small for the multitudes who thronged to hear, so he lectured in the convent garden. Florence had by this time become both a commercial and a collegiate city, and it was a motley group which the friar gathered around him. There were merchants, scholars, priests and princes. Here might be seen the Bohemian, privileged, above others, with the eucharistic cup; there, the cultured but sceptical adversary of ecclesiastical pride. Here would be the enterprising Lombard, there the zealous Wickliffite, and yonder, looking askance at the gathering, some wary stranger from Rome; and as the tall spare form of the monk stood forth, with the sky for the roof of his cathedral, the rosary for his chancel, and for his incense the sweet breath of a thousand flowers; and as he thundered out his denunciations of the corruptions of the Papacy, and the godlessness of the new philosophy into which many of its adherents had recoiled; every one felt that a power to control and to command abode in that emaciated frame.

As superior of the convent he was thrown into a new relation towards Lorenzo; this relation became at first an embarrassment and then a cause of quarrel. It is difficult to exonerate

Savonarola from the charge of ingratitude. His independence revolted from being the Duke's minion, but the fear of being so regarded became a morbid one, and induced a studied discourtesy towards his patron which was as marked as it was bold and unlovely. San Marco had been built by the Medici, by them enriched with a costly library, raised by their munificence to a position of prosperity, and even of grandeur. Savonarola himself was indebted to Lorenzo for his introduction to Florence, and for the office which gave him all his power. There was a respect which would have been graceful, and a courtesy which he might have paid without compromising his principles by the breadth of a hair. The monk, however, was haughtier than the Medici, and, in his scorn of patronage, exhibited the proverbial "falsehood of extremes." It was a custom to pay a visit to Lorenzo when the new Prior was installed. Savonarola refused to go. "Who elected me Prior, God, or Lorenzo?" Of course the monks said God. "Then to God I will give thanks, and not to mortal man." The Duke, anxious to conciliate, sent some valuable presents. These Savonarola coldly received and coarsely alluded to: "the good dog will always bark to defend his master's house, and, if a thief comes, and tries to quiet him by throwing him a bone or a morsel, the good dog just picks it up, drops it on one side, falls a barking again, and bites the thief." Lorenzo was present when Savonarola spoke these words, and could hardly fail to make the application. This irritating collision, however, was soon ended by Lorenzo's untimely death. On his death-bed he gave the most unequivocal mark of confidence by sending for Savonarola in preference to his own confessor, "for," he said, "I have not found another religious except him." It is said that in this latest interview the monk insisted upon three conditions before he would absolve the dying man. First—a spiritual one,—that he should exercise a lively faith ; second—a pecuniary one,—that he should restore whatever had been acquired by unlawful means ; and third—a political one,—that he should loose Florence from the Medicean yoke, and re-establish the republic as of old. Lorenzo promised the two first, but demurred to the last, shrewd enough to see that to give such a promise was utterly out of his power ; honest enough to refuse to disinherit his children of the authority which the State had conferred upon his family ; and manly enough, even with the death-dews on his brow, to protest against political conditions of salvation, and to shake loose from the intolerable tyranny which would gag the departing spirit, and hide from it, beneath the cloak of a spurious patriotism, the Cross of an insulted Saviour.

After the death of Lorenzo, Savonarola entered with holy boldness upon that wider career in which we may follow him with admiration almost kindling into rapture. A preacher, famed for eloquence ; a prophet, stern as Ezekiel in the inspired, or Cassandra in the fabled canon ; a vigorous reformer both in church and state ; a legislator among distracted counsels ; he seemed to be possessed with the great idea of destiny, and went on his course heedless of discord or danger. He knew that it was impossible to speak as he had spoken without gathering against himself a rancorous opposition, and the hatred of that relentless enemy which dogs its victims to the death. "Do you ask me," he says, "*in general* what will be the end of the conflict? I answer, Victory! But if you ask me *in particular*, then I answer Death. But death is not extinction. Rather it serves to spread abroad the light." His own mind, though it had largely freed itself from errors of morality, was still, and indeed always, bound by superstitions of doctrine. He stood among the ages, midway between two great periods, orphan of the old, prophet of the new, like Noah among the worlds of God. While behind him was the thick darkness, and before him the glorious morning, he lived and died in the gloaming, with dim ideas of truth and power which it was never given him fully to comprehend. Hence sacramental efficacy and personal trust in Christ ; reverence for the Scriptures and pretension to an immediate revelation ; the profoundest humility and the most marvellous fanaticism, alternated from his lips and in his life.

Under his influence the reformation of morals in the city was wonderful. Monasteries became pure, the churches crowded. His was no Ash Wednesday denunciation, following upon a permitted carnival. The carnival itself was restrained in its excesses, and religious entertainments were publicly given, to which the masses of the people thronged. Eight thousand children were banded into a sort of juvenile republic, and were called " The Children of Jesus Christ." They attended service in procession, stood by little portable altars in the streets on feast-days, soliciting the offerings of the people, and went from house to house, begging for immodest pictures, and vanities of apparel or furniture, which were given up to them to be destroyed. On the last day of Lent there was a grand and general burning. A pyramid was reared in one of the large squares, the inside of which was filled with combustibles, and on the steps of which, rising to the apex, were the motley vanities which were to be given to the fire. Latin and Italian poems, music-books, cards, lutes, pictures, false hair, looking-glasses, wigs, beards, masks, chequer-boards, cosmetics and perfumes, all were devoted in this harmless *auto-da-fe*. Four captain-boys, each with his torch, fired a corner when the trumpets gave the signal, the bells rang, the people shouted, the flames rose and swelled, and in a few moments luxuries and works of art and imagination, the hair-dresser's stock-in-trade, the life-labours of the artist and the poet, were reduced to ashes. The intention of all this was doubtless good, and if the heart went with the sacrifice, and it was not a self-righteous complacency in trampling upon pride with greater pride, it might be a consecration as sublime as the burning of books at Ephesus ; if otherwise, it was a notable act notwithstanding ; it is a perpetual testimony of Savonarola's power.

Meanwhile the breach between the monk and the Papacy grew wider day by day. Alexander VI., who then filled the papal chair, perfidious, licentious, venal, covetous, cruel, to a degree so shameless that he, Borgia of the Borgias, stands on a bad eminence of his own, was not likely to commend himself to the Florentine monk's good will. The Pope first silenced him in the pulpit, but by the interference of the magistrates the inhibition was withdrawn. The next step was an endeavour to bribe him. " Give him a red hat, and so make at once a cardinal and a friend." Savonarola answered from the pulpit of St. Mark, " I will have no other red hat than that of martyr-dom, coloured with my own blood." Then came the trial to get the monk into his power, by the proposal, in a very affec-tionate letter, of a journey to Rome. His answer was that his preaching was very useful in Florence, and that he begged to be excused. After the invitation came a brief, commanding him to appear in Rome. He answered the letter, but did not obey the summons, and, after a few weeks' silence, preached again in disregard of the Pontiff, saying he was urged to do so by Him who is prelate of prelates and pope of popes. Attempts were made to take his life, by stiletto and poison, and ruffian hands —all of which were frustrated by the Providence of God, and by the watchfulness and valour of his friends. Invitation, inhibition and brief having failed to subdue the unconquerable spirit, Alexander proceeded further, and, in the Lent of 1498, fulminated the Bull of Excommunication. But the monk had got long past the age at which so very harmless a thing could make him tremble. Hear his answer: " He who commands a thing contrary to the law of Christ, is himself excommunicated. On what side then wilt thou stand? Shall they be blessed whom the Pope blesses, although their life is the curse of Christendom, or shall they be excommunicated whom he excommunicates, although all the fruits of the Spirit be displayed in their life. I may have failed in many respects, for I am a sinner, but I have not failed, inasmuch as I have preached the Gospel of Christ freely and without fear of man. They threaten, too, that they will not bury us. That will give me no concern when I am dead. Fling me into the Arno if you will, my body will be found in the judgment, and that is enough."

Florence, however, was not equally brave. She had before her the terrors of interdict, and war, and the possible extinction of the state, so that her fickle people and her cowardly magistrates became the betrayers of the man who had deserved so well of their city. He was arrested under a safe conduct, after a night attack upon the convent, and upon his friends in the streets, which, in its measure, was a minor St. Bartholomew. Of course the safe conduct was violated. It could not be otherwise, when fear and hate combined to make his death a necessity. The closest examination furnished no proof either of sedition or impiety. Then the torture was applied, until beneath its agony he was weary of his life. Still there was nothing to criminate him, until a heartless rogue, Ser Coccone by name, altered and interpolated one of his written statements, so as to serve the purpose of his foes. And on this forged confession, brought about by an artifice which Savonarola disdained to expose, the iniquitous mockery ended, and he was adjudged to die. The official record says : " On the said 23rd day of May " (that is, May, 1498) " Friar Jerome, Friar Dominic, and Friar Silvester were degraded at 13 of the clock, and then burnt in the Piazza de Signori." Three platforms were erected in front of the palace. Savonarola was taken up into the presence of a Bishop, clad in priestly robes. Then, piece by piece, the vestments were removed in the presence of the multitude, and the Bishop pronounced the degradation : " I separate thee from the Church Militant and from the Church Triumphant." " Nay," said the intrepid spirit, " from the Church Militant if you please, but not from the Church Triumphant, that is more than you can do." He then mounted the pile, uttered but one sentence, " O Florence, what hast thou done this day ? " Soon there was a glowing heap of ashes, from whose heart, as if in a fiery chariot, a *man* had arisen to the throne of God.

The re-action soon set in. Ere yet the flames of the martyr-fire were quenched, noble matrons and citizens, faithful to the last, snatched some of the charred bones as treasures more precious than gold. By order of the commune the ashes were thrown into the river, that they might be scattered beyond recovery. But, as in the case of all such impotent persecution, they could not kill the living words nor the immortal memory. That memory became an inspiration to the Italian people. It stirred them to a deep-seated anger against both ecclesiastical and civil oppression. Priests who courted popularity were forced to emulate Friar Jerome the martyr. Medals were struck in his honour, and sold under the eye and with the approbation of a future pope. Poetry embalmed his virtues, and associated him with freedom and piety; at this day the friends of religious liberty inscribe his name upon their banners; and as his words of fire "*Italia renovabitur*" (Italy shall be renewed,) pass monthly into thousands of Italian homes, they stir every worthy purpose into life, and at once eloquence and prophecy shrine him in a remembrance as fragrant and more inspiring than the violets which for centuries regretful Florence was wont to strew upon the pavement of his doom.

The present state of Florence, and indeed of all the cities of the free Italian Kingdom, entails solemn responsibility upon the witnesses for God. The successive blows which have been already struck at the Papacy, and the bolder political changes which are sure to come, have of necessity brought with them much spiritual unsettlement and indecision. The whole country is in transition. Popery, as a vital force creative of other forces, a power from the heart upon the life, has lost its hold. It survives, a ceremonial, as a tradition, as an engine of political power, but as a conviction, a faith, an incarnation of the Divine, it lives no longer. There is fear lest in the fierce rebound from its discovered vanity, the nation should rush into infidelity defiant and terrible. Now is the time for Christian work. The people enquire. There is hunger of heart for knowledge. The people are filled with strange yearnings. There is hunger of heart for rest. The people are elate with the new intemperance of freedom. Can there be a nobler opportunity or a stronger need for Catholic-hearted Christianity to satisfy the avarice for knowledge by the revelation of God and His Christ ; to still the quick trouble by the Gospel's divinest peace ; to tell to the liberated, even in the fever of their joy, that

> " He is the freeman whom the Truth makes free,
>   And all are slaves beside."

Yes ! Italy shall be renewed. There is an inner truth which like a sound of power goes ringing through the ages, in Savonarola's prophetic word. The light, which was the morning twilight to him, has climbed higher up the sky, and is broadening fast into a noon of splendour. Yes ! Italy shall be renewed. The pure truth shall win its way, in spite of hindrance and insult, against banded foes, or traitorous or time-serving friends. The historical prestige of Popery has departed from it. France will never reproduce a House of Guise, nor Spain a Duke of Alva. The great wild souls who united a brilliant chivalry with a prostrate faith, have passed away. No martial Julius or strong-souled Leo will fill the Papal chair. The world is moving on. Men's minds march to its progress. The flowers upon the martyrs' graves will suggest the harvests which their offspring may gather, till

> " They who have strewn the violets reap the corn,
>   And having reaped and garnered, bring the plough
>   And draw new furrows 'neath the healthy morn,
>   And plant the great Hereafter in the Now."

Meanwhile, let the Anglo-Saxon race see to it that it be not again enslaved. The onset is steady and determined. Warders slumber at ease upon their posts. Traitors play into the enemy's hands. Already the light is in the eye, and the boast upon the lips, as if with the assurance of victory. And shall it really be so? Discrowned and fugitive in the lands where it has been accustomed to be honoured, is the error to find shelter and royalty in lands whose freedom dates from the shivering of her yoke of old? With the sun shining in the heavens, are we to choose the crypt for a dwelling? With the healing air at hand, shall we abide in the red-crossed houses where the plague waits for its prey? The wizards "peep and mutter," and croon in their distempered age—is it among homes of liberty that their ancient spells are to prevail? I am no prophet, nor the son of one, but I know this, if such a day should come it will be in an oblivion of history and in an eclipse of faith ; it will be from a fatal indifference or from a spurious charity ; it will be when Anglo-Saxons shall have sunk into a degenerate manhood, whose eye kindles with no holy pride as they recall their gallant sires. Never more than to-day were needed the men of calm and resolute faith. Brothers, to your knees and to your ranks ! To your knees in humblest supplication—to your ranks in steadfast bravery which no foe can cause to quail. Stand forth in courage and in gentleness for the Truth which you believe to be allied to Freedom, and Progress, and God. Be so strong that you are not afraid to be just. Cherish a tender humanity and a catholic heart. In your righteous anger against destructive error, show your manly compassion for the souls which bad systems enslave. Then take your stand, calm and moveless as the stars, and say to ultramontane insolence and error : " The advancing tide shall not be rolled back with our good will. Our civil freedom ! Our reformed faith ! Our unsealed and open Bible ! These are our landmarks, and they shall not be taken away. Amid many divisions these are our points of rallying. We abide here. Touch not this ark of our covenant. We will guard it, we will possess it, until we die!"

THE HUGUENOTS.

THE HUGUENOTS.

FROM the Reformation may be dated a new era in the history of history. As presented to us in the writings of the older historians, history consisted, for the most part, of the bare recital of events, unaccompanied by philosophical reflections, or by any attempt to discover the mutual relations and tendencies of things. After the Reformation the adherents of the rival churches, each from his own standpoint, moralised upon that wondrous revolution, and upon the circumstances, political and social, which introduced and attended it. That which had been chronicle thus became controversy. Writers not only narrated events, but fringed them with the hues of their own thought, and impressed upon them the bias of their own opinions, and as one result of this there sprang up the Philosophy of History. Men began to think that if the Reformation, and the events connected with it, might be canvassed in their sources and issues, all national changes, all events upon the mighty stream of tendency, might be legitimately subjected to similar criticism. Gradually this survey of the past took a loftier stand, and spread over a wider range. The causes of the rise and fall of empires, the elements of national prosperity or decline—the obsoleteness or adaptation of various forms of government—the evidences of growth and transition among the peoples of mankind,—all in their turn were made matters of historical inquiry. Thus history, at first narrative and then polemical, has become, in our day, a record of progress, a triumphal eulogy of the growth of civilization.

But both writers and readers of history form an unworthy estimate of its province if they restrict it within such limits. They only realise its mission who see in its transitions the successive developments of Providence, ever working, without pause and without failure, the counsel of the Divine will. It is not enough, if we would study history aright, that we should follow in the track of battle, and listen to the wail of the vanquished and the shouts of conquerors; it is not enough that we should philosophically analyse the causes of upheaval and remodelling; it is not enough that we regard it as a school for the study of character, and gaze, with an admiration that is almost awe, upon the "world's foster-gods," the stalwart nobility of mankind; it is not enough that we should regard it as a chaos of incident, "a mighty maze, and all without a plan :" we realise the true ideal of history only when we discover God in it, shaping its ends for the evolution of His own design, educing order from its vast confusions, resolving its complications into one grand and marvellous unity, and making it a body of completeness and symmetry, with Himself as the informing soul.

Let this faith be fastened on our spirits, and history becomes a beautiful study. The world is seen linked to Christ—an emerald rainbow round about His throne. In His great purpose its destiny of glory is secure. There is sure warrant for the expectation of that progress of which the poet-watchers have so hopefully sung ; progress unintermitting, through every disaster of the past, heralding progress yet diviner in every possibility of the future. The eye of sense may trace but scanty foreshadowings of the brightness ; there may be dark omens in the aspects of the times—and the wistful glance, strained through the darkness, may discern but faint traces of the coming of the day ; but it *shall* come, and every movement brings it nigher— for " the Word of the Lord hath spoken it," and that Word " endureth for ever."

In our study of the history of France, or, indeed, of any other nation, we must remember certain peculiarities which, though apparently of small account, are influential elements in national progress, and means towards the formation of national character. Each race, for example, has its distinctive temperament, which it transmits from generation to generation. The character which Cæsar gave of the Gallic tribes two thousand years ago is, in its most noticeable features, their character still. " They are warlike, going always armed, ready on all occasions to decide their differences by the sword ; a people of great levity, little inclined to idleness ; hospitable, generous, confiding and sincere." This transmission of qualities, while it fosters the pride of a nation, stamps upon it an individuality, and prevents the adoption of any general changes which have no affinity with the national mind.

In like manner the traditions of a nation are potent influences in national culture. The memory of its heroes, and of the battle-fields where their laurels were won ; of its seers of science, its prophets of highest-mounted mind ; of its philosophers, the high priests of nature ; of its poets, who have played upon the people's heart as upon a harp of many strings ; of its great men, who have excited wonder ; of its good men, who have inherited love ; all the old and stirring recollections of the romantic past which flush the cheek and brighten the eye ; all these are substantive tributaries to an empire's education, and aid us in forming our estimate of its career and destiny.

But more potent than either of the causes we have mentioned are those external agencies which from time to time arise, in the course of events, to stamp a new form and pressure on the world. The sacred isolation of the Hebrew commonwealth—the schools of Greece—the militocracy of Rome—the advent of the Redeemer—the Mohammedan imposture—feudalism, with its blended barbarity and blessing—the Crusades—the invention of Printing—the Reformation,—all these were not only incidents but POWERS, each of them exerting an appreciable influence upon the character of the nations of mankind. In tracing the history of the Huguenots, therefore, we are not merely following the fortunes of a proscribed people, nor reciting a tale of individual suffering—we are depicting the history of France, we are evolving the subtle cause of that mysterious something which has been, through a long course of years, an element of national disquiet, which has alternately impelled the attack of passion or furthered the schemes of tyranny, and under which that sunny and beautiful land has groaned in bondage until now.

The doctrines of the Reformation took early root in France. The simultaneous appearance of its confessors in different countries is one amongst the many collateral proofs of its divine origin. Movements which men originate are local and centralised, arranged in concert, and gathering ripeness from correspondence and sympathy. When God works there is no

barrier in geographical boundaries, nor in the absence of intercourse.   He drops the truth-seed, and it falls into world-wide
furrows.   When the hour is ripe—full-grown, heroic, and ready—
there springs forth the MAN.   Events had long been preparing
the way for the mighty change.   In the Church, whether through
ignorance or faithlessness, pagan ceremonies had been grafted
upon the "reasonable service" of the worship; discipline had
become rather a source of immorality than a guard to holiness;
and the traffic in indulgences had shaken the foundations of every
social and moral bond.   Former protests against encroachment
and error, though crushed by the strong hand of power, were
not utterly forgotten.   The voices of Claude and Vigilantius
yet echoed in the hearts of many; traditions of Albigensian
confessors, and of saints in Vaudois valleys, were in numerous
homes; the martyr songs of the Lollard and the Hussite lingered
—strange and solemn music—in the air.   By and by, in cotem-
poraneous blessing, came the revival of learning and the invention
of Printing.   The common mind, waking from its long, deep
slumber, felt itself hungry after knowledge, and more than three
thousand works were given to appease its appetite in the course
of seventy years.   The sixteenth century dawned upon nations
in uneasiness and apprehension.   Kings, warriors, statesmen,
scholars, people, all seemed to move in a cloud of fear, or
under a sense of mystery, as if haunted by a presentiment of
change.   Everything was hushed into a very agony of pause, as
Nature holds her breath before the crash of the thunder.   Men
grew strangely bold and outspoken.   Reuchlin vindicated the
claims of science against the barbarous teaching of the times.
Ulrich von Hütten, who could fight for truth if he had not felt its
power, flung down the gage of battle with all the knightly pride

of chivalry. Erasmus, the clear-headed and brilliant coward, lampooned monks and doctors, until cardinals, and even the pope himself, joined in the common laughter of the world. All was ready,—the forerunners had fulfilled their mission, and the Reformation came.

In 1517, Tetzel, the indulgence-peddler, very unwittingly forced Luther into the van of the battle, and the ninety-five propositions were posted on the cathedral at Wittemberg.— In 1518, Bernardin Samson, another craftsman in the sorry trade, performed in Switzerland the same kind office for Ulrich Zwingli ; and in 1521, while Luther was marching to the Diet of Worms, Lefevre, in a green old age, and Farel, in a generous youth, proclaimed the new evangel in the streets and temples of one of the cities of France. The city of Meaux was the first to receive the new doctrine, and Briçonnet, its bishop, a sincere protester against error—though not made of the stern stuff which goes to the composition of heroes—published and circulated widely an edition of the four gospels in the French language. So rapid was the spread of the truth, so notable the amendment in morals throughout the provinces which were pervaded by it, so loud were the complaints among the monks and priests of lessened credit and diminished income, that the dignitaries both of Church and State became alarmed and anxious ; and, as the readiest way of putting the testimony to silence, they began to proscribe and imprison the witnesses.

The doctors of the Sorbonne had already declared Luther's doctrine to be blasphemous and insolent, " such as should be answered less by argument than by fire and sword." The parliament, though no friend to monkish rule, could not understand why, when people were satisfied with one form of government, they should want two forms of religion. The court, remembering that the pope had an army at his back which would have astonished St. Peter not a little even in his most martial moments, and wishful to secure the aid of that army in the wars of Italy, favoured the spirit of persecution. Louisa of Savoy, queen-regent in the absence of her son, who was then a prisoner at Madrid, asked the Sorbonne, in 1523, "by what means could the damnable doctrines of Luther be soonest extirpated from the most Christian kingdom ;" and the clergy, not to be outdone in zeal, held councils, at which cardinals and archbishops presided, in which they accused the reformer of "execrable conspiracy," exhorted the king "to crush the viper's doctrines," and proposed to visit yielding heretics with penance and prison, and to hand over obstinate ones to the tender mercies of the public executioner.

This combination of purpose soon resulted in acts of atrocity and blood. The names of Leclerc, Pavanes, and the illustrious Louis de Berquin, deserve to be handed down to posterity as the proto-martyrs of the Reformation in France. In 1535 there was a solemn procession through the streets of Paris. Never had such a pomp of relics been paraded before the awestruck faithful. The veritable head of St. Louis, a bit of the true Cross, one of the nails thereof, the real crown of thorns, and the actual spear-head which had pierced the body of the Saviour—all were exhibited to an innumerable crowd of people, who swarmed upon the housetops, and sat perched upon every available balcony or abutment of stone. The shrine of Ste. Geneviève, the patron saint of Paris, was carried very appropriately by the corporation of butchers, who had prepared themselves for the occasion by a fast of several days' duration. Cardinals and archbishops abounded, until the street was radiant with copes, and robes, and mitres, like a field of the cloth of gold. In the midst of the procession came the king, bareheaded, as became a dutiful son of the Church, and carrying a lighted taper, for the blessed sun was not sufficient, or its light was too pure and kind. High mass was celebrated, and then came the choicest spectacle of the raree-show. Six Lutherans were burned. With their tongues cut out, lest their utterances of dying heroism should palsy the arm of the hangman or affect the convictions of the crowd, a moveable gallows was erected, which alternately rose and fell—now plunging them into the fire, and now withdrawing them for a brief space from the flame, until by the slow torture, they were entirely consumed. Such was the villanous punishment of the estrapade—a refinement of cruelty which Heliogabalus might have envied, and which even the Spanish Inquisition had failed to invent for its Jewish and Saracen martyrdoms. The executions were purposely delayed until Francis was returning to the Louvre. He gazed upon his dying subjects, butchered for no crime, and the eyes of ecclesiastical and courtly tigers in his train glared with gladness at the sight of Lutheran agony.

Shortly after came the yet more horrible butcheries of Mérindole and Cabrières, by which the Vaudois of Provence, a whole race of the most estimable and industrious inhabitants of France, were exterminated because of their religion. Men, women, and children were slain in indiscriminate massacre, some in the frenzy of passion, others, more inexcusably, after a show of trial, and therefore in cold blood. Their cities were razed to the ground, their country turned into a desert, and the murderers went to their work of carnage with the priests' baptism on their swords, and were rewarded for its completion by the prayers and blessings of the clergy.

The usual results of persecution followed. In the fine old classical fable the dragons' teeth were sown in the field, and the startling harvest was a host of armed men. It is a natural tendency of persecution to outwit itself. A voice is hushed for the while, but, eloquent though it may have been in its life, there issues from the sepulchre of the slain witness more audible and influencing oratory. A community is broken up, and companies of worshippers are scattered in many lands of exile; but though there be dispersion of families, unlike the banishment of Babel, there is no confusion of tongues; each in his far-off wandering becomes a centre of truth and blessing, until "their sound has gone forth through all the earth, and their words to the end of the world."

There is something in the inner consciousness of a religious man which assures him that it must be so. You may practise on a corpse without let or hindrance. Wrap it in grave-clothes, it will not complain; perpetrate indignities upon it, it will be sealed in silence; let it down into the cold earth, no rebuke will protest against its burial. But life is a more intractable thing. With a touch of the old Puritan humour, it abides not the imposition of hands; it *will* move at liberty and speak with freedom. Cast among barbarous peoples, when men babble in strange speech around him, the man who has divine life in his soul will somehow make it felt; the joy of his bounding spirit will speak and sparkle through the eye, if it cannot vibrate on the tongue; the new song *will* thrill from the lips, though there be only the echoes to answer it; how much more when there is the neighbourhood of sensitive and impressible men!

Hence you will not wonder that it happened to the Reformed as it happened to the Israelites of old, "the more they were vexed, the more they multiplied and grew." The progress of the Reformation during the closing years of the reign of Francis I., and during that of his son and successor, Henry II., was rapid and continual. Several large provinces declared for the new doctrines ; and " some of the most considerable cities in the kingdom,—Bourges, Orleans, Rouen, Lyons, Bordeaux, Toulouse, Montpellier, and 'the brave' Rochelle,—were peopled with the Reformed." It was calculated that in a few years they amounted to nearly one-sixth of the entire population, and almost all classes ranged beneath the Reformation banner. The provincial nobles were nearly all secretly inclined to it. Merchants who travelled into other countries witnessed the development, under its influence, of industrial progress, and the display of the commercial virtues, and brought home impressions in its favour. The people of the *tiers-état*, who had received a literary education, perceived its intellectual superiority, and on that account were prejudiced to give it welcome. " Especially," says Florimond de Remond, a Roman Catholic writer, with a simplicity that is amusing, but with an ingenuousness that does him credit,—" Especially painters, watchmakers, goldsmiths, image-makers, booksellers, printers, and others, who in their crafts *have any nobleness of mind*, were most easily surprised." There were, indeed, scarcely any classes which collectively adhered to Rome, except the higher ecclesiastics, the nobles of the court, and the fanatic and licentious mob of the good city of Paris. This was the purest and most flourishing era of the Reformation in France. They of the Religion, as they were afterwards called, meddled not with the diplomacy of cabinets, with the intrigues of faction, nor with the feuds of the rival houses of the realm. "Being reviled, they reviled not again ; being persecuted, they threatened not, but committed themselves to Him who judgeth righteously ;" and the record of their constancy and triumph is on high.

The Reformation in France may be considered as having been fully established at the time of the first Synod. This was held at Paris in 1559. From this assembly, to which eleven churches sent deputies, were issued the " Confession of Faith " and the "Articles of Discipline," which, with little alteration, were handed down as the doctrinal and ecclesiastical standards of the Protestants of France.

The reign of Henry II. was mainly distinguishable for the Edict of Chateaubriand, which made heresy a civil as well as an ecclesiastical offence, and for the massacre of the Rue St. Jacques, and the arrest and sentence of the celebrated Anne Dubourg. The martyrdom of this distinguished and pious councillor, which the king's death by the lance of Montgomery did not suspend, inspired many with the persuasion that the faith professed by such a man could not be a bad one, "melted the students of the colleges into tears ;" and more damage accrued to Rome from that solitary martyr-pile than from the labours of a hundred ministers, with all their sermons.

Meanwhile the affairs of the kingdom were daily involved in more embarrassing complications. The new king, Francis II., the husband of the unhappy Mary Stuart, was imbecile in mind, and had a sickly constitution of body. The factions of the realm, which had been partially organized in the preceding reign, practised upon his youth and feebleness, that he might aid them in their struggles for power. There were at this time three notable factions in the field, and it may be well for a moment to suspend our interest in the narrative, that the *dramatis personæ* may appear upon the scene.

The leaders of the various parties were all remarkable men. The real heads of the Catholic party were the two celebrated brothers of the house of Guise. Claude de Lorraine, the ancestor of the family, came to seek his fortune in France "with a staff in his hand, and one servant behind him; but his immediate descendants were all in high places, and wielded, some of them, a more than regal power. Francis, Duke of Guise, the eldest son, was a skilful and high-spirited soldier, whose trusty blade had carved its way to renown in many a well-fought field. He possessed a sort of barbaric generosity, but was irascible, unscrupulous, and cruel. He pretended to no learning save in martial tactics, and held his religion as a sort of profitless entail, which, with his name, he had inherited from his father. "Look," said he to his brother, after the massacre at Vassy, "at the titles of these Huguenot books." "No great harm in that," replied the clerkly cardinal; "that is the Bible." "The Bible!" rejoined the Duke, in extreme surprise; "how can that be? This book was only printed last year, and you say the Bible is fifteen hundred years old." Knowing little, and caring less, about religious controversies, a man of ceaseless energy and ready sword, he was the strong hand which the crafty head of the cardinal wielded at his will.

His brother, Charles de Lorraine, Cardinal and Archbishop of Rheims, of courtly address and pleasing elocution, sagacious in foresight and skilful in intrigue, was the soul of all the projects which, ostensibly for the honour of the Holy Church, were really for the advancement of the fortunes of the house of

Lorraine.   He was a man of no personal valour, but influential enough to make a jest of his own cowardice.   The pope of that time—for, in spite of presumed infallibility, popes and cardinals do not always see eye to eye—was uneasy at his ambition, and was accustomed to call him "the pope on the other side the mountains ;" and, in fact, it was the dream of his restless life to see the crown of France upon his brother's brow, and the tiara of the supreme pontificate encircling his own.

The chiefs of the Politiques, as they were called, the middle party in the state, who counselled mutual concession and forbearance, were the Chancellor l'Hôpital and the Constable de Montmorency.   The chancellor was one of those statesmen of whom France has reason to be proud.   A man of stern integrity, and of high principle, he worked his way through various offices of trust into one of the highest positions in the Parliament of Paris.   As superintendent of the royal finances, by his good management of affairs, and by his inflexible resistance to the rapacity of court favourites, he husbanded the national resources and replenished the exhausted treasury.   Wise in counsel, tolerant in spirit, and with views broader than his age, he was the unfailing advocate of religious freedom.   For his efforts in this behalf he was ultimately deprived of his seals, and ran in danger of being included in the massacre of St. Bartholomew. So great was his peril that the queen-mother sent a troop of horse with express orders to save him.   When they told him that those who made out the list of proscription had forgiven him, "I was not aware," was his sublime reply, "that I had done anything to merit either death or pardon."

The Constable de Montmorency was a rough-hewn, valiant knight, rude in speech and blunt in bearing, of an obstinate disposition and of a small soul. He had two articles in his creed,—the first, that he was the first Christian baron—and the second, that the kings whom he served were Catholics. From these he deduced the very substantial corollary that it was his duty to shew no quarter to heresy, wherever it was found. Hence it is almost wonderful that he should have allied himself with the Moderates in counsel, but the Chatillons, the chief Huguenot family, were his nephews, and he had an old-fashioned loyalty towards the princes of the blood. The Abbé Brantôme has transmitted to us the particulars of his extraordinary piety; he fasted regularly every Friday, and failed not to repeat his *paternosters* every morning and every night. It is said, however, that he occasionally interjected some matters which were not in the Rubric. " Go and hang such a man for me ; tie that other to a tree ; make that one run the gauntlet ; set fire to everything all round for a quarter of a league ;"—and then, with exemplary precision, would begin again just where he had left off, and finish his *aves* and *credos* as if nothing had happened.

The individual whom circumstances rather than merit had thrown into the position of one of the leaders of the Huguenot party, was Antoine de Bourbon, the husband of the heroic Jeanne D'Albert, and, through her, titular King of Navarre. Indolent and vacillating—a mere waif thrown upon the wave— a Calvinist preachment or a Romish auto-da-fè were equally in in his line, and might both rejoice in the honour of his patronising presence. Destitute both of energy and principle, his character shaped itself to the shifting occurrences of each successive day, or to the wayward moods of each successive companion. The purpose of his life, if that may be so called which attained no definiteness and resulted in no action, was to exchange his nominal sovereignty for a real one, over any country and upon any terms. He was one of those whom the words of the poet accurately describe :

> " So fair in show, but, ah ! in act
> So overrun with vermin troubles,
> The coarse, sharp-corner'd ugly Fact
> Of Life collapses all his bubbles ;
> Like a clear fountain, his desire
> Exults and leaps towards the light ;
> In every drop it says ' Aspire,'
> Striving for more ideal height ;
> And as the fountain, falling thence,
> Crawls baffled through the common gutter,
> So, from his bravery's eminence,
> He shrinks into the present tense,
> Unking'd by sensual bread and butter."

To say that he abjured his faith were to do him too much honour. The pope's legate, the cardinals, the princes of Lorraine, and the Spanish ambassador, angled for him as for an enormous gudgeon, and they baited the hook with crowns. Tunis in Africa was suggested as a somewhat desirable sovereignty. Sardinia, which was represented fertile as Arcadia, and wealthy as Aladdin's cave, might be had on easy terms. Nay, Scotland dangled from the glittering line, and the poor befooled hungerer after royalty put up his conscience to perpetual auction, and, like others of such unworthy traffickers, " did not increase his wealth by its price." The Reformation owes nothing to Antoine of Bourbon. By him the selfish and the worldly were introduced into its claims, and, shorn of its spiritual strength, it dwindled in after reigns into a politico-religious partisanship, a menial at the levee of ministers, a sycophant in the audience rooms of kings. Shame on thee, Antoine of Navarre ! renegade and companion of persecutors ! the *likeness* of a kingly crown is decoration enough for a puppet-head like thine. Pass quickly out of sight ! for we are longing to look upon a MAN.

Behold him ! Of ordinary stature, his limbs well proportioned, his countenance tranquil, and with a lambent glory resting on it, as if he had come recently from some Pisgah of divine communion—his voice agreeable and kindly, though, like Moses, slow of speech—his complexion good, betokening purity amid courtly licentiousness, and temperance in an age of excesses —his bearing dignified and graceful—a skilful captain, an illustrious statesman, magnanimous in good fortune, unruffled in disaster—a patriot whom no ingratitude could alienate—a believer whose humble piety probed its own failings to the quick, but flung the mantle of its charity over the errors of others— Behold a MAN ! That is Gaspard de Coligny, Admiral of France, the military hero of the Reformation, whose only faults seem to have been excessive virtues—who was irresolute in battle because too loyal to his king—who was lacking in sagacity because, his own heart all transparent, he could scarcely realise the perfidy of others—Gaspard de Coligny, who lived a saint—Gaspard de Coligny, who died a martyr. France engraves upon her muster-roll of worthies no braver or more stainless name.

Whilst the rival leaders were contending for power, another influence, which all by turns feared and courted, was that of the queen-mother, the many-sided Catharine de Medicis. It is humiliating to our common nature to dwell upon the portraiture which, if history says sooth, must be drawn of this remarkable woman. Her character is a study. Remorseless without cruelty and sensual without passion—a diplomatist without principle and a dreamer without faith—a wife without affection and a mother without feeling—we look in vain for her parallel. She stands "grand and gloomy in the solitude of her own originality." See her in her oratory! Devouter Catholic never told his beads. See her in the cabinet of Ruggieri the astrologer! Never glared fiercer eye into Elfland's glamour and mystery—never were philter and potion (alas! not all for healing) mixed with firmer hand. See her in the council-room! Royal caprice yielded to her commanding will ; soldiers faltered beneath her glance who never cowered from sheen of spears nor blenched at flashing steel ; and hoary headed statesmen, who had made politics their study, confessed that she outmatched them in her cool and crafty wisdom. See her in disaster! More philosophical resignation never mastered suffering; braver heroism never bared its breast to storm. Strange contradictions are presented by her, which the uninitiated cannot possibly unravel. Power was her early and her lifelong idol, but when within her grasp she let it pass away, enamoured rather of the intrigue than of the possession—a mighty huntress, who flung the game in largess to her followers, finding her own royal satisfactions in the excitement of the chase. Of scanty sensibilities, and without natural affection, there were times when she laboured to make young lives happy—episodes in her romantic life during which the woman's nature leaped into the day. Toiling constantly for the advancement of her sons, she shed no tear at their departure, and sat intriguing in her cabinet, while an old blind bishop and two aged domestics were the only mourners who followed her son Francis to the tomb. Sceptical enough to disbelieve in immortality, she was prudent enough to provide, as she imagined, for any contingency ; hence she had her penances to purchase heaven, and her magic to propitiate hell. Queenly in her bearing, she graced the masque or revel, smiling in cosmetics and perfumes—but Vicenza daggers glittered in her boudoir, and she culled, for those who crossed her schemes, flowers of most exquisite fragrance, but their odour was death. Such was Catharine de Medicis, the sceptred sorceress of Italy, for whom there beats no pulse of tenderness, on whom we gaze with a sort of constrained and awful admiration, as upon an embodiment of power,—but power cold, crafty, passionless, cruel—the power of the serpent, which cannot fail to leave impressions on the mind, but impressions of basilisk eye, and iron fang, and deadly gripe, and poisonous trail.

The first false step of the Protestants was the enterprise known as the conspiracy of Amboise. Exasperated by petty persecutions, and goaded by the remembrance of their wrongs, they plotted to expel the Guises from the land, and to restore the real government to the king. Terrible was the vengeance which succeeded. Twelve hundred conspirators were put to death without investigation or trial, until the Loire was choked with the corpses of those who had been flung into its waters to drown. The immediate results of this ill-concerted scheme were to establish the Duke of Guise as lieutenant-general of the kingdom, with a powerful army at his bidding, and to enable the cardinal to fulminate an edict against heresy, by which it might be judged and doomed at an Episcopal tribunal. This roused the Huguenots to passion, and in some parts of the provinces to arms.

Then followed the Fontainebleau assembly, at which, in presence of the king and nobles, Coligny presented the petition of the Reformed, asking for the free performance of Protestant worship. "Your petition bears no signature," said Francis. "True, Sire," was the admiral's reply; "but if you will allow us to meet for the purpose, I will undertake, *in one day*, to obtain fifty thousand signatures in Normandy alone." Such an assertion, from such lips, was no unholy gasconade, but indicated a threatening and deep reality of danger. As the result of the debates which followed, as no one seemed able to grasp the great idea of liberty of conscience, it was agreed that a national council should be summoned to determine upon the religious faith of France. The princes of Lorraine had prepared for this convocation arguments that were somewhat peculiar. One was the assassination of the princes of Bourbon; the other was the banishment of every one who refused to sign a creed of the cardinal's devising—"a creed," says Jean de Serres, "that no man of the religion would have either approved or signed for a thousand lives." The first of these projects failed from some touch of humanness or cowardice which arrested the kingly dagger; the second failed because a pale horse, in the meanwhile, stood before the palace gate, and the rider passed the wardens without challenge and summoned the young king to give account at a higher tribunal. The death of Francis was, in fact, a revolution. For awhile the court became Calvinist, feasting in Mid-Lent upon all the delicacies of the season, making sport of images and indulgences, of the worship of the saints, and of the authority of the pope. Another intrigue, however, restored the Guises to power, and their return was marked by the edict of 1561, which shewed at once the animosity and the caution of the princes of Lorraine. The private worship of the Huguenots was sanctioned, but their public celebrations were forbidden, and they were promised a national council to adjust all differences of religion. This council met in the convent of Poissy, on the 9th of the following September. The boy-king, Charles IX., sat upon the throne. Six cardinals, with him of Lorraine at their head, and doctors, whose name was legion, appeared as the Catholic champions. Twelve ministers and twenty-two deputies from the Calvinistic churches were by and by admitted, rather as culprits than as disputants. The Genevese prized the safety of Calvin so highly that they required securities for his protection, in the absence of which the more courtly and eloquent Beza appeared in his stead. The discussion, like all others, failed utterly of the purpose which it was intended to effect. A dispute arose about the laws of the combat, and about the very issue that was put upon its trial. What were to be the questions of debate? "The whole round of the doctrines," said the Huguenots. "The authority of the Church, and the Real Presence in the sacrament," said the creatures of the cardinal. What was to be the test? "Holy Scripture as interpreted by tradition, and by the Fathers and Councils," said the followers of the Papacy. "Holy Scripture alone," was the sturdy reply of the Reformed. Who are to adjudge the victory? "The civil government," said Beza and his friends. "The Church authorities," was the Romanist rejoinder. Why dispute at all when all the conditions of controversy seem so hopelessly involved? Both parties agree in the answer—"Not to overcome our antagonists, but to encourage our friends." We shall not wonder, after this, that the colloquy at Poissy came to a speedy and resultless conclusion. The Huguenots were at this time estimated by the chancellor to amount to one-fourth of the population, and though such calculations are of necessity uncertain, it is evident that they were no obscure sectaries, but a compact and powerful body, who could demand privilege in worship and redress from wrong. The Guises, however, were incessant in their hostility ; and after the secession of the frivolous Antoine of Navarre, who, with the proverbial animosity of the renegade, was rancorous in his hatred of his former friends, they sought aid for the extirpation of heresy from the forces of Spain. As the Duke of Guise was marching to Paris in support of this enterprise, he heard the bells of the little town of Vassy, in the province of Champagne, summoning the faithful to their prayers. With an oath he exclaimed, "They shall soon Huguenotize in a very different manner," and he ordered them to be attacked. Unarmed as they were, they could only defend themselves with stones. It is said that one of these stones struck the Duke upon the face, and that in his anger he let loose upon them all the fury of his armed retainers. Sixty were left dead upon the spot, and two hundred more were severely, some mortally, wounded. The news of this onslaught was carried speedily to Paris, and the Duke on his entry had a triumphal ovation from the populace, whom the priests had taught to regard him as the Judas Macca-bæus of his country—the heaven-sent and heaven-strengthened defender of their endangered faith. Encouraged by his success he seized upon the persons of the queen-mother and her son, and kept them in strict though gentle captivity. Then the whole land was roused. The butchery of those unarmed worshippers was the red rain which made the battle-harvest grow. Fearfully was the slaughter of those slain witnesses avenged ; for from the massacre at Vassy, and from the seizure of the king, may be dated the commencement of the sad wars of religion ; and of all wars there are none so fierce and so terrible as those of intestine strife, when fanaticism sounds the clarion and nerves the frantic hand—

> " When rival nations, great in arms,
> Great in power, in glory great,
> Rush in ranks at war's alarms,
> And feel a temporary hate ;
> The hostile storms but rage awhile,
> And the tired contest ends ;
> But oh ! how hard to reconcile
> The foes that once were friends."

It is not our province to dwell largely upon the sad period which followed, nor to enter here into the vexed question as to how far the use of the sword is, under any circumstances, defensible for the maintenance of religion. War is a terrible scourge, one of the direst and most appalling of the effects of sin. There is no more Christianity in the consecration of banners than there is in the baptism of bells ? They who battle for the glory of renown, or for the lust of dominion—*sin*. The conqueror, who fights for conquest merely, is but a butcher on a grander scale : and even in the sternest necessity that can compel to arms, so deceitful is the human heart, so easily can it mistake pride for patriotism, and baptize the greed of glory with the inspirations of religion, that we must ever feel that the camp should not be the chosen school for godliness, and that they have deepest need to claim a Saviour's intercession who have to meet their Maker with sword-hilt stained with slaughter, and with the hands, uplifted in the dying litany, all crimsoned with a brother's blood. The sentiments of Agrippa d'Aubigné, a historian of the sixteenth century, (whose name has again become illustrious in the field of historic literature in the person of Dr. Merle d'Aubigné, his lineal descendant,) are worthy of being mentioned here. " It is ever worthy of note that, whenever the Reformed were put to death under the form of justice, however unjust and cruel the proceedings, they presented their necks, and never made use of their hands. But when public authority and the magistrates, tired of kindling the piles, had flung the knife into the hands of the mob, and by the tumults and wholesale massacres of France had deprived justice of her venerable countenance, and neighbour murdered neighbour by sound of trumpet and by beat of drum, who could forbid these unhappy men opposing force to force, and sword to sword, and catching the contagion of a just resentment from a resentment destitute of all justice? Let foreign nations decide which party has the guilt of civil war branded on its forehead."

Both parties asked for aid from other nations in the struggle. Spearmen from Spain, and soldiers from Italy, obeyed the summons of the pontiff to the new crusade ; Germans and English enrolled for the assistance of the Huguenots; and the Swiss, with mercenary impartiality, stood ready for the cause which had the longest purse and readiest pay. Both sides put forth manifestoes, both professed to be moved with zeal for the glory of God, and both swore fealty to their lawful sovereign. At the commencement of hostilities the Huguenots gained some advantages, but they wasted their time in useless negotiation while their adversaries acted with vigour. They laboured, indeed, under the misfortune of being led by the Prince de Condé, who, though a brave soldier, was of the blood-royal of France, and might one day, if he did not commit himself too far, be lieutenant-general of the kingdom. It is a grievous thing, in a struggle for principle, to be cursed with a half-hearted commander. Fancy the sturdy Puritans of our own country led to battle by some gay Duke of Monmouth, instead of "trusting in God, and keeping their powder dry" at the bidding of Ireton and Cromwell!

The death of Antoine of Navarre, who was mortally wounded at the siege of Rouen, the fall of Marshal St. André on the field of Dreux, and the assassination of the Duke of Guise, which to the soured temper of the homicide seemed but a legitimate act of reprisal, were the occasions of that suspension of hostilities which resulted in the hollow treaty of Amboise. It satisfied neither party, and was at best only an armed truce, during which frightful enormities were committed on both sides. War speedily broke out again, and the Catholics triumphed on the plains of St. Denis, though the Constable de Montmorency, the last of the triumvirs, died of a wound which he had received upon the field. Again, during the progress of the conflict, did the Huguenots appear to prevail; but again did the matchless cunning of the queen-mother triumph over the unstable leader, and he signed the peace of Longjumeau, "which," says Mezerai, "left his party at the mercy of their enemies, with no other security than the word of an Italian woman." The treaty never existed save on paper; the foreign mercenaries were still retained in the kingdom; the pulpits resounded with the doctrine that no faith should be kept with heretics; the streets of the cities were strewed with the corpses of the Huguenots, ten thousand of whom, in three months of treaty, were barbarously slain. The officer of the Prince de Condé, while carrying the terms of peace, was arrested and beheaded, in defiance of the king's safe-conduct; and the prince and the admiral, fleeing from an enemy whom no ties could restrain nor oaths could bind, flung themselves into the city of Rochelle. Thither came the heroic Queen of Navarre with an army of four thousand men ; thither flocked also the most renowned captains of the party ; so that, at the commencement of the third war of religion the Huguenots had at command a more considerable force than ever, and Coligny repeated the aphorism of Themistocles— "My friends, we should have perished if we had not been ruined." On the bloody fields of Jarnac and Montcontour, where the Duke of Anjou, afterwards Henry III., won his first spurs of fame, their ruin seemed to be complete, for their army was well nigh exterminated ; and of their leaders, the Prince de Condé and d'Andelot, the brother of Coligny, were slain ; and the admiral himself was carried, weary and wounded, from the field. But nothing could daunt the spirit of this brave soldier, and while the victors were quaffing their nectar of triumph, and carousing in the flush of victory, he appeared before the gates of Paris at the head of a still stronger and better disciplined army. Again peace was concluded, and the Reformed in appearance obtained more favourable terms. The leaders came to Paris, and were received with fair show of amity by the king and court; but it was only a brief interval of repose, soon to be succeeded by dismay and confusion, for even then the dark Italian and the fanatic Spaniard were brooding over the fierce tragedy to follow.

For the honour of humanity let us pass rapidly over the massacre of St. Bartholomew—that premeditated and most infamous atrocity. On the 24th August, 1572, at the noon of night—fit time for deeds of blood—the queen-mother and her two guilty sons were shivering in all the timidness of cruelty in the royal chamber. They maintained a sullen silence, for conscience had made cowards of them all. As they looked out uneasily into the oppressed and solitary night, a pistol shot was heard. Remorse seized upon the irresolute monarch, and he issued orders to arrest the tragedy. It was too late, for the royal tigress at his side, anticipating that his purpose might waver, had already commanded the signal, and even as they spoke the bell of St. Germain aux Auxerrois tolled, heavy and dooming, through the darkness Forth issued the courtly butchers to their work of blood. At the onset the brave old admiral was massacred, and the Huguenots in the Louvre were despatched by halberdiers, with the Court ladies looking on. Armed men, shouting " For God and the king," traversed the streets, and forced the dwellings of the heretics. Sixty thousand assassins, wielding all the weapons of the brigand and the soldier, ran about on all sides, murdering, without distinction of sex or age, or suffering, all of the ill-fated creed ; the air was laden with a tumult of sounds, in which the roar of arquebus and the crash of hatchet mingled with blaspheming taunt and dying groan.

> " For hideously, 'mid rape and sack,
> The murderer's laughter answered back
> His prey's convulsive laughter."

The populace, already inflamed by the sight of blood, followed in the track of slaughter, mutilating the corpses and dragging them through the kennels in derision. The leaders, the Dukes of Guise, Nevers and Montpensier, riding fiercely from street to street, like the demons of the storm, roused the passion into frenzy by their cries—" Kill, kill ! Blood-letting is good in August. By the king's command. Death to the Huguenot ! Kill ! " On sped the murder, until city and palace were gorged.

Men forgot their manhood, and women their tenderness. In worse than Circean transformation, the human was turned into the brutal, and there prowled about the streets a race of ghouls and vampires, consumed with an appetite for blood. The roads were almost impassable from the corpses of men, women, and children—a new and appalling barricade; "The earth was covered thick with other clay, which her own clay did cover." Paris became one vast Red Sea, whose blood-waves had no refluent tide. The sun of that blessed Sabbath shone, with its clear kind light, upon thousands of dishonoured and desolate homes; and the air, which should have been hushed from sound until the psalm of devotion woke it, carried upon its startled billows the yells of blasphemers, flushed and drunk with murder, and the shrieks of parting spirits, like a host of unburied witnesses, crying from beneath the altar unto God, "How long, O Lord, how long!"

The massacre was renewed in the provinces. For seven long days Paris was a scene of pillage. Fifteen thousand in the capital, and one hundred thousand throughout the whole of France, are supposed to have perished, many by the edge of the sword, and many more by the protracted perils of flight and of famine.

Consider all the circumstances of St. Bartholomew's massacre; the confederacy which plotted it in secret; the complicity of the king and court; the snares laid for the feet of the Huguenots; the solemn oaths of safety under whose attestation they were allured to Paris; the kisses by which, like the Redeemer whom they honoured, they were betrayed to ruin; the dagger of wholesale murder, whetted upon the broken tables of the Decalogue, and put by priests and nobles into the hands

of a maddened crowd ; the long continuance of the carnage—
the original as it was of the Reign of Terror ; and, lastly, the
uplifting of red hands in thanksgiving, the ringing of joy-bells
at Madrid and Rome, and the baptism of all this horrible
butchery by the insulted name of religion ;—and we cannot
avoid the conclusion that nothing in the annals of human
history involves such flagrant violations both of earthly and
heavenly law ; that there is a combination of atrocious elements
about it for which we look elsewhere in vain ; and that it stands,
in unapproachable turpitude, the crime without a shadow and
without a parallel.

We dwell upon the wars of religion and the tragedy of St.
Bartholomew, not to keep alive old animosities, but to induce
our thankfulness that we live in kindlier times ; to inspire a
more reverent appreciation of the priceless heritage of religious
freedom ; and, not least, to impress upon our hearts the truth
that banded armies and battle's stern array are no meet mission-
aries of " the truth as it is in Jesus."   Oh, never, we may boldly
say it, never did the cruelties of war, nor the tortures of tyranny
advance one iota the cause of our holy religion. The Crusader's
lance reclaimed no Saracen from his error.   The scimitar of the
Moslem might establish a military domination, but the fear of it
wrought no spiritual change.   Covenanters still gathered in the
dark ravine, and raised the perilous psalm, though the sleuth-
hound tracked them through the wild wood, and some, whom
the soldiers of Claverhouse had slaughtered, were missing from
each successive assembly.   With the torture and the stake in
prospect the coward lip might falter, and the recreant hand might
sign the recantation, but the heart would be Protestant still.
Christianity is a spiritual kingdom, and no carnal weapons

glitter in her armoury. To her zealous but mistaken friends who would do battle for her she addresses the rebuke of her Master, " Put up thy sword into its sheath again, for they that take the sword shall perish with the sword."   A beautiful and healing presence ! she comes to soothe, not to irritate—to unite, not to estrange. Oh, believe me, Christianity forges no fetters for conscience ; she rejoices not, but shudders, at the stream of blood ! While, on the one hand, it were insult to the sincerity of faith to proffer boon in requital for devotion ; on the other, it were felony of the crown-rights of man to " rob even a beggar of a single motive for his worship ;" and that were an unworthy espousal which would wed the destiny of heaven to the intrigues of earth, and " hang the tatters of a political piety upon the cross of an insulted Saviour."

Alas ! that in our fallen nature there should be such a strange disposition to make persecution coeval with power. Calvin raised no voice in the Genevan Council against the sentence which adjudged Servetus to the stake. The fanatic Roundhead, in his day of power, searching the baronial hall for hidden cope and missal, was to the full as brutal and, because he had clearer light, more criminal than was the roystering cavalier. The Pilgrim Fathers, men honoured for conscience' sake now as much as they were despised a century ago, were not long established in their Goshen home, when, unmindful of their own sharp discipline, they drove out the Quakers into the Egypt of the wilderness beyond. The fact is that persecution generates persecution, the lash and fetters debase as well as agonise the races of the captive and the slave.

While, however, we admit this tendency, and watch over its beginnings in ourselves—while we confess that in the sad wars of religion there were Michelades as well as Dragonades, Huguenot reprisals as well as Romanist massacres, we ought not to omit to notice one essential difference which should be ever kept in mind : When Protestants persecute, they persecute of their own " malice aforethought," and in direct opposition to the rescripts of their holy religion—in the other system, persecution is no exotic growth, but springs, indigenous and luxuriant, from the system itself.   Persecution, in the one case, is by Protestants, not of Protestantism ; in the other case, it is not so much by Romanists, as of Popery.   I rejoice to believe that there are multitudes of high-hearted and kindly Roman Catholics who are men, patriots, aye, and Christians too, in spite of their teachings in error.   And I am proud of my country and of my humanity, when, in the breach and in the battle, on the summit of Barossa or in the trenches at Sebastopol, I see nationality triumph over ultramontanism, and the inspiration of patriotism extinguish the narrowness of creed.   But if the spirit of persecution be not in the heart of the Catholic, it is in the *book* of Popery, in the decretal, in the decision of the council, in the fulmination of the Pope.   The Church of Rome can only save her charity at the expense of her consistency.   Let her erase the "Semper Eadem" which flaunts upon her banner. There is an antiquated claim of infallibility put forward on her behalf sometimes, which she had better leave behind her altogether.   But she cannot change.   When she erases penal statutes from her registers, and coercion and treachery from her creed—when we see her tolerant in the countries where she lords it in ascendency, as she would fain have us think her in our own, where, thank God, she yet only struggles for the mastery—when she no longer contemplates aggression—when lady tract distributors are no longer incarcerated, and when Madiais are free—when papal protection comes not in the form of grape-shot over Tahitian women—when metallic arguments are no longer threatened from French corvettes against King George of Tonga—when all these marvels come to pass (and when they do, there is hope of the millennium), then, possibly, we may listen more willingly to the advances of Popery ; but until then, it is the duty of us all, while careful to preserve our own charity—wanting neither gags, nor gibbets, nor penalties, nor prisons, allowing the fullest liberty to hold and to diffuse opinion, robbing of no civil right, and asking for no penal bond —to take our stand, as did our brave and pious fathers, by the altars of our faith, and to cry in the homesteads of our youth, and in the temples of our God, " All kindness to our Romanist fellow-subjects, but a barred door to Popery, and No PEACE WITH ROME."

Horrible as was the massacre of St. Bartholomew, the subsequent celebrations of it were yet more revolting.   Rome and Madrid were intoxicated with joy.   Pope Gregory and his cardinals went to church, amid the jubilee of citizens and the booming of cannon, to render God thanksgiving for the destruction of the Church's enemies.   A medal was struck to commemorate the event to the faithful, and a picture of the massacre embellished the walls of the Vatican.   Protestant Europe was struck with astonishment and horror.   Germany began to hold the name of Frenchmen in abhorrence.   Geneva appointed a day of fasting and prayer, which continues to this day.   Knox, in the Scottish pulpit, denounced vengeance for the deed, with all the boldness of the Hebrew Prophet ; and when the French ambassador made his appearance at the court of Queen Elizabeth, she allowed him to pass without a word of recognition through files of courtiers and ladies clad in the deepest mourning.

Shortly after these events, Charles IX. miserably died; consumed with agonies of remorse, and, whether from corrosive sublimate, or from some new and strange malady, with blood oozing out of every pore of his body. Henry III., his brother and successor, was a strange medley of valour and effeminacy, of superstition and licentiousness. His youth of daring was followed by a voluptuous and feeble manhood. He was crafty, cowardly, and cruel. One of the chief actors in St. Bartholomew's tragedy, he afterwards caused the assassination of his *confrère*, the Duke of Guise, who was poniarded in the royal presence-chamber. When revolt was ripe in his provinces, and treason imperilled his throne, he would break off a council, assembled on gravest matters, that he might sigh over the shipwreck of a cargo of parrots, or deplore in secret the illness of some favourite ape. The Leaguers hated him, and preached openly regicide and rebellion. The Huguenots distrusted him, and Henry of Navarre routed his armies on the field of Coutras. Gifted with high talents, and of kingly presence, he shrank into the shadow of a man—a thing of pomatums and essences— the object of his people's hate and scorn. His reign was a continual succession of intrigue and conspiracy between all the parties in the realm; and, in 1589, he fell by the knife of Jacques Clement, who was canonised by the Pope for the murder; and the Vicar of Christ, seated in full consistory at Rome, dared the blasphemous avowal that the devotion of this assassin formed no unworthy comparison with the sacrifice of the blessed Redeemer.

In Henry III. terminated the "bloody and deceitful" race of Valois, "who did not live out half their days." Francis I. died unregretted; Henry II. was killed by the lance of Montgomery; Francis II. never came of age; Charles IX. expired in fearful torments; Henry III. was murdered by a Dominican friar; the Duke d'Alençon fell a victim to intemperance; Francis and Henry, successive Dukes of Guise, fell beneath the daggers of assassins. The heads of the persecutors came not to the grave in peace. It is not without an intelligible and solemn purpose that retribution should thus have dogged the heels of tyranny. Oh, strange and subtle affinity between crime and punishment! Lacratelle, in his "History of the Wars of Religion," has accumulated the proofs that nearly all the actors in the massacre of St. Bartholomew suffered early and violent deaths. In the earlier persecutions of the Reformed, the clergy instigated the cutting out of the tongues of the victims to stifle their utterances of dying heroism. See the sad example followed by the frantic populace against the clergy two hundred and fifty years afterwards, in the Reign of Terror! In the time of the Cardinal of Lorraine, the Loire was choked with common victims; in the time of Carrier of Nantes, it ran with noble blood! Henry, Duke of Guise, kicked the corpse of Coligny on the day of St. Bartholomew, with the exclamation, "Thou shalt spit no more venom." Sixteen years passed over, and the monarch of France, spurning the slain body of this very Duke of Guise, exclaimed, "Now, at length, I am king." Charles IX., in the frenzy of cowardice, or in the contagion of slaughter, pointed an arquebus at the flying Huguenots; two hundred years after, Mirabeau brought from the dust of ages that same arquebus, and pointed it at the throne of Louis XVI. Beza spoke truly when he said, "The Church is an anvil upon which many a hammer has been broken." "Verily there is a God that judgeth in the earth," and though "the heathen have raged, and the kings of the earth taken counsel together against the Lord, and against His anointed," drifted corpses on the Red Sea shore, Babylon's monarch slain in his own palace, scattered vessels of a proud Armada, wise men taken in their own craftiness, the downfall of a fierce oppressor, the crash of a desolated throne,—all these have proved that " He that sitteth in the heavens doth laugh, the Lord doth have them in derision."   The bush in the wilderness has been often set on fire, flames have been kindled on it by countless torches, flaring in incendiary hands ; but the torches have gone out in darkness, the incendiaries have perished miserably, and

> " The bush itself has mounted higher,
> And flourish'd, unconsumed, in fire."

Henry of Navarre succeeded to the throne, but found himself in the peculiar position of a king who had to conquer his kingdom.   The Leaguers refused allegiance, and set up as king the old Cardinal of Bourbon, under the name of Charles X.   The Duke of Mayenne had convened the states-general in Paris, and was ready to be the Catholic champion, and many of the nobles attached to the party of the court refused to march under a Huguenot leader.   The Protestant captains remained faithful and were less exacting.   The chief of them, the Duke de Bouillon, de Chatillon, the son of Coligny, Agrippa d'Aubigné, Lanoue, the illustrious Duplessis Mornay, and the still more illustrious Baron de Rosny, afterwards Duke of Sully, rallied round him and inspirited his small army of seven thousand men.   At the head of this army, scanty in numbers but sturdy in valour, and having the new obligation of loyalty added to the old obligation of religion, Henry joined battle with his adversaries, and triumphed both at Arques and on the memorable field of Ivry. A few days before the latter battle, Schomberg, general of the German auxiliaries, demanded the arrears of payment for his soldiers. The finances fell short, and the matter was reported to the king. In the first moment of impatience he said, " They are no true men who ask for money on the eve of a battle." Repenting of his ill-judged rebuke, he hastened, before he went into action, to offer reparation. " General," said he, in the presence and hearing of his troops, " I have offended you ; this battle will perhaps be the last of my life. I know your merit and your valour ; I pray you pardon and embrace me." Schomberg replied, " It is true, Sire, that your Majesty wounded me the other day ; but to-day you have killed me, for I shall feel proud to die on this occasion in your service." In the hour of danger Henry called to mind the instructions of his pious mother. Raising his eyes to heaven, he invoked God to witness the justice of his cause. " But, Lord," said he, " if it has pleased Thee to ordain otherwise, or if Thou seest that I shall be one of those kings whom Thou givest in thine anger, take from me my life and crown together, and may my blood be the last that shall be shed in this quarrel." Then riding through the ranks cheerful as a lover speeding to his bridal, he thus addressed his soldiers : " You are Frenchmen, I am your king, and yonder is the enemy." Pointing to a white plume which he had fastened in his helmet, " My children," he said, " look well to your ranks. If the standards fall, rally round my white plume, it will shew you the short road to glory." Animated by strains like these, the soldiers fought like heroes, the Leaguers were utterly routed, and the French historians say that this single field of Ivry has

covered Henry of Navarre with a wreath of immortal fame. It
has indeed immortalized him, though in a manner on which
they would hardly calculate, for it has throned his memory in
the stanzas of Macaulay's undying song:

> " Oh, how our hearts were beating when, at the dawn of day,
> We saw the army of the League drawn out in long array;
> With all its priest-led citizens, and all its rebel peers,
> And Appenzel's stout infantry, and Egmont's Flemish spears.
> There rode the brood of false Lorraine, the curses of our land;
> And dark Mayenne was in the midst, a truncheon in his hand:
> And, as we looked on them, we thought of Seine's empurpled flood,
> And good Coligny's hoary hair all dabbled with his blood;
> And we cried unto the living God, who rules the fate of war,
> To fight for His own holy name, and Henry of Navarre.
>
> The King has come to marshal us, all in his armour drest,
> And he has bound a snow-white plume upon his gallant crest.
> He looked upon his people, and a tear was in his eye;
> He looked upon the traitors, and his glance was stern and high.
> Right graciously he smiled on us, as rolled from wing to wing
> Down all our line a deafening shout, 'God save our lord the King.'
> 'And if my standard-bearer fall, as fall full well he may,
> For never saw I promise yet of such a bloody fray;
> Press where ye see my white plume shine amid the ranks of war,
> And be your oriflamme to-day the helmet of Navarre.'
>
>   *   *   *   *   *   *
>
> A thousand spurs are striking deep, a thousand spears in rest,
> A thousand knights are pressing close behind the snow-white crest;
> And in they burst, and on they rushed, while, like a guiding star,
> Amidst the thickest carnage blazed the helmet of Navarre.
> Now, God be praised, the day is ours. Mayenne hath turn'd his rein,
> D'Aumale hath cried for quarter. The Flemish count is slain.
> Their ranks are breaking like thin clouds before a Biscay gale;
> The field is heaped with bleeding steeds, and flags, and cloven mail.

*　　*　　*　　*　　*　　*

But we of the religion have borne us best in fight,
And the good Lord of Rosny hath ta'en the cornet white.
Our own true Maximilian the cornet white hath ta'en,
The cornet white with crosses black, the flag of false Lorraine.
Up with it high; unfurl it wide; that all the host may know
How God hath humbled the proud house which wrought his Church such
　　woe;
Then on the ground, while trumpets sound their loudest point of war,
Fling the red shreds—a foot-cloth meet for Henry of Navarre.

"Ho! maidens of Vienna; Ho! matrons of Lucerne;
Weep, weep, and rend your hair for those who never shall return.
Ho! Philip send, for charity, thy Mexican pistoles,
That Antwerp monks may sing a mass for thy poor spearmen's souls.
Ho! gallant nobles of the League, look that your arms be bright;
Ho! burghers of Saint Genevieve, keep watch and ward to-night:
For our God hath crush'd the tyrant, our God hath raised the slave,
And mocked the counsel of the wise and valour of the brave.
Then glory to His holy name, from whom all glories are,
And glory to our sovereign lord, King Henry of Navarre!"

After this spirit-stirring eulogy it may seem rather an anti-climax to question whether the cause of the Huguenots has in the long run been furthered or damaged by the patronage of Henry of Navarre. Indeed, it was in many respects a grievous misfortune to the interests of Protestantism in France that it was allied for so many years to the fortunes of the house of Bourbon. It was deserted and betrayed by them all. Anthony of Navarre forsook it in hope of a sovereignty; his brother, Louis of Condé, for the chance of becoming lieutenant-general; the younger Condé, to save his life on St. Bartholomew; Henry IV., not content with one apostasy, was recreant twice, first for the preservation of his life, and then for the preservation of his crown ; and the three following Bourbons "persecuted this way unto the death." Surely, if they of the Reformed had been docile scholars, apt to learn the lessons of experience and wisdom, they would have profited earlier by the admonition "Put not your trust in princes, nor in the son of man, in whom there is no help." The abjuration of Protestantism by Henry IV. has found some earnest and zealous defenders. It is said that by adhering to the Reformed Church he would have prolonged war, dismembered France, been a king without a crown and without a kingdom, abdicated in favour of the Guise, and delivered up the defenceless Huguenots to the blind fury of the Leaguers and their party. On the other hand, by returning to the Romish communion he restored peace, secured toleration, established an empire, and transmitted a dynasty. With what reason, say they, in the prospect of such consequences, could he persist in the maintenance of a creed to which he had only given, at any time, a traditional and thoughtless adhesion ? Such apologists are worse than any accusers. Henry of Navarre, with all his faults, was a truer man than these defenders make him. He was no hypocrite when he led his gallant troops at Coutras and at Ivry ; and to suppose that for long years he conducted one of the deadliest civil wars which France has ever known without one honest enthusiasm, is to fasten upon him the brand of a colossal blood-guiltiness for which history would scarcely find a parallel. Some ascribe his apostasy to a humane and politic foresight ; others, quite as plausibly, to the absence of commanding principle, the power of seductive influences, and a weakness for sensual pleasure. But whether prompted by godless expediency or by fatal flexibility to the influences of evil, it was a great sin.   It deserves sharp and stern reprobation. Taking the best view of it, it exalted human sagacity above God's great laws of truth and right, which cannot be violated with impunity.   Taking the worst view of it, it was an impious blasphemy against all sacred things,—in the strong, but just words of a modern French historian, " a lie from beginning to end."   But honesty is the best policy as well as the noblest practice; and it may be questioned fairly whether the abjuration was not, *à la* Talleyrand, " worse than a crime—a blunder;" whether the political results of it were not fraught as much with mischief as with blessing. It conciliated the Catholics, but by presenting religion as a profession which might be changed like a garment, it tended to sap the foundations of all piety, and prepared the way for those godless philosophising ideas which cursed the France of the future with infidelity.   It gave the Huguenots a comparative and mistrusted toleration, but it robbed them of their severer virtues, and imperilled their consistency by the contagion of its example. It secured to himself a reign of seventeen years, but they were years of vice and error, abruptly terminated by the assassin's dagger. It rescued France from the rivalry of a disputed succession, but it entailed upon her two centuries of misrule and despotism. It transmitted the crown to seven of his posterity in succession; but one was a monkish hypochondriac, one has left an infamous name, three were deposed by their tumultuous subjects, and one perished on the scaffold.   Louis XIV. seems to be the only exception to the fatality which, like a weird spirit of disaster, waited upon the house of Bourbon, and even he—a despot and a debauchee, a prodigal and a persecutor—entailed ruin, if he did not suffer it, upon his name and race. So true are the maxims of the Holy Book : " A lying tongue is but for a moment, but the lip of truth shall be established for ever." "The righteous shall be in everlasting remembrance, but the memory of the wicked shall rot."

We have said there was in the character of Henry of Navarre a fatal flexibility to evil influences, and we are inclined to think that if we regard him as too indolent to rebel against the pressure of present advisers, constant only in fickleness, we shall explain many of the seeming inconsistencies of his conduct and of his reign. He seems to have had, mingled with the bravery and intellect which he undoubtedly possessed, a marvellous ductility, which yielded to well nigh every touch of interest or passion. He never seems to have said " No," to any one. " My son," said Jeanne d'Albret, " swear fealty to the cause of the Reformed." The oath was taken. " My brother," said Charles IX., " don't bury yourself in the country, come to court." Henry came. "Don't you think you had better marry Marguerite of Valois ?" No objections. " The mass or the massacre," thundered out the assassins on the day of St. Bartholomew. " Oh, the mass, by all means." " Follow after pleasure," whispered Catharine de Medicis ; " kings and princes are absolved from too strict adhesion to the marriage vow." Henry too readily obeyed. " Let us form an alliance," said Henry of Valois, although he had told the States at Blois that they were not to believe him, even if he promised with most sacred oaths that he would spare the heretics. " With all my heart," was the reply of Navarre. " Become Catholic," shouted the nobles of the court, " and we will swear allegiance." " Wait a bit," was the answer of the king. " Abjure," was the soft whisper of the all powerful Gabrielle d'Estrées ; " the pope can annul your marriage, and then ours shall be love and gladness." Henry abjured. "Sire, we look to you for protection," respectfully said the Reformed. "Oh, of course; only if I should seem to favour the Catholics, remember the fatted calf was killed for the prodigal, and you are the elder son." "Sire, don't you think it is rather hard upon the Jesuits that they should be banished from France? May they not come back again?" "Oh, certainly, if they wish it;" and they came—and among them Ravaillac the assassin. Throughout the whole of his life there is scarcely a recorded instance of his maintenance of an individual opinion, or of his assertion of a commanding will. Oh, these men who cannot say "No;" what mischief they have wrought in this world! Their history would be a sad one if we could only trace it. Advantages thrown away, opportunities of golden promise slipping by unheeded, fortune squandered, friends neglected; one man drawn into difficult controversy, another involved in ruinous speculation, a third wallowing in the mire of intemperance, a fourth dragged into the foul hell of a gaming-house. Gambling, drunkenness, felony, beggary, ruin both to body and soul, all because men could not say "No."

Believe me, he who can say "No," when to say it is to speak to his own hurt, has achieved a conquest greater far than he that taketh a city. Let me exhort you to cultivate this talent for yourselves. You need not mistake sauciness for strength, and be rude, and brusque, and self-opinionated in your independence. That extreme were as uncomely as the other. But let it be ours to be self-reliant amid hosts of the vacillating—real in a generation of triflers—true amongst a multitude of shams; when tempted to swerve from principle, sturdy as an oak in its maintenance; when solicited by the enticements of sinners, firm

as a rock in our denial. I trust that yours may never be the
character which, that you may be the more impressed by it, I
give you in the poet's pleasant verse :

    " ' He had faults, perhaps had many,
       But one fault above them all
    Lay like heavy lead upon him,
       Tyrant of a patient thrall.
    Tyrant seen, confess'd, and hated,
       Banish'd only to recall.'

    " ' Oh ! he drank ?'   'His drink was water !
      'Gambled ?'   ' No ! he hated play.'
    ' Then perchance, a tenderer feeling
      Led his heart and head astray ? '
    ' No ! both honour and religion
      Kept him in the purer way.'

    " ' Then he scorned life's mathematics,
      Could not reckon up a score,
    Pay his debts, or be persuaded
      Two and two were always four ? '
    ' No ! he was exact as Euclid,
      Prompt and punctual—no one more.'

    " ' Oh ! a miser ? ' ' No.' ' Too lavish ? '
      ' Worst of guessers, guess again.'
    ' No ! I'm weary hunting failures.
      Was he seen of mortal ken ?
    Paragon of marble virtues,
      Quite a model man of men ! '

    " ' At his birth an evil spirit
      Charms and spells around him flung,
    And with well concocted malice,

Laid a curse upon his tongue ;
Curse that daily made him wretched
Earth's most wretched sons among.

" ' He could plead, expound, and argue,
Fire with wit, with wisdom glow ;
But one word for ever failed him,
Source of all his pain and woe:
Luckless man ! he could not say it,
Could not, dare not, answer—No !' "

The sole result of advantage immediately flowing from the kings's apostacy, was the power which it gave him to promulgate the celebrated Edict of Nantes, the great charter of the French Reformation. In the preamble it was acknowledged that God was adored by all the French people, with unity of intention though in variety of form ; and it was then declared to be a perpetual and irrevocable law—the main foundation of union and tranquillity in the state. The concessions granted by it were,—1. Full liberty of conscience (in private) to all; 2. The public celebration of worship in places where it was established at the time of the passing of the Edict, and in the suburbs of cities ; 3. That superior lords might hold assemblies within the precincts of their chateaux, and that gentlemen of lower degree might admit visitors to the number of thirty to their domestic worship ; 4. That Protestantism should be no bar to offices of public trust, nor to participation in the benefactions of charity , 5. That they should have chartered academies for the education of their youth ; 6. That they might convene and hold national synods ; and 7. That they should be allowed a certain number of cautionary towns, fortified and garrisoned to secure against infractions of the covenant. This Edict, though as it appears to us recognising an *imperium in imperio*, and as such giving freedom but in grudging measure, was for eighty-seven years the rule of right, if not the bulwark of defence, for the Protestants of France. Those years, after all, were years of distrust and suspicion, of encroachment on the one hand and of resistance on the other. The fall of Rochelle, and the edict of pardon in 1629, definitively terminated the religious wars of France, and the Protestants, excluded from court employment and from the civil service, lost their temptations to luxury and idleness, and became the industrial sinews of the state. They farmed the fine land of the Cevennes and the vineyards of Berri. The wine-trade of Guienne, the cloths of Caen, the maritime trade on the seaboard of Normandy, the manufactures in the north-western provinces, the silks and taffetas of Lyons, and many others which time would fail us to mention, were almost entirely in their hands; and, by the testimony of their enemies, they combined the highest citizenship with the highest piety, industry, frugality, integrity—all the commercial virtues hallowed by unbending conscientiousness, earnest love of religion, and a continual fear of God.

The Edict of Nantes was revoked on the 22d October, 1685. The principal causes which led to this suicidal stroke of policy were the purchased conversions and the Dragonades. Louis XIV. had a secret fund which he devoted to the conversion o his Protestant subjects. The average price for a convert was about six livres per head, and the abjuration and the receipt, twin vouchers for the money, were submitted to the king together. The management of this fund was entrusted to Pelisson, originally a Huguenot, but who became a convert to amend his fortunes, and a converter to advance them. The establishment was conducted upon strictly commercial principles. It had its branches, correspondents, letters of credit, lists of prices current, and so forth, like any other mercantile concern. There is extant a curious letter, perhaps we should say circular, of Pelisson's, which shews that, amid all his zeal, he had a keen eye for business, and was not disposed to be imprudent in his speculations with the consciences of others. "Although," he says, "you may go as far as a hundred francs, it is not meant that you are always to go to that extent, as it is necessary to use the utmost possible economy; in the first place, to shed this dew (O blessed baptismal dew !) upon as many as possible ; and besides, if we give a hundred francs to people of no consequence, without any family to follow them, those who are a little above them, or who bring a number of children after them, will demand far larger sums." Pelisson's success was so great that Louvois was stimulated with the like holy ambition, only his converting agency was not a charge of money, but a charge of dragoons. Troops were quartered upon Huguenot families, and the soldiers were allowed every possible license of brutality, short only of rape and murder. All kinds of threat and indignity were practised to induce the Protestants to abjure ; the ingenuity of the soldiers was taxed to devise tortures that were agonising without being mortal. Whole provinces were reported as being converted. One of the agents in the Cevennes wrote to the Chancellor thus: "The number of Protestants in this province is 240,000. I asked until the 25th of next month for their entire conversion, but I fixed too distant a date, for I believe that at the end of this month all will be done." No day passed without bringing to the king the news of thousands of conversions; the court affected to believed that Protestantism in France was at an end, and the king, willingly deluded, no longer hesitated to strike the last blow. On 22d October 1685, he signed the revocation of the Edict of Nantes. The following were the chief provisions : The abolition of Protestant worship throughout the land, under penalty of arrest of body and confiscation of goods. Ministers were to quit the kingdom in a fortnight, but if they would be converted they might remain and have an advance of salary. Protestants schools were closed, and all children born after the passing of the law were to be baptized by the priests, and brought up in the communion of Rome. All refugees were to return to France in four months, and to abjure, otherwise their property was declared confiscate, under pain of the galleys for men, and imprisonment for women. Protestants were forbidden to quit the kingdom, and to carry their fortunes abroad. All the strict laws concerning relapsing heretics were confirmed; and finally, those Protestants who had not changed their religion might remain in France *until it should please God to enlighten them.*" This last sentence sounds bravely pious and liberal, and many of the Protestants began to rejoice that at least private liberty of conscience remained to them ; but they soon found that the interpretation of it was, " until the dragoons should convert them as they had converted whole provinces before." The provisions of the edict were carried out with inflexible rigour. The pastors were driven into immediate banishment, the laity were forbidden to follow them; but in spite of prohibitions and perils, in the face of the attainder and of the galleys, there were few abjurations and many refugees. Some crossed the frontier sword in hand, others bribed the guards, and assumed all sorts of disguises ; ladies of quality might be seen crawling many weary leagues to escape at once from their persecutors and their country. Some put out to sea in frail and open boats, preferring the cruel chances of wind and wave to the more cruel certainty of their fierce human oppressors ; and fair women, who had lived all their lives in affluence, and whose cheeks the air of heaven had never visited too roughly, fled without food or store, save a little brackish water, or gathered snow by the road-side, with which the mothers moistened the parched lips of their babes. Protestant countries received the refugees with open arms. England, America, Germany, Switzerland, Denmark, Sweden, Russia, Prussia, Holland—all profited by this wholesale proscription of Frenchmen. It is difficult to estimate the numbers who escaped. Vauban wrote, a year after the Revocation, that France had lost 100,000 inhabitants, 60,000,000 of francs in specie, 9000 sailors, 12,000 veterans, 600 officers, and her most flourishing branches of manufacture and trade. Sismondi considers the loss to have exceeded 300,000 men; and Capefigue, the latest writer on the subject, and an adversary to the Protestant cause, reports that at least 225,000 quitted the kingdom. But all are agreed that the refugees were among the bravest, the most loyal, and the most industrious in the kingdom, and that they carried with them the arts by which they had enriched their country, and abundantly repaid the hospitality which afforded them in other lands that asylum which was denied them in their own.

So early as the latter half of the sixteenth century thousands of French fugitives had taken refuge in England from the persecutions which followed the massacre of St. Bartholomew. The first French church in London was established in 1550, and owed its origin to the piety of King Edward VI., and to the powerful protection of Somerset and Cranmer. Churches were subsequently founded, by successive emigrations, in Canterbury, Sandwich, Norwich, Southampton, Glastonbury, Dover, and several other towns ; so that at the period when the Edict of Nantes was revoked, there were centres of unity around which the persecuted ones might rally. It is estimated that nearly eighty thousand established themselves in this country during the ten years which preceded or followed the Revocation. About one-third of them settled in London, especially in the districts of Long Acre, Seven Dials, and Spitalfields. Scotland and Ireland received their share of refugees. The quarter in Edinburgh long known as Picardy, and French Church Street in Cork, are attestations of their presence there. The French Protestants were very efficient supporters of William of Orange in those struggles for principle which drove the last of the Stuarts from the throne. The revolution in England was effected without bloodshed ; but in Ireland numbers of the refugees rallied round the Protestant standard. A refugee, de la Melonière, was brigadier at the siege of Carrickfergus ; a refugee, Marshal Schomberg, led the troops at the Battle of the Boyne ; and when William was established in London, and, breaking off diplomatic relations, enjoined the French ambassador to quit within twenty-four hours, by one of those caprices which are strangely like retribution, a refugee, de l'Estang, was sent to notify his dismissal ; and a refugee, St. Leger, received orders to escort him safely to Dover.

The influence which the refugees exerted upon the trade and manufactures of the country was more widespread and more lasting. The commercial classes of England ought, of all others, to feel grateful to the Protestants of France ; for the different branches of manufacture which were introduced by them have mainly contributed to make our "merchant princes, and our traffickers the honourable of the earth." They established a factory in Spitalfields, where silks were woven on looms copied from those of Lyons and of Tours; they taught the English to make "brocades, satins, paduasoys, velvets, and stuffs of mingled silk and cotton." They introduced also the manufacture of fine linen, of Caudebec hats, of printed calicoes, of Gobelin tapestry, of sailcloth, and of paper. Most of these things had previously been obtained only by importation; where native manufactories were at work they produced articles of coarser material and of less elegant design. It has been ascertained, by calculation, that the manufactures introduced into this country by these same despised Huguenot traders deprived France of an annual return of £1,800,000. There is an old proverb, "Whom the gods would destroy they first madden;" and certainly the revocation of the Edict of Nantes was not only an atrocious wickedness, but an act of unparalleled folly.

Many of the refugees and their descendants attained honourable positions, and well served the country of their adoption in art, and science, and statesmanship, and jurisprudence, and literature, and arms. Thomas Savery, a refugee, was the inventor of a machine for draining marshes, and obtained a patent for it so long ago as 1698. Dennis Papin, a refugee, realised, a century before Watt watched the tea-kettle, the great idea of steam power, and had a notion, which they called "a pretension" then, of navigating vessels without oars or sails. Saurin burst into the reputation of his eloquence at the Hague; but at the old French church in Threadneedle Street he "preened his wings of fire." Abbadie discoursed with mild and earnest persuasion in the church at Savoy, and then wrote, with ability and effect, from the deanery of Killaloe. The first literary newspaper in Ireland was published by the pastor Droz, a refugee, who founded a library on College Green, in Dublin. The physician Desagulièrs, the disciple and friend of Newton; Thelluson (Lord Rendlesham), a brave soldier in the Peninsular War, more distinguished than notorious; Thelluson, the million-aire, the eccentric will-maker, more notorious than distinguished; General Ligonier, who commanded the English army at the battle of Lawfield; General Prevost, who distinguished himself in the American War; General de Blaquière, a man of high personal valour and military skill; Labouchère, formerly in the cabinet; Lord Eversley, who, as Mr. Shaw Lefèvre, was Speaker of the House of Commons; Sir John Romilly, the present Master of the Rolls; Sir Samuel Romilly, his humane and accomplished father; Majendie, some time Bishop of Chester; Saurin, once Attorney-General for Ireland; Austen Henry Layard, the excavator of Nineveh,—all these, it is said, are descendants of the families of the French refugees.

The descendants of the Hugenots long remained as a distinct people, preserving a nationality of their own, and entertaining hopes of return, under more favourable auspices, to their beloved fatherland. In the lapse of years these hopes grew gradually fainter, and both habit and interest drew them closer to the country of their shelter and of their adoption. The fierce wars of the Republic, the crash of the first Revolution, and the threatened invasion of England by the first Napoleon, severed the last ties which bound them to their own land, and, their affinities and sympathies being for the most part English, there was an almost absolute fusion both of race and name.

One hardly knows, indeed, where to look for a genuine Saxon now, for the refugee blood circulates beneath many a sturdy patronymic whose original wearer one might have sworn had lived in the Heptarchy, or trod the beechen glade in the time of Eanwolf and Athelstan. Who would suppose for a moment that there can lurk anything Norman in the colourless names of White and Black, or in the authoritative names of King and Masters, or in the juvenile name of Young, or in the stave-and barrel-suggesting appellation of Cooper, or in the light and airy denomination of Bird? Yet history tells us that these are the names now borne by those who at the close of the last century rejoiced in the designations of Leblanc, Lenoir, Loiseau, Lejeunes, Le Tonnellier, Lemaitre, Leroy. The fact was, that when Napoleon threatened to invade England, to which they owed so much, they felt ashamed of being Frenchmen, and translated their names into good sturdy Saxon. Thus did these noble men—faithful witnesses for God, brave upholders of the supremacy of conscience—enrich the revenues and vindicate the liberty of the land which had furnished them a home; and then, as the last tribute of their gratitude, they merged their nationality in ours, and became one with us in feeling, in language, in religion.

Protestantism in France—oppressed by many restrictions, suffering equally under a parricidal republic and under a "paternal despotism"—yet lives and struggles on. Though small in its numerical extent, it does no unworthy work; though unostentatious in its simple worship, it yet bears no inglorious witness against apostasy and sin. There is hope for the future of France—hope in the dim streaks of the morning, that the day will come—hope in the hoariness of Popery, for it is dismally stricken in years—hope in the inability of scepticism and philosophy, falsely so called, to fill a national heart, around which an unsatisfied desire keeps for ever moaning like the wind around a ruined cairn—hope, above all, in the unexhausted power of that Divine Word which, when it has free course, *will* be glorified ; and in the sure promise, faithful amid all change, that "the kingdoms of this world shall become the kingdoms of our God and His Christ, and He shall reign for ever."

And England, what of her ? The dear old land, rich in ancestral memory, and radiant with a younger hope ; the Elim of palms and fountains in the exile's wilderness—whose soil the glad slave blesses as he leaps on her shores a freeman : England —standing like a rock in mid-ocean, and when the tempest howls elsewhere, receiving only the spent spray of the revolutionary wave ; or as the Ark in the Deluge, the only mission of the frantic waters being to bear it safely to the Ararat of rest ; England—great by her gospel heritage, powerful by her Protestant privileges, free by her forefathers' martyrdoms! What of her ? Is she to be faithful or traitorous, gifted with increasing prosperity—or shorn of her strength, and hasting to decay? The nations of old have successively flourished and faded. Babylon and Carthage, Macedon and Persia, Greece and Rome —all in their turn have yielded to the law of decline. Is it of necessity uniform? Must we shrivel into inanition while "westward the course of empire takes its way?" I may be sanguine, that is an error of enthusiasm ! I may be proud of my birthland, of all pride that is the least unholy—but both the patriot's impulse and the seer's inspiration prompt the answer, No—a thousand times No !—if only there be fidelity to principle, to truth, to God. Not in the national characteristics of reverence and hope—reverence for the struggling past, hope in the beautiful future; not in the absence of class antagonisms, or in the fine community of interest in all things sacred and free; not in the true practicalness of the British mind, doing, not dreaming, ever; not in any or all of these, valuable and influential as they unquestionably are, put we our trust for the bright destiny of England. Her history has facts on record which we would do well to ponder. "*One uniform connection,*" as Dr. Croly has accurately shewn, "*between Romish ascendency and national disaster—between Romish discountenance and national renown.*" To the question of Voltaire then, "Why has England so long and so successfully maintained her free institutions?" I would not answer, with Sir James Stephen, "because England is still German," though that may be a very substantial political reason; but rather "because England is still Protestant, with a glad gospel, a pure altar, an unsealed, entire, wide open Bible." Let her keep her fidelity and she will keep her position, and there need be no bounds to the sacred magnificence of her preservation. For nations, as for individuals, that which is right is safe. A godless expediency or an unworthy compromise are sure avenues to national decline. Oh, if we would retain that influence which, as a nation, we hold in stewardship from God, there must be no adulterous alliances between Truth and Error, no conciliations at the expense of principle, and an utter abhorrence, alike by church and cabinet and crown, of that corrupt maxim of a corrupt creed, that it is lawful "to do evil that good may come."

> "Do ill that good may come, so Satan spake.
> Woe to the land deluded by that lie;

> Woe to its rulers, for whose evil sake
>   The curse of God may now be hovering nigh :
> Up, England, and avert it ! boldly break
>   The spells of sorceress Rome, and cast away
> Godless expedience. Say, is it wise,
>   Or right, or safe, for some chance gains to-day,
> To dare the vengeance from to-morrow's skies ?
>   Be wiser, thou dear land, my native home,
> Do always good—do good that good may come.
>   The path of duty plain before thee lies,
>   Break, break the spells of the enchantress Rome."

And now, at the close, let me repeat the sentiment advanced at the beginning. God is working in the world, and therefore there shall be progress for ever. God's purpose doth not languish. Through a past of disaster and struggle, " Truth for ever on the scaffold, Wrong for ever on the throne," through centuries of persecution, with oppressors proud and with confessors faithless, amid multitudes apostate and shame-hearted, with only here and there an Abdiel, brave, but single-handed— God has been always working, evolving, in His quiet power, from the seeming the real, from the false the true. Not for nothing blazed the martyrs' fires—not for nothing toiled brave sufferers up successive hills of shame. God's purpose doth not languish. The torture and trial of the past have been the stern ploughers in His service, who never suspended their husbandry, and who have " made long their furrows." Into those furrows the imperishable seed hath fallen. The heedless world hath trodden it in, tears and blood have watered it, the patient sun hath warmed and cheered it to its ripening, and it shall be ready soon. " Say not ye, there are yet four months and then cometh harvest ! Lift up your eyes," and yonder, upon the crest of the mountain, the lone watcher, the prophet with the shining forehead, looking out upon God's acres, announces to the waiting people—" The fields are white unto the harvest; thrust in the sickle, for the harvest is ripe." But the Lord wants reapers. Who of you will go out, sickle in hand, to meet Him? The harvest is ripe ; shall it droop in heavy and neglected masses for want of reapers to gather it in? To you, the young, in your enthusiasm—to you, the aged, in your wisdom—to you, men of enterprise and ardour—to you, heirs of the rarest endurance, and affection of womanhood—to you, the rich in the grandeur of your equalising charity— to you, the poor, in the majesty of your ungrudging labour, the Master comes and speaks. Does not the whisper thrill you? "Why stand ye here all the day idle?" Up, there's work for you all —work for the lords of broad acres, work for the kings of two hands. Ye are born, all of you, to a royal birthright. Scorn not the poor, thou wealthy—his toil is nobler than thy luxury. Fret not at the rich, thou poor—his beneficence is comelier than thy murmuring. Join hands, both of you, rich and poor together, as ye toil in the brotherhood of God's great harvest-field—heirs of a double heritage—thou poor, of thy kingly labour—thou rich, of thy queenly charity—and let heaven bear witness to the bridal.

> The rich man's son inherits lands,
> And piles of brick, and stone, and gold,
> And he inherits soft white hands,
> And tender flesh that fears the cold,
> Nor dares to wear a garment old :
> A heritage, it seems to me,
> One scarce would wish to hold in fee.

The rich man's son inherits cares,—
The bank may break, the factory burn,
  A breath may burst his bubble shares ,
And soft white hands could hardly earn
A living that would serve his turn :
A heritage, it seems to me,
One scarce would wish to hold in fee.

  What doth the poor man's son inherit ?
Stout muscles and a sinewy heart,
  A hardy frame, a hardier spirit ;
King of two hands, he does his part
In every useful toil and art :
A heritage, it seems to me,
A king might wish to hold in fee.

  What doth the poor man's son inherit ?
A patience learn'd of being poor,
  Courage, if sorrow comes, to bear it,
A fellow-feeling that is sure
To make the outcast bless his door :
A heritage, it seems to me,
A king might wish to hold in fee.

  Oh, rich man's son ! there is a toil
That with all others level stands,
  Large charity does never soil,
But only whiten soft white hands ;
This is the best crop from thy lands :
A heritage, it seems to me,
Worth being *rich* to hold in fee.

  Oh, poor man's son ! scorn not thy state
There is worse weariness than thine
  In merely being rich and great ;
Toil only gives the soul to shine

And makes rest fragrant and benign :
A heritage, it seems to me,
Worth being *poor* to hold in fee.

    Both, heirs to some six feet of sod,
Are equal in the earth at last,
    Both, children of the same dear God,
Prove title to your heirship vast
By records of a well-fill'd past :
A heritage, it seems to me,
Well worth a life to hold in fee.

A PILGRIMAGE

TO

TWO AMERICAN SHRINES.

A PILGRIMAGE

TWO AMERICAN SHRINES.

IN an old country, where almost every plain has been a battle-field, and every hill top an altar of freedom ; where castled crag and fairy glen have each a legend of their own ; where in every journey you light upon a spot which some hero has glorified, or of which some minstrel has sung—shrines are so numerous, and so often trodden by pilgrim feet, that they lose somewhat of their venerableness because they are so accessible and common. America, too young, by comparison, for history, and too stirring and real for romance, has but few holy places ; but these are treasured with a solemn affection in the hearts of the choicest of her sons. Two days in the month of August, 1869, are days that will live in my memory, as the days on which I became familiar with places which for many years I had longed to see—the one the sepulchre of an Apostle—the other the birthplace of a nation. Leaving Portland (in Maine) by the Eastern Railway, a ride of some seventy miles along the Atlantic coast brings the traveller to a small town in the State of Massachusetts, called Newburyport. There is nothing to distinguish it from an ordinary New England village ; and as you pass along its narrow streets, not overcrowded with traffic or passengers, it does not strike you as looking like the scene of anything stirring or memorable. But come with me, down a lane somewhat narrower than the rest; pause before this building, now two comfortable residences, but in the former time the parsonage of the old Federal Street Church—with spacious entrance hall, out of which the fine oak staircase led into the rooms above. It was here, on the evening of the 29th of September, 1770, that a blue-eyed evangelist—tall, manly, earnest, though in feeble health, and older in constitution than in years—gazed on an eager crowd, who filled the hall and stretched out on the pavement beyond, craving some loving message from the lips on which they were wont to hang. It was on this staircase that he paused; and, as if with a sense of opportunity that was rapidly vanishing, and moments that were more precious than gold, gathered up his fast waning strength and delivered his latest exhortation upon the things of God. It was in the room above that, on the following night, amid the pomp of watching stars, the brave spirit wrestled with its agony; and it was here that, when the Sabbath sun was just rising over the neighbouring waters, the chariots of God came, and GEORGE WHITEFIELD, the later Elijah, "was not, for the Lord had taken him." Passing up the lane again, you enter the church, large and elegant, and so perfectly constructed that a whisper will travel to its farthest extremity. Near the altar, a massive marble monument commemorates the great evangelist. You are then taken behind the pulpit, and the guide takes a lantern in his hand and lifts up a trap-door. As it is lifted it is impossible to avoid seeing, and smiling as you see, what American shrewdness has "calculated" to catch the eye. There is indeed a mathematical exactness in the angle at which the light is made to fall upon the words, " Please to remember the sexton." You descend into a crypt and thence into the vault, where, with two former pastors of the church, is the open coffin of the Prince of Preachers, in which, all exposed to view, are his decaying bones. Some years ago the right arm was stolen and carried to England, but remorse of conscience, or the dread of popular anger, so scared the anti-quarian felon that he was moved to make restitution. Hence it is part of the sexton's lesson to inform you that Whitefield crossed the Atlantic thirteen times, but his right hand has been fourteen times across ; and then, when you are sufficiently astonished, he proceeds to expound the riddle. You can take the skull into your hand and muse upon this dome of thought, with its breadth of brow and brain. This handful of dust : is it all that is left to us of him who to hundreds of thousands was as the angel in the sun ? I could not gaze into that coffin un-moved, nor without a multitude of thoughts within me—thoughts of mortality and hope, thoughts of high emprise and ambition that were not all unholy. How mighty the work ! How fra-grant the memory of the great spirit whose dust lies here ! Beneath his surpassing renown how mean is the glory of " all great self-seekers, trampling on the right !" Oh, for a race of such apostles ! strong-souled and lipped with flame, who shall preach as he preached, or, if not with equal eloquence, with equal sincerity and zeal. If, as the great moralist has said, " Patriotism grows warm upon the plains of Marathon, and piety is enkindled amid the ruins of Iona," surely each pilgrim to George Whitefield's grave will leave it with a holy purpose, and breathe over it a self-consecrating prayer.

I travel on to the quaint city of Boston, but do not linger in the American Athens just now, though it has much to stay the footsteps ; and Cambridge is hard by, and especially Mount Auburn, that beautiful city of the dead. I leave it at the old Colony Depot, and pass through a country which presents few points of interest to a stranger ; so I betake myself to reverie, in which I picture the scene as it once was—unbroken forest and inhospitable shore, serpents writhing in the swamp and deer bounding on the hills—an ocean innocent of ships and a land free of inhabitant, save when some lordly Indian trapped his game in the wildwood. Then, too, I wander into speculations as to the subtle causes which affect and determine the growth of nations and of men, until my reverie is broken by the announcement of the conductor of the train—" Plymouth !" I step out of the cars, and realise, though with some difficulty, that I am in the first settlement of the Pilgrim Fathers. In these days of fast living and haste to be rich, when even in America " westward the course of empire takes its way," Plymouth has shared the fate of many of the smaller New England towns, and is looked down upon somewhat as a laggard behind the age. Well, it may be so ; but it is all the better fitted for the memories which it is called to preserve and embalm. It enshrines a spirit nobler than the trade spirit, and a heritage costlier than gold. Plymouth consists of one or two principal streets, and a number of tributary lanes branching off into the country and towards the sea. The streets are lined with neat frame houses, with verandahs to shade from the sun, up whose trellises creeping plants are climbing. There are a fine State house and one or two excellent hotels. Rows of elms—the *arbor domesticus* of New England—are planted on either side of the road, and are of such stately growth that the branches meet in the centre, suggesting poetry while they contribute shade. It is a meet spot for the dwelling of a quiet spirit; such a spot as Izaak Walton would have gloried in; or in which, except that he would have missed the church's ivied tower, George Herbert might have warbled of contentment, or gazed, enraptured, upon "the lace of Peace's coat."

Nearest to the railway station, after passing the "Samoset Hotel," so called after the friendly Indian who welcomed the pilgrims, we come to the "Pilgrim Hall," a substantial stone building with a wooden vestibule, built in 1824 by "The Pilgrim Society," with the laudable object of perpetuating the memory and gathering the relics of "the forefathers." In front of the hall is a piece of the veritable "Rock" on which the pilgrims landed, surrounded by an iron railing, for all the world like the railing of a tomb. In the iron are cast the names of the signers of the compact in the cabin of the "Mayflower." This piece was detached from the main body of the rock as a sacrifice to Plymouth patriotism.

In 1775, during the excitement which preceded the revolutionary war, the people of the town were anxious to show their zeal and patriotism; and, not being under very reasonable guidance, a mob of them formed the notion of removing the rock to the town square, and planting a flagstaff by its side from which the flag of Liberty should wave. So they met, with screws and levers and shouting, and proceeded to lift the rock, intending to draw it to its destination in a carriage drawn by thirty yoke of oxen. Suddenly it burst asunder. Strange and sinister omen! There were many Cassandras in the crowd, who regarded it as a mute prophecy of separation from the mother country—while, possibly, some thoughtful ones deemed that it illustrated the proverbial separation between fools and their wits. After long consultation they lowered one part into its place again, and drew the other to the town square in triumph. There it remained until, in 1834, it was removed to its present position in front of the Pilgrim Hall.

Entering the hall we find many genuine relics of the pilgrims, and many other things which have but little connection with their history. Near the door are the old oak chairs of Governor Carver and Elder Brewster—substantial enough once, but, partly from the lapse of time and partly from the "whittling" of irreverent relic-hunters, too frail for occupancy now. In the cabin of the "Mayflower" these old chairs have assisted at many a "Diet" of heroic faith and patient hope, and long meditation of the things of God. There is an inlaid dressing-case belonging to William White, and a deed signed by his son Peregrine, the child born on board the "Mayflower," who obtained a grant of two hundred acres of land on the strength of his petition that he was "the first Englishman born in these parts," and who lived to the great age of eighty-three. This deed, signed by Peregrine White, is witnessed by "Miles Standish," the redoubtable warrior of the pilgrims, whose exploits contributed, under God, to secure their early and peaceful settlement, and whose "courtship" Longfellow has set to such skilful music. Here also are his last will and testament, the iron pot in which his stews were cooked, and an enormous pewter dish on which he was accustomed to have them served, savouring, from its size, of the "giants" that were "in the earth in those days." Hard by these lies his sword, on the back of which is an Arabic inscription, indicating that it was one of those "glittering Damascus blades" which were formerly held in such special repute. It is not large nor elegant, but made for work, and has evidently seen and done real service. Hanging against the wall is a sampler wrought by "Lora," or as she signs herself, "Lorea" Standish, his daughter—a worthy specimen of an art known to our mothers, but now gone, with spinnet and spinning-wheel, into forgetfulness. The sampler reads thus :

LOREA STANDISH IS MY NAME.

———

Lord, guide my hart that I may doe thy will,
Also fill my hands with such convenient skill
As may conduce to vertue, void of shame
And I will give the glory to Thy name.

We may not dwell upon a multitude of other relics ; noticing simply the cap of King Philip, the Indian ; a plate of Governor Bradford ; a charter signed by Edward Winslow ; Thomas Clark's pocket-book, a wallet capacious enough to absorb a score of more degenerate size ; and a copy of the Bishop's Bible, the treasured property of John Alden, the proxy wooer of Miles Standish's Priscilla, and the successful one who ran away with the bride—John Alden, of whom tradition says that he was the first to leap upon the rock when the pilgrims landed, and the latest of the band who survived.

But we are all this while detained from the actual spot of landing, and are impatient to tread, if we may, where first " they, the true-hearted, came." Passing beneath the elms in front of the neat court-house and the bank, we turn down a rather steep descent to the left, and are on our way to the Fore-fathers' Rock. To the right of us is an abrupt ridge, called Cole's Hill, from which a flight of steps is cut to the rock beneath. This was the original burying-place of the pilgrims during the mortality of the first sad winter. The God's Acre has become man's acre now, for the ridge is covered with dwellings, and no stone or memorial remains. Formerly this eminence overhung the beach, and immediately underneath it was the cove in which the shallop grounded, and the projecting boulder which received the first tread of freedom. Now the whole is altered. The rock is eight feet above the water, and some rods further in shore than the high water mark. It is sup-posed that the whole neighbourhood has been lifted and filled up with gravel, to make the road and wharves which commer-cial enterprise has needed. It is averred, however, and this is some consolation to our chilled enthusiasm, that it lies immedi-ately *over*, if not actually *on*, the original spot of landing. By a series of uninterrupted testimony, stretching back to the very days of the forefathers, the " Rock " is declared to have been the identical one on which they leaped to shore, so that when you stand beneath the canopy of Quincy granite, and place your feet on the piece of rock about two feet square, which is all that, for fear of the sacrilegious, dare be left exposed, you may be sure that you stand where have stood the *conditores imperiorum*—the founders of empire, to whom Lord Bacon assigns the highest meed of earthly fame, and who deserve a higher eulogy than his, because they planted not for dominion or renown, but for freedom, for conscience, and for God.

From the rock we re-ascend into Leyden street, so called from the city which afforded the pilgrims shelter for so long, then climb the steep pathway to Burial Hill, 165 feet above the sea. This is the hill on which the fort was erected, at once a watch-tower and a stockade. It is high enough to cover the settlement and to guard against surprise, but not high enough for isolation from the neighbourhood below. Here, like the ancient Hebrews, they wrought, armed with sword and trowel, and up the slopes of this hill they toiled, with exemplary steps, when the Sabbath summoned them to worship. From this elevation all the places made sacred by the pilgrims are visible. Down below, a little to the east, is the harbour where the little vessel was guided by a skill more prescient than that of the bewildered pilot at the helm. Far in the distance, indistinctly seen through the haze, is Cape Cod, the scene of five weeks' weary waiting. Within the bay, to the south-east, is the Manomet Ridge, crested with pines, by which the pilot guided his bark to the place where he wished to land. To the north is Clarke's Island, where the first Sabbath was spent, and where

> " Amidst the storm they sang,
> And the stars heard, and the sea."

On the north-east is the green hill of Duxbury, where Standish made his home, and where, linking gloriously ancient heroism and modern progress, the French Atlantic Cable takes possession of American soil. Across the Town Brook, to the south, is Watson's, formerly Strawberry Hill, where Massasoit, the friendly sachem, appeared with his followers, and where the treaty was made which was so faithfully observed on both sides. The place teems with their memories, and to the eye and heart of those who are in sympathy with their cause, every spot is hallowed ground. On the hill itself, though a populous city of the dead, we look in vain for the forefathers' graves. It may be that some of the moss-covered old stones just peeping above the soil cover the dust of heroes ; but we cannot tell. The pilgrims died, but "no man knoweth of their sepulchres." Haply they are hidden lest superstition should canonize, or avarice make merchandise of their bones. A column rises to the memory of Governor Bradford, bearing this inscription : "Under this stone rest the ashes of William Bradford, a zealous Puritan and sincere Christian, Governor of Plymouth Colony from April 1621 to 1657 (the year he died, aged 69), except five years which he declined." The descendants of the early settlers are all buried here. It needs only to wander amongst the tombs to be impressed with the longevity which prevails in a community established upon Bible laws, and to be impressed, also, with the quaint Puritanism which would fain have made Plymouth a Theocracy, extending to the minutest detail of the ancient pattern, and perpetuated even in the names. In a ten minutes' ramble I saw upon the gravestones the following Scripture names, which, I do not doubt, might have been multiplied by farther search :—Abigail, Bathsheba, Bethiah, Drusilla, Ebenezer, Elisha, Esther, Experience, Elnathan, Eunice, Gideon, Heman, Ichabod, Job, Jerusha, Jabez, Joanna, Lemuel, Lois, Mercy, Miriam, Priscilla, Phœbe, Patience, Phineas, Rufus, Rebecca, "that virtuous woman, Ruth," Sylvanus, Seth, Thankful, Zabdiel, Zoeth, Zilpah, Zaccheus. But with quaint manners and quaint names these men had the hero heart and the confessor's faith. Their faith was, indeed, their strength. Strong in the supremacy of conscience, in that real earnestness which springs from conviction and which prompts to enterprise ; far-sighted in political sagacity, because seeing Him that is invisible; shrewd enough to know that the truest policy for the life that now is, is a reverent recognition of the life that is to come, they were brave in endurance and patient under trial; and, never losing sight of the principle for which they struggled, and of the purpose of their voyage afar, they "won the wilderness for God."

This age needs to be reminded of them. It is hard, unreal, materialistic, money-loving. There is corruption in its high places. It is tainted with the lust of dominion, and defiled with the greed of gain. It were happy for it, and for all of us, to visit in person, or by proxy, these Massachusetts shrines, and to learn from them that Faith is the highest virtue, and labour for God the most exalted calling; and that, as a promised recompense of Faith and Labour, "the righteous shall be in everlasting remembrance, while the memory of the wicked shall rot."

KINDNESS TO THE POOR.

KINDNESS TO THE POOR.

"If there be among you a poor man of one of thy brethren within any of thy gates, in thy land which the Lord thy God giveth thee, thou shalt not harden thine heart, nor shut thine hand from thy poor brother; but thou shalt open thine hand wide unto him."—Deut. xv. 7, 8.

"For the poor shall never cease out of the land."—Deut. xv. 11.

IT does not need that I should remind you at any length of the circumstances under which this command was given. It occurs in that grand valedictory service to which Moses, the great Jewish lawgiver, summoned the children of Israel, and in the course of which he repeated the commandments of the law, and urged upon them to be consistent and faithful in the land of promise which they were about to inherit. There was a pathos in his utterances—for he knew that he spoke his latest counsels to the people who had often tried him, who had often rebelled against him, but whom he loved with a love stronger than death. And there was also the deeper pathos of the remembrance that he, and the few elders who survived, had forfeited their own entrance into Canaan—and that by the decree of an unchangeable penalty each silver-haired ancient who had started from Egypt, and had been concerned in the condemning unbelief, must lay his bones in the wilderness, while the speaker himself could but gaze in one brief trance of rapture upon the people's inheritance, and then lie down and die. In this farewell charge, which comprises the whole Book of Deuteronomy—not only are motives to obedience pressed upon them with overwhelming power—but circumstantial directions are given upon all matters connected with the establishment of their new life. There are denunciations of idolatry—the one crowning sin which was the cause of their sacred isolation—and then follow regulations touching the four great principles of theocratical government: 1. Worship and sacrifice; 2. The institution of the family, and its concurrent obligations; 3. The consecration of time, with the Sabbath as God's especial portion; and 4. The consecration of the substance, and its apportionment to the requirements of personal and family need—of legitimate business—of the sanctuary—and of the calls of charity. In the last of these comes the injunction of the text. As if, by provident foresight, God had ordained the existence of the poor on purpose to be the check upon the rich man's selfishness, and the outlet for the rich man's bounty; it is predicted that they shall "never cease out of the land;" and the duty of the now highly favoured in regard to them, and the specialty of the claim upon the ground of a common nationality, are both included in the words I have read. And let no man suppose that the command is of any less obligation, or that it comes with sanction less divinely authenticated, because spoken from Hebrew lips, and addressed to one wayward people's needs. But there is in many respects a close analogy between our circumstances and theirs. We are not newly enlightened, the last trophies of some venturous mis-sionary's toil, as were many of those to whom the Apostles wrote; if there do linger about us any remnants of our Paganism, it is because we have cherished them for years, and habit has made us fond of the badges of our darkness and shame. We revel in the light which only dawned greyly on the former time; we dwell beneath institutions which will begin to cast forth shadows soon. To us it is fitting that the prophet's lips should speak; we may be aptly rebuked by the faithfulness of the seer's warning. The principles enunciated for the guidance of the Jewish people, so far at any rate as high religious ethics are concerned, are principles which must govern us to-day. This is an interesting service which has gathered us, a time when in the far country we evoke the memories of home, those deep-lying and long lasting instincts which years have no power to stifle, and which even hard usage and all the buffetings of a pitiless world cannot utterly destroy. Here we summon our patriotism to prompt our charity—haggard strangers loom through the sea-fret, ever coming near to us with their cry of distress and need—and as they approach us through the parting mists, we find that they are brethren, heirs with us of glorious history and traditions which make the blood leap the fleeter through the veins—children of the dear island mother from whom our own breath was drawn, and who sits in sceptred state, shaking her tresses of freedom to the winds, and girt about in loving embrace by the arms of the triumphant sea. It is an occasion, therefore, in some sort, of national concern and sympathy, and those especially who have named the name of Jesus, and so march under more sacred banners than that of the old Cappadocian hero, are bound to be helpful in their measure, that our good may not be evil spoken of, and that our religion, in one of its comeliest developments, may come before the observation of men. No

great elaboration is necessary to impress upon you the principles which the text embodies and enforces. *The claim is that
of the poor man within thy gates, who never ceases out of the land,
and the claim becomes the stronger because of the peculiar circumstance that the poor man is one of thy brethren.* Let us illustrate
these thoughts for a brief while. " God has made of one blood
all nations of men, for to dwell upon the face of the whole earth."
This is the announcement of a grand fact, which has never yet
been successfully disproved. " One blood "—there is the dis
tinct, individual unity of the human race ; one family—though
sundered by climate and language ; one deep underlying identity, however chequered by the varieties of external condition.
This relates man to man everywhere, makes all the world a
neighbourhood, and founds upon universal affinity a universal
claim. The old Roman could say, with a far-sighted perception of this great truth : " I am a man ; nothing, therefore, that
is human can be foreign to me," and Christianity has exalted
this sentiment into a perpetual obligation, and stamped it with
the royal seal of heaven. This general law, however, must be
divided into minor modifications, or it will be practically useless. It is not intended to contravene nature, but to assist and
regulate its affections ; and if it be the world at large which is
the object of pity, the very magnitude of the area will induce a
mental vagueness which will fritter away the intenseness
of the feeling. That is a suspicious affection which attaches
itself to nobody in particular, which makes no heart its centre,
which brightens no hearthstone by its light. Its words may be
loud and swelling ; like the blast of March it may sweep noisily
about men's houses and drift the dust about in clouds, but they
are conscious only of discomfort when it blows ; they do not

trust it; it "passes by them like the idle wind, which they respect not." Hence all private affections are recognized and hallowed, and are indeed the source from which all public virtues spring. They are not inconsistent with the love of the whole race; they prepare for it, and lead to it, and scoop out the channels through which the tributes of its bounty may flow. Who shall sympathize with oppressed peoples but the patriot-heart which rejoices in the sacredness of its own roof-tree, and in the security of its own altars? Who shall be eloquent for the rights of others but he who is manly in the assertion of his own? Who shall succour breaking hearts, and brighten desolate houses, but the man who realizes in daily up-welling the unutterable happiness of home? These two obligations, therefore, the claim of universal sympathy and the claim of particular relationships, are not incompatible, but fulfil mutually the highest uses of each other. God has taught in the Scriptures the lesson of a universal brotherhood, and man must not gainsay the teaching. Shivering in the ice-bound, or scorching in the tropical regions; in the lap of luxury or in the wild hardihood of the primeval forest; belting the globe in a tired search for rest, or quieting through life in the heart of ancestral woods; gathering all the decencies around him like a garment, or battling in fierce raid of crime against a world which has disowned him, there is an inner humanness which binds me to that man by a primitive and indissoluble bond. He is my brother, and I cannot dissever the relationship. He is my brother, and I cannot release myself from the obligation to do him good. I cannot love all men equally; my own instincts, and nature's provision, and society's requirements, and God's commands, all unite in reprobation of that. My wealth of affection must be in home, children, kindred, country;

but my pity must not lock itself in these, my regard must not compress itself within these limits merely—my pity must go forth wherever there is human need and human sorrow; my regard must fasten upon the *man*, though he has flung from him the crown of his manhood in anger. I dare not despise him, because there, in the depths of his fall, as he lies before me prostrate and dishonoured, there shines, through the filth and through the sin, that spark of heavenly flame—that young immortal nature which God the Father kindled, over which God the Spirit yearns with continual desire, and which God the Eternal Son offered his own heart's blood to redeem. Yes—there is no man now who can rightfully ask the infidel question of Cain. God *has* made man his brother's keeper. We are bound to love our neighbour as ourselves; and if, in a contracted Hebrew spirit, you are inclined to press the enquiry, "And who *is* my neighbour?" there comes a full pressure of utterance to authenticate and enforce the answer, *Man.* Thy neighbour! Every one whom penury has grasped or sorrow startled ; every one whom plague hath smitten or whom curse hath banned ; every one from whose home the darlings have vanished, and around whose heart the pall hath been drawn.

> " Thy neighbour ! 'Tis the fainting poor
> Whose eye with want is dim,
> Whom hunger sends from door to door
> Go, thou, and succour *him*."

I observe further that the last clause of the text is as true to-day as in the time of its original utterance, the " poor shall never cease out of the land ;" and although in this new Dominion, with its large acred wealth of soil, and comparatively scanty population, you can know nothing of the overgrown pauperism which is at once a fault, a sorrow, and a problem to the rulers of older states, yet here, as in every age and in every clime, there are distinctions of society in the world. It must be so from the nature of things; it is part of God's benevolent allotment, and of His original economy. He makes no endless plains, or uniform mountain ridges. He has stamped His own deep love of beauty on the undulating woodland, and on the flower-sprent hill, and on the pleasant varieties of peak, and copse, and stream. A level creation were not the creation of God, and it is so with society. It has its inequalities of necessity; men may fret against them, but they cannot help themselves. Nothing can alter the irreversible law, and if by the fury of some revolutionary deluge, all things were reduced to a drear level of waters to-day, you may be sure that some aspiring mountain-tops would struggle through the billows to-morrow. Society could not cohere as a union of equals; there must be graduation and dependence. God hath set the poor in his condition as well as the rich, for " He that despiseth the poor reproacheth his Maker;" and the announcement of the Saviour, "The poor ye have always with you," is at once the averment of a fact and a perpetual commendation of them, as Christ's clients, to the help and succour of His church. In the text, benevolence towards them is positively enjoined, and enjoined because of their abiding existence as a class of the community. Hence it has been well said, " Poverty is the misfortune of some and the disgrace of more, but it is the inheritance of most." There will always be those who will need and claim the friendliness of their fellows above them. Some by native energy, or favouring circumstances, will raise themselves in the social scale, (and here are ampler opportunities than most other lands afford,) but the mass will toil on through a lifetime in the condition in which they were born, with few reliefs and fewer aspirations, the mouth demanding and absorbing the ceaseless labour of the hands. There is that also in the constitution of society which requires that the class from which the ranks of clamant poverty are recruited should be always the largest class amongst us. The pyramid must stand upon its base. The wants of the population, naturally large, have been increased by the refinements of civilization. The poor are the stalwart purveyors to the necessity, and to the comfort of life. Who shall say that in seasons of exigency they have not a claim upon the state they serve, and upon the charity which is but the justice of others; some of whom have risen from their ranks; some of whom have been enriched by their toil. Once recognize the relationship, and the claim will inevitably follow, the sense of service rendered and obligation created thereby will make that claim more sacred, and religion, attaching her holiest sanction, lifts the recognition of the claim into a duty which may not be violated without sin. "I will have mercy, and not sacrifice." "Whoso seeth his brother have need, and shutteth up his bowels of compassion, how dwelleth the love of God in him?" Nay, Christ himself, once poor in the travail of His incarnate life, and therefore touched with the feeling of their infirmities, "adopts them as His own peculiar care, and pointing to them as they shiver in rags, or parch from hunger, commends them to His church, that they may be warmed and fed," adding the benediction which is itself a Heaven: "Inasmuch as ye have done it to one of the least of these, ye have done it unto Me." There are, moreover, peculiarities in the poor man's lot, of which I may here briefly remind you, which tend to the enforcement of the claim which both Reason and Scripture commend. Think then of *the nature of the occupations in which so many pass their lives.* It is true that there is an inherent dignity in labour. It is not, as some have erroneously supposed, a penal clause of the original curse. There was labour, bright, healthful, unfatiguing, in unfallen Paradise. By sin labour became drudgery — the earth was restrained from her spontaneous fertility, and the strong arm of the husbandman was required, not to develop, but to "subdue" it. But labour in itself is noble, and is necessary for the ripe unfolding of the highest life. But how many are there to whom the days pass in dreary monotomy, little to task the intellect, to engross the affections, or to call into play the finer sensibilities of the man. It is "Work, work, work, as prisoners work for crime." The man within the man is degraded by the unintermitting toil; the task-work is performed, the holidays come but seldom, and when they do come, he is too listless to enjoy them. Day after day rolls wearily along, and there is no prospect of retirement; a family grows up around him, and the children are clamorous for bread. Each morning summons him inexorably to labour; each evening sets unpitying on his weariness. The frosts gather upon his head; the lithe limbs lose their suppleness, there is a strange sinking at the heart, but he must work, until at length infirmity disables him; then he dies, and there is his wife exposed to the cold world's buffetings, and his children to a stranger's charity or an early grave. Think again how *the poor are circumscribed from many ordinary sources of enjoyment.* Though sin has sorely afflicted humanity, there are yet open many sources of pleasure, and from books, and friends, and intellectual conversation, and taste, and rambles among the flowers, or the woodland, or on the pine-clad hills, or by the fringe of the living sea ; as well as from those exercises which belong to Christian fellowship, benevolence, and enterprise, there can be realized a rapture which mitigates the curse, and which leaves no remorse behind. But from many of these the poor are, by the necessities of their position, debarred. They do not start fairly with their fellows in the race of intellectual acquirement. To them, as a rule, the sciences are sealed. It is but rarely that they can kindle before a great picture, or travel to the spots renowned in song or story, or be thrilled beneath the spell of a great Poet's mighty words. Not for them the pleasures of sense, the ample board, the convenient dwelling, the gathered friends, the appliances of comfort with which wealth has carpeted its own pathway to the Tomb. Their life is a perpetual struggle beneath the winner and the spender, and unless they are happy at home, and blessed by the consolations of religion, existence will be a joyless peril, a weariness which ceaseth not, or, if there be a respite, it will be one which gives " no blessed leisure for love or hope, but only time for tears." Think again of *the pressure with which the ordinary ills of life fall upon the poor.* There is no part of the world where the curse has not penetrated. Man is born to trouble amid Arab hordes, and in Siberian wilds, as well as in royal courts and teeming cities. The cloud, like the sun, is no respecter of persons. Everywhere disappointment tracks the footsteps, and sickness steals into the dwelling, and Death waiteth at the door. But these ills, common to all men, fall most heavily upon the poor. They have to bear the penalty in their condition as well as in their experience. They cannot purchase the skill of many healers, the comforts which soothe the sickness, the delicacies which restore the strength. They cannot afford the time to recover thoroughly, for effort is required to keep ahead of the world, and to the quickened apprehension there are many visions of the wolf of Hunger glaring in through the panes of the uncurtained window. Their very maintenance is dependent upon contingencies which they can neither foresee nor control. Their prospects in life, their hopes of supply, their only chance of provision for emergency, are derived from their labour. That labour is contingent upon the state of trade, upon the measures of government, upon the yield cf harvest, upon the price of money. Sometimes upon the caprice of their employers, sometimes upon the coarse tyranny which they exert over each other, and sometimes even upon the thoughts, purposes and quarrels of a people whom they never saw, and from whom they are separated by a waste of waters upon whose breast they never cared to sail. If labour fails, bread fails and hearts fail. The more provident can struggle for a while on the results of their thrift and care, but if the scarcity be protracted, and if no friendly succour interpose, you can trace the inevitable progress downward. The little savings for which the industry of the past had toiled, and on which the hopes of the future rested, are frittered away to supply the need which will not wait ; the cottage comforts vanish one by one, and there is a sickness at the heart as they go, for long habit has made them grow up into familiar friends, until, in extremest desolation, the picture of the poet is realized :

> " A shattered roof—a naked floor,
>   A table—a broken chair,
> And a wall so blank, their shadow they thank
>   For sometimes falling there."

Then sickness comes—the fever follows hard upon the famine. The comfort is gone—the strength is gone—the hope is gone.

Death has nothing to do but take possession. They have neither power nor will to resist him. Not hopeful, but sadly, strangely, terribly indifferent, they await his approach, and if you tell them of their danger, they might answer in the words of the strong and gentle spirit from whom we quoted before :

> " But why do you talk of Death,
> That plantom of grisly bone,
> We hardly fear his terrible shape,
> It seems so like our own."

And this is no fancy sketch or fevered dream. There are homes of your countrymen where the Ruin is in progress to-day. I enlarge no further but to remind you that there is a specialty in the case of the poor for whom I plead, in that *they are at once " strangers, and of your brethren"—of the one blood, but in a strange land.* In many aspects the lot of the emigrant is a painful one. However, if he attains a position in a new country, he may become proud of its institutions and rooted in its soil. The parting from the home of his youth cannot be without a pang. Even those who come, blithe venturers for fortune, under the patronage of youth and hope —own to the first feeling of desolation as they realize the stranger's loneliness ; and when, as in many cases, the emigration has been constrained by adversity, and the man must part per-force from old associations, and friends, and belongings—there is a cruel wrench of the tenderer fibres of the soul ; and if, in addition to the regretful memories of the past and the sickening sense of homelessness—there be the forebodings of an uncer-tain future—and the fear comes creeping over the spirit ot exhausted means and a pining family ; of the Want which is a deadly tempter, and of the Hunger which is a sharp thorn. Oh that is a condition surely of extremest need, and, I tell you, a word of kindness in such a strait is welcome as the smile of an angel, for it may redeem from hopelessness and despair; and a helpful hand-grasp, with something in the hand the while, is worth a hundred-fold its cost, for it may have ransomed for all future time the most kingly thing on earth, *the manhood of a man*, for industry, and society, and God.

I do not know much about the real or mythical personage—I am unable to determine which—who, alleged to have been born in some Cappadocian fastness, has been adopted as the patron saint of England, whatever that may mean. I cannot separate the fact and the fable. I know not whether or not he slew the monster who is represented to be transfixed by his spear, and delivered some fair princess Aja, beautiful exceedingly, from durance or from doom, but I know this, that in the heart of this legend there are underlying symbols of the Christian warfare in which all who love the Lord Jesus should be valiant for the truth upon the earth. What is our life-work but to release, in ourselves and in each other, the maiden graces of the Christian character, which have been in bondage to the tyrant of the Fall? What is the whole work of our Religion but a warfare with the Dragon—that old and cruel serpent who still creepeth to empoison and destroy. Sirs, if ye would not shun the plainest meanings of the symbols under which ye gather, embody these teachings in your lives. Let your daily experience shew that you have learned this secret of life, that it is not a mere provision for the flesh to fulfil the lust thereof—that it is not an hour of idleness, to be wasted "in rioting and drunkenness, in chambering and wantonness, in strife and envying," but that it is a stewardship to be accounted for hereafter— an earnest gift, full of earnest longings, and tending to earnest ends—something to be given primarily to Christ, who redeemed it, and for His sake to be employed for men.   Let your Religion be the base of your character, and there will be a goodly superstructure of Enterprise and Patriotism and Charity.   It is right that on this occasion you should remember the land of your birth or of your fathers.   The pride of patriotism is a pride that is not all unholy.   Not in vaunting but in thankfulness—not captive by the rivers of Babylon, but happy in the beneficent outgrowth of ancient blessings on the soil of a New Dominion, the descendants of the dear old mother-isle gather in this fair Canada the comeliest of her daughters to recall her advantages, and to be generous to her fugitive sons.   She is worth all our love and pride. Secure from invasion, prolific in produce—of tiny extent but of tremendous influence—a speck upon the world's charts but an emperor in the world's councils—the school of the wise and the home of the free—her sails whitening all waters, and in all latitudes her flag flying upon some fringe of coast—girding the globe with her possessions, and owning archipelagos of isles —while, as the late National Thanksgiving proved, in the remotest dependency there throbs the great heart-pulse of home, "She is the anointed cherub that covereth, and God hath set her so." But not in these things are her safety and her strength. They are in her equal laws, and in her national honour, in the fact that, over cottage and palace alike, the ægis of the constitution rests, and in that all the machinery of justice is set in motion to protect the peasant's nome if high-born wrong assail it ; and to guard the beggar's conscience, if he but fancy it aggrieved ; above all in her adhesion, though imperfectly rendered, to the

Gospel of Christ, and to the grand principles of morality, and charity, and godliness, which that Gospel has established among men.   Let her decay from these, let there come corruption in her high places, the repudiation of national honour—the reign of encroaching error—the supremacy of a fell infidelity in the national mind—and her condemnation will not slumber, and, with her proud forerunners in empire, her greatness will be forgotten as a cloud.   Let her hold to these great principles, widening through the ages into increasing reverence for Truth, and Peace, and God, and her greatness shall be assured until the last fires blot out the sun.

> "This England never did, nor ever shall
> Lie at the proud foot of a conqueror,
> But when it first did help to wound itself.
> Come the three corners of the world in arms,
> And we shall shock them.   Nought shall make us rue
> If England to herself do rest but true."

Dear Brethren, to the duty which awaits you you need not be further urged.   Your countrymen, forced to stranger shores by blighted hope and ruined fortune.   *These are our clients.* "Inasmuch as ye did it unto one of the least of these, ye did it unto Me."   *This is our Divinely furnished argument.*   "Ye know the grace of our Lord Jesus Christ, who, though he was rich, yet, for our sakes He became poor."   *This is our example.* "She hath done what she could."   *This is to be the measure o, our giving.*   "He that hath pity upon the poor lendeth unto the Lord.   And look ! what he lendeth, He will pay him again." *This is our surety.*   "Thou hast been faithful over a few things, I will make thee ruler over many things.   Enter thou into the joy of thy Lord."   *This is our exceeding great reward.*

SALVATION OF ISRAEL.

THE SALVATION OF ISRAEL.

"Oh that the salvation of Israel were come out of Zion! When God bringeth back the captivity of his people, Jacob shall rejoice, and Israel shall be glad,"—PSALM liii. 6.

THIS is one of those Psalms which were wailed out at intervals during the time of captivity; when, though the hope of deliverance was still inertly cherished, the day which was to realize it had not yet dawned even upon the clearest vision. All these Psalms have a plaintive character of their own, such as might have been expected when all the outward circumstances were untoward, and no joy of home or freedom quivered in the heart whose fingers swept the strings. Yet the prisoners were "prisoners of hope." Throughout all disastrous changes confidence in the brighter future existed within them, as a principle too firmly established to be shaken either by tyrannous exactions or by fleeting years. Brethren, the centuries have rolled away, each with its own burden of vicissitude, and with its own record of progress; but there is a long captivity which has never once been lifted from one fated nation, and beneath which it is languishing to-day. The mournful story which Vespasian's medal tells is the story of the Jewish nation now. The weeper still sits beneath the palm-tree, the one hand listless alike from music and labour, the other covering the eyes, whose lids droop heavily; and she makes her sad plaint to a world which has too often scorned her, and to a church which has too often been indifferent to her claims. In the meet language of ancient prophecy, "Is it nothing to you, all ye that pass by? Behold, and see if there be any sorrow like unto my sorrow, which is done unto me, wherewith the Lord hath afflicted *me* in the day of his fierce anger." (Lam. i. 12.) It is my purpose—a purpose which I fear I shall very imperfectly fulfil—to present before you, in condensed fulness, the condition and the destiny of the once favoured race of Israel, reminding you:

I. That their salvation is needed;

II. That their salvation is promised;

III. That Christians are bound to seek it by personal effort and prayer.

I. There is nothing which more strongly moves the sympathies of the thoughtful than to behold some impoverished descendant of an ancient house gazing mournfully upon the demesne which he once called his own, but which has passed into the hands of the stranger; or some scion of the De Courcys and Plantagenets starving in the destitution to which his spendthrift habits have reduced him. The inspiring associations of the past do but deepen the present desolation, and our pity for his fall is the deeper because of the contrast with his former heritage of rank and fortune. Here is, not an individual but a nation, thus homeless and ruined; a nation that could once outrival the proudest and most highly privileged. If it be considered that the antiquity or a family, and the great names won by those who have belonged to it, aggravate the calamity of its fall, then your pity for this prostrate people may be intenser, because in their case both these conditions exist. The haughtiest noble who boasts of Norman blood has not an ancestry half so renowned, or a lineage half so pure, as the poor Jew pedlar on whose vagrancy he thinks with pity, or whose sordidness he rebukes with scorn. The Jew had had a history for long years before the Babylonian empire laid the foundations of its power; before a dwelling rose on the Capitoline hill; before the confederate Greeks assembled beneath the walls of Troy. While the records of other nations are lost, or have drivelled into the veriest fable, you have accurate records, drawn under Divine guidance, of patriarchal customs, and times when this wondrous people were chosen to be witnesses for God. When the antiquarian eye glistens before some fragment of the ancient Babylon, it may be that he gazes on the disinterred handiwork of some Jewish builder. When the traveller is wearied with the climbing of the Pyramids, he may remember that it is not improbable that the Jews piled up their steep stairs of stone. When the explorer penetrates into the royal tombs at Thebes, there stares out at him from the walls the very Hebrew physiognomy which is so familiar in the midst of us to-day. Hebrew chieftains were brave, and Hebrew shepherds wealthy, when time itself was young. It will be remembered, also, that theirs are some of the most illustrious names which the annals of the world record. Why should they despair of statesmanship for whom Moses enacted his wise and patient lawgiving, and in whose veins the blood of Daniel flows? Why should not they be brave who are the descendants of Joshua and of the valiant Maccabeus? Why scorn them, as if they were incapable of genius, when they are of the kindred of Ezekiel the fiery-eyed, or Isaiah the glorious, or the minstrel-monarch of Israel? Who shall say that all their wealth of wisdom was monopolised by Solomon ; that all their power of command was translated with Elijah ; that all their marvels of eloquence ceased with the last words of Paul? Who will not weep that they should ever be stubborn and degraded, " of whom, as concerning the flesh, Christ came, who is over all, God blessed for ever." But this nation, thus venerable in its history and rich in its renowned sons, has vanished. It is now " scattered and peeled," and its children inherit the displeasure which, as we believe, eighteen hundred years ago their fathers invoked upon themselves. The prophet promised by Moses rose up in the midst of them, but they refused to hearken to his words. The Messiah " came to his own, but his own received him not." The day of visitation dawned in clearness and brilliancy, but they trifled or opposed through its noontide to its twilight, until it set before their eyes. Their own obduracy in the rejection of the Saviour issued in their own *rejection from being the privileged people, and in their exile from the land where such glorious opportunities had been given.*

Just look more largely at each of these thoughts for a moment. The whole ritual of Jewish service supposes that there is a living heart in the worshipper ; otherwise there is nothing in the services to redeem them from formality, or to distinguish them from any other ceremonies of unmeaning symbolism. In Levitical times this inspiring heart was the hope and promise of Messiah : in the times of the Redeemer's incarnation, it was the belief in the Messiah who had come, and whose coming had been approved by miracles, announced by angels, and attested by divine sanctions of impressiveness and power. But to the mass of the Jewish people this heart, this trust, was lacking. To them first were the tidings proclaimed—their ancestral rights and the boundlessness of Christ's compassion alike necessitated that—but they "rejected the counsel of God against themselves." By consequence the vitality languished out of their system; the symbol of God's presence abode no longer in the temple, and the temple itself was by and by "razed to its foundation, so that not one stone was left upon another." How remarkable a fulfilment has there been of the woes of Hosea's prophecy, "For the children of Israel shall abide many days without a king, and without a prince, and without a sacrifice, and without an image, and without an ephod, and without teraphim." (Hosea iii. 4.) From that time there has been no king of the Jews, nor even the remnant of a nation over which he could reign. They have now no high priest—for their genealogies are lost—and they know not who are of the tribe of Levi, and who of the family of Aaron. Their sacrifice is no longer presented, for the chief rabbi is an officer unknown to their law, and invested with no mediatorial authority; and in burdensome ceremonies they spend the annual day of expiation, ceremonies which cannot possibly profit them. The Mishna and Gamara of their Talmuds have so encumbered the law, that they no longer study it with reverence as their fathers did; and though there are reactionary symptoms here and there, and some are evidently panting after the true light of the Word, of the mass it may be said with truth, that now, as in the days when Paul wrote to Corinth, "when Moses is read the veil is upon their heart." Not a few of them, from this fatal neglect of God's Word, have relapsed into a species of

Deism, and multitudes into a total and eclipsing worldliness, which renders them practically Atheists in the world. Their worship is more a bodily than a spiritual service, and there is mournfully little either of instruction for the mind or of the cultivation of purity for the heart. They cling yet vainly to the dream of the coming Messiah, but are readier to anticipate their uplifting from their manifold afflictions and their restoration to their patrimonial home, than the circumcision of the heart and the mastery over human passion which we have learnt to be the highest glories of His kingdom. Alas! for them. They have been so often mocked with shadows that it is said they have a curse for him who shall calculate the time of the Redeemer's advent. Alas! for them. If they are sincere and earnest, their consciences are but lashed into accusing activity to be lulled into a delusive repose. Alas! for them. To a crouching fear of death they are all their lifetime subject to bondage, and at the best have but a glimmering ray with which to light their pilgrim footsteps in their travel to the dark unknown. Surely they need the kind offices of Christian compassion, and the prayer unceasingly offered that their eyes may be delivered from their films of blindness, and the "hearts of the disobedient turned about to the wisdom of the just."

If you take the other thought—their dispersion into all lands—their condition will be still more appreciated in its painfulness and ruin. It is not idly that Jeremiah says, "God hath delivered them to be removed into all the kingdoms of the earth for their hurt, to be a reproach and a proverb, a taunt and a curse, in all places whither I shall drive them." (Jer. xxiv. 9). How marvellous their history has been and continues to be in this matter! They are scattered, but one in the mighty sympathies which have defied all the disasters of the years to denationalize them. There you see them, present everywhere, but having nowhere their belongings, rising up in the midst of national combinations —like a strange chemical element which refuses affinity with everything with which men try to mingle it—always identical, but always homeless. There never was possibly a more terrible siege, either in ancient or in modern warfare, than the siege of Jerusalem. The mind sickens over the recital of the combined horrors of the slaughter and the famine, as they are recorded in the annalist's pages; but there were darker woes and fiercer cruelties behind. Decrees of banishment succeeded the downfall of the city. The first wild attempt at insurrection was expiated by the destruction of half a million of the remnant that was left. In the time of Hadrian the heaviest penalties were threatened upon any Hebrew who remained in Jewry. He might not oar the blue waters of Tiberias, nor own a rood in the fertile Sharon, nor, save by stealth, even glance upon the hill ot Zion; and, cruellest of all, he could not even have in Hebron the poor comfort of a grave, for

> " He must wander witheringly
>   In other lands to die;
> And where his father's ashes were
>   His own could never lie.

Throughout succeeding ages, though surrounding governments ran through all grooves of change, no reversal of the attainder came upon the disinherited Jew. Jerusalem had been overrun by sucesssive hordes of strangers. All religions but the purest had been professed within its walls. All alien tribes could find shelter and traffic—but it was inexorably barred against the entrance of its own children. From the minarets there might wave the crescent of the Ottoman, or shine the bright lances of the tameless Arab, or gleam the crucifix of the Papist—the Jew was still proscribed. Or if now and then there dawned a milder policy or more merciful times, he lived in his own home by sufferance ; and in literal fulfilment of the prophecy, " he had a trembling heart and failing eyes, and sorrow of mind, and feared day and night, and had none assurance of his life." (Deut. xxviii. 65, 66). And now, though they have larger immunities than before, they are practically in banishment still. They have no portion in Jerusalem, and scarcely a memorial. They owe their tolerated presence in the holy city to the protection which the British flag gives to its own subjects everywhere ; or they have bargained for a foothold, and, to regain this inalienable birthright, have " purchased the gift of God with money." Not only are they exiled still from Jerusalem, exiled so thoroughly that it is computed that at this day there are fewer Jews in Palestine than in London, but there has been no colonization among them by which they have become politically considerable in any other country, and have gathered to a head of power. The scattering has been complete and perpetual. This marvellous people have a sort of ubiquity. They live in every nation of Europe. They swell the tide of emigration, and turn up, mysterious and shrewd, at the Antipodes. They shiver in Siberia and Greenland, and scorch in Africa's heart ; they bow before the simoom of the desert, and lave their wearied limbs in Gunga's sacred stream. In all countries where they have wandered, persecution and contempt have awaited them. In the East their sufferings have been multiplied. The lazy Turk rouses himself to express his momentary anger against the

Hebrew. Chivalrous France, classic Italy, romantic Spain, tolerant and thoughtful Germany—all in former days have treated the Jew with cruelty, and in later times with slander and with scorn. And in England, free, enlightened, happy, there are dark historic pages which record the calamities of the Israelite; how avarice was rapacious, and chivalry unknightly, and honour, even royal honour, belied, and the common laws of right and honesty forgotten where their interests were concerned; how Saxon thane and Norman noble alike thrust them from the courtesies of life; and how even the swineherd and the jester dared insult the velvet gaberdine with ribald oaths and with unseemly-scorn. It is but lately that all the reproach of persecution has been wiped away; and even now there are but few of us that have felt as we ought for this people, still, after so many ages, branded with their original curse, still without a prince and without a sacrifice. Think with Christian sympathy of their political dispersion and of their religious danger, and I am sure that there will be struck upon your hearts such a consciousness of needed salvation that you will cry out in the entreaty of the text, "Oh that the salvation of Israel were come out of Zion! When God bringeth back the captivity of his people, Jacob shall rejoice, and Israel shall be glad."

II. We come to notice that *their salvation is attainable.* The harp is not always to hang idly upon the willows, nor to be swept by troubled fingers to wild and plaintive music. The penal curse is to be reversed. The malediction, though it has hung over the unhappy race for ages, is not eternal.

There are many proofs that a widespread belief of this has obtained in the Christian Church. When you feel tenderly towards this disinherited elder brother of the family, and long for his reinstatement in the inheritance which he has " sold for nought," you feel that you have both warrant for your tender wishes, and hope that they will be realized, in the love and words of the Father. But what do we mean when we speak of the salvation of Israel? It is perhaps necessary to explain our terms, as the Word may be variously understood. We at once affirm our meaning to be the conversion of the Jewish nation unto Christ—their "looking upon Him whom they have pierced," not in rage as many of them do now; not in remorse and hopelessness, as in the quick recoil of conviction they might be tempted to do,—but in contrite and godly sorrow. All other meanings which may be put upon the Word are lacking if they include not this first and highest. Some look for political deliverance—a social elevation beneath whose amenities they shall be refined into that higher character from which their long persecutions have debased them. But if you invest them with all rights of citizenship here—or bring them to their own land with all the spontaneous gladness of a jubilee—and do not at the same time change their hearts, the curse which has cleaved to them in their wanderings would cleave to them equally in the city of their solemnities—" an abomination of desolation " more hateful than the Roman Eagle flaunting in " the holy place." Some look for mental emancipation—an emergence from the bondage of the Rabbinical law into a sort of free-thinking liberalism which is cousin-german to absolute infidelity. Some expect only to see· the Hebrews come over to a speculative adhesion to the Messiahship of Christ, or to a mere nominal adoption of the Christian name. Brethren, if all we do by our efforts be but to dislodge the Jew from his ancestral faith ; to unsettle his cherished ideas, and to supply him with nothing better, we incur a very alarming responsibility, and accomplish a very doubtful good. If we persuade to an intellectual assent only—though we secure silence from the blasphemers and removal of the prejudice—we are just hiding light in darkness, and making darkness denser by the sad eclipse. If we are content with a nominal profession of Christianity, we give premiums to the crafty and the sordid, and lay ourselves open to the perpetration of those discreditable frauds upon us which have already created a *prima facie* impression of distrust against a converted Jew. Nothing will at once fulfil the mission of the Christian Church, and satisfy her pants of roused desire, but the real renovation of the Jewish race; that they may individually become heirs of the grace of pardon, reconciled to God through Christ—"having their fruit unto holiness, and the end everlasting life." That this result will be accomplished we do verily and in truth believe, and that not by special miracle, not by any process other than that which makes every conversion miraculous, but by the power of the Holy Ghost, acting in persuasive might upon their own free power of choice, and making effectual the appeal of the ministry or the utterance of the Word. Surely there is no irreversible hindrance in God, nor invincible stubbornness in Hebrew hearts against the truth. It is true that the curse has been pleaded in bar of Christian endeavour to reclaim them—just as it was pleaded in justification of the accursed system of slavery, but "God hath not cast off his people whom he foreknew." It is true that the Jews themselves acknowledge a peculiar hardness about Jewish nature, and that many others would be inclined to the opinion which Luther somewhat roughly affirms: "A Jewish heart is hard as a stock,

V

as a stone, as iron, as the spirit of evil;" but it is the "stony out of the flesh" which God has specially promised to remove. Rooted as are their prejudices they can be rooted out by Gospel husbandry.   It was not only for a witness that Christ's pitying tenderness enjoined "the beginning at Jerusalem" of the tidings of great joy; and as if to shame and silence for ever Gentile indolence and unbelief, God gave, in the initial campaign of the Apostles, a glorious Pentecostal type of the conversion of Israel, in the three thousand Jews who were smitten and saved under Peter's rousing word.

There are many circumstances, moreover, which exalt our hopes for the conversion of the Jewish people.   It is not for nothing surely, but in fulfilment of some Divine purpose, that they have preserved their individuality through so many centuries of years, and that the land of theirfathers has been held in such marvellous abeyance of possession.   Interpreting the future by the past, we may well conclude that His mercy yearns over them, "though his hand is stretched out still."   Mercy hid herself behind all their sufferings in the former time.   Behind the bondage of Egypt was the education for a magnificent nationality, and the prestige which came upon them by the manner of their deliverance and the destruction of their enemies. Behind the wandering in the wilderness was the training, never interrupted during the forty years, for the Canaan of inheritance and rest.   Behind the Assyrian and the Babylonish captivities there was purpose to disgust them with idolatry, and to make their witness to the Divine unity more distinct and impressive. Some gracious design is manifested in each painful infliction or seeming abandonment.   And why should it not be so now?   Is it not astounding that they should continue to exist?   Aboriginal tribes of the forest have died out before advancing civilization. The Jew has had more persecutions than any of them, but he lives still. Violence and strife have pursued him unrelentingly. He has been driven before Pagan lances, and scorched by Roman faggots, and gashed by Turkish scimitars with cruel wounds; all the enginery of torture and all the exactions of tyranny have been employed to exterminate him—and yet he lives! Empires have decayed, and he seems to have risen from the ruins. Kingdoms have been born, he has assisted at the birth. Everywhere he wanders on his separate way—amid Bourses of Europe, beneath the glare of tropic suns — amid costly archipelagos of ocean. His distinction even of suffering is as glorious to him as were the displayed phylacteries to the Pharisees of old. Amid many temptations to coalesce—though not the balance only, but the entirety of temporal motive inclined to persuade him to amalgamate —though with but little difficulty he might at one time have united with the Mohammedan power and so have secured impunity and the chance of revenge, yet through all hazards he has maintained his separation, exclaiming, with all the fervour with which men express a passion of their souls : " I am a Jew, I can never be anything else but a Jew. I may become a Christian, I can never become a Gentile." Thus wearing his national reproach as a fallen king his diadem, and faithful to the traditions of his ancestors even in his altered fortunes, " as the sun-flower turns to the sun when he sets the same look which she turned when he rose."

If you add to this consideration that which invests it with a still greater marvel, namely, that it is computed that there has not only been preservation of race, but an approximate equality in number—and that there are three millions and a-half of Jews in the world to-day, just as there were when the "chariots drave heavily" after them, and the Red Sea rolled back at their glorious leader's signal,—you cannot refuse the conviction that all this has not been an arbitrary impulse, but a Divine arrangement; that the Father has tracked the prodigal in all his wanderings; and that by and by there shall be the best robe and the music of the festival because of the "dead that is alive again, and of the lost that is found."

There are not wanting indications, moreover, in the feeling of all thoughtful men, of an awakened interest in this great matter of Israel's salvation. The mind of Christendom is no longer indifferent. Christians of every name have interred their ancient prejudices against the Hebrew, and vie with each other to atone for the criminal apathy of the past by being no longer laggards nor idlers—but by compassing this cause with the tenderness of sympathy, with the diligence of faithful labour, and with the importunity of prayer. Among the Jews themselves there are strivings and quickenings as of a nascent birth. Many questions and customs, which the Rabbinism of the ages have enjoined, have been discarded by their modern intelligence, and there has been struck in many hearts a chord of earnest feeling which has led them to the study of the Prophecies, only to be dismayed by the conclusion that the Messiah has already come. Their prejudices against Jesus have in many instances been diminished. There is an eagerness to receive, and an insatiableness to devour, the New Testament Scriptures, amongst many who a few years ago would have scorned to touch them as unclean. And last, not least, many among them have been actually converted, and evidence, in consistent living and earnest missionary toil, that they have "passed from death unto life."

In this review of probabilities I have abstained from the mention of that which forecloses the entire argument, while yet it is a sure resting-place for Faith—the absolute promise of God. It is, however, impossible to read many parts of Jeremiah, Ezekiel and Hosea's prophecies, or to follow the Apostle's argument in the eleventh chapter of the Epistle to the Romans, without resting upon the assurance, as clearly revealed as any part of the Divine Will, that "if the casting away of them be the reconciling of the world, what shall the receiving of them be but life from the dead." (Rom. xi. 15.)

Yes, Israel shall be saved! God hath promised it—and it shall be so. Vain shall be all the efforts of the world and the devil to hinder it. Through the degeneracy of character, and through the incrustation of prejudice, through the inveteracy of habit and through the teeming slaveries of years—the conquering word of Jesus shall make its resistless way. In deepest sorrow for the great wrong they did to the crucified, "the land shall mourn, every family apart," until, sprinkled with the blood they shed, they shall rejoice in His purity and healing. And in the great day when the multitudes shall gather for the coronation of the Son of Man, there shall be the Jew, eldest born among the aristocracies; with an ancestry that dates before parchments; "concerning the flesh" of the kindred of the king; bending the knee, foremost in the homage, lifting the voice most tuneful in the praise; and, with an eagerness that no other can outrival, bringing forth the royal diadem, "to crown Him Lord of all." Brethren, to hasten this consummation all of you may contribute. The Hebrew people have many claims upon you. They are men, and they appeal to you for the common pitifulness of manhood. They are men in need and in peril, and their sorrows, like the wounds of the ancient Greeks, are their advocates before you. Much of our present privilege came to us by their means. Their bards sang for us, their prophets thrill us yet. The grand fishermen and tent makers whom they sent forth are inspirations to us at this hour. They kept through a long dark night, and amid a horde of prowling enemies, the " lively oracles of God." We have to atone to them for the wrongs of ages. Children of those who oppressed them, and who killed their prophets, we should do better than " build their sepulchres," we should teach them how holily to live, and how hopefully and triumphantly to die. God has not finally cast them away. Christ died for them, and intercedes in His royalty for their recovery. The Spirit strives with them with a power which many of them are unwilling to acknowledge. Now your duty is before you, to work and to pray for their salvation, and to let the active benevolence testify to the sincerity with which the lips have breathed the prayer: " Oh, that the salvation of Israel were come out of Zion ! When God bringeth back the captivity of His people, Jacob shall rejoice, and Israel shall be glad."

THE LORD'S SUPPER.

THE LORD'S SUPPER.

"For as often as ye eat this bread, and drink this cup, ye do show the Lord's death till He come."—1 Cor. xi., 26.

THE Apostle Paul sustained to the Corinthian church the relation of a father to his child. By him the Gospel had been first preached in the rich and sensual city,—by his instrumentality the first converts had been won to Christ ; and with all a father's yearning did he watch over their welfare, counsel them in their ever recurring perplexities, and guide the heedless footsteps which were too prone to go astray. To his fatherly care for their interests we owe the circumstantial account which he has given us in this chapter, of the institution of the Lord's Supper, in the celebration of which, among the Corinthians, certain abuses had crept in. His account of it, here recorded, is a valuable and welcome revelation. He was not present in the upper room. He was not among the awe-stricken company who were thrilled with horror by the announcement that amongst them was a foul betrayer, and who, scarce recovered from the shock of such sad tidings, were invited to join in the tender and prophetic feast ; and yet he had not been left to the hazard of a traditional knowledge, nor received his impression of the scene from the glowing descriptions of another. He distinctly repudiates the thought that he "had either received it, or had been taught it of man," and expressly states that "he had received it" directly "from the Lord." So distinguishing was the honour put upon the Apostle of the Gentiles, and so important the institution itself, that there was given to him a new revelation—that its Divine paternity might be placed beyond all cavil, and that it might be authenticated by yet weightier evidence, and more firmly homed in the hearts of believers, in the perpetuity of its obligation unto the end of time.

To the Lord's Supper, then, with its hopes and memories, with its delights and duties, standing out as a Divine institution, solemn and beautiful, our attention is to be directed, and, as our object is not critical but practical, we shall but briefly refer :

I. To the nature of a Sacrament ; and more largely

II. To the aspects under which *the* Sacrament of the Holy Communion ought to be considered.

The word Sacrament, derived from the Latin, and in use among the armies of Rome to denote the great military oath by which they swore allegiance to their country, was used by the early church to signify any of its ceremonies, especially those that were figurative and typical. Gradually, however, it became of more restricted meaning, and in the narrower sense it is commonly understood now. In the general definition of a Sacrament, it may be said to be a sign and seal of a covenant, and to distinguish it from a ceremony it is further necessary that it should be expressly of Divine institution. The creative power of the Papacy has swelled the Sacraments into seven—the less mystery-loving genius of Protestant Christianity is content with the two which are admittedly of Divine appointment—Baptism, by which we are initiated into the fellowship of the church, and the Lord's Supper, by which we commemorate the Redeemer's death.

There are various views entertained of the nature of the Holy Communion, into the discussion of which we cannot largely enter, and of which we can only hastily remind you. There is the opinion of the Church of Rome, which believes that after the act of consecration the bread and wine lose their essence, and are verily and indeed transmuted into the "body and blood, soul and divinity, bones and nerves of the Son of God." We object to this monstrous dogma because, in certain instances connected with the administration of the Eucharist, it has led to gross and revolting impiety; because it brings us back from the dispensation of the spiritual into the age of material symbol, which is the church's childhood; because it is plainly opposed to the whole scope and genius of Scripture; and because, in the quaint words of a German critic, "it creates a new Christ—a dead Christ by the side of the living one." In opposition to this theory, and in extreme recoil from its absurdity, some have deprived the Sacrament of all religious significance, and have commended it solely on account of the salutary influence which it may have upon the mind—like reading of the Scripture, or the act of prayer, or any other duty of the Christian life. We object, likewise, to this bold and dishonouring interpretation, because it is an affectation of independence to forms which the Scripture will not sanction; because it strips into unworthy bareness an act official and solemn; because it does injustice to the memory of the Saviour, takes the beauty from His ordinance, and the heart and force out of

His words.   There is another view which approximates to the first mentioned, and is sometimes held conjointly, though it is likewise affirmed by those who would hesitate to be classed amongst the adherents of the Church of Rome—that the elements after consecration have in them an inherent virtue, irrespective altogether of the disposition and desire of the person by whom they are received.   Who has not deplored the prevalence of this notion among the darkened masses of our land? In many instances, though the life has been consumed in sin, and in neglect of or scoffing against religion, its minister is hastily sent for in the mortal sickness ; and, by the giving of the sacred emblems it is presumed that the enemy is cheated of his prey, and the spirit charmed into the happiness of the sky. We need hardly utter our protest against this doctrine of necessary efficacy.   We object to it because God makes no unconditional covenants or promises of blessing ; because, by inducing indifference or slumber, it has been largely used by Satan as a device to ruin souls ; because it introduces other terms of salvation than those which Christ has solemnly declared ; and because it transforms a holy rite into the mere trick of a conjuror, a "lying wonder" of perverse and manipulating wizardry.   Our view of the Supper of our Lord is that there is in it no virtue of atonement or power to subdue the rebellion of a sinner, nor even any exclusive conveyance of grace or comfort ; but that, rightly and reverently used, it is a blessed means of grace ; an ordinance in which there couches much spiritual profit ; and which, perhaps above all others, draws aside the veil for the faithful, and reveals to the rapt soul already somewhat of the lustre and ecstacy of Heaven.

II. By one or other of the sacred writers the Sacrament of

the Lord's Supper is presented under certain aspects which unfold to us its design and blessings. They tell us that it is :

1st. *A commemorative ordinance.* "This do in remembrance of me." It is no uncommon thing in the history of nations to commemorate events of national importance by expressive symbolism. Medals are struck to celebrate a victory or to perpetuate the prowess of a hero. The statues of the wise and of the valiant are niched in their country's temples—columns rear their tall heads on the mounds of world famed battle-fields, or on some holy place of liberty—processions and pageants of high and solemn festivity transmit from generation to generation the memory of notable days and deeds. And it is right that it should be so. We are no friends to the ruthless utilitarianism that can see no good in these things, and that would shear off all the trappings from State, and all the pageantry from Power. They are unsubstantial, and expensive too, sometimes, but they are expressions of something great and true, and by how much they are invested with imposing grandeur, by so much is the likelihood that they will be fastened upon the memory and the heart. There is hope of a nation when its gratitude lives, though the exhibitions of that gratitude may be extravagant and unseemly. If you come from the national to the individual, how memory clings round some relic of sanctity bestowed on us by some far off friend, some dear gage of affection ; the gift, perhaps in the latest hour, of the precious and sainted dead. As we gaze upon them—mute but eloquent reminders of a past that has fled for ever, how closely they seem linked with our every conception of the giver, and in what an uncounted value we hold them for the giver's sake. Surely then there is a fitness in the institution of the Lord's Supper as a standing memorial, by which the church at large may commemorate the grandest act, and by which the heart of each individual believer may be reminded of his dearest friend. You, who have learned to love the Saviour, will prize His ordinance for the Saviour's sake. You who rejoice in the salvation purchased by His dying, will not fail with gratitude and faith to " show the Lord's death until he come."

The time at which the ordinance was instituted was the time of the Feast of the Passover. There was a memorable deliverance wrought out for the children of Israel. Think of a land retiring to slumber under the threat of a terrible destruction ; some of its dwellers unconscious, some scornful, others apparently heedless, but haunted by a strange misgiving—and in the dead of night, when all the world was still, hark ! that frantic wail resounding through the midnight, rising in simultaneous sorrow from palace, and mansion, and cottage ; rich and poor brought into closer fellowship by the great leveller, trouble— echoed far out into the darkness, and amid the glare of torches and the tramp of hasty feet, each cheek blanched into an ashen paleness, and on each lip the same dread words of agony. Gradually the knowledge is gathered that the destruction is a common one, and that from every dwelling the fondest and most treasured had departed, for " throughout the whole land there was not an ' Egyptian' house in which there was not one dead." Well might there be " a cry in Egypt, such as there was none like it, nor shall be like it any more." But see in the land of Goshen, those dwellings whose doorposts are sprinkled with blood ; dwellings which the proud sons of Egypt would have scorned to enter, dwellings of menials and slaves, but within them on that night of disaster there is no bleeding heart ᴊor slain beloved one, but everywhere songs of thanksgiving, firm reliance and a chastened and solemn joy. God has set his token upon those dwellings of Israel ; they were the Lord's well-favoured ones, and as he passed them by the Avenging Angel smiled. See them thrust out in haste, enriched with the spoil of their oppressors ; driven into liberty before the blast of a nation's fear ; leaving the land of bondage behind them ; journeying enfranchised and happy from Rameses to Succoth ; and then pitching their tents as freemen, beyond the lash of the taskmaster ; and do you wonder that hearts should feel and voices sing, " It is a night to be much observed unto the Lord." This was the memory uppermost in the minds of the disciples when the Saviour "took bread and blessed it, and brake it, and gave to them ;" and though the veil was on their hearts just then, so that they knew not the full significance of the act, nor comprehended the grandeur of their Master's mission, in the aftertime, when they had been schooled in the upper room, and had shared in the Baptism of Pentecost, they would understand it better, and would see, as we see in the light of a perfected Revelation, how fitly on the night of the Passover was instituted the memorial of deliverance from a bondage greater than Egyptian, and from the deadlier perils of a death that never dies.

But if the minds of the disciples were filled with thoughts of the Passover and its great salvation, what were the thoughts of the Redeemer? He was just entering within the shadow of His Passion. There stretched out before His conscious eye the whole course of suffering which He had set himself bravely to travel. His betrayal, His arrest, the Garden, the Judgment Hall, the Cross, the Sepulchre, that strange contact with sin, that mysterious curse-bearing which was to His pure soul the greatest of all possible humiliation—that drear and lonely moment of desertion by the Father—the most terrible of all possible endurance, all these were before Him; and distinct and near He saw the approach of the sorrow. "It was the same night on which He was betrayed." It was the *last* Supper Table. He gazed with ineffable tenderness upon the disciples whom He had chosen, and who were so soon to be orphaned of His love. He knew them, save the betrayer, to be true at heart though infirm of purpose, and earthly in conception, and dazzled with high imaginings of a temporal kingdom. "With desire,"—*then* broke out the strong affection which many waters could not quench—"With desire I have desired to eat this Passover with you before I suffer;" as if He had said, My time is at hand, I can no longer delay the completion of my solemn purpose. I have forewarned you of this. I go to my Father and ye see me no more—yet a little while and I must die. Ye are my sheep whom I have led, but the sword must awake against the shepherd, and the sheep must be scattered abroad. This is the Feast of the Passover. Ye have been remembering its deliverance, but ye will soon have a tenderer memory. Take, eat this bread, it is my body, soon to be broken for sinners. Take, drink this wine, it is "the New Testament in my blood." Forget me not when ye no longer see me, "This do in remembrance of me." Deeply would the words sink into the hearts of those faithful disciples, and as deeply should they sink into ours, for the words have come thrilling on, sounding with a deepening pathos "through the corridors of time." We, too, must enter into the Saviour's sorrow. For us, if we believe in Him, He breaks the bread and pours the wine, and when we eat and drink we do "show the Lord's death until He come." His death, not His life, though that was lustrous with a holiness without the shadow of a stain. His death, not His teaching, though that embodied the fulness of a wisdom that was Divine. His death, not His miracles, though His course was a march of mercy, and in His track of blessing the world rejoiced and was glad. His death! His body, not glorious but broken; His blood, not coursing through the veins of a conqueror, but shed, poured out for man. On the summit of the Mount of Transfiguration, when the hidden Divinity broke for a while through its disguise of flesh, and Moses and Elias, those federal elders of the former time came down in conference, and the awe-stricken disciples feared the baptism of the cloud, "they spake of His decease, which He should accomplish at Jerusalem." HIS DEATH! Still His death! Grandest and most consecrating memory both for earth and Heaven.

> "See Him set forth before your eyes,
> That precious bleeding Sacrifice !
> His offer'd benefits embrace,
> And freely now be saved by grace.

You are to remember His death ; you are to see your sins, all loathsome and unsightly, laid upon Him! Your souls, polluted and impure, washed by Him! Your doom, accursed and terrible, reversed by Him! Your life, present and eternal, secured by *Him !* Then "show the Lord's death until He come."

2. *It is a confirmatory ordinance.*—It is manifest from the solemnity of its inauguration, and from the singular reverence with which it was regarded by the early Christians, that the Lord's Supper was not intended to be a thing of one generation,

W

but to be a precious and hallowed memorial to the end of time. So broad and deep was the impression of its perpetual obliga-ion, that in every age of the Church, alike when it was crushed by persecution, and when it had degenerated into worldly alliance and conformity, the continuity of this great festival sustained no interruption; it remained in general acknowledg-ment through all external changes. This perpetuity of the Sacrament seems to stamp it as a confirming ordinance—con-firming man's faith in God, confirming God's fidelity to man.

The disciples had long cast in their lot with the Master, and with leal hearts had followed his fortunes "through evil and through good report," but they were more faithful witnesses after that night's solemnity than they had ever been before; and when their Master walked no longer with them; and when their minds recalled Him, as they saw Him last, receding from their view in his chariot of cloud; and when, in obedience to His command, they partook of the ordinance which He had bequeathed to them, it is no wonder that they should come away from each successive celebration of the communion of His body and blood with braver courage, more valiant in His service, both to dare and to do. And it is so with God's people still. By thus waiting upon the Lord in His own endeared ordinance, they renew their exhausted strength, "mount up as eagles," on the wings of spiritual thought, and "run" on errands of charity, or "walk" in consistent conduct, "without weariness or fainting."

The Sacrament confirms the two things which it exhibits— the atonement and the second advent of the Lord. It links the humiliation and the royalty, the scornful trial and the session of judgment, the accomplished part and the assured future, together. The gone and the coming converge in its blissful present. It is the Lord's sign on the earth, as the sun is in the heaven. It is like a pause in eloquent conversation, which yet is not a pause, because the eye takes up the tale of the tongue, and "fills with light the interval of sound." It is the wedlock of the believer's memory and hope : memory which lingers round the Cross, hope which already revels in the glory of the throne. It is the "angels' food," which the children of Israel did eat in the wilderness, again dropping from heaven for the nourishment of the believer's life. We are now in circumstances closely similar to theirs. They had a past of bondage and a future of blessing ; the deliverance from Egypt to remember, the inheritance of Canaan to anticipate ; and all through the weary desert journey fell God's sign—the manna. We have to remember the time when He died for us, and to expect the time when He shall come to "be admired of" us, with tens of thousands in His regal train ; and we, too, are in a desert land, and sickened Hope, and drooping Faith, have often asked the question, "Can God furnish a table in the wilderness?" Can He? Yes, He spreads it in His own banquet hall—a feast of royal dainty and generous welcome— and He speaks to his disciples in the words of invitation now, "Come, eat and drink ; eat, my friends ; eat abundantly, oh, my beloved !"

For the confirmation of your faith and of your devotedness God has set up the sacramental sign. Now come with docile hearts and learn its mystic meanings. It is to confirm your faith in His death—*in its reality* that it was not a prolonged swoon, nor counterfeit of dying, nor simulation of martyrdom as the crowning cheat of the grand imposture of His life ; but that He *died*, that His body was broken, and that the water and the blood issuing from the spear-wound of the Roman soldier were the signs of life actually departing from its tabernacle. It is to confirm your faith in His death ; *in its vicariousness*, that He was offered, not for His own sins, but for the sins of others —for the unjust, for the leprous, for the abandoned, for all, for *you*. It is to confirm your faith in His death ; *in its efficacy* as an accepted atonement, as an oblation which has made it *just* for God to pardon you ; as an all-comprising and perpetual reconciliation, which has made "at one" both earth and heaven, "to show forth His death until He come." It is to confirm your faith *in the certainty of His coming*. He *shall* come ; the Church is not for ever orphaned of His presence ; the disciples need not mourn over a dead Christ ; the weeping Virgin may dry her tears, for her son liveth, glorified, exalted, King of Kings and Lord of Lords. It is to confirm your faith in *the recompense* that awaits you at His coming ; all wrongs redressed, all mysteries cleared, the prisoning stone rolled away from the door of every sepulchre ; no flaming sword at the gate of the new covenant Eden ; all temptation overcome ; sorrows woven into elements of stronger character ; the image of the earthly faded, the burning of the fiery trial having purged the features into the reflected beauty of the King ; sin eradicated, Satan trampled under feet, death destroyed, the glad welcome, the abundant entrance, the triumphal honours, the everlasting joy ! Of all these, believer, the sacramental sign speaketh ; it sparkles for thy strengthening with all this fulness of joy.

You are called, those of you who believe in Jesus, to meet the Saviour in this confirming and witnessing ordinance though there is no necessary efficacy of conversion about it, do not thou, poor penitent, earnest and sin-hating seeker after mercy, be discouraged and imagine that its comfort is not for thee. If thou seekest Jesus, surely He will not send thee empty from His own table. But for you who have not met with the Saviour; who, amid outward decorum, keep your hearts alien and your habits worldly, there is no grace in the sacrament for you. It is rather a confirming than a covenanting ordinance. Like the blessed sun and kindly rain, it will shine and fall upon the stone, and the stone will remain insensible, because it hath no hidden principle of life ; but it will foster the growth and develop the blossom of the flower, because the life is there. Give yourselves first unto the Saviour. Make your humble confession of sin and your solemn consecration of service. "Repent and be converted ;" then the sacrament will be a precious means of grace ; then, through its influence, "the times of refreshing shall come from the presence of the Lord." You will be strengthened by it for effort or for trial, and your souls, like so many passion flowers warmed into beauty by the sun, will exhibit the tender memory of the Saviour's passion, and thus "show forth His death until he come."

3. *It is a covenanting ordinance.* The definition of a Sacrament seems to lack completeness, unless it be regarded not only as a sign but as a seal—a solemn federal act which involves mutual pledges, of fidelity on the one hand and of blessing on the other. The expression of the inner dispositions by appropriate symbol is by no means of uncommon occurrence in the Sacred Writings. When the Psalmist speaks of his own deliverances, and, in astonishment at their extent and magnitude, asks "What shall I render ?" he replies, as the most public and graceful utterance of his gratitude, " I will take the cup of Sal-

vation and call upon the name of the Lord ;" and the next verse
may be regarded as the translation of the symbol into language,
"I will pay my vows unto the Lord now in the presence of all
His people." And your participation of the Holy Communion
must be thus regarded as the fresh act of your espousals, as the
solemn renewal of your covenant ; as your surrender, entire and
unhesitating, to the service of the Lord. It is thus that you
confess Christ and witness of Him to the world. If you eat
and drink without discerning this great purpose, you eat and
drink unworthily ; if you repudiate such purpose, either in
thought or act, you crucify in your measure "the Son of God
afresh, and put Him to an open shame." By your profane use
of the means of grace without the slightest desire for the grace
of the means, it is as if you cut and wounded the Saviour in this
the house of His friends, and sharpened the daggers of your
treachery upon the tables of the violated law. But I am
speaking to those who love the Saviour ; who will rejoice to
confess their discipleship, and to renew their covenant in the
ordinance of bread and wine. Your heart longs to express its
devotion, and throbs with affection and reverence towards the
Lord who has redeemed you, but within you there lurks a not
unnatural fear, and you shrink from involving yourself in the
obligations of a covenant so solemn. That this Holy Sacrament may be for your comfort, and that the cup may be "a cup
of blessing ;" remember that there are two parties to the covenant ; and that the Sacrament is the divinely instituted seal of
the fidelity of God's promise to you, just as—in allusion to the
ancient custom of ratifying covenants—the presence of the Lord
under the symbol of "the smoking furnace and the burning
lamp" passed between the portions of the divided sacrifice

which Abraham had offered, that he might know thereby that he should inherit the land. So the presence of the Lord, not in the fire, but in the still small voice, comes down in the Sacrament for your consolation and mine. Hark ! the Lord speaks to the Father of the New World as He looks from the altar of Ararat upon the earth from which the waters had but recently assuaged, " I do set my bow in the cloud," and it shall be for a token of the covenant between me and the earth. You can imagine how the patriarch would impress it on his children, and they to their posterity in lengthening succession. And you can fancy how some grey father of a later time, some pious Hebrew of the next generation, would hush the ailing, and would soothe the fretful, and would cheer the timid, as he pointed in the hurricane to the brilliant arch that spanned the angry cloud. " It will subside by-and-by, there's the rainbow ; never mind the blackened Heaven and the howling tempest, *there's the rainbow.*" Do you tell me that the " skies pour out water," and the river has burst its banks, and the " fountains of the great deep are broken up," *there's the rainbow.* God has set it in the cloud, and for the sake of His plighted word, of which that is the token and seal, He will say to the proud waters " Hitherto shalt thou go, and no further."

Brethren, here in the sacrament is the rainbow of the new and better covenant, the ever renewed pledge of salvation purchased, and strength imparted, and blessing conferred on the believing soul. And now, as in *your* covenant you pay your vows, time, talent, influence, property, life, *all God's,*—He, the Infinite, in boundless condescension stoops to whisper, " My light, my strength, my grace, my purity, my joy, my Heaven, all yours." " Thou hast avouched the Lord this day to be thy

God, to walk in His ways, and to keep His statutes, and His commandments, and His judgments, to hearken to His voice ; and the Lord hath avouched thee this day to be His peculiar people, as He hath promised thee." And thus, brethren, in a mutual covenant of blessing, you do "show forth His death until He come."

The Lord's Supper is the privilege of believers—the banquet of the servants in the house of the Master whom they confess and whom they serve.

That same Master has provided a great supper, to which He has bidden me to invite you all. Come, for all things are now ready.

That same Master, Jesus, our Immanuel, will receive you if you come, pleading no worthiness ; trusting in no name but His. And when the probations of earth are over, and the gospel invitations have ceased, and the typical ordinances are not necessary, because of the fulness of the vision, you shall sit down, if faithful unto death, at the Marriage Supper of the Lamb.

THE TRANSFIGURATION

OF CHRIST.

THE TRANSFIGURATION
OF CHRIST.

"And this voice, which came from Heaven, we heard when we were with Him in the Holy Mount."—ii. Peter, i. 18.

THE Apostle is writing to the churches at a time when scoffers had begun to cavil against the truth, and when a swarm of false teachers had put the faith of believers in peril. He encourages their endangered confidence by reminding them of the evidences of Christianity ; evidences of which he had a right to testify, for he " could not but speak which he had heard and seen." One of the chosen witnesses to the Lord's Transfiguration won early the crown of martyrdom ; but the two survivors both allude to that wondrous scene, which they used to strengthen the confidence of others while it had fastened itself upon their own minds, at once an inner strength and an indelible memory. Peter speaks of it in the text as the best possible proof to him that he had not followed a " cunningly devised fable." John, reverently recognising the Divinity incarnate, tells us that " the Word was made flesh and dwelt among us, and we beheld His glory, the glory as of the only begotten of the Father, full of grace and truth." Brethren, I want you to stand with me upon the Holy Mount this morning : a spot haunted by such hallowed memories must have a charm and a lesson of its own. It is in Galilee, so we shall be in the footsteps of Jesus. It is "apart," so it is suitable for a Sabbatic ramble. It is high, so our thoughts will rise in sympathy, and we shall become the heavenlier for our climbing. Let us enquire :

1st. What are *the circumstances.*

2nd. What are *the purposes* of the Transfiguration of Christ? These will furnish us with ample material, both for thought, and faith, and love.

The second year of that loving and instructive ministry is now fast drawing to a close. Already have the miracles been multiplied, and the faith of the disciples, at first tremulous, has expressed itself without wavering in the confession of Peter, the ever ready spokesman of the rest. They are prepared to believe in Him as the Christ, though they are yet intensely Jewish in their ambition for a temporal kingdom. It is time now that their faith should enter upon its higher education, and that they should be fitted for their work of witness-bearing by the study of the mystery of suffering. Hence it is with the first intimation of the coming trouble that the narrative of the Transfiguration properly begins. " From that time forth began Jesus to show unto His disciples how that He must go into Jerusalem, and suffer many things of the elders and chief priests and scribes, and be killed, and be raised again the third day." About six days " after these sayings," when time had been given for them to sink deeply into the hearts which had doubtless been perplexed concerning them, with imaginings diverse and sad, Jesus takes Peter and James and John to be the sharers of His hours of midnight prayer. They wend their way together to the "high mountain apart," perhaps some bold hill of the Hermon ridge, where, in the majestic solitude of night upon the hills, He was accustomed to commune with his Father. While He prays the fashion of His countenance is changed. The inner radiance shines through the serge and sackcloth of His incarnate life ; and for once they "see Him as He is,"—"the brightness of the Father's glory and the express image of His person,"—and they wonder at the awful grandeur of the Divinity which the Man of Sorrows possessed, but which He had veiled even from their vision until now. And see! there are two forms appearing, whom, by some instinct or instruction, they know to be Moses and Elias ; the one a disembodied spirit, clothed for the time in some material vehicle ; the other yet wearing the body of which he had cheated death. and which had gone to "put on immortality" by another road than his. They speak, and the disciples listen in a sort of sorrowful trance, for the talk is of some "accomplished decease." They are startled by the sound, and willingly "slow of heart to comprehend." And now there encompasses them a luminous cloud, and from the midst of it an authoritative voice speaks, attesting the Divine Sonship and Mission of the Master whom they loved so well. These poor frail mortals faint beneath the privilege which has so highly favoured them, and when they recover from their swoon of awe the dazzling vision has vanished. There are the stars shining in the clear and far off sky ; the piercing night wind blows keenly upon the hill, and on its summit there is nothing living but themselves— themselves and "Jesus only." By and by they descend and rejoin their fellows, but it is with a great secret in their hearts, which they were straightly charged to conceal, except in the contingency, whose remoteness would seem to them almost as an everlasting seal, "until the Son of Man be risen from the dead." This is the great sight which, in the calmness of this Sabbath morning, when our eyes are not heavy with sleep, we may turn aside to see ; and with the added light which the interpreting years have cast upon its significance, we may learn its lessons of suggestiveness and wisdom.

"He took Peter and James and John." There seem to have been distinctions among the Apostolic band, although the Saviour had said "All ye are brethren." The three whom we now see in the Holy Mount would appear to have been the innermost circle round the Lord ; the nearest in intimacy ; the most favoured in fellowship ; the chosen to testify any special revelation of His love. Their very names were significant of the great purpose for which Christ came into the world, that the "gift or mercy of God," founded upon a "rock" of impregnable strength, should "supplant" all idolatry and error. If then, the first power of Christ over death is to be displayed in the weeping household of the ruler of the synagogue, whose little daughter had faded into the beauty of the tomb, Peter and James and John must be the only witnesses of her miraculous recovery. If there is to be a revelation of "God manifest in the flesh" on the Mount, or a mysterious burst of more than mortal agony in the Garden, the same witnesses must watch until their eyelids droop and close, wearied with the twin excitements of the joy and sorrow. If great truths are to be proclaimed in the hearing of the nations, who so fitting to declare them as those "first three," He, the Man of Rock, and they, the sons of thunder ?   If every variety of character is to be joined in " bearing witness " to the truth, you secure constancy in the person of the earliest apostolic martyr, fearless and ardent advocacy in the impetuous Peter, and intelligent affection in the " disciple whom Jesus loved."   There they stand, those fit and chosen witnesses ; their frames thrilling with a strange emotion ; their weather-beaten faces shining in the reflected glory of the transfigured Saviour.   Who of us does not feel his heart within him tremble to their words : " Lord, it is good for us to be here."

" And there appeared unto them Moses, and Elias talking with him."   These are the parties summoned to this solemn mountain conference ; representatives from the invisible world, whose constituency were " the law and the prophets."   Moses and Elias—the one girt with the awful honours of Sinai, the other bright with the remembered triumph of Carmel.   Moses and Elias—the one, whose death was hastened on account of sin, but over whose dying Death had no cause to rejoice, for he had a God-prepared sepulchre and a divinely ordered funeral ; the other, whom God summoned in such haste that he had no time to die, and went off to heaven, as kings travel home, with the " chariots and horsemen of Israel."   Moses and Elias— the viceroys rendering up their commissions of delegated sovereignty because the Monarch is enthroned : the servants hastening humbly to discharge themselves of their trust in the presence of the well-reverenced Son.

" Talking with him ;" both in their ancient garb and in their familiar speech ; treading a planet which they had for ages ceased to visit ; using voices which for long years had never spoken with tongues ; unrecognizable by the Apostles ; not living upon earth; and yet consciously and happily alive; bright strangers from the spirit-world, who had risen to tell the living that the dead *can* rise.

And what shall be their theme when they converse together? these immortals, fresh from the presence of the Holy One. What heavenly intelligence shall fire their willing lips? What newer discovery of harmonious perfection shall animate them to loftier praises of the Divine? They, newly initiated into Heaven's secret—the Son of God, who had been the "Wisdom of God" from the beginning—what shall be the subject of their solemn midnight converse? Oh marvellous condescension of the Divine! Oh wonderful exaltation of the interests of the human! They spake of His decease, which "He should accomplish at Jerusalem." Their interest centred on that coming Agony and on that lifted Cross. Their highest topic was the topic of Redemption. Not on the might and marvel of creation; not on the omnipotence which sustained each minute or vaster organism in its native design; not on the general adaptedness and harmony of all things: not even on those heavenly bands of bright obedient mind, the eldest born of God, did these shining visitants dwell; but on the glory which was to suffer sad eclipse so soon; on the over-mastering mercy which vanquished Death for others by the agonies of its own dying; on the "grace which stooped so low to succour human woe." In blessed sympathy with those who kept their first estate, these glorified ones desired to look into the fellowship and the mystery of the Cross. This was their chiefest interest and their grandest contemplation; this, which believers on earth rejoice in with exceeding joy; this, whose symbol John in heaven beheld "as in the midst of the throne;" this, upon which, alas! sinners trample, and "account it an accursed thing."

"And He was transfigured before them." It has been well observed that this was *not* the Transfiguration : the Mount but showed him as He was—the actual Transfiguration was in the humiliation of the incarnate life. He, essentially glorious, was "transfigured" into poverty and shame. But now, lest any lingering doubt should lurk in the minds of the Apostles, which might make their future utterances falter, they see His glory ; they had suspected it before. There was a heavenliness in His teaching, and a lustre from His miracles, and a brightness in His spotless life, which, amid the meanness, had betrayed the God ; but here the inner Divinity shines forth through its fleshly covering, and the attesting Shechinah comes down in the encompassing cloud. Well might the mortal spirit live, and the mortal senses faint, before a revelation like this, while yet the desire struggles with the awe, and the bewildered Peter would fain have been busy with the " tabernacles " in which the illustrious visitors might rest. Who of us, even at this far distant period endeavouring to contemplate this scene, as he looks at the Redeemer's form thus lighted up with its own glory of Godhead, but must declare in the Psalmist's words, " Grace is poured into Thy lips ;" " Thou art fairer than the children of men."

But it is time, secondly, that we enquire into *the purposes* of the Transfiguration. What were the designs for which it was arranged, and the lessons which it was intended to impress ?

The first and great design, as we have already intimated, was *the solemn inauguration of Christ as the supreme lawgiver in His Church.* This was the " honour and glory " which He received of the Father, as the Apostle in the context distinctly declares. The exposition of the whole transaction, then, is in "the voice from Heaven." After Moses had received his commission he prophesied of a greater than himself: "The Lord thy God will raise up to thee a Prophet from the midst of thee, of thy brethren like unto me; unto Him ye shall hearken," and on this solemn occasion was the promise fulfilled. If you keep this idea in mind you will see the fitness of the appearance of Moses and Elias, rather than any other of the old Testament saints. They were the representatives of the law and the prophets; the two great authorities of the Jewish Church; the rigid jurists who upheld, in all its strictness, the rubrical exactitude of the law. There was strong contention among the early Church, many of whose members believed that the ceremonial and moral laws should be of equal force for ever; and the Apostles, in the First Council, were called to legislate on matters affecting the Church's spiritual freedom from the yoke of ancient observance. Now, unless there had been some formal abrogation of authority, the laws of Moses, which God had solemnly enjoined, and to the violation of which He had annexed heavy penalties, must have continued in force. But only He who anointed the lawgiver could supersede Him. The same authority which enacted the law must be the power to revoke its provisions. This authority was here given—given in the presence of the man by whose lips the former law was spoken, and of the man by whom it was championed, when degenerate Israel had forgotten it. The voice spake from the cloud for the confirmation of the words of Christ, just as at His baptism it had spoken in acceptance of His person. The servants were henceforth to stand aside. They had done their work, and done it well; but they were not needed now, and on the crest of the mountain they were to render up their commission to the Son. In the last chapter of Malachi they appear, Moses and Elias, closing up the old covenant. In the 17th of Matthew they appear at the instalment of the new. It is not a little remarkable that the circumstances attendant upon the giving of the law furnish almost a parallel to the circumstances of the Transfiguration in which that early lawgiver was superseded by a higher. Aaron, and Nadab and Abihu, instead of Peter, James and John; Mount Sinai instead of the Mount in Galilee; the face of Moses shining with reflected glory instead of the indwelling brightness radiating from the incarnate Son. With these points of difference there was the same pomp of legislation, the same solemnity of utterance, and the same glorious and encompassing cloud.

The conclusion of the marvellous scene answers to all the rest, like the last stamp of the signet-ring, sealing and confirming the whole. When the fainting disciples recovered consciousness and looked around, " they saw no man, save Jesus only." Moses and Elias had been aforetime the objects of their devoutest reverence—the recognized teachers whom they felt themselves bound to follow. Where are they now? They have renounced all claims to empire—they retire willingly from the field. There is but one royal lawgiver. There must be no division of authority, no admixture of legislative claim. " Jesus only " reigning in unchallenged and sole lordship over each heart and mind. Brethren, for us as well as for them was this solemn instalment given. Christ is the lawgiver to His Church for all time. Prophets and Apostles—they are valuable to us only as they repeat the words of Christ. Holy men and confessors!

We rejoice in them because they give to us transcripts of Christ —laws, decretals, confessions, catechisms, creeds—we accept them only as they are embodiments of the words of Jesus. Let a thousand rubrics or canons condemn what Christ hath not condemned, we may snap them as Samson the withes with which they sought to bind him. Let a thousand enactments enforce what Christ hath forbidden, and disobedience becomes a Christian duty, and brave death were preferable to life unworthy and dishonoured. "Jesus only,"—no surrender of personal thought and freedom ; no binding of the conscience with the scorpion yoke of a consistory, or at the bidding of a man who "as God sitteth in the temple of God." "Jesus only!" Then rejoice, believers, in your freedom, and in all matters of perplexed meditation "appeal" directly "unto Cæsar." Listen submissively to the faintest syllable from the lips which cannot err. Render a homage more dutiful and willing than you have ever rendered yet. Look for ever into this "perfect law of liberty," that you may be blessed in your deed. Our souls exult to feel and to proclaim that there is but one authoritative teacher ; and just as one fond spot in a landscape, hallowed by some tender or pensive memory, may fasten the gazer's eye until he is insensible to the charms of woodland and waterfall, and copse and spire—so we, waking in bewildered trance and dim memories of shining visitants on the Holy Mount, seek not for accessories and backgrounds to the picture which fills the soul and fastens the eye— we see "no man save Jesus only."

We cannot help thinking, however, that the Transfiguration must be regarded also as *the solemn baptism of the Saviour into His priestly and mediatorial office.*

The great purpose of the Incarnation, as you are aware, was

the offering upon the Cross. They who do not keep this in mind fall grievously short in their comprehension of the mystery. It is not enough to explain the Incarnation as designed only for the spiritual teaching, or for the loving miracles, or the exhibition of the illustrious and perfect pattern. These were all collateral and subsidiary. They are not unimportant, any of them. It is necessary that we should learn God's will from lips that are authorized to declare it. It is necessary that that will should be authenticated by signs following. It is necessary that we should see humanity uniform and consistent in its bright obedience. But the teaching was glorified by the dying, and the miracles were the smaller illustrations of that mercy whose crowning act was the draining of its own heart in sacrifice, and the obedience was an " obedience unto death." Present ever before the Saviour's mind was the grand issue to which His earthly sojourn tended—to make an atonement for the world's sin. This was " the Father's business" which He had offered, and was embodied, to do. For the accomplishment of this end " it behoved Christ to suffer," and there was not a moment of His incarnate life, whether He taught in synagogues or prayed on hill-side altars, or rested from His incessant toil in the brief holidays of Bethany, when this purpose was absent from His mind. He did not for some time declare it to those who followed him. You do not harass a child, while his education is proceeding, by setting before him the probabilities of orphanage· His children must be instructed in His doctrines, and trained for the fulfilment of their mission before they were told. But the influence of the thought may be traced from His very earliest years—did not leave Him in the temptation and in the triumph

—enstamped itself indelibly on each word of the lip and on each action of the life.

The inner connection between the first announcement of the sufferings and the more formal consecration to them on the summit of this mountain is preserved by St. Luke, who tells us that it was about "an eight days after these sayings," that is, six days intervening, one on which the sayings were spoken and one on which the Transfiguration took place—"about an eight days *after these sayings* " that He went up into the Mount to pray. This was, so to speak, the meridian of his incarnate day. His sun began after this to go down towards the clouds, which awaited its setting. The first shadow of His approaching suffering now darkened upon the sky.

It will not be uninteresting to remember the history of the three heavenly voices of which we read in the lifetime of Jesus. You will find that they do not speak capriciously—even as to the moment of their utterance there is an arranged and intelligible plan which they are designed to aid in its working. The first voice spake at Christ's baptism, when, in fulfilment of the great design which required Him to be " made like unto" sinners, he was baptized by John in Jordan, not in confession of sin—but as he himself declared, " to fulfil all righteousness." There is force in that argument which represents the baptism of Christ as the closing up of the old covenant—the obedience to the " baptism of repentance " which John preached, and which was the last external commandment given by God unto Israel. But the significance of the act would not be completely discerned if you exclude the prophetical character—if you do not recognize that beneath the Divine humility which says " thus it becometh us to fulfil all righteousness," there is a reference to that other baptism, that baptism of agony and blood, about which Christ declared Himself " straitened until it was accomplished." Now it was at this first anointing of the person of Jesus that the voice from Heaven spake, " This is my beloved Son, in whom I am well pleased." The last occasion on which the voice spake was when Christ had entered upon His passion, and felt already the sharpness of its mental anguish : " Now is my soul troubled, and what shall I say? Father, save me from this hour? But for this cause came I unto this hour. Father, glorify Thy name. Then came there a voice from heaven, saying, " I have both glorified it, and will glorify it again." Midway between these voices spake the one upon the Holy Mount. Is it not evident that there was unity of purpose and harmony of counsel between the Son and the Father? The continued watchfulness in heaven of the working out on earth of the scheme of Redemption—the attestation never failing to be given when it might authenticate the work, or encourage the brave worker in His trial?

Not only, therefore, do we witness on the Holy Mount the installation of the royal lawgiver, but of the great high-priest. It is a grand valedictory service in which He is re-ordained to duty—as the banners are blessed before the army marches to the field. And the voice speaks from Heaven as a sovereign gives audience to a chosen commander, and cheers him with the encouragement of royal favour. With what reverence, brethren, should we, sinners, look upon the scene ! As we see Him standing alone upon the mountain—fresh from His ordination of glory—calm, and kingly in His heaven-imparted strength ; and then as we see Him, with firm step, treading the dark avenue which, through desertion, agony, insult, abandonment, terminates in His death upon the Cross—surely our distrust should vanish, and in reliance upon such a champion we should have "joy in believing." Surely our indignation against the vile sin which made all this suffering necessary should be roused within us. Surely our hearts should bound with a fervour of devotion and gratitude which the obedience of a lifetime can only inadequately express. Surely we shall mark His track and follow in his footsteps, triumphant in the endurance of our own portion of sorrow, and, quaffing bravely the cup which He, who drained the bitterest has mingled, go on our patient way, singing :

> "O Lord, my God, do thou thy holy will,
>   I will lie still.
> I will not stir, lest I forsake thine arm,
>   And break the charm
> Which lulls me, clinging to my Father's breast,
>   To perfect rest."

It hardly comes within our scope to educe the various lessons which may be taught us in the Holy Mount. Our aim, very imperfectly fulfilled, has been to elicit the meaning of the great event before us, if haply some of its thoughts may linger in our hearts—like chimes heard within doors—softened by the silence and the comfort in which we sit and hear them, and ringing on, long after the actual sound has ceased, in the melody of each remembered tone. We can but suggest how, when we have recovered from the thrilling consequent upon the glorious vision, we might learn much of collateral instruction and blessing. Gospel narratives teach truth and scatter fragrance incidentally, as the sick folk were healed "by the *shadow* of Peter passing by."

We might learn, for example, the immortality of the soul, from the real appearance of two men, who had long ceased to be inhabitants of earth, again revisiting the glimpses of the moon. We might learn the conscious existence of the spirit after its separation from the body, that it does not sleep, as some affirm through dishonoured and inactive ages, but is possessed of intellectual vigour, and, in the case of the righteous, of a residence in glory. We might learn that Christ crucified is the grand theme of contemplation and converse, both to believing hearts on earth and to the ransomed spirits of the sky ; and our faith in the one offering which has redeemed us might become, therefore, more precious than ever. We might learn that God prepares for coming trial by special manifestations of His favour, and that though we may " fear" as we " enter into the cloud," we shall come out of it with manlier hearts and truer courage. Those who are not, alas ! partakers of Christ, might learn, and shudder as they learn, the value of that Divine communion from which they sinfully exclude themselves, and of that inherit-ance of glory which they sell for nought or alienate with scorn-ful hands. Those who have believed, and rejoice in mountain fellowship with Jesus, might learn that, refreshing as is the diffi-cult air, bracing as is the steep ascent, rare and elevating as is the glorious companionship, we must not " build our tabernacles there." In the valley below there is work for us to do, and we must hear our Master's voice as He asks us to descend, and leads us down into the great field of toil and travail and triumph :

> " Think not of rest, though dreams be sweet,
> Start up and ply your heavenward feet.
> Is not God's oath upon your head,
> Ne'er to sink back on slothful bed,

Never again your loins untie,
Nor let your torches waste and die,
Till, when the shadows thickest fall,
Ye hear the Master's midnight call.
He calls you angels—be your strife
To live on earth the angels' life."

www.ingramcontent.com/pod-product-compliance
Lightning Source LLC
Chambersburg PA
CBHW021541110726
47902CB00004B/968